I0760498

BOOKS BY TIM MCBAIN & L.T. VARGUS

The Violet Darger series

The Victor Loshak series

The Charlotte Winters series

The Scattered and the Dead series

Casting Shadows Everywhere

The Clowns

LONESOME HIGHWAY

a Violet Darger novel

L.T. VARGUS & TIM MCBAIN

COPYRIGHT © 2022 TIM MCBAIN & L.T. VARGUS

SMARMY PRESS

ALL RIGHTS RESERVED.

THIS IS A WORK OF FICTION. NAMES, CHARACTERS, BUSINESSES, PLACES, EVENTS AND INCIDENTS ARE EITHER THE PRODUCTS OF THE AUTHOR'S IMAGINATION OR USED IN A FICTITIOUS MANNER. ANY RESEMBLANCE TO ACTUAL PERSONS, LIVING OR DEAD, OR ACTUAL EVENTS IS PURELY COINCIDENTAL.

LONESOME HIGHWAY

PROLOGUE

The highway stretches into the night. An asphalt stripe etched into the foliage. A black line that slices some 1,908 miles from just south of downtown Miami all the way up the east coast through Maine, where it dead-ends at the Canadian border.

I-95. The interstate.

Traffic pulses down the road at all hours like blood cells surging through an artery. Sedans and SUVs twitch from lane to lane, booming up entrance ramps and coiling aside on the exits, red taillights gleaming as they drive away.

Though lonely sections of the freeway go dark for long intervals, the interstate itself never sleeps. Not fully. There's always a motorcycle fluttering here, a minivan jiggling there.

Throbbing engines. Sweeping headlamps.

All those hungry animals hunkered over their steering wheels. Hurrying somewhere. Agitated.

Here, in rural North Carolina, the interstate is quiet. Not dead, but quiet.

A rabbit stirs in the greenery along the shoulder. Its nose twitches. The smell of rain is still strong here, though the storm has passed. The animal nibbles at the clover, keeps its black eyes aimed into the emptiness where the road lies, vaguely conscious of the danger the asphalt presents.

The bunny senses the silence expanding over the freeway, the pregnant atmosphere of the lull in traffic. It feels faint bristling along its arched back at the awareness, but the rabbit is not disturbed.

The small creature will never know what horror has taken

place just off the next exit, will never grasp the malignant psychology that inspired the act.

Only humans can know that.

Something changes in the air. Fresh vibrations. The rabbit's ears perk up a second before the sound arrives.

A semi engine growls in the distance, a tiny sound at first but growing. That chunky diesel thrum reaches out over the empty land, disrupts the stillness, fills the space with mechanical ugliness.

The rabbit stops chewing. Watches the dark highway. Waits.

And then the truck crests a hill, two beams thrusting out of it, the headlamps set around the gridwork of the grill.

The semi is a muscular thing. Hulking. Imposing. Something harsh in all the planes and angles of its form. Rigid and boxy.

The truck rushes down the hill. Wet asphalt glitters where the headlights touch it. The glow reaches farther down the strip of black freeway, flitting over the plant life along the side of the highway, grasping toward the bunny's hiding spot.

The rabbit shivers and hops away from the road.

☾

Lightning paled the sky, flaring and relenting. The rain had moved on almost an hour ago, but the last forks of brightness still flashed in the distance, thunderless like a silent movie.

Dwayne Kunkle limped out toward the back lot where the truck still rumbled. He'd waited for this moment. In between mopping sessions and running garbage bins out to the dumpster in the drizzle, he had kept an eye on the traffic flowing in and out all night. He had someone to meet.

Lonesome Highway

Even with the lightning sheening off the wet asphalt, the lot at Big Jon's Travel Center seemed surprisingly dark tonight. Moonlight shimmered on the tops and sides of the trailers, reflecting panels of silvery light, but the places between the rows of semis held shadowy.

Kunkle glanced over his shoulder. His eyes traced up the twin poles along the road. The big sign, the one visible from the freeway, glowed bright as ever way up high. The spotlights aimed five white beams at the Big Jon's logo, gleaming day or night, rain or shine. He noted, however, that the neon lights beneath the big logo remained dark.

Sam forgot to turn on the sign again. Typical.

In the second-to-last row of the lot, Kunkle strode into the headlights of the semi that had just pulled in. He raised a hand to his brow and squinted to beat back the glare, and then he could see the shape of one Randall Hendy hunched behind the wheel. A little smile curled Kunkle's lips at the sight of his friend, but not out of any warmth or kindness. Hendy owed him a hundred bucks.

Friends were one thing. Money was another.

The trucker killed the engine, and the headlights winked off a second later. Kunkle gaped at the fresh darkness around him, all the shapes suddenly indistinct, charcoal smears where the contours had been. The North Carolina humidity seemed to swell in the gloom, the night air still heavy from the recent rain.

Lightning bugs flitted around. Blinked out signals to each other with their yellow butts. Right now they looked like specks in the abyss to Kunkle — tiny flares in a vast nothingness.

The truck door cracked open, and a wedge of dome light drifted down to the asphalt, sculpting solid shapes in the night once more. It helped Kunkle make sense of reality. He watched the beanpole trucker climb down, the man's lack of a chin and giant Adam's apple somehow looking all the more cartoonish in silhouette.

"Christ, my legs," Hendy said, stepping down to the asphalt. His twang made *legs* sound more like *laigs*. "How sitting in a truck all day can so thoroughly fuck a man's legs, I'll never know. But it sure as shit works that way, don't it?"

He stood still then, let his eyes flick over Kunkle a couple seconds before he spoke. A cigarette bobbed in the trucker's mouth, flapping up and down with each syllable.

"Didn't know the welcome committee would come all the way out to greet little ol' me. Cripes. You're worse than the IRS, you know that?"

Kunkle grinned.

"You got my money, then?"

"Nice to see you, too, good buddy. Jesus."

Hendy hit the cigarette. Exhaled smoke. Otherwise, he didn't move.

Kunkle's smile cut out. He pressed his lips together into a tight line and braced himself for tonight's excuse.

Great. Here it comes. This asshole is gonna stiff me again. Unbelievable.

In the past six months, Hendy had used a menagerie of pretexts to squirm out of paying up. Family emergency, dental emergency, dog emergency, plumbing emergency — all of the major emergencies, now that Kunkle thought about it.

What'll it be this time? Gerbil emergency? Soap poisoning?

After a couple more seconds of silence, though, Hendy shook his head. He reached into his back pocket, took out a floppy wallet with deep creases crushed into the leather, and fished a couple of 50-dollar bills free. He sniffed and made a face as he handed them over.

"No offense, Kunkle, but you… uh… smell a little ripe."

Kunkle wheezed out a laugh as he shoved the money into the breast pocket of his jumpsuit. Then he shrugged.

"I'm a janitor, dipstick. Part of the job to get elbow deep in the stanky stuff. Sometimes, anyway. But for 22 dollars an hour, I can deal with that. Way I see it, we're all debasing ourselves for cash, one way or another."

Hendy hit his cig again, considered, and then he bobbed his head a couple times.

"Beats sitting in a truck all day. Pissing in a damn bottle. Hell, my legs feel like rubber tubes, dude. Dead meat. Hurts just to stand here — like, shooting pains from my heels all the way up into my ass crack."

Kunkle wheezed again, harder this time. He watched his laugh slowly infect Hendy, who smiled and then chuckled a little himself.

And then he heard it. They both did.

Their heads turned. Their laughs cut off. They listened.

Nothing. Now.

But there had been something. Kunkle was sure of it.

Something… off.

It was a little scuffing sound and then a bulk plopping and splashing into a puddle. Something heavy. Quiet, though. The volume barely stronger than the whisper of the breeze kicking through the lot even now.

Probably nothing.

So why did it make the hair prick up all over Kunkle's body?

Hendy plucked the cigarette from his lip and whispered. He must've been spooked pretty good, too.

"Fuck was *that*?"

Kunkle shook his head. Then he pointed deeper into the lot, two fingers jutting toward where the sound had come from.

They both stared another few seconds. Quiet.

Kunkle didn't want to go look. Felt queasy at the thought of venturing out toward the noise. His gut all disturbed like a pond someone had just dropped a cinder block into.

Still, he hobbled that way, stepped out in front, and Hendy followed. They crept for it, not discussing it, maybe both knowing they shouldn't be doing this. Kunkle knew for damn sure he shouldn't, in any case — his thundering heart told him that much. But his legs kept going anyway, each step tremoring electricity down the length of the limbs in slow motion, easing him over the asphalt.

A stillness wafted over the night, a silence punctuated by their soft footsteps. Faint wind slithered over the hoods of the trucks now and then. All else was placid.

As they advanced toward the darkest corner of the lot, thick shadows swaddled them. No lightning seared in the heavens now. Even the fireflies seemed to have gone dark.

Kunkle slowed as he came upon the space between the last two trucks. He scanned the darkness, not quite sure what he was seeing.

Hendy gasped. A scraping sound in the trucker's throat. So sharp that it made Kunkle cringe, shoulders aquiver.

And then he saw it, too.

Not it.

Her.

The girl. Face down in a mud puddle. Naked. Sort of pretzeled into an awkward shape with something holding her there. Rope, maybe.

Yeah. Hog-tied.

Kunkle's throat clicked. A shaky breath entered him. His lips popped and parted as though he might say something, but no words came.

He wanted to go back into the light and call for help, call the police, call an ambulance. All those things a person's supposed to do in a situation like this. But now his legs wouldn't move.

He stood and stared. Felt his mouth hanging wide open, that muggy night air creeping past his lips, wriggling over his teeth.

Death.

The girl's skin shone purple in the dusky light. Almost looked phosphorescent against the blacktop, like those mushrooms that glow in the dark.

Murky water obscured most of her face. She wasn't breathing. That was for sure.

Death.

A body. A dead body. Right here in the parking lot at Big Jon's.

Death.

The dark lines drawn into her skin only came clear then, after a second. Slashes all over her back. Wounds opening, yawning to reveal slivers of red tissue.

She's all… slit.

Kunkle made a noise then — a moan or a groan released in an exhale, so soft. His own sound startled him, refreshed the goose bumps pebbling the surface of his body.

And part of him knew that nothing would be the same. Not after this. He knew that these few seconds would stick with him forever. The experience would scrawl something deep into his being with permanent ink, something that would come to him in dreams, something that would stay with him to the grave.

Death.

He'd seen death up close many times in his 42 years. In hospital rooms. On the highway. Once in a neighbor's garage where he'd found a suicide strung up from the rafters, face all turning black after eight days of dangling there alone.

He would almost think he'd have grown used to it by now. Hardened to it. Impervious.

But no matter how many times he brushed up against mortality — the finality, the fragility, they never failed to shock. Especially when the death crept up and caught him unaware.

He blinked. Let his eyes crawl over those gashes in her skin. Still wet.

And he thought of the lightning bugs in the murk again — those tiny glowing flares in a vast nothingness.

That's us, a voice spoke inside him. Fragile. Temporary. Little flashes in the darkness. There for a second and then gone forever.

Hendy gasped again, a sucking sound. Kunkle flinched and looked over, so shocked he'd almost forgotten the other was even there.

The cigarette dangled from the corner of the trucker's mouth, stuck to his bottom lip, adhered there by a thin film of saliva even though his lips were opened wide. The smoldering tube of tobacco wobbled next to where the chin should be, its red cherry pointed straight down.

CHAPTER 1

Darger stood in her kitchen, drizzling melted butter over a bowl of popcorn. The odor wafted into her face and made her mouth water.

"You pick out a movie yet?" she asked.

Owen's voice drifted in from the living room.

"I think I've narrowed it down to two. Would you rather watch *Alien* or *The Thing?*"

"Tough choice." Darger considered it while she sprinkled salt on the popcorn. "But I'm going to go with *Alien.*"

"You got it," Owen said.

Darger grabbed the popcorn and a bag of Reese's Pieces and entered the living room as the opening credits were starting. She handed Owen the bowl and plopped down beside him on the couch.

White text appeared on the screen: *A JAMES CAMERON FILM.*

Darger flinched. Her eyes narrowed to slits.

"Uh… stop the movie."

Owen picked up the remote, but he didn't finger the stop button. Instead he swiveled his head toward Darger, and his eyebrows scrunched together.

"Wait. I'm stopping it… why?"

"Wrong movie. Stop it."

Darger jabbed a finger at the screen while she spoke, but her eyes stayed locked on the remote in his hand. He held it across his body from her, curiously distant as though he might need to keep it away from her. Maybe he did.

The black box shifted in his hand. His thumb hovered out over the number pad in slow motion. He still didn't press any buttons.

Up on the screen, the title popped up in glowing blue letters: *ALIENS.*

"Wrong movie? What the hell are you talking about? You picked *Aliens.*"

Darger stopped herself from lunging for the remote and took a breath.

"No. I picked *Alien.* Singular."

"Well, you couldn't have picked *Alien,* because *Alien* wasn't among the choices."

Darger stared at him.

"You asked me to choose between *Aliens* and *The Thing*?"

"Yeah."

"Well that's lunacy. Obvious choice would be *The Thing,* but to even suggest *Aliens* without watching *Alien* first? It borders on sociopathic."

Owen snorted. He paused the movie at last, and Darger felt a weird surge of relief as the image held still on the screen.

"So any time I want to watch an *Alien* movie, I have to watch the entire franchise in order? Is that it?"

"No, but it makes sense to at least watch the first one, seeing as it's the best."

"Not a chance." Owen shook his head and shoved a handful of popcorn in his mouth. "*Aliens* is the best of the series."

Darger blinked.

"The first movie is the perfect blend of science fiction and horror. The pacing… the atmosphere… flawless. The sequel is like… *Rambo in Space.*"

Owen squinted at her like she was speaking a foreign language.

"Rambo in space… and that's supposed to be a bad thing?"

Darger took another deep breath.

"I don't mean to be dramatic, but this conversation is making me reconsider our entire relationship."

"Oh, it's too late for that," Owen said, scooting closer. "You're stuck with me now."

He leaned in as if to kiss her and then latched his hand over her face.

"Quit," Darger said, swatting at his arm.

He kept his hand on her face, cackling.

"There's no stopping a facehugger, Violet. Just try to relax. Once it's implanted the juvenile xenomorph, it will unlatch under its own power."

Darger squealed and wriggled away from him.

Owen reached out an arm, and she sent a playful kick his way, thinking he was trying to grab her again.

"Ouch!" He recoiled and then reached again, this time plucking her phone from the coffee table. "Your phone is ringing."

"No calls during movie night."

"I know, but it's Loshak, and I figure if he's calling at this hour..."

"Son of a bitch."

Darger sighed and took the phone. She thumbed the "Answer" icon and pressed the plastic slab to her ear.

"What's up?"

"Just got a call," Loshak said. "A serial case in North Carolina. I usually wouldn't call so late, but if we head out now, we can be on the scenes while they're still fresh."

"Scenes? As in more than one?"

"Yeah. Three victims. Two separate crime scenes."

She glanced at Owen, who shrugged.

"Alright," she said. "Give me twenty minutes."

When she hung up and explained the scenario to Owen, he smirked.

"It's OK. I know this is all just an elaborate ruse to get out of watching *Aliens*."

"You saw right through me," Darger said, heading into the bedroom.

She dragged her suitcase from where she'd dropped it after her last trip, which she hadn't even bothered to unpack yet. She plopped it on the bed and traded out the dirty clothes with fresh ones. In the bathroom, she swept a collection of toiletries into a small zippered bag, found her travel toothbrush, and chucked that into the suitcase as well.

As she changed out of her ancient t-shirt and dinosaur-print pajama pants and into a set of work clothes, she got a distinct whiff of coffee. Dark roast by the smell of it. Her favorite. And now her mouth was watering again.

She rolled her suitcase to the door and hesitated there for a second. Then she poked her head into the kitchen.

Owen stood in front of the coffee pot, pouring steaming black liquid into a giant travel thermos.

Darger wrapped her arms around him from behind.

"Have I ever told you how much I love you?"

"Does this absolve me of my take on *Alien* versus *Aliens*?"

"Let's not get carried away," she said, nipping at his neck.

A car pulled into the driveway, and the headlights flashed twice.

"Loshak's here. Gotta go." She spun Owen around and pressed her lips to his. "I'll call you in the morning."

"Not too early," he said, handing over the thermos. "You know I need my beauty sleep."

The suitcase went *thump-thump-thump* down the porch

steps as she made her way to the car. The big sedan wasn't Loshak's personal vehicle, meaning he must have borrowed one of the loaners from Quantico.

Loshak popped the trunk, and after depositing the suitcase inside, she climbed into the passenger seat.

There was a sensory battle happening in the interior of the car: the lingering odor of Swisher Sweets from whoever had previously used the car versus the "vanilla-rama" scented air freshener dangling from the dash. Darger rolled down her window, hoping the fresh air outside would reign supreme over both smells.

Loshak's eyes locked on the coffee thermos immediately.

"What have we here?"

"Coffee. Courtesy of Owen."

Loshak nodded approvingly as he backed out of the driveway.

"You know, I've always liked him."

They coasted down Darger's darkened street, porch lights dotting the blackness here and there. A crescent moon hung over them, cloaked in a layer of gauzy clouds.

Darger swiveled in her seat.

"OK, answer me this. You've seen *Alien*, right?"

"The movie?"

Darger nodded.

"Of course."

"And you've seen the second movie? *Aliens*?" She emphasized the *S* sound.

"Sure."

"Which one's better?" Darger asked.

Loshak's brow wrinkled.

"The first one. Obviously."

"Thank you!" Darger said, slapping one hand on the dash.

"Owen was just trying to sell me on *Aliens* being the best of the franchise."

"That's crazy talk."

"That's exactly what I said."

Loshak put on his turn signal and merged onto the highway, and Darger was forced to roll up her window. The cigarillo smell had faded some, but the phony vanilla fragrance was as strong as ever.

"So? What are we heading into?"

"I only have the barest of details so far. Three bodies, most likely sex workers according to the locals. The first was discovered about two hours ago at a truck stop near Roanoke Rapids. While they were busy with that, they got another call. Two more bodies in a nearby motel."

"Yikes. And they're sure the two scenes are connected?"

Loshak nodded.

"Apparently the bodies were in pretty rough condition. Extensive stab wounds and mutilation. Bite marks. The whole nine yards of piquerism."

"Lovely."

The dark highway blurred past. White line dotting the way, dividing the lanes. At some of the interchanges, streetlights illuminated the road, the sickly yellow glow barely beating back the gloom. The only other colors visible in the blackness were the periodic bursts of fast food signs. A splash of red here and blue there.

After a long stretch of silence, Loshak spoke again.

"I expect you've had some experience with these types, back when you were in Victim Services. Truck stop sex workers, I mean."

"Yeah. There's a lot of opportunity for sex trafficking in that kind of location. The population in the area is extremely transient. Most of the truckers are only stopping for the mandatory rest periods, and then they're back on the road."

"There's a name for them, right? The girls who work truck stops specifically?"

"Lot lizards," Darger said. "They generally don't like the moniker, though."

"I wouldn't imagine so." Loshak took a sip of coffee. "There's a certain less-than-human connotation to the word 'lizard.'"

Rain pattered the windshield now, and the wipers beat out a rhythm like a metronome.

Darger's eyelids felt heavy, but she knew that sleeping now would lead to grogginess when they reached their destination. She unscrewed the top of the thermos and took a big swallow of coffee.

"How prevalent would you say it is?" Loshak asked. "I mean, I've been to my fair share of truck stops, and maybe I'm blind, but I couldn't say I've ever seen any obvious signs of prostitution."

"Well, from what I understand, it's not all truck stops. In fact, a lot of them are pretty vigilant about keeping it away, especially the big chain operations. The last thing they want is to get a seedy reputation that scares away the quote-unquote 'respectable' clientele. Families and whatnot. So they'll crack down hard if they find evidence of drugs or prostitution. Many of them employ rent-a-cops to patrol the lots. I suspect a lot of the places that allow this kind of thing are owned by people who are getting some kind of kickback or are possibly partaking in the goods themselves."

Darger yawned and leaned her head back into the seat.

"But even if you had found yourself in such a place, you probably wouldn't have been in a position to notice. If you think about it, most truck stops keep the regular traffic completely separate from the semi traffic. Separate gas pumps. Separate parking lots. And from what I recall, the so-called 'party row,' which is where most of the illegal activity takes place, is in the very back row of truck parking."

"Like how back in high school, the back row was the goof-off row."

"Exactly. Just about as far as you can possibly get from the prying eyes of the regular folk."

"Huh. Kind of wild to think about how many times I've probably stopped for gas at one of these places just a few hundred yards from a hotbed of lawless iniquity."

The two agents fell quiet then. The highway stretched out before them, mostly vacant as the hour grew late. They plunged into the endless dark, the drone of the tires on the road somehow creating an aura of sleepiness inside the car. Darger's chin bobbed to her chest a few times, but the coffee kept her from fully going under.

When they curled down the exit ramp, centrifugal force pulled Darger's stomach to the side and woke her up fully. Her eyelids fluttered open and closed, and then she saw it.

Big Jon's Travel Center was a compound comprised of multiple buildings, all of it surrounded by a sea of asphalt. Pink neon light glinted down over everything, reflecting off the wet pavement in marbled patches.

Darger spotted three different gas stations, four fast food chains and a sit-down restaurant, a tire shop, and several other buildings with less obvious signage. This oasis of convenience was a glowing beacon enveloped by a whole lot of darkness, a whole lot of nothing.

Swampy-looking woods bordered the truck stop on three sides, with vines and ivy shrouding the trees and growing up the telephone poles like coils of green facial hair. Something about it gave Darger a creepy feeling.

Loshak veered into the parking lot and around the back side of a Bojangles. Beyond the front facades of the various businesses, Darger got her first glimpse of the crime scene.

The spiraling police lights. The cordoned-off area surrounded by yellow tape. The techs fluttering around between two semi-trailers.

The car drifted into a parking space between a police cruiser and an ambulance and came to a halt. It felt strange to stop so suddenly after all that driving, all that momentum. Three straight hours of pressing forward like a shark. And then stillness.

Darger took one last swig of coffee from the thermos and climbed out into the night.

CHAPTER 2

A whitewashed brick facade coated the diner, the building nearest to where the body had been discovered. It looked clean and modern. Manicured bushes rose out of beds of porous red gravel, decorating each side of the front door. Beyond that, bright light gleamed in the boxes of the windows dotting the rest of the building, hollow screens that exposed the booths and tables inside.

Despite the late hour, a crowd of gawkers milled around there in front of the bricks, just beyond the border of the crime scene tape. Mostly men, decked out in flannel and jeans and trucker hats. Smoking cigarettes and drinking from gigantic Big Gulp-style cups.

Darger studied the group as she crossed the lot, wondering if the killer might be among them. She looked for anyone who seemed unduly nervous, but the whole lot of them seemed jittery and restless. More than one of the men rocked from foot to foot. Another chewed his nails. Darger knew that the notion of all truckers being on speed was a stereotype, but she supposed even the clean ones probably chugged caffeine by the liter. Throw in a grisly crime scene and it made sense that they'd be keyed up.

When they reached the line of the crime scene tape, a uniformed police officer manning the barricade held up his hands.

"Sorry, no one's allowed past this point."

He was pale-faced and impossibly young. Peach fuzz dusted his top lip. Trying (and failing, Darger thought) to grow a proper cop 'stache.

Loshak pulled out his badge.

"We're FBI."

The uniform squinted at the badge, mouth hanging slightly agape.

"OK. But, um… I'm not supposed to… uh… Hold on just a sec."

He turned and beckoned to a middle-aged Black woman in a suit standing to one side of an evidence van.

"Detective Bledsoe?"

Bledsoe raised her eyebrows.

"The, uh… there's two people here… Fed-uh… F…"

The uniform gave up and jogged over to her.

Darger watched him gesticulating as he explained the situation. Before he was finished, Bledsoe was marching toward them, shaking her head.

"You the folks from the FBI?" she asked, lifting the crime scene tape so they could step under it.

"That's us," Loshak said, and they took turns introducing themselves.

"Sorry about that," Bledsoe said with a flick of the eyes toward the young policeman. "Some of these rookies take things like, 'Don't let anyone past the tape,' too literally."

"It's no problem," Loshak said.

"Well, we appreciate you coming down on such short notice. My partner's over at the second scene when you wrap things up here."

She led them to the back of the evidence van where the tech equipment was set up. She handed them each a pair of booties, gloves, and a bunny suit.

"We know anything about the vic, yet?" Loshak asked.

Bledsoe nodded.

"Name's Tara Bemis. Twenty-six years old. Has a few priors for solicitation and possession."

When they were properly suited up, Bledsoe waved them around a line of privacy screens set up to block the crowd's view of the actual crime scene.

They rounded the barrier, and Darger caught her first glimpse of the body, lit up under the artificial glow of the portable lights.

The girl lay on her stomach, nude save for a pair of strappy high heels. Her wrists and ankles were bound together behind her back, curving her body into something like the letter "L." She was partially submerged in a puddle, the murky water obscuring the left side of her face.

The glaring lights made the girl look very small and pale. Darger's first thought was a nonsensical one: *She must be freezing. Someone should dry her off. Give her a blanket.*

She grimaced. The absurdity of the blanket idea made goosebumps ripple over the backs of her arms.

Then the fear hit — that cold, familiar feeling she got whenever she walked the scenes. Something cleansing in it. Stark and purifying.

The chill saturated her flesh. Her breathing suddenly felt loud and fluttery inside her head.

The fright always made her feel lonely, singular, even when she was surrounded by others. Cold and distant.

With the fear sharpening her senses, she studied the scene again. Pierced the surface of the morbid spectacle and really looked at the details.

The girl seemed a fragile thing. Frail and bony and exposed by the harsh lighting. She remained somehow apart from all the activity flitting around her.

She's lonely, too.

Death, like fear, eventually made each of us lonesome, Darger supposed.

The ligature marks came clear then. A dark coil of bruising wrapped around her neck like a black snake. Textured like a rope, a braided pattern. Fainter, shadowy lines above and below the first.

Then her eyes swept back to the bulk of the corpse, and the wounds filtered into focus. Red lines slashed roughly into the skin, some of the openings parting enough to reveal bits of stringy muscle tissue.

Loshak was right about the piquerism angle. Even from a distance, Darger could see that the cuts on the body were extensive. Her back was riddled with stab wounds and bruises.

She stepped closer, squatted next to the body, and examined the girl's face. It was mottled and swollen, and two dark tracks down her cheeks showed where her mascara had run when she cried. The death had been neither quick nor painless.

Her eyes drifted lower on the face. Hovered on the lips.

Something there. Protruding.

The cold gripped Darger more tightly all of a sudden. More goosebumps crawling over her.

A fluttering of her eyelids obscured her sight. Involuntary.

She tried to re-steady her vision on what she'd just seen. Couldn't.

"There's something in her mouth," she said. "Looks like… fabric."

CHAPTER 3

Darger fought to get her eyelids to stop fluttering, some panic already gnawing in her gut. She sat back from the corpse and took a deep breath. It helped.

The lights over the lot whirled another second, and then they settled. When she could see straight again, she cranked her head around to the woman standing just behind her.

Detective Bledsoe pursed her lips. Her voice came out low, like maybe she thought it wise to keep the details quiet for now. Darger could respect the instinct for discretion.

"Yeah, I noticed the fabric too. Guess we won't know exactly what it is until the M.E. does the post-mortem."

Darger nodded once and stood. The fear seemed to be rolling away from her still, an ebbing tide pulling off of the beach. She couldn't decide if the bustling techs on the periphery of the scene made the twinge of anxiety better or worse.

Would it better to be out here alone?

Realizing Loshak had barely made a peep since they'd come within sight of the body, Darger glanced over at him. She expected to find him quietly brooding over the disturbing tableau, but instead, he was fiddling with a sheaf of papers attached to a clipboard.

"You OK over there?" she asked.

"Who, me?" He paged through the documents. "I'm fine."

Darger stood again and scanned the lot. The body had been dumped right at the back edge of the property, only a few feet from the chain-link fence and the inky darkness of the forest beyond. Crickets shrieked out an endless zithering chorus, and Darger could smell the unmistakable green funk of a not-so-distant swamp.

She turned and looked past the crowd, studying the non-law enforcement vehicles in the lot. Several dozen semis, plus the regular consumer traffic. It was going to be a hell of a lot of potential suspects to sift through. She hoped this place had decent security footage.

Her eyes slid back to the crowd of onlookers behind the barricade, and she noticed a lone woman standing off to one side. There was something in her eyes. A haunted look. She'd known their victim, Darger was sure of it.

"Have you taken any witness statements?"

Bledsoe nodded.

"We talked to damn near everyone who was here when it happened. The ones who didn't flee when they heard the cops were coming, anyway." She gestured with a flick of her chin at the gawkers. "Guy in the camo hat is the one who found her. Randall Hendy. Him and another guy…"

Bledsoe flipped through her own notes.

"Dwayne Kunkle."

"Both truckers?"

"Hendy's a driver, but Kunkle works here at the truck stop. He's a sort of janitor-slash-maintenance man. He got called away to take care of some sort of plumbing emergency, but he should be around here somewhere."

Now Bledsoe wagged her elbow at the girl Darger had noticed moments before.

"And then the girl on the far end of the crowd there, the one in the denim cutoffs, is a friend of the deceased. Another working girl. Name's Candace Delaney."

Loshak tucked his clipboard under his arm and raised his

eyebrows at Darger.

"Lots of options on who to talk to. What do you think?" Loshak asked.

"Let's talk to the girl first. The victim's friend."

He nodded once, and they set off across the asphalt.

CHAPTER 4

As they approached the barrier of the crime scene, some of the wary eyes in the crowd turned their way. Darger saw pain and suspicion in the expressions there. Sallow faces. Clenched jaws.

She reminded herself that the scrutiny wasn't personal as she stepped over the line and into the mob. People were upset. Leery of outsiders. It was a natural response to something like this.

They picked their way through the cluster, a mix of flannelled bodies turning sideways to get out of their way. When they reached Candace, Darger stepped out front to take point.

The woman's hair was curly and wet-looking, shellacked into tight coils with some kind of gel or mousse. She wore a belt with skull studs on it and a pair of giant heart-shaped earrings with the word "Bitch" engraved in the middle. Her eyes were ringed with a thick outline of eyeliner and decked out with artificial lashes.

Darger didn't think she could be older than 25. Still a kid in most ways.

After making the proper introductions, Darger asked if they could talk for a minute.

"Sure," the girl said. "And you can call me Candy. Everyone does."

Her eyes kept returning to the police barrier, and Darger realized it was probably going to be difficult for Candy to concentrate if they tried to interview her within sight of the crime scene.

"Why don't we go inside?" Darger suggested, pointing at the restaurant at one end of the lot.

Candy's gaze flicked over to the spinning sign on the roof of the place that advertised "Big Jon's Ribs & More… BREAKFAST - LUNCH - DINNER!"

"Oh, I'm not allowed inside."

"Why not?"

The girl's mouth twitched into something that wasn't quite a smile.

"It's a rule. If you look like me, they… make assumptions."

Darger nodded.

"Well, if they have a problem with it, they can take it up with me. Unless you wouldn't feel comfortable?"

Candy stared at the place for a few moments and then smiled a little for real.

"Nah, it'll be funny to see the looks on their faces. Those snobby waitresses in there? They're not gonna like bein' forced to serve the likes of me."

The three of them crossed the lot to the entrance of the restaurant, Candy's platform espadrilles scraping and clunking over the asphalt.

A sign in the entryway read, "Please take a seat." There were only a few tables occupied — Darger suspected there'd be more if not for the crowd of rubberneckers outside.

They chose a table far from the other patrons, a booth next to a large fake fig tree.

A waitress bustled over, her saccharine smile souring when she spotted Candy. She looked poised to say something, but then Darger caught her eye.

"I'm Special Agent Violet Darger. I hope you don't mind if we sit here and talk for a bit."

The waitress's eyes went from the agents to Candy and back

to the agents. She tried to compose her face into something pleasant again, but she was only marginally successful.

"Of course not. Can I get y'all anything?"

"I'll have some coffee and a slice of coconut cream pie," Darger said. "How about you, Candy? You want anything?"

There was a mischievous look on the girl's face as she perused the menu.

"Could you tell me what y'all's specials are today?"

The waitress blinked.

"We've got the meatloaf, and the turkey dinner."

"Mm," Candy said, pursing her lips. "And what's the soup du jour?"

"Minestrone."

Candy clicked her tongue.

"Could you tell me what comes with the patty melt?"

The waitress's face was like stone.

"You have a choice of fries, salad, or baked potato."

"And are those shoestring or steak fries?"

"Steak," the waitress said through gritted teeth.

"Oh my, you make that sound so good, I think that's what I'll go for. The patty melt with fries. Please and thank you."

Candy batted her eyelashes as she handed her menu to the waitress.

Loshak ordered coffee and stuffed French toast.

When the waitress walked away, Candy let out a little chuckle.

"Good lord, did you see her face? Just wait 'til I tell—"

The words cut off, and Candy's face fell.

"Shit," she pressed her lips together. "I keep forgettin' that she's…"

She didn't finish the sentence, but Darger finished the thought for her internally.

I keep forgettin' that she's dead.

Darger opened her mouth to say something reassuring, but Candy spoke again before she could.

"You know what's really fucked up?"

"What?"

"I haven't even cried. I mean, that's my best friend out there. Shouldn't I be a fuckin' mess right now? Instead, I'm in here fuckin' with the waitress for shits and giggles."

"That's normal," Darger said. "You're probably still in shock. The reality of it hasn't fully hit you yet, you know?"

Candy inhaled and let out a shaky breath.

"I guess. But it sure as hell should have hit me. I mean, I saw her body, for Christ's sake. Rushed straight over after Randy started hollerin'. This was before the police got here and put up that barrier. I ran right up on her, my toes like an inch shy of the… the puddle. Stared down. Had this almost out-of-body experience when I seen that it was Tara. Like it was almost too private, seeing her that way… Like Tara, she should have been able to keep that to herself or somethin'."

Darger remembered her own urge to cover the girl's body.

"How long have you known Tara?"

"Two, three years. We first met down in Florida. Outside of Jacksonville. We were both just startin' out then. Kinda learned the trade together. Then we kicked around St. Augustine awhile. Only came up here a few months ago."

"Was there a reason you left Florida?"

Candy shrugged.

"Just got kinda stale, you know? It happens sometimes. The lot we were workin' at originally got too crowded, and we heard from one of the drivers that there was places up north with less competition. Nice places, too. Big Jon's is sort of a beloved truck stop among the drivers. One of the busiest in the state, even if it's kinda out in the boonies. Or maybe because it is. So we said, what the hell? Hitched a ride and been here ever since."

The waitress returned with their food, setting it down and leaving without a word.

Candy stared down at the patty melt, as if she didn't understand why it was there.

"Is something wrong?" Darger asked.

"I don't think I can eat this." She swallowed and pushed the plate away. "I'm sorry, it's just the idea of food right now..."

"No need to apologize," Darger said. "I understand."

Darger picked up Candy's plate and set it on the table on the booth behind them. Instinct told her it was better out of sight.

Candy gave a weak smile.

"Waitress probably had the kitchen staff spit in it anyway."

Loshak grimaced a little as he took a bite of his own food, clearly imagining his French toast loaded with loogies, but Darger kept the conversation rolling.

"Why do the waitresses have so much animosity toward you?"

"It ain't just the waitresses. It's damn near everybody that works here. They think they're better than us because they work for The Man and conform to what society says you're supposed to do. They think I degrade myself, doin' what I do. But let me ask you something. What's more degrading? Working forty hours at this shithole, gettin' paid maybe four hundred bucks a week, and still havin' to make ends meet with food stamps? Or working for yerself, makin' four hundred in a single night, and doin' whatever the hell you want the rest of the time? Not to mention the fact that we serve the same clientele. Now, 95 percent of these drivers are solid guys.

Decent folk, you know? Raised right. But that other five percent? Complete fuckin' animals. At least when they cop a feel with me, I get paid for it. These girls have to grit their teeth and offer them a refill on their coffee."

"Do you know where Tara was from? Anything about her family?"

"Only bits and pieces. We had sort of an unspoken rule, I guess. No pasts. We never talked about where we came from or what things were like before this. Part of it is that we didn't need to. Most of us didn't get here by way of private school. Not a lot of Ivy Leaguers working the lots, ya know?"

Something resembling a smile tugged at the corners of Candy's mouth for half a second before she went on.

"I know she was a runaway, like me. Except where I was running away from foster care, I think Tara had a home. But probably not a good one. Otherwise, why leave, right? And she definitely spent some time on the streets. That's one of those things you get used to spotting in a person. But we have a place now. It's not the nicest, but it's ours."

Candy shook her head and picked at the chipped nail polish on her thumb.

"Or… it was. Guess it's just mine now."

"What can you tell us about tonight?" Darger asked. "Did you see who Tara was with at any point?"

With a sigh, Candy turned and stared out the window at the lot.

"We usually try to get here before dark, but we were late today. Tara was out of cigarettes, so she went inside, and I headed for the lot. Spotted one of my regulars almost immediately, so I didn't see her at all after that until there was all the fuss over the radio about someone finding something in the lot. Someone said the cops were on their way, and I figured that was my cue to skedaddle. The last thing I needed was to get hassled by the po-po tonight. I figured Tara'd be thinkin' the same thing, and I was expecting to meet up with her at the car, but then…"

Darger knew there was a reel playing the scene over again in Candy's head. The moment she'd toed up to the mud puddle, discovered Tara's body. The images and sounds of that split second in time would be burned into her mind forever.

"Do you have any idea who Tara might have been with tonight?"

Candy closed her eyes.

"I wish to fuck I did. I wish I knew who he was so I could pay him back for what he done."

Her fingers curled into fists, squeezing so hard they shook slightly.

"You said before that you work for yourself. Does that mean you're independent?"

The question brought Candy back. She snapped her head around, nodding emphatically.

"Goddamn right. That's another reason we left Florida. Fuckin' dirtbag pimps. The first time, this guy came around and tried to lay claim to the whole track. Said we belonged to him now. Tried to set a quota and brought in this mean-lookin' Bottom to collect. So we got the fuck out. Snuck away in the middle of the night so they couldn't try to shake us down. Found somewhere new. Things were OK for a few months, and then some guy moved in his whole stable of girls. He mostly left us renegades alone, but the competition killed business for us, so the result was the same."

"And that's when you and Tara moved up here?"

"Uh-huh."

"You mentioned that you spotted a regular customer. Did

Tara have any regulars?"

"Oh, sure. Some of the guys have routes like clockwork, and they'll stop pretty much anytime they come through here. Some of 'em end up here two, three, even four nights a week, depending on their routes."

"Anyone she ever complained about?"

Candy drummed her fingers on the tabletop.

"There was this guy a few months back who stiffed her on payment. When she tried to raise a stink about it, he grabbed her by the hair and practically threw her out of his truck. But we haven't seen him around since then."

"What about Johns who wanted something extra? Bondage or that kind of thing?"

Candy was already shaking her head.

"No. Tara steered clear of any of that. She had a… bad experience. This was years ago, before we met, and I don't really know the details. Again, no pasts. But she said more than once that she wasn't about to let anybody tie her up or put handcuffs on her, not for any amount of money." She crossed her arms over her chest, hugging herself. "I mean, shit. That was one of the reasons we worked the lots. Most of the drivers, they're not lookin' for nothin' too wild, usually. The guys on the corner, you never know what whackadoodle stuff they might want. Not to mention the turnover. Trucks comin' in at all hours, you know? A constant flow of potential customers, and you don't even have to leave the lot. Plus, it's safer."

"Safer? How?"

"I mean, everyone sees you get into a truck, right? There's witnesses. No one's gonna…"

The words seemed to choke out all of a sudden, and Candy's face fell.

"No one's gonna try anything crazy," she said, her voice

cracking. "Or that's what I thought, anyway. Before tonight."

Something clicked deep in the girl's throat. Her eyelashes fluttered like moth wings.

And then, at last, Candy was crying.

CHAPTER 5

Back outside, the wet asphalt still gleamed under the lamps shining down on the lot. The mob of people trying to sneak a peek at the crime scene edged right up to the sawhorse barrier holding them back.

Darger and Loshak found Randall Hendy in roughly the same spot in the crowd as before. They pulled him around the side of one of the buildings, out of earshot from the rest of the onlookers.

Hendy stood with his back almost up to the wall with his arms crossed over his chest, the grid of brickwork behind him looking harsh in the half-light. Shadows swathed one side of the trucker's face, leaving only a fraction of the weak jaw visible in the glow slanting down from the streetlight. His tiny chin reminded Darger of a cat's somehow.

She cleared her throat before she began the questioning.

"Can you tell us what happened here tonight?"

Hendy peeled the camo trucker hat off his head and raked his fingers through his hair.

"Jesus, it's still kind of a blur, really. Have to keep reminding myself it's real."

"Start from the beginning," Loshak said. "What were you doing just before you discovered the body?"

"I was talking to Dwayne."

"Dwayne Kunkle? What were you two talking about?"

"Nothin', really. I owed him some money, and he'd come to collect." He shook his head. "Practically jumped on me as soon as I pulled in here. Didn't even give me a chance to take a leak before he's breathing down my neck for his hundred bucks. Tight ass."

He blinked a couple of times before he went on, eyes looking far away now, lost in thought. Then he seemed to come back to the moment.

"Anyway, we were just standing there, shootin' the shit, and we heard something."

"What did you hear?"

Hendy fiddled with the brim of his hat.

"A sort of scraping sound and then a splash. Like someone stomping their foot into a mud puddle or somethin'. But just the once, and then utter quiet. I swear even the crickets stopped makin' noise just then." He blinked again, eyes shifting around. "All I know is that it gave me the heebie jeebies right off. I can't say why. If I stop and think about it, I have a hard time figurin' why I even paid it any mind at all. It was just a little noise in a truck stop parkin' lot. So what?"

Hendy paused and licked his lips.

"But then I saw Dwayne's face, and I could see he was spooked, too. It was like we both already knew something bad was going down, somehow. Instincts and shit. What do they call it? A gut feelin'."

"Can you show us where you were standing when you heard the sound?"

Hendy swiveled around and gestured at one of the trucks.

"That's my truck there, with the red cab and American flag mud flaps. We were standing just next to the driver's side door." He swept his arm over the rest of the lot. "Now you have to picture that there were more trucks parked out here. There was a truck on either side of the, uh… body… when we found it… or her. Once word got around that the police were coming, a bunch of the guys just took off. Especially the ones in party row."

He swallowed then, his Adam's apple bobbing up and down like a peach pit jutting out of the skin covering his neck.

"Anyway, we heard the sound, and we went to check it out. Didn't even say nothin' to each other, just started walking over. I… When I first seen her, I thought it must be a joke. A doll or something, you know? They sell all sorts of weird shit inside the adult bookstore, with the porno and whatnot. A couple years back, as a prank, one guy tied a blowup doll to another guy's truck. Everyone had a laugh. So that was my first thought." He gave his head a little shake. "But... not this time."

His eyes flicked from Darger's to Loshak's and back to Darger's.

"Guess I was in shock once I realized it wasn't no doll. Everything's kinda fuzzy after that. All jumbled up. I kinda remember callin' the cops, or… more like I remember that it had happened, that I *had* called 911 or whatever, more than I actually remember doin' it, I guess."

"Do you remember anything about the trucks that were parked near the body?" Darger asked.

"No, ma'am," he said, frowning. "There coulda been a circus elephant settin' out here, and I don't think I'd remember seeing it."

Again Darger hoped the truck stop had decent security footage. Sorting out the trucks closest to the body would give them another angle to pursue.

"What about the victim? Did you know her?"

"I'd seen her around, I think, but I didn't know her name or nothin'. Never spoke to her. But she looked familiar some, yeah. There's a lot of 'em, the girls that work the lot. They come and go. And then there's a lot of these lots, too. All up and down the highway. Sometimes the names and faces start to bleed together. Guess I end up sleeping at damn near all of the truck stops, one time or another."

He shrugged, and Darger noted a little quiver in the muscles connecting his neck to his shoulders.

"I used to be into the party scene, the drug scene, when I first started drivin'. But it takes a toll on you. Especially the speed." He shook his head. "I been clean for five years. Don't touch any of that stuff anymore. I thank my wife for that. She stood by me while I went through treatment. Got some counseling. I still drink, but that's just alone in my truck at night so I can sleep. Truth is, I haven't enjoyed alcohol's effects in some years, even before I got cleaned up. I still feel that warmth come over me and, like, sense my thoughts slow down, of course, but there's no joy in it. Not anymore. The euphoria I used to feel is just *pfft,* gone."

"Is there a reason you parked so close to the back row?" Loshak asked. "I understand that's where a lot of the party scene is, in most lots."

"Sure, sure. I usually stay the hell away from party row. Don't want anything to do with it. Not to mention the fact that the girls'll come knocking at all hours when you're parked back here. Hell, sometimes they'll knock no matter where you're parked, but I still try to keep my distance. Not for temptation's sake, mind you. It's just that it don't interest me none. Anyway, the lot was damn near full up when I pulled in this evening. So it ain't like I had a lot of choice but to park all the way back here."

"What time did you get here?"

"It was around a quarter of nine. Got the exact time in my logbooks, if you want it." He sighed. "I was really looking forward to havin' myself a shower inside and the meatloaf special, but I don't think I could eat a bite now. Don't know how I'm gonna sleep after all this, either. Guess I'll probably just put on my headphones and watch *Twister* in hopes I doze off at some point."

Loshak glanced up, eyebrows raised.

"The tornado movie? With Bill Paxton?"

Hendy smiled then.

"Hell yeah. It's one of my favorites. Probably seen it two hundred times." He shrugged. "Sometimes you're so beat after driving all day, you can't watch something new, 'cause that would require concentration, you know? So I have a rotation. Maybe a dozen classics that I watch over and over. That way it don't matter if I zone out or fall asleep."

"Sounds like the job takes a lot out off you."

Hendy let out something that was half laugh, half scoff.

"Shoot, you can say that again. I've been sayin' to myself I'm only gonna do so many more runs. That I gotta figure out something else. Because Jesus…" He smeared a hand over his face. "No one should have to see what I just saw. Shit, maybe this is a sign that it's time to get away from all this for good. Stayin' clean myself is one thing. No trouble there. But just being around it. Seeing what goes on here. I don't want to do that anymore. I mean, every girl I see on the lot from now on is gonna make me think of that girl in the puddle back there. Maybe that's a selfish way of lookin' at it. I ain't the one who died. I'm standin' here breathin' and talkin' and whatever the hell. But goddamn. It gets under your skin, ya know? I can't… I can't look at this shit anymore and pretend it don't bother me."

CHAPTER 6

After wrapping up their talk with Randall Hendy, Darger and Loshak went in search of their second eyewitness. An electronic chime sounded as they stepped through the automatic doors of the truck stop, and it took several seconds of slitting her eyelids for Darger's eyes to adjust to the bright fluorescent lighting inside the convenience store.

Without a word, Loshak made a beeline for a shelf of energy drinks. Darger had already had the same thought — it was going to be a long night, and they'd need the caffeine. She moved past him to the coolers and grabbed a cold brew coffee for herself.

The cashier was in her mid-20s and wore dark purple lipstick and an eyebrow ring. Her eyes went wide when she glanced up from her phone and got a look at them. The expression made her look like a curious raccoon.

"Y'all here 'cause of the murder?"

Darger smiled.

"We're that obvious?"

The cashier snapped her gum and shrugged.

"We don't get a lot of folks in suits."

As Darger tapped her credit card against the card reader, she remembered that Candy had told them about Tara coming into the truck stop to buy cigarettes.

"She came in here tonight, right? The victim, I mean."

The cashier nodded.

"Yeah. She was in here. Bought a pack of Camel Lights."

"Was she by herself?"

"Yes, ma'am."

"Did you see her talking to anyone?"

"No. I mean, that's one of the rules."

"The rules?"

"The lot, uh, girls can come in here for smokes and stuff, but they can't... you know... solicit inside the premises, or whatever. So they tend to be in and out pretty quick."

Darger made a mental note to get security footage from inside the various businesses on the truck stop premises in addition to the exterior footage.

There was a trilling sound that reminded Darger of a landline telephone ringing. The cashier glanced at one of the many screens behind the counter and held up her hand.

"Just one second." She pressed a button and spoke into a small microphone attached to an intercom system. "Shower Customer Number 92, your shower is ready. Please proceed to Shower Four."

She repeated the message a second time, her voice echoing out from the loudspeakers mounted at various locations in the ceiling on a slight delay.

When the cashier finished her announcement, she returned her attention to Darger and Loshak.

"Anything else I can help y'all with?"

"Yes," Darger said, grasping her coffee drink and giving it a shake. "Can you tell us where to find Dwayne Kunkle?"

"Try the laundromat. One of the washing machines went ka-doosh earlier, so he was cleaning up and sh-stuff." She pointed a finger lacquered in dark green glitter at a pair of double doors painted a garish pumpkin orange. "Through those doors and hang a left. There are signs on the wall and whatnot. You can't miss it. And if he's not there, he might be mopping up in the lounge, opposite end of the hall."

Darger gave her a nod.

"Thanks."

She and Loshak moved toward the orange doors. The moment Loshak pushed through the threshold, Darger heard the unmistakable sounds of a pornographic movie coming from the so-called "lounge."

The doors of the darkened room were open wide so that anyone in the hallway could see inside. It was set up like a home theater, with rows of seats and a large screen on the wall. Two men were seated at opposite sides of the room.

Nothing weird going on here, Darger thought to herself. Just two strangers watchin' a porno together at a truck stop in the middle of the night.

"Wholesome," Loshak said.

Darger snorted, causing one of the men to whip his head around. She stepped back from the door, chuckling.

They went left, moving on to a brightly lit room farther down the hall. Rows of commercial washing machines and dryers lined the walls.

One of the washing machines was pushed forward from the rest of the row. A toolbox rested on top, the metal surface covered completely with multiple layers of stickers: Woody Woodpecker, Pepsi-Cola, a parody of the Starbucks logo that said, "Stealin' Yo Bucks," and dozens more that were either unfamiliar or obscured by the other stickers.

Darger couldn't see anyone as they entered, but a few faint *clinks* and *clanks* could be heard from behind the cockeyed washing machine.

"Dwayne Kunkle?"

A head popped up — a middle-aged man with bright green eyes and dark hair slicked back. It almost looked like his head was floating behind the machine, disembodied.

"That's me."

"I'm Agent Darger." She aimed a thumb beside her. "This is my partner, Agent Loshak. Do you mind if we ask you a few questions?"

He stood up and set a socket wrench on top of the machine. He came out from behind the metal box then, revealing a lanky frame encased in a janitor's brown jumpsuit that didn't quite seem long enough in the arms or legs — a Jack Skellington build on this one, Darger thought.

Something youthful shone in the half-smile on his face, gleamed in his eyes. He maybe could have passed for mid-30s, Darger estimated, but the intricate creases of the crow's feet encircling his eyelids revealed his real age to be 45 or so.

"This is about Tara, I expect," he said, wiping his hands on the chest of his jumpsuit. "I talked to the detectives earlier, but I kinda figured there'd be more questions to answer."

"You knew her?"

"Tara?"

He lifted one shoulder and let it fall back down. A child's gesture. He went on.

"A little. Shared a six-pack with her after my shift a few times. Made small talk. 'Course I never figured it'd end up the way it did, me and Hendy finding her out there in the lot… like she was. I didn't even reco'nize her. Not at first. But then…"

He scowled as he spoke, lips puckering like he'd tasted something bitter. His skin suddenly seemed waxy and moist, a flu-ridden pallor. Darger decided to redirect him toward the nature of his prior relationship with the victim to keep him talking.

"It seems like most of the other employees here make it a point not to be friendly with the girls on the lot."

"Yeah, well… some of the lizards are mean as hell, so I

don't blame them. It's not really their fault, of course. That's a rough trade they're in, and it hardens 'em up pretty good." He adjusted his jumpsuit with a sniff. "But they're not all like that. Some of 'em are real kindhearted souls. Wouldn't hurt a fly. I guess most of the people here ain't interested in spotting the difference."

"And Tara was one of the kindhearted ones?"

"I'd say so. Didn't have an ounce of aggression in her that I could see, anyway."

"And what did you talk about?"

Kunkle leaned against the washer and picked at one of the stickers on the toolbox with his thumbnail.

"Oh, little bits of everything. The last time we talked, she said she was thinkin' about making a change. Saving up and getting out of the trade."

Darger raised an eyebrow.

"Really? Did she say what she wanted to do?"

"She was talking about a cousin of hers. Lives out in California and started up some kind of Jane Fonda-type thing. You know, whatever they call it when the ladies dress up in the tights and the spandex leotards..."

Darger couldn't help but smile at the description.

"Aerobics?"

He snapped his fingers and pointed at her.

"Bingo. But Tara said this was different because it was set to music, and there's dancing involved. It had some kind of cutesy name I can't remember. I guess she and this cousin used to take dance classes together as kids, and she was thinking that if her cousin could do this thing, then, by God, she could do it too."

"Do you think she was serious about it?"

He clicked his tongue and winced.

"Eh... not to be an asshole, but a lot of 'em say that kind of stuff. They've always got big plans, big dreams, you know? Claim that this here is just a temporary thing. Those are the ones who are honest about what they do. Then there's the ones who insist they ain't doing what they're doing. Knew this one lizard who insisted she'd never had sex for money. Not once. Meanwhile, she's turnin' ten tricks on a Tuesday night. Knew another one who always told tales about how the drivers were all in love with her and would propose to her. I guess everyone has a story they gotta tell themself to get by." He inhaled. "Of course, I didn't tell her that."

"What did you tell her?"

He flared his nostrils before he answered. Crossed his arms over his chest.

"I mentioned that I used to be a driver back in the day, before this job."

"You drove a truck?" Loshak asked.

Kunkle nodded.

"What made you decide to leave it?"

"Well, I like to say that the universe made the decision for me. I knew I couldn't keep on drivin' forever. See, I got this herniated disc, and all the hours of sitting was just killin' my back. Could hardly sleep from the pain of it. And one day I was comin' through here and got to talkin' to Ernie — he was my predecessor. He says to me that he's fixing to retire and move down to Sarasota, was actually supposed to have retired the month before, but he didn't want to leave Big Jon's until he'd found a replacement. The problem was finding someone skilled enough to do the job who also didn't mind that we're kind of out in Bumfuck, Nowhere… His wife was hot to trot and gettin' more pissed by the day at Ernie's feet-dragging. So I started asking him about the job. Now, the starting money wasn't what I was makin' on the road, but there's always a trade-off, isn't there? And he said management, for the most part, was hands off. Unless there's some kind of emergency, they leave you be. Ernie even made his own schedule. So I told him I was interested, but I wanted a few days to think on it. Had to finish my run anyway. But I knew I was gonna take the job before I drove out of the lot. It's like I said, the universe made the decision for me."

"Is that what you told Tara?"

"It is. And she wanted to know if I had any regrets. Now, I was honest. There are parts I miss. Like I said, the pay was better. But also, I enjoyed that sense of forward momentum. That feeling like I had a singular purpose. When you're drivin' truck, all of existence boils down to moving from point A to point B. Something made sense about that. A kind of peace in the simplicity of it. But I wouldn't go back. You can't beat sleeping in a real bed at night. Especially not with a fucked-up back."

He sighed and straightened, picking up the socket wrench and thumping it against the leg of his paint-stained jumpsuit.

"Anyhow, it's a real shame what happened to her. Then again, these girls know what they're getting into. Trouble just follows all of 'em. Eventually it bests 'em. Especially a girl like Tara. Too nice for her own good, you know? You gotta be hard to make it, this kind of work, this kind of world."

He paused and shook his head slowly.

"It's a real sorrowful thing sometimes, but it's the way of the world."

CHAPTER 7

When they'd finished with Kunkle, they thanked him and left him to tinker with the broken washing machine. There were still animalistic grunts and moans emanating from the lounge as they passed, but Darger found the porn noises less amusing this time.

She was pondering the type of killer who preyed on prostitutes. Treated them as disposable. And was it any wonder? She recalled the look on the waitress's face when she was forced to tolerate Candy's very presence.

It wasn't just the killers who thought of sex workers as trash. Society as a whole often took a "this is what happens" attitude when a prostitute met a bad end.

The callousness wasn't confined to the public, either. For years, the LAPD had referred to crimes against prostitutes as NHI — No Human Involved.

Darger was familiar with the grim statistics surrounding the matter. One study said that 75% of serial murder victims were sex workers. Another study found that murder was the number one cause of death among those who worked in prostitution.

"Kind of ironic," Loshak said.

Darger shook her head slightly to clear her thoughts.

"What?"

"Well, Kunkle said he got out of trucking because 'the universe decided for him.' I was just thinking about how Tara had wanted out, and in a way, the universe decided for her, too." He sighed. "She's out, alright. Just not in the way she would have hoped."

☾

The Cozy Motor Lodge — the site of the second crime scene — was located less than a mile from Big Jon's Travel Center. Emergency vehicles clogged the parking lot, some with flashers glittering, some gone dark. Loshak found a spot on the road and parked there, his car straddling the line where the gravely shoulder gave way to a sloped embankment of grass.

Darger climbed out, stretched, and felt something pop along her spine, not unpleasantly. Then she turned and took in the details of the motel, humid night air coiling around her as she did.

Between the vintage neon sign and the room doors painted Pepto Bismol pink, she figured the place was built in the mid-to-late 60s. And given the state of it, she didn't think any maintenance work had been done on it since.

Half the bulbs in the big red arrow on the sign were burned out. The siding had faded to a lifeless gray shade that reminded her of spoiled meat, and the pink paint on the doors was cracked and peeling in places.

It was only after studying the building that Darger noticed the sheer amount of trash in the parking lot. Empty beer bottles and red Solo cups. Crumpled fast food bags and wrappers. Cigarette butts and used condoms. She stepped over a flattened brown thing she thought was a piece of fried chicken. A thigh, maybe.

They had less trouble getting past the line of crime scene tape this time, and a burly man greeted them at the door.

"I'm Detective Glenn. Bledsoe told me you'd be coming over."

The bristles of his silver crew cut glistened under the square doorframe, backlit by the lighting rigs the tech crew had set up inside the room. Only when she stepped closer could Darger see the wide-set jaw and chiseled features take shape in the gray blur his face had been. Detective Glenn looked like a prototypical drill sergeant, she thought, except his eyes looked kinder than that. Something clever flickered in the brown irises.

"What can you tell us about this place?" she asked, shaking his hand.

"Well, it has somewhat of a reputation among the truckers coming through. If you want to party all night… this is the place to go."

"As opposed to party row at the truck stop?" Loshak asked.

Glenn shrugged.

"I guess this is the spot for when you want more of a full-blown party atmosphere. I mean, you can only cram so many people in a truck cab, right? So if you score some drugs or girls and want to share…"

"I see."

"We get called out here probably once a week. Breaking up fights. People so high or drunk they're passed out in the parking lot."

"Any witnesses to what happened tonight?"

Glenn glared out the door at the handful of gawkers beyond the tape.

"No one saw anything. Damn near everyone we talked to is high as a kite on something or other. Only one who might be sober is the front desk clerk, and even then, I wouldn't put any money on it."

"Whoever's working the front desk at least should have seen who rented the room."

The detective nodded and held up a plastic evidence baggie. Inside, a New Jersey driver's license slid down and settled at the bottom of the plastic sleeve.

"One of the victims booked the room. This place accepts cash, and if you put down a hundred-dollar deposit, they only require you to leave an ID."

Darger's eyes went to the photo first. The girl had light brown hair and a little cupid's bow of a mouth.

The name on the license was Dawn Sawiki. Doing quick math in her head, Darger determined the girl had been twenty-two years old based on the listed birthday.

"I take it she's not local, based on the Jersey ID?" Loshak said.

"None of the local police recognize either girl so far," the detective explained. "So yeah… right now we're thinking they're out-of-towners."

"No name on the second victim?" Darger asked.

"Not so far."

They followed him inside the room, which proved to be just as dated as the exterior. Dark wood-paneled walls. Aged shag carpet the color of old guacamole.

Darger thought it looked like a place fit to film a porn scene circa 1981.

A claustrophobic feeling constricted around her ribcage as she stepped fully into the place, gently increasing the pressure with each step. She had to remind herself to breathe.

Immediately to one side of the entryway was a dank bathroom, the bright light in the doorway catching her eye and pulling her closer. Three evidence techs crammed their bunny-suited bodies into the small space, white vinyl swishing against white vinyl, so Darger and Loshak merely stood at the threshold and peered inside.

Tiles in a cat puke beige lined the floors and walls, with darker spatters and smears that Darger knew were blood. The sink faucet dripped out a steady rhythm in the background.

Glenn pointed out two soggy towels on the floor.

"Our killer took a shower before he left."

"Might be able to get touch DNA from the towels," Loshak said.

"That's what we're hoping," Glenn agreed.

They left the bathroom and moved further inside. The harsh yellow light from an overhead fixture was punctuated by bright white flashes coming from the camera held by one of the techs.

Along with the coppery smell of blood, there was a strange medicinal scent that reminded Darger of Vaseline.

The first body was on the bed. Naked, except for her shoes. Eyes open wide and utterly vacant.

She was on her back, arms and legs spread, with her wrists and ankles tied to the four opposite corners of the bed. Darger recognized her face from the driver's license.

Like Tara Bemis, Dawn Sawiki's body was covered in stab wounds and circular impressions that Darger was pretty sure were bite marks. A wad of silky-looking pale pink fabric protruded from her mouth.

That tightness clenching around Darger's torso squeezed harder. She fought for breath now. Loshak gave her a look as though to ask if she were OK, but she shook her head, shook him off.

A tall man in a lab coat stooped over the body, using a long metal thermometer to take the liver temperature. Comparing that to the rectal temp would give them the time of death.

Darger studied the scene. There was a tremendous amount of blood on the bed, and the woman had a pale, exsanguinated look to her.

"Looks like she bled out," she said.

The man in the lab coat straightened, and his gaze locked onto Darger's.

"That's exactly what happened." He pointed to a laceration on the girl's upper right arm. "Nicked the brachial artery here."

Something severe shined in his gray eyes. Intense. Forlorn. But Darger thought he looked more weathered than grim. Now he gestured at a blood-soaked rag on the floor.

"It appears there was some attempt to stanch the wound, but without medical attention, it was only a matter of time before she expired."

"This is our medical examiner, Dr. Moody," Detective Glenn said.

The doctor gave a brief nod and handed the thermometer to his assistant. He tapped at a tablet and muttered silently to himself.

"Time of death is between 1730 and 1930 hours."

Glenn scribbled this down on a pad of paper.

"So that confirms it. These two were killed before the girl at the truck stop."

"That's right," Dr. Moody said. "And there's something else."

Darger glanced around the room. Aside from a few small blood stains and a tangle of sheets and blankets, the second bed was empty, and she'd forgotten there were supposed to be multiple victims here until Glenn had said, "these two."

Then she noticed that Dr. Moody was moving toward the closet, and she spotted the legs protruding from within.

Dr. Moody nudged the door further open with his foot and got down on one knee.

Like the other two victims, this victim was naked except for her shoes. And Darger spied dark impressions on her wrists and ankles, as if they had also been tied to the bed at some point.

She was scrunched up in a sort of semi-fetal position, with her face mashed into the floor and her knees tucked partially underneath her. Something about her position made Darger think she was rather unceremoniously dumped in the closet, like a rag doll. Unconscious or already dead.

He pointed at a few angry red marks on the victim's thighs. They almost looked like inflamed insect bites.

"See here, how there's much less blood coming from the wounds compared to the girl on the bed?"

Glenn nodded.

"That's because they were inflicted post-mortem."

"Seems like there are less wounds overall," Darger said, studying the body in the closet.

"Yes. I counted maybe a dozen wounds on Jane Doe. And they're primarily shallow, slashing cuts. Not very deep." Dr. Moody reached up and adjusted his glasses. "But the one on the bed? Many, many more. Twenty, at least. And most of them are deep stab wounds."

"And Tara Bemis?"

"He did a number on her, both before and after she was dead. She had the most wounds by far. I counted something like three dozen antemortem slash wounds and bite marks. The few deep stab wounds were all inflicted after she was dead."

Darger wondered at this change in pattern. It made some sense… an increase in violence over the course of the night. An escalation. And yet, she couldn't shake the sense that she was missing something. Some piece that would complete the puzzle and lay the meaning bare.

Dr. Moody conferred with one of the techs nearby and then tucked his tablet under his arm.

"Let's pull this one out of the closet now. Nice and easy."

The doctor and his assistant were surprisingly gentle as they maneuvered Jane Doe's body from the closet.

"Lay her out right here, on her back."

This woman appeared to be of East Asian descent. She had jet black hair and a smattering of freckles over a small, elfin nose.

Dr. Moody used a pen light to study her face, which was swollen and discolored. A faint trickle of blood coming from her nose.

"Some kind of fabric gag in her mouth, just like the other two." He angled the flashlight under her chin. "Ahh… this s interesting."

"What?"

He shone the light on the woman's neck, tracing along a dark line.

"See the ligature mark here on Jane Doe? How high it is?" He used one gloved hand to gesture to his own throat. "All the way up under her chin. And here. See the bruising and swelling? When I get her on the table, I'd bet money that I'll find a broken hyoid bone."

"Is that fatal?" Glenn asked.

"Not necessarily, but depending on the severity, it can cause internal lacerations. And if it isn't treated, the swelling can cut off the upper respiratory tract and lead to asphyxiation. I think that's what happened here." He fiddled with his glasses again before he went on. "It's a lot more common with manual strangulations, but every once in a while you see it with a ligature strangulation if the garrote is placed in the right position. Or perhaps the wrong position, in this case."

The detective held up a hand.

"What does that mean?"

Dr. Moody walked over to the bed, directing the light to

Dawn Sawiki's throat area.

"Take a look at the ligature marks here," he said. "Not only was the cord placed much lower, but notice there are at least three different impressions? That happens when a ligature is tightened and loosened several times over."

Darger considered this. Sexual sadists commonly used strangulation as a means to incapacitate and control their victims. Often they would strangle a victim to the point of unconsciousness before assaulting them. When the victim began to wake up, they'd be strangled again.

Strangle, assault, repeat.

"That's why Jane Doe has less wounds than the others," Darger said, the words coming out of her mouth almost before she had time to fully make sense of them. "He killed her too quickly. Once she was dead, he lost interest."

Glenn frowned.

"OK, but why put her in the closet?"

Loshak jumped in.

"He was probably angry at himself. Maybe even embarrassed, you could say. These guys are all about control. That kind of screw-up could be a big blow to his self-esteem."

Darger stepped closer to the bed and swept a hand over the grisly tableau there.

"So then he takes that anger out on Dawn Sawiki. Stabs and bites her repeatedly. And in his frenzy, he ends up slashing her artery. She bleeds out."

Loshak was nodding now.

"Now he's really losing it. He's killed both girls before he intended. So he goes out and finds a third girl. Tara Bemis." He raised his finger and wagged it back and forth. "And this time around, he's determined not to mess up. He takes his time. He's methodical about only inflicting non-fatal wounds until he's ready."

Darger felt a wave of satisfaction at figuring it out. Solving the puzzle. But just as quickly, the triumphant feeling faded and was replaced by a trickle of disquiet.

Because a man capable of this kind of brutality was very dangerous indeed. And he was still out there.

CHAPTER 8

Detective Glenn spent a few moments furiously scribbling in his notepad before tucking his pen behind his ear and clearing his throat.

"OK, so here's the timeline I've got so far. Dawn Sawiki checks in around five this evening. Maybe there's some preamble to the murders, where he takes some time to set the girls at ease. Or maybe he gets right down to it. We don't really know yet. But he incapacitates the girls somehow, maybe even just convinces them that this is just a little harmless bondage play. Either way, he gets them tied up. Starts in with the torture. Somewhere over the course of that, he accidentally strangles Jane Doe to death. This sets him off, and he goes berserk on Dawn Sawiki. Slices her brachial artery, and she bleeds out over the course of..."

He paused and glanced at Dr. Moody.

"Anywhere from five to twenty minutes, approximately."

"Alright. He tries to stop the bleeding, and when that fails, he gives up. Takes a shower and goes off to find victim number three." Glenn flipped to the next page. "At 7:31 P.M., dispatch gets a call from one of the other rooms about a possible domestic dispute. Caller says they heard screaming from inside the room. But there was a car accident on the highway, real nasty. Took a while for a unit to get out here, and in the meantime, we get the call about the body at the truck stop. That was around 8:45. So it was over an hour from the domestic dispute call before a car made it out here."

"And what happened then?" Darger asked.

"Officers on the scene knocked, got no response. They went to the office, found the door locked. Took almost ten minutes before the clerk came around. Said he was asleep in the back."

"That's convenient," Darger said.

"Right?" Glenn agreed. "Anyway, by the time they finally convinced the clerk to get the keys to the room and let them in, twenty minutes had passed. He unlocks the door, and they find this."

He gestured at the girl on the bed.

"So we know at least one of the girls was still alive at 7:30, when dispatch got the call about the possible domestic dispute?" Darger asked.

Glenn sighed.

"That's where things get murky. When the cops first came in, the volume on the TV was cranked all the way up, and there was some kind of horror movie on. A remake of one of those old 80s slashers. So it could have been one of the girls someone heard screaming… or it could have been the TV."

"Either way, that leaves at least an hour window for him to leave here, go to the truck stop, pick up Tara, kill her. Mutilate her body. Dump her…" Loshak said, scratching at his chin. "Doable, but… Jesus."

"Reminds me of Bundy in Tallahassee," Darger said.

Loshak nodded.

"I was thinking the same thing."

"Bundy?" Glenn repeated. "As in, Ted Bundy?"

"Right," Loshak said. "After Ted Bundy escaped from jail the second time, he fled to Florida. In the early morning of January 15th, he attacked five women in the span of about one hour. Killed two and severely wounded the other three. Kind of went into rampage mode, for lack of a better term."

The detective's jaw worked as he considered this.

"How many people did Bundy kill in total?"

"He confessed to thirty murders, but there are probably more," Darger said.

Glenn grimaced.

"So — and I hate to ask this because I think I already know the answer — does that mean our guy has probably killed before?"

"Oh, I'd say it's almost a certainty," Loshak said. "Which reminds me…"

He pulled out the clipboard he'd had at the previous scene and began shuffling through the pages. Darger wondered why he'd suddenly abandoned his trusty yellow legal pad.

"Where is it?" he muttered to himself. "Ah. Here we go. Section five."

"What is that?"

"Crime analysis report." He looked up from the clipboard. "For ViCAP."

Darger crossed her arms.

"I understand that you might have printed it out back in the olden days… but you know it's all digitized now, right?"

Loshak rolled his eyes.

"Yes, I do know that. But if I take notes now, we can get a head start. Of course, we won't have a complete report until Dr. Moody here does his thing, but my guess is we'll get hits with just what we have here. I already called Quantico, asked them to loan us a ViCAP analyst."

Darger considered it. Looked at the bodies.

He was right. The signature was quite specific. The bindings. The ligature strangulation. The fabric gag stuffed in each victim's mouth. That alone would be enough to start a preliminary search for matches in ViCAP. But if you added in the victim typology, the stabbing, cutting, and biting... If this guy had killed before — and she agreed with Loshak that he almost definitely had — they'd have to come up with matches. An unsub didn't develop the kind of ritual they were seeing here without a lot of practice.

Loshak held up his pen and addressed the medical examiner.

"Dr. Moody, I know this is an unusual request, but I was wondering if you might be willing to remove one of the gags?"

The doctor pursed his lips and glanced down at the body on the bed.

"I'd normally wait until the full post-mortem examination to do so… but I don't see why not. As long as we deposit it directly into an evidence bag, there's little risk of cross-contamination."

Dr. Moody's assistant handed him a pair of pre-sterilized forceps. The doctor removed the wrapper and bent over Dawn Sawiki's body. He clasped a piece of the baby pink fabric and pulled it gently from the victim's mouth.

"Ah, Christ," Glenn said.

Darger looked hard at the item of clothing after it unfurled, not sure she was seeing it right.

"Are those…?"

The detective nodded.

"Gagged with her own panties."

CHAPTER 9

Dr. Moody murmured something to his assistant, who wove around the various people in the room and went outside.

"We're going to bag the victims for transport now, if no one has any objections?"

"Fine with me," Detective Glenn said. "Agents?"

"We're good."

The assistant returned with a gurney, and he and Dr. Moody transferred Jane Doe's body from the floor into a thick blue body bag. The vinyl crinkled and swished as it closed over her face.

Loshak finished scribbling and checking boxes on the ViCAP form and then folded the pages back down.

"I say we go have a chat with the concierge," he said.

Darger's eyes were on a large brown water stain in the vague shape of the state of Louisiana covering one corner of the ceiling.

"I think that's too fancy a word for this place."

"Concierge. Night clerk. Whatever," Loshak said. "Shall we?"

Back outside, Darger gave the crowd a once over. They appeared just as twitchy and agitated as the truck stop onlookers, but instead of huddling at the police barrier, these people loitered near the open doors of their rooms. As if to give them the chance to retreat should they be approached by any of the law enforcement officers.

She and Loshak strode over to the office, entering through a door with an antique shopkeeper's bell that jangled when it was opened. Inside, the odor of some kind of lemony disinfectant perfumed the air, and the same outdated wood paneling they'd seen in the motel room covered the walls.

A gaunt man with sagging jowls shuffled a deck of cards behind the counter. Glenn had told them the clerk's name was Clint Torbert.

Torbert glanced up as they came in, pausing in his shuffling. His pitted face was topped with a dull, greasy skullet — bald on top, party in the back. He had strange pale eyes, and combined with the rest of his features, Darger couldn't help but think of the CryptKeeper from the old *Tales from the Crypt* TV show.

"Mr. Torbert?"

The pale eyes narrowed.

"Now what?"

"Could we ask you a few questions?"

He began shuffling the cards again.

"Agin? I already answered every damn question in the book 'bout a hunderd damn times."

"Just once more, if you don't mind," Darger said.

"Fine."

He made a show of setting the cards aside, face up, and that was when Darger noticed the cards featured photos of naked women. Torbert leered at her, as if expecting a reaction, so she made it a point to appear completely undisturbed by the dirty playing cards.

"Let's start with who rented out the room."

He rolled his eyes.

"Like I told them other officers before, it was one of the… one of the women they found in there, all cut up. The brunette."

"And she paid with cash?"

"Uh-huh. That's usual for that type."

Darger cocked her head to one side.

"That type?"

Torbert pressed his lips together and inhaled deeply.

"Look, I seen enough of that type of girl to know what she was on sight."

"And what was that?" Darger asked.

He tittered.

"You know... a lady of the evening?"

When Darger said nothing, he went on.

"Jesus. She was a whore."

He pronounced the word as if it had two syllables and rhymed with "sewer."

A hoo-er.

"Had you seen either victim before?"

"Don't think so. Then again, all the customers' faces tend to fog together, and I make it a point to not pay much attention to 'em."

"And why is that?"

He shrugged and scratched behind his ear.

"I don't make it my business to know what these folks are up to. They pay for a room. I give 'em a key. That's about it."

"And you and your boss are fine with the fact that there's illegal activity happening under your roof?"

He smirked.

"Like I said, it's not my business. I ain't the po-lice. If I see anyone anywhere doin' something shady, is it my responsibility to put a stop to it? Make a stink? That ain't how I was brought up. If you're an adult, nothin' you do on your time is my concern, expecially if it don't impact me none."

"So you just… look the other way?"

He shrugged again, crossing his arms as he did.

"Costs me nothin' to mind my own business. Might cost me an awful lot to go stickin' my nose where it don't belong."

"Are you ever compensated for looking the other way?"

"Pardon?"

"Do any of the guests offer you money for allowing certain illicit activity on the premises?"

He grinned, showing off teeth marbled yellow and brown by years of tobacco use.

"People offer tips from time to time, but I've always assumed that was a reflection on my exemplary hospitality."

Darger resisted the urge to roll her eyes.

"You know, places like this end up being prime locations for sex trafficking. But then, I guess that's also none of your business?"

Torbert sat up a little straighter, pointing a finger at her.

"Hey now. You folks are the ones with the guns and the badges and the shiny cars with sirens. I'm just a guy at a desk. Like, if the ice machine breaks, I gotta fix it. That's *my*, whaddya call it, uh… jurisdiction. Other than that…" He licked his lips. "I mean, if you're suggestin' that what happened to them girls is my fault, well, I don't think that's fair."

His face went serious for the first time, his mouth puckering.

"Maybe our usual clientele ain't exactly the hoity-toity type. But this deal here is something altogether different. Because whoever done *that* to those girls is some kind of devil."

There was a glassy look in his eyes now, and Darger was certain he was remembering the grisly scene in the motel room. He might also have been on something, like Detective Glenn had suggested.

"Mr. Torbert?"

He twitched and blinked, coming out of the daze.

"Huh?"

"Are there any security cameras on the premises?"

His previous demeanor seemed to have returned in full force, and he snorted.

"What do you think this is? The Ritz?" He chuckled at his own joke. "Security cameras."

She glanced over at Loshak, who interjected for the first time.

"When the police first arrived on the scene, they said the office door here was locked."

"Uh-huh."

"Why was that?"

"I was takin' a nap. I always lock the door when I take a nap."

"Why?"

"Because the last time I left it unlocked, one of those damn tweakers came in here, dropped trou, and took a B.M. in the potted fern." Torbert gestured at an empty corner of the office. "Well, it's not there anymore because we had to throw the whole thing out on account of the smell, but yeah, I keep the door locked now if I know for sure I'm gonna nod off."

"Do you know how long the door was locked?"

Torbert made a show of thinking on it.

"Well, I suppose it was right after I gave that dead gal the key."

When Loshak paused to write this down, Torbert piped up again.

"It ain't against the rules, you know. Locking the door or not locking the door is up to my discretion, and if you want to talk to my manager—"

"I'm sure it's fine," Loshak said.

"Sleeping, too. No rules against it. Everyone who works the

overnights does it. It's one of the perks, to be honest, though I doubt I'll be gettin' anymore sleep tonight. Not after what I seen."

The haunted, glazed look returned to the man's eyes. Darger slid a business card across the counter.

"If you think of anything else..."

He made no move to pick up the card. Instead, he snatched up the dirty playing cards and began shuffling them again.

"Yeah, yeah. Give you a call."

Darger led Loshak back out through the glass door onto the sidewalk. That humid air seemed to be thickening around them as the night progressed. They didn't speak again until they were several paces away from the building.

"You thinking what I'm thinking?" Darger asked.

"I believe so," Loshak said, nodding. "If he had the office locked up from the time the girls first arrived — with no one to alibi his exact whereabouts — then he could have killed the girls in the room and made it to the truck stop and back before the cops showed up and started knocking at the door. I'd say he makes the 'Persons of Interest' list for sure."

Loshak's phone let out an electronic blip. He glanced at the screen.

"Message from Chief Hall. There's a task force meeting scheduled first thing in the morning."

Darger checked the time on her phone.

"That only gives us a few hours to put together a profile," she said, rubbing her eyes.

"Guess we better get to it then," Loshak agreed. "But first, we're going to need to find more coffee."

CHAPTER 10

Composing the profile was no easy task given the fact that an official report had yet to be filed. That meant they had to draw entirely from what they'd observed at the scenes and heard from the various witnesses — no photos or files to sift through to refresh their memories about the finer points.

Darger and Loshak took turns typing furiously while sipping fast food coffee, working up to the last possible minute before hopping in the car to head over to the local police station.

Daylight leaked over the horizon now, exposing the little North Carolina town in gray twilight. Old brick buildings leaned over the narrow streets, equal parts charming and 1950s drab. Kudzu vines seemed to engulf most everything at the edges of town, swelling over porches and crawling up telephone poles.

The police building sat at the center of Roanoke Rapids, a big grey windowless box. Darger wondered if it had once been a movie theater or some other kind of business that would have purposely eschewed sources of natural light.

Inside, the air was stale but cool. A welcome relief from the constant subtropical humidity outside.

The desk sergeant led them upstairs and into a conference room. A dozen or so people milled about, some from the local department and some from the County Sheriff's office, chatting with small Styrofoam cups of coffee clutched in their hands.

Detective Bledsoe spotted them as they entered and waved them up to the front of the room.

"Agent Darger. Agent Loshak." She gestured at a squat man with a silver mustache. "This is Chief Hall."

He shook each of their hands.

"Really appreciate you coming down here. It's not every day that we get a triple homicide, and certainly not one so… horrific."

"We're happy to lend assistance in any way we can," Loshak said.

Chief Hall inhaled through his nose.

"I think we're going to need all the help we can get. Now, I understand you'll be putting together a profile, but I know you only got in a few hours ago, so if you need more time…"

"Actually, we were able to work up a preliminary report," Darger said. "We'll be able to fine-tune it after the autopsies are complete, but we can at least start laying the groundwork today."

"That's great." Something caught the chief's attention at the back of the room. "Would you excuse me for a moment?"

As soon as the Chief had gone, a young woman with an FBI badge swooped into the space where he'd been standing. Her big eyes locked onto the two of them.

"Agent Loshak and Agent Darger?"

"That's us."

The woman put out her hand. She had reddish hair cut into a shag.

"I'm Ellie Gummer. The intelligence analyst from ViCAP?"

"Yes! Excellent," Loshak said, fiddling with his trusty clipboard. "Now, I know we'd usually wait until there was an official case file before entering these murders into the system, but I'd like to see if we get any matches just from the notes I took at the scenes."

He handed over a stack of papers.

"I filled out the pertinent areas of the form for each victim, mostly focusing on the sections for the 'Offense M.O.' and 'Condition of the Victim.'"

"Oh wow," Gummer said, flipping through the pages. "You have the original forms and everything. I've never actually seen them printed out. Everything's in digital format these days."

Loshak shot Darger a sour look.

"So I've heard."

"Crazy that you used to have to do this whole thing by hand." A dimple appeared in each of Gummer's cheeks when she smiled. "Anyway, I can start entering these reports into the database, and then we'll see what we come up with."

Gummer took a seat near the door and opened her laptop.

A hollow thumping noise sounded from the front of the room, and Darger turned to see Chief Hall banging the flat of his hand on top of a podium there.

"Let's find a seat, everyone. We're about to get started."

Chairs scraped and voices murmured as the group settled in.

"First things first, I'd like everyone to welcome Agent Loshak and Agent Darger from the FBI. They were generous enough to drive down here to assist with the investigation."

There was a smattering of applause. Darger couldn't stop herself from thinking, *Golf clap.*

"Before I hand things over to them, I'll run down what we have, though it isn't much. And I doubt y'all haven't heard most of it through the old rumor mill already as it is, but I'd like to be sure we all have the facts before we begin."

Papers ruffled as Chief Hall thumbed through a file filled with loose pages.

"Dr. Moody is doing his best to expedite the autopsies, but obviously there's only so much the one man can do. That being said, he was able to give me a rough preliminary report on the victims."

He used a magnet to secure a printout of Jane Doe's morgue photo to the white board behind him.

"Our first victim is Jane Doe. Found in a closet at the Cozy Motor Lodge. Estimated time of death, between 5:30 and 7:30 P.M. Cause of death is consistent with asphyxiation secondary to hyoid bone fracture caused by ligature strangulation."

He held up a second morgue photo and placed it next to the first. Bloodless white flesh against the stainless steel background of the morgue slab.

"Second victim is Dawn Sawiki. Twenty-two. ID says she's originally from Camden, New Jersey. We've been in touch with the locals there in an attempt to locate next of kin or any kind of background. We're hopeful that if we find something on Sawiki, that might lead to an ID on our Jane Doe. Estimated time of death, also between the hours of 5:30 and 7:30. Cause of death, exsanguination due to laceration of the brachial artery."

He added a third photo to the lineup.

"Victim number three is Tara Bemis. Twenty-six. Local girl. Known to frequent Big Jon's Travel Center, where her body was found. Estimated time of death, somewhere between 7:45 and 8:45 P.M. Cause of death, asphyxiation secondary to ligature strangulation. Not that there were any doubts on the matter, but the manner of death in all three has officially been ruled homicide."

Now he held up three photos showing the purplish lines encircling the wrists and ankles of the three women.

"All three victims were bound, and the cord he used to bind the girls in the hotel appears to be identical to the bindings on Tara Bemis. I'm going to assign a team of investigators to go around to the various hardware stores in the area to see if we can find a match that-a-way. Dr. Moody will also be sending samples of the cord to the lab. One way or the other, we're hoping we can find the source of the cord."

Next came close-ups of the neck of each victim.

"Likewise, all three victims appear to have been strangled with a cord with a diameter that matches those of the bindings. Dawn Sawiki and Tara Bemis have multiple ligature marks, meaning the cord was tightened and loosened several times over the course of the attack. It's Dr. Moody's opinion that Jane Doe was perhaps inadvertently killed the first time the ligature around her neck was tightened, which is why she alone has a single ligature mark."

Chief Hall flipped through his notes.

"All three victims show signs of sexual assault. Rape kits were negative for semen, which means our perp was probably wearing a condom. No surprise there.

"Each victim was to some degree beaten, cut, stabbed, and bitten. Dr. Moody counted twelve wounds on Jane Doe. More than twice that on Dawn Sawiki. And at least forty on Tara."

Detective Bledsoe raised her hand.

"Does he have an idea of what kind of weapon he's using?"

The chief licked his thumb and shuffled through the file.

"Where was it…" he muttered to himself. "Ah. Here it is."

He brought out another autopsy photo, this one a close-up shot featuring multiple wounds.

"See here, the variance in the widths of each of these cuts?"

Bledsoe nodded.

"According to Dr. Moody, the width of the cuts corresponds directly to the depth. These smaller cuts here are where the perpetrator only pressed the tip of the weapon through the skin. Now, he emphasized that this was only a preliminary theory, but coupled with the clean edges of the wounds, Dr. Moody believes he's using a box cutter or craft knife. Something with a straight, angled blade."

Chief Hall closed the folder and pressed both palms into the top of the podium.

"I think that brings us up to speed as far as what we've got from the medical examiner's office. Let's move on to what we know about our victims, which, frankly, isn't much.

"Given the fact that Dawn Sawiki has an out-of-state ID, New Jersey, and that so far no one recognizes her or Jane Doe, right now we're running on the theory that they were picked up outside of our jurisdiction and brought here.

"The motel has no security cameras. The truck stop does, and we have footage of Tara Bemis in the gas station buying cigarettes, but we have been unable to find any footage after she leaves the gas station. So as of now, we know virtually nothing about our killer. Not his age, race, what kind of vehicle he's driving. That's where this comes in."

He presented an evidence baggie containing a McDonald's drink cup. The end of the straw was stained bright red with lipstick.

"We found this in the motel room trash. Looks like our girls stopped at McDonald's at some point before they got to the motel. I wanna know which one."

There was a groan from one of the uniformed men.

"That's right, Malone. You know what it means. Each squad car is going to be assigned a list of McDonald's restaurants in the surrounding area to canvas. I want a witness who saw these women, and who they were with. Sergeant Anthony is putting together assignments now, so make sure you see her at the conclusion of this meeting to get your list."

Chief Hall's gaze flitted over the faces in the room before settling on Darger and Loshak.

"I think that about does it for me. Agents… if you're ready?"

CHAPTER 11

Loshak stepped to the podium while Darger began handing out a paper summary of the profile they'd assembled over the last few hours.

"Good morning. Chief Hall has already introduced myself and my partner, but we have another colleague here as well. Sitting in the back of the room, please welcome Ellie Gummer. She's an intelligence analyst helping us fast-track these cases into the ViCAP database."

Gummer didn't take her eyes from her screen, but she stopped typing long enough to stick her hand in the air and wave.

"Two things before I begin," Loshak continued. "First, I'd like to caution everyone that the profile Agent Darger is passing out right now is just a preliminary version. It's a bit unusual for us to come into a case so early on in the process. We usually have a complete case file and full autopsy reports to consult. So I just want to give fair warning that once we're able to see the full picture, there's a good chance we'll have to tweak the profile a bit. That being said, what we observed tonight still gave us plenty to go on."

Loshak unbuttoned his jacket and planted his hands on his hips.

"Second, if you have a question at any point, please speak up. No need to wait until the end. There's also no such thing as a stupid question, in my opinion. Chances are, if you're wondering about it, one of your colleagues is too."

Darger watched Loshak's gaze sweep over the room as he

looked for small, nonverbal signs that his message had been received. He nodded once and began.

"Now, one of the most noteworthy details in this case is the level of what we call 'expressive violence.' That is to say, violence beyond what is necessary to control or kill the victim. We also sometimes refer to this as 'overkill.' However, the term 'overkill' can also be used to describe the kind of violence that occurs when someone is in a psychotic state or a fit of rage and ends up inflicting wounds they don't even remember. Expressive violence, on the other hand, stands apart in that it is both intentional and deliberate."

Loshak gestured at the collection of morgue and crime scene photos tacked to the board.

"If you consider the cutting on all three victims, I think it's quite clear that most of the wounds have that deliberateness to them. A majority of the cut marks are straight and shallow. Not meant to kill, but to inflict pain."

He paused and held up a finger, which he then used to point at the fatal wound found on Dawn Sawiki.

"All, perhaps, but the series of stab wounds that resulted in Dawn Sawiki bleeding out. Our current theory is that the killer inadvertently strangled Jane Doe to death before he was ready. When he realized what he'd done, he flew into a rage and inflicted the deep, penetrating wounds we see on Dawn Sawiki. Now, having killed both victims faster than he'd prefer, and without having been able to complete his violent ritual to his liking, he was compelled to go out and find a third victim."

Loshak uncapped a marker and wrote "PIQUERISM" on the board.

"I believe this is a textbook case of piquerism, which is a rare sexual paraphilia that focuses on cutting, stabbing, and slashing the skin with a knife or another sharp object. Could be anything from a screwdriver to an ice pick or a razor. Biting is also included. Inflicting the wounds is, for all intents and purposes, a sexual act for the perpetrator. The wounding behavior may accompany more expected forms of sexual assault, but it is not unheard of for the stabbing to take the place of penile penetration completely."

Detective Glenn raised his hand.

"So when you say it takes the place of penetration completely… I mean… these guys are still able to, you know… get off?"

Loshak nodded.

"Yes. One of the most notable piquerists was Andrei Chikatilo, the Red Ripper. Chikatilo's first murder victim was a nine-year-old girl named Yelena Zakotnova. When he attempted to rape the girl, he was unable to achieve an erection. He strangled her and stabbed her three times, and it was while stabbing her that Chikatilo said he spontaneously ejaculated. Thus began his foray into serial murder, as after the killing of Zakotnova, he claimed he was unable to achieve orgasm without stabbing his victims. He totaled over fifty kills before anyone could stop him. On one occasion, when he found himself with a victim and no knife, he used his teeth and a stick."

Detective Bledsoe was sitting a few chairs over from the podium, so even though the woman's voice was barely above a whisper, Darger was still able to make it out.

"Lord have mercy."

Loshak went on.

"Albert Fish was another serial killer who not only engaged in this kind of deviance with his victims, but with himself as well. At the time of his arrest, it was discovered that he had twenty-nine needles stuck into his body, mostly in and around his genitals."

One of the uniformed officers near the front recoiled at that, his face going pale.

"Obviously, with our three victims today, there are clear signs of sexual assault in addition to the numerous stab wounds," Loshak said. "But when we look for other potential victims, it would be unwise to prematurely toss out any who present with evidence of piquerism but without other signs of sexual assault."

Now it was Bledsoe raising her hand.

"How can you tell the difference between a regular stabbing and this piquerism thing?"

Loshak crossed his arms.

"That's a good question," he said, squinting thoughtfully. "If there are no obvious signs of sexual assault, it can sometimes be difficult to determine whether a stabbing is motivated by piquerism or not, but there are certain hallmarks. The perpetrators in these cases very often target specific areas: the breasts, groin, and buttocks. There is very often post-mortem mutilation. And these cases often include some manner of posing the victim. For instance, I don't think it's an accident that he left Dawn Sawiki tied to the bed with her arms and legs spread-eagle. Likewise with Tara Bemis being left hogtied in a public place. Another telltale sign of piquerism is when the offender inserts objects into the various body cavities of their victims."

"Like shoving panties in the victims' mouths?" Glenn asked.

"Exactly," Loshak said, pointing his uncapped marker at the detective.

Loshak drew a large arrow after the word "PIQUERISM" and then wrote out "SEXUAL SADISM."

"Now, piquerism is really a highly specific subcategory of sexual sadism. A sexual sadist is someone who finds pleasure, excitement, and arousal by the expression of fear and pain in their victims. To a sexual sadist, violence is a fetish. And the probable piquerist behavior isn't the only thing screaming 'sexual sadist' in this case."

He held one finger in the air.

"Bindings were found to be an increased predictor of sadism in the offender in one study of sex crimes. Restraints like rope, handcuffs, and chains are physical representations of the near complete control the offender has over the victim, which is why the use of bindings is very often part of a sadist's signature. Whereas some killers may tie their victims up to make them easier to deal with or to prevent escape, the sadist gets specific enjoyment out of the act of binding."

Loshak put up a second finger.

"Strangulation is another common element in the signature of many sexual sadists. One study found that strangulation was found in 59% of serial sexual murders, and yet another analysis found that ligature strangulation in sexual murders was a mark of increased cruelty and deliberateness. And that makes sense. Whereas strangling someone with your hands may come about in a fit of rage, ligature strangulation requires a tool. Even if it's improvised — say, with an electric cord or some other item found at the scene — it suggests a certain premeditation to the act. In our case, given that the cord used for the ligature appears to have been brought to the scene by the killer, this implies pure premeditation.

"For our unsub, the closeness required for strangulation is something akin to intimacy. Sexual sadists almost always prefer a hands-on method of killing — knives, blunt instruments, ligatures. They rarely use firearms. Stabbing, bludgeoning, and strangulation are more personal, more stimulating, and are thus more sexually gratifying to this kind of offender."

Loshak held up a photo of a hollow-cheeked man with dark wavy hair.

"To quote Richard Ramirez, the Night Stalker, 'Killing with a knife is very personal. You are actually holding it as it goes in, and when death comes, you can feel your victim dying through the knife. It's like sex.'"

CHAPTER 12

Loshak paused to sip from a bottle of water, and Detective Glenn piped up again.

"Dr. Moody found evidence that the ligatures on Tara Bemis and Dawn Sawiki had been tightened and loosened several times over. Is there any significance to that?"

Loshak was already nodding as he screwed the cap back on his water.

"There is. It shows the unsub wanted to prolong these assaults. The strangulation is not simply a means to an end, i.e., a way to kill the victim efficiently and quietly." Loshak shook his head. "No. This guy *enjoyed* the act of strangling these women. Enjoyed the complete control he had over them when he cut off the flow of blood and oxygen to the brain and they lost consciousness. Again, this is a calculated, premeditated act that serves some function in the killer's fantasy. And fantasy is everything to a sexual sadist."

Loshak put his hands together, steepling his fingers.

"These offenders are always men who, at their core, are deeply insecure. Their feelings of worthlessness are intolerable to them, and their fantasies try to quell those feelings by casting them in a role of exaggerated power. It's not a phenomenon limited to serial killers. Not at all. In fact, I think it's quite common for people who feel powerless to imagine scenarios in which they have strength and authority and influence."

He looked out over the people gathered in the room.

"Who here hasn't been in conflict with someone and later thought of all the things they should have said to put the other person in their place? Well, on the most basic level, that's not dissimilar from the dynamic we see with sexual sadists. Except that their fantasies evolve, push past the normal. Instead of influence, they want dominance or possession. Instead of respect, they want to elicit full-blown terror. Violence becomes the way they inflict these feelings on others. Witnessing the terror of their victims gives this type of killer a sense of ultimate power and control."

Loshak raised his eyebrows in Darger's direction, and she readied herself.

"I've brought with me some excerpts of an interview with Ted Bundy, which I think will better illustrate some of these ideas."

Darger had cued up the pertinent quotes on the computer earlier that morning. When Loshak gave her the OK, she pressed play, and Bundy's disembodied voice filled the conference room.

"I saw myself as meek. I perceived myself to be easily intimidated. And somewhat unsophisticated. Uninteresting... even unattractive."

Loshak nodded again, and she played the next audio clip.

Bundy's voice was low and relaxed as he described himself in the third person. Conversational.

"One of the primary reasons he did this... uh, committed the murders... was a search for the release of stress or feelings of low esteem or anger, hostility, resentment, whatever... it was channeled for some reason toward women."

The audio clip ended. Loshak tucked one hand in his pocket as he spoke.

"This contrast between the meek and unsophisticated internal feelings and the brutal domination illustrated by Bundy's crimes is the essence of pretty much all sexual sadists.

"These offenders are filled with a near-constant inner tension fueled by their feelings of isolation and inferiority. They concoct fantasies — often sexual — to counteract that tension. These fantasies are frequently quite specific and are honed over time. But eventually, the fantasies aren't enough, and they act out, violently."

Loshak ticked his chin, and again Bundy's voice spilled out from the speakers, sounding eerie as he once more described his own motivations in the third person.

"The fantasy is always more stimulating than the aftermath of the crime itself. He should have recognized that what really fascinated him was the hunt, the adventure of searching out his victims. And, to a degree, possessing them physically, as one would possess a potted plant, a painting, or a Porsche. Owning, as it were, this individual."

Loshak scrawled "POSSESSION" on the board in spiky sharpie lettering.

"Again, we come back to this idea of possessing the victim. Because to a sexual sadist, the victim is primarily an object with which they can act out their fantasies."

Chief Hall cleared his throat.

"Maybe this isn't exactly pertinent to our investigation, but… why does Bundy sometimes speak in the third person?"

Loshak smiled.

"Ah, yes. I should have explained that in the beginning. Bundy vehemently denied any involvement in the murders he was convicted of right up until his impending execution. So his interviewers devised a clever scheme that would allow him to talk about his crimes without admitting his own guilt: since he'd taken some psychology classes and gone to law school, they asked him to analyze and speculate on the murders as an 'expert.' Bundy, being a classic narcissist, couldn't resist the opportunity to show off this so-called expertise."

With a final nod from Loshak, Darger played the last excerpt of the Bundy interview.

"I think we see a point reached — slowly, perhaps — where the control, the possession aspect, came to include, within its demands, the necessity... for purposes of gratification... the killing of the victims. Perhaps it came to be seen that ultimate possession was, in fact, the taking of the life. And then purely... the physical possession of the remains."

Loshak paced back and forth behind the podium.

"I think the end of this quote is particularly pertinent in our case, since we've seen some degree of post-mortem wounding. Again, it troubles people that someone would bother to inflict wounds on a person who is already dead. What's the point? If they're dead, they can no longer show pain and fear. Well, in the case of many sexual sadists, they are able to continue to act out their fantasies even after the victim is beyond screaming, crying, and begging for their lives."

Halting in front of the board, Loshak hastily scribbled down two words.

"Now, a forensic psychologist by the name of Louis B. Schlesinger divides sexual murders into two types: catathymic and compulsive. A 'catathymic' murder would be characterized as an abrupt act of violence prompted by underlying stressors. The murders are almost like explosions set off by some sort of trigger."

Beneath the word "CATATHYMIC," Loshak wrote, "RIDGWAY."

"Gary Ridgway, the Green River Killer, is a great example of this. Though he killed at least 49 times, he did not kill every prostitute he met with. He often cited the provocation for killing as when the woman seemed disinterested or tried to rush him. He was also more likely to kill if he'd had a bad day at work or a fight with his wife. On at least two occasions, he suggested that a loud and noisy environment was the trigger. Regardless of the specifics, there are clear external factors that play a causal role in bringing these murders about. The crimes are impulsive and generally not planned, or at least not to the degree of a compulsive killer.

"On the opposite end of the spectrum, 'compulsive' murders are motivated almost entirely by internal factors. There is some sort of pathological urge to kill and to do so repeatedly. This group includes Ted Bundy and John Wayne Gacy. Where Gary Ridgway could still have what we'll call 'normal' sex — or at least sex devoid of violence — for the compulsive sexual killer, sex and violence have become irrevocably entwined."

Loshak wrapped his two index fingers around one another and held them before him.

"Given what I've seen with this case, I believe we're dealing with a compulsive killer. That means he is driven. He is planning both the crimes and how to get away with them. He kills because he likes it. He kills because it's the only thing that gets him off."

Loshak paused and stared out at the people in the room.

"And that compulsion will not go away."

CHAPTER 13

It was Darger's turn now, and she swapped places with Loshak. The fluorescent bulbs buzzed faintly overhead as she got up in front of the task force, the sound seeming to match the low-level thrum of tension in the quiet room.

"So my partner has given you a pretty good idea of *why* he does what he does. So let's talk now about *who* he is."

Darger held out her hand, and Loshak passed her the marker he'd been using to write on the board.

"Given the ages of the victims, we believe we're looking for a man 25 to 35 years of age. Probably White."

She scrawled these details down on the white board as she continued to speak.

"He very likely came from a chaotic family environment, which a lot of times we assume to mean either serious neglect, abuse, or abandonment. But it could also mean he experienced unstable living arrangements as a child — perhaps he was homeless, institutionalized, or moved frequently. Another possibility would be some sort of dysfunction with one or both parents — incarceration, substance abuse, frequent domestic disputes. It's also possible he was raised by someone other than his biological parents, perhaps someone unfit to perform the parental duties."

Darger capped the marker and turned back to face the room.

"The key here is that something in his childhood left him a deeply insecure person with very limited coping mechanisms. Given the level of sadism and expressive violence, my personal hunch is that we're looking for someone who experienced overt and severe physical abuse as a child. Childhood abuse is very common for this type of offender, but there are outliers."

Darger showed a photo of a fleshy-faced man with a 70s porn 'stache.

"This is Richard Cottingham, the Times Square Torso Killer. He tortured and mutilated his victims in a manner quite similar to what we're seeing here, and yet he reportedly had a very normal, non-violent childhood."

She tucked the photo back into her personal file and continued on.

"It's common for this type of killer to have some kind of psychosocial deficit, though I think in this case it might be mild or non-existent based on the fact that Dawn Sawiki checked into the motel, seemingly of her own volition. Add to this that no one reported hearing any sort of violent struggle at the truck stop when Tara Bemis was killed. That means it's almost certain that he's using a 'con' approach to attract victims versus 'blitz' or 'surprise.' He may simply solicit them as prostitutes, or he may use some other ruse: offering drugs or alcohol or some other non-sexual enticement.

"The point is that he is able to talk these women into going with him, which suggests some degree of social competence. At the very least, he has the ability to appear rational and non-threatening. In fact, he seemed trustworthy enough to Dawn Sawiki and Jane Doe that they followed him into that motel room. And don't forget, these are women who tend to have decent radar for what they call 'bad dates.'"

Darger leaned one elbow on the podium as she went on.

"Also noteworthy is that he was able to take on two victims at once. It's possible he was able to convince Dawn Sawiki and Jane Doe to let him bind them, but Tara's friend Candy was adamant that she never would have agreed to being tied up. That makes me think he's using a different approach. It might be that he drugs them or otherwise incapacitates them in order to tie them up. With the two victims in the motel room, if he didn't convince them or drug them, he likely would have separated them so he could deal with them one at a time. Maybe he sends Jane Doe to get ice or something while he disables Sawiki. When Jane Doe returns, he takes her by surprise and binds her as well.

"No matter how he manages to do it, two victims radically increases the risk of being caught. If something goes wrong, if one of them gets away from him or screams before he has the gag in place, it could all be over for him. So he has an extraordinary level of confidence at this point, probably built up from previous crimes."

Chief Hall sat forward.

"I have a question, if I may?"

"Go ahead."

"It's just that you and your partner talk about previous murders as if it's a near certainty. Shouldn't we wait to see what comes up in ViCAP, if anything, before we start to make that assumption? I know you're the experts on this stuff, but I'm wary of jumping to conclusions this early in an investigation."

Darger suspected there might be pushback on this point, and she was ready.

"I understand and appreciate your caution on this point. But killing three victims in such a short period of time is a clear sign of escalation. Something he's worked up to. Like Agent Loshak explained earlier, the crimes of a sexual sadist stem directly from their sexual fantasies. Those fantasies are almost like an addiction, and much like someone using a particular substance, the offender builds up a tolerance over time. The same old things simply aren't as stimulating anymore. They need more. And so we often see an increase in violence. More torture. More sadism. And more victims.

"In addition to that, he's probably started to get cocky, believing that because he hasn't been caught for the others, he won't get caught for these. Which might not be a bad thing in terms of the investigation. We often see an increase in the sophistication of a killer's M.O. over time. They get, for lack of a better term, smarter. But we also often see a certain degeneration in some cases. They become sloppier, more reckless. This might be related to drug and alcohol use, but it is often simply an issue of complacency."

Darger displayed another serial killer photograph.

"John Wayne Gacy is a great example. His first known victim was a boy named Timothy McCoy, a stranger he'd picked up at the bus station. Someone he had no ties to. His next known victim was an employee of his. John Butkovich. Butkovich's parents were immediately suspicious of Gacy, but police treated the missing boy as a runaway. Perhaps realizing that killing people known to him was inherently riskier, Gacy switched to killing primarily strangers. At some point, however, he began killing acquaintances again. Gacy's final victim, and the one that ultimately resulted in his capture, was a boy he'd offered a job, Robert Piest. Piest had told both his current coworkers and his parents that he was meeting a Mr. Gacy about a job, which is what led police to Gacy as a suspect. Gacy got smarter for a while… and then he got dumber."

Darger set the photo down and grasped both sides of the podium.

"This erosion of Gacy's M.O. is not the only reason I bring him up. Because like the Gacy case, which stemmed from a single missing boy and ultimately revealed that he'd killed at least 33 young men and boys, I believe the three victims tonight are only the beginning of what we'll find when it comes to our killer."

Darger studied Chief Hall, trying to determine if she'd convinced him or not. But he had too good a poker face.

In the end, it didn't matter what the chief or anyone else thought.

Her eyes went to the FBI analyst in the back of the room. They'd either get a ViCAP hit, or they wouldn't.

And she knew in her gut that they would.

CHAPTER 14

Chief Hall's question had required that Darger deviate from her main profile notes, and it was a moment before she found where she'd left off. Those fluorescent bulbs hummed again in the meantime, that odd tension of what they were here to do somehow swelling in the idle moment. Someone's breath whistled in their nostrils.

"Now that same core insecurity and emotional immaturity we talked about earlier would result in unstable romantic relationships. But since our guy appears to have some social proficiency, I think it's possible that he's been married, possibly more than once. Again, he might be savvy enough to attract a mate in the first place, but I doubt he can keep them for long. His underlying issues will always come to the surface given time.

"Given his penchant for violence, one might assume a history of domestic abuse, but I think it more likely that, similar to Gary Ridgway and Ted Bundy, this guy holds back all of his aggression for his victims. He doesn't attack the actual sources or targets of his anger. He doesn't let off steam in his regular life."

Darger placed a photo of Ridgway next to where Loshak had written his name on the board.

"Much like the Bundy quotes we heard before, Ridgway, too, spoke often of a deep sense of insecurity. In particular, he had chronic feelings that women were unfair to him and controlled him. His first two wives had affairs and eventually divorced him. As an adult, he lived with his domineering mother, who took his paychecks and only gave him money for things she approved of. He resented his female coworkers, whom he believed got preferential treatment at work. Despite all of this ill will toward specific women in his life, he only ever killed sex workers."

Darger had her own set of audio clips at the ready, and she played the first. Ridgway's voice was softer than Bundy's. Almost a whisper.

"Back then I was just a… I was just a wimp, and then when I was… I had control when I was…" Ridgway paused, as if struggling to get the words out. "… when I killed the women."

She played the next clip.

"Pleasure in killing is to uh, get… you know, be in control. To have sex with 'em if I wanted afterwards, and to uh, take away another woman so she won't hurt anybody else."

Darger underlined some of the words Loshak had already written on the board.

Inferiority.

Control.

Pleasure.

"Ridgway illustrates that inferiority-control loop Agent Loshak was talking about, clear as day."

Darger found a blank spot on the board and began a new column.

"Let's move on to the criminal history angle. According to one study, only a quarter of this type of offender would have no prior criminal record, so it's more than likely our guy has a rap sheet. Probably for non-violent crimes — substance abuse charges, drunk driving, petty theft. Again, this is someone who is uncomfortable confronting his problems head-on. Instead, he seeks out indirect ways of relieving stress."

"What about sex crimes?" Detective Bledsoe asked.

"If there is a history of sex-related convictions, it would be much more likely to be for something lesser, like peeping or public masturbation versus rape," Darger said. "Of course, that doesn't mean he hasn't raped before. It only means he probably hasn't been caught."

The marker squeaked and squawked against the board as Darger wrote out the next item.

"Interestingly, killers who use ligatures were found to have an extremely high incidence of alcohol dependence — 66% in one study — and an even higher number were intoxicated at the time the murder occurred, around 72% in the same study.

"Adding to that, sexual predators who use expressive violence have a high correlation with antisocial tendencies. As a child, he likely ran away from home or was disruptive in a school setting. He would have a short temper and a compulsion to rebel against authority figures. Aside from the likelihood that he uses alcohol or other substances, he might also engage in other so-called 'risk-taking behaviors.' Drunk driving, gambling, unprotected sex, etc. In terms of more covert antisocial traits, we'd consider things like lying, theft, burglary, and fraud. Lastly, there are non-sexual violent behaviors that mark someone who is antisocial: cruelty to animals, assault, repeatedly making threats against others, armed robbery, and so on."

"There's something I've been wondering about," Glenn said. "What's up with the gags? The fact that he used the victim's own, uh, undergarments… that has to mean something, right?"

Darger nodded.

"Using the victim's underwear as a gag is almost certainly meant as a way to further humiliate them, and humiliation of the victim is a highly significant profiling detail. Combined with the expressive violence, I'd expect this offender to score high on the sexualization scale. There are a variety of behaviors associated with this: addiction to pornography, compulsive masturbation, promiscuity. Specifically, humiliation of the victim has a very high correlation to having watched pornography directly prior to committing the crime. As such, I'd expect him to have an extensive porn collection, with a heavy focus on violence and sadism."

Darger couldn't help but think of the "lounge" at the truck stop seemingly playing porn on a non-stop loop. The ape-like grunts coming out of the speakers, day and night.

"As my partner pointed out, we're dealing with a type of killer whose crimes are meticulously fantasized about. He thinks about his murders in great detail beforehand. That level of planning and premeditation means he probably has some sort of kit with the tools necessary to subdue and bind his victims along with whatever implements he uses to torture them. He also might wear some sort of disguise. Glasses he doesn't need, a fake mustache, maybe even a wig. This would be for the benefit of any potential witnesses more than for the victims, but it would also add another dimension to the ritual. Like an actor donning a costume for a movie role."

"What about the fact that the personal effects of our victims are missing?" Bledsoe asked. "So far we haven't found a purse or a wallet for any of the girls. Is he trying to make it look like a robbery, or does he just have sticky fingers?"

"It's more likely that he takes these items as trophies. My guess is that sometime over the next few weeks, you'll find the purses and other effects dumped somewhere. If the girls had money in their wallets, it'll still be there. All of it. But something will be missing. A key chain. A tube of lip balm. Trophies serve as a sort of concrete touchstone for when he's reliving the crimes, which he does often. Again, this goes back to his obsession with the fantasy he's created."

Darger stared at the notes already written out on the board and tapped the marker against the palm of her hand.

"The location of the crime scenes gives us more clues about this guy. The truck stop, the motor lodge… these are places used by people who are on the road a lot, and they also serve a predominantly working-class clientele. So I think we're looking for an out-of-towner with a blue-collar job."

"Why not a local?" Glenn asked. "You know, a John or maybe even a pimp who's gone off the deep end?"

One of the uniformed men sat forward.

"Or how about that creep who works at the motel?"

"We should absolutely look into Clint Torbert's background, but as I said before, this is not a first timer. This is someone who has built up to this level of brutality. Not just with the violence inflicted but with the multiple victims in a short period of time. Another thing I neglected to mention before is that we usually see a cooling off period between crimes with serial offenders. This is a period of time in which the perpetrator experiences some psychological release, followed by a period of believing they won't do it again."

As she spoke, Darger noticed that Gummer had left her station at the back of the room and was whispering something in Loshak's ear. Had she found something? Discovered a match in ViCAP?

Darger forced herself to keep talking. To focus on finishing the profile.

"It's very much like an addiction. And like an addict, it takes time for someone to work up a tolerance like this. Again, let me remind you that he brutalized not one, but two women in that motel room before he sought out Tara Bemis. Because apparently what he did to Dawn Sawiki and Jane Doe wasn't enough. That's the only reason it would make sense to target a third victim so soon after. So if he's a local, and it's almost definite that he has killed or attacked before, where are the other victims?"

"Maybe he traveled elsewhere to do them," Glenn suggested.

Darger lifted her shoulders in a noncommittal gesture.

"That's possible, but then it doesn't really make sense for him to start killing here, at home. Serial killers are usually specific about that. They either kill on their home turf, or they don't."

Now Loshak was back at Gummer's laptop. Frowning at the screen.

Shit. Did that mean there'd been no hits from ViCAP?

But how could that be? She was certain this guy had killed before. His signature was too distinct.

Darger cleared her throat.

Stay on track, she thought to herself.

"Also, the fact that the two crime scenes were in a very limited geographic range tells me he doesn't like straying too far from his travel route."

Darger didn't realize she'd trailed off until Loshak glanced up and met her eyes.

"We got something," he said. "From ViCAP."

"A hit?" Darger asked, feeling relief.

Loshak shook his head, and Darger felt a pang of confusion before he went on.

"Not *a* hit. Eight of them."

CHAPTER 15

Darger and Loshak huddled around Gummer's laptop along with both detectives and Chief Hall, all of them packing tightly behind her chair. Someone smelled like Old Spice — probably Detective Glenn, Darger thought.

Her eyes ran down the list of dates first. The most recent murder was just a few months back. The oldest had occurred almost three years ago.

All eight of the victims were women. Collectively, they'd been raped, beaten, cut, and strangled, and they spread from Florida to Massachusetts.

Darger's eyes flicked across the screen. She found herself disturbed that each of these victims had been reduced to a few lines of text here. A name. A place. A couple lines of details to summarize each crime.

One had been left under an overpass. Another had been found under a bed in a motel room with a length of copper pipe jammed into her vagina. The coldness of the terse descriptions only seemed to sharpen the violence somehow. It made Darger squirm in place.

Chief Hall extended a finger and tapped one side of the screen.

"What's this column here, marked HSKI?"

"It stands for Highway Serial Killings Initiative," Darger said and then glanced at Loshak. "You want to explain it?"

He nodded and took a step back from the computer.

"Back in 2004, an analyst from the Oklahoma Bureau of Investigation noticed a string of killings along I-40 that spread from Texas, Oklahoma, Arkansas, and Mississippi. This information was passed on to ViCAP, and our analysts determined that there was not only a consistent pattern here, but along other highways as well. In the original case from Oklahoma, it was noted that many of the victims had last been seen at truck stops. This led to the theory that the killer might be a trucker. Turns out they were correct. John Robert Williams and his girlfriend Rachel Cumberland are believed to have killed at least four people together, most of them sex workers. Williams has claimed a total death count of over thirty, and I don't doubt that he killed more than four, but these guys also have a tendency to exaggerate."

Loshak shrugged.

"Anyway, they started the HSKI to keep track of killings that fit this geographic pattern of following a particular highway. The database has identified 500 murders that occurred along major trucking routes."

He pointed at a section of the screen that showed each murder as a red dot on a map of the US.

"And if you look here, most of our matches are in the vicinity of I-95, which is likely why they've been flagged as potential HSKI cases."

Detective Glenn thrust his hands in his pockets.

"So we're looking for a trucker?"

"Well, I wouldn't say that. Not just yet." Loshak waved a hand at the screen. "A match in ViCAP only means so much. There are similarities between these murders and ours, but that doesn't necessarily mean that they're all the same perpetrator. We'll need to follow up with the local detectives to determine whether these killings were actually committed by our guy."

Gummer raised a timid hand.

"If I might make a suggestion?"

"Go for it," Loshak said.

"Well, aside from maintaining the unsolved murders database, the HSKI also has a database of potential suspects. You should talk to Elizabeth Morris. She's the analyst who oversees the HSKI."

Loshak clapped her on the shoulder.

"That's good thinking, Gummer."

The young woman blushed.

"Alright, then," Loshak said. "It sounds like we have a plan."

CHAPTER 16

Bright and early, before the sun could begin cooking the blacktop outside the Roanoke Rapids police station into a supple goo, a series of phone calls launched the investigation into motion up and down the East Coast.

After dividing up the ViCAP matches among themselves, Darger and the rest of the task force began the somewhat tedious task of tracking down the lead investigator on each individual case. In several instances, given the early hour, the detectives in question had to be rousted from their beds, a circumstance that didn't exactly breed cordiality. The first detective Darger spoke to, in fact, had a few choice words.

"Are you telling me you got me up at the ass crack of dawn for a fucking cold case?"

Still, their diligence paid off, and they were able to rule out two of the original eight ViCAP matches.

The murder of Annalise Geiger was crossed off the list when Loshak spoke with the lead detective and found out that Geiger had been a lawyer. Along with forensic anomalies in the case, this didn't match their killer's victim typology: transients, sex workers, and otherwise marginalized women.

Darger was able to remove Miranda Gonzalo from the list because, though her body was discovered only two miles from the I-95 corridor, Gonzalo was murdered in her own home. The locale of the primary crime scene didn't match the rest.

That left six photos on the wall. Six cold case murders that appeared to be the work of the same man who'd killed the three women last night.

All of the victims were found completely unclothed, except for their shoes. All had been bound at the wrists and ankles. All had pre- and post-mortem cut wounds. All had been strangled with ligatures. Four victims had been gagged with their own undergarments. One had a sanitary pad stuffed in her mouth. The earliest victim, Debra Smith of Newark, had been gagged with duct tape. Four of the six victims were known sex workers. All six had been dumped within a twenty-mile radius of I-95.

The fourth and fifth victims, chronologically, had been found together in a motel room outside of Miami, an eerie echo of the scene at the Cozy Motor Lodge.

For each confirmed victim of their killer, they recruited an investigator from the respective jurisdiction to their cause. Boston. Miami. Newark. Savannah. Fayetteville. New blood flooded into the task force, not unlike a Sheriff handing out deputy badges in a crisis.

And almost at once, those new investigators splayed out into the field to gather information, given the fresh angle to chase down. These were no longer isolated homicides spread up and down the East Coast. They were working a serial murder case.

Credit card records were gathered in Miami. Surveillance footage in Savannah was analyzed and uploaded to the task force headquarters in North Carolina. New witness statements were taken in Boston.

So it would go. With detectives hitting the streets just after dawn, the task force's intelligence would grow exponentially over the course of the day.

All the rocks would be turned over, and they'd get a good, long look at what lay wriggling beneath.

CHAPTER 17

Detective Andrew Kassab plodded over the parking lot at Mr. Freddy's Trucks and Gas. The mom-and-pop gas station sat in an industrial stretch on the outskirts of Boston.

An awning hung over the front of the cinder block structure, its formerly red vinyl now faded to grapefruit-flesh pink. Sun-bleached. There was something awfully dreary about the color, Kassab thought, like the life of this neighborhood had slowly been sucked out over the years, and here was the hard evidence.

The place was small. Hell, it was tiny. Freddy's was one of those dinky buildings so crammed with cartons of cigarettes and soft drinks it left just enough room to let a customer inside. Closer to a walk-in closet than a place of business.

Kassab didn't think he would've noticed the lot full of ten or twelve semis behind the building if he hadn't been looking for it. The wooden fence-enclosed asphalt slab was ostensibly all that made the place a "truck stop" instead of a simple gas station. The tops of a few trailers rose up over the planks and caught the morning sun.

Yeah. It didn't look like much to Kassab. Yet, from what he'd learned this morning, this dumpy little gas station had been connected to a serial murder case that spanned roughly 1,500 miles up and down the East Coast.

He smoothed his hand over the prickles of his thinning hair, felt a faint tingle there at the thought. It'd be hot later, but this early, a cool breeze breathed pleasantly on the back of his neck.

Now that the connections between the various murders had been made by some FBI hotshot, Kassab found himself assigned to the task force and working the case. It wasn't how he'd thought his morning would go, but surprise was part of the job.

As a homicide cop in an urban police department, it wasn't unusual for shifts to pass without catching a murder. Quiet days spent trying to shift the puzzle pieces of old cases around while they waited for the next calamity to pop up.

The call didn't always arrive on time, but it always arrived, and when it did, those humdrum stints of anticipation got replaced with frantic bursts of activity.

On a fresh murder investigation, he often worked 48-72 hours straight trying to close the case before it went cold. No sleep. Meals that came out of vending machines. Kassab had a feeling this one would take him right up to the edge of his limits, along with all the others in the task force.

Nevertheless, he would attack this case like he did all of them. That was the job, and he didn't just take it seriously. He reveled in it.

He relished closing the loops, taking another murderer off the streets. The lost sleep and poor diet were small prices to pay for the satisfaction and sense of purpose he'd found in his career.

Frankly, he didn't know how other people got through their lives, doing work that was mostly meaningless by comparison. He often drove through the guts of the city, staring out a bustling world that looked to him about as meaningful as the ants swirling a hill. All those people. How the hell did they all keep going?

When he reached the glass door of the gas station, he stopped and gazed back down the road. He could see the overpass in the distance, perhaps a half-mile down the way. The body had been dumped underneath it some eight months back. Found face down on the sloped concrete. Tucked back in the shadowy place where the steel girders of the overpass butted up to the land.

Sandra Colson. That was the victim's name. Thirty-eight years old. A mother of three. She'd worked the truck stop behind Freddy's, among others.

The pictures from the file flashed through Kassab's head. Before and after. Whole and harmed. Alive and dead.

Then he turned back. Pushed into the gas station. Here, the work would begin.

Over the next twenty minutes, he'd get the rundown from the owner — which companies sent trucks through here, especially the regulars. The list would be cross-referenced to those from the other crime scenes, and the process of whittling that down to something small enough to be useful would begin.

☾

Meanwhile, some 1,494 miles away, Detective Barb Mustafa of the Miami PD quested after similar information at the Forty Winks Motel in one of the roughest suburbs of Vice City. She waited in the lobby while the clerk went to get the manager, trying not to dwell on the faintly fishy odor present here.

She checked her watch. She was four hours and forty minutes away from flying up to North Carolina as part of the task force, and she wanted to bring some good information with her.

The manager appeared in the doorway behind the counter. Round face. Silver comb-over. Sheepish smile.

Mustafa didn't dally. She hit the questions hard and fast like she was working the speed bag. Jotted down notes as the manager spoke.

"Yeah. Yeah, we get truckers out here. Parked out back in the big lot, and they'll rent a room or two. They don't come too often. Maybe once or twice a week, and then nothing for a couple weeks. Usually for partying more than sleeping, if I'm being honest."

Mustafa's pen swooped over the notebook in her hand. She had her phone recording the conversation, but she liked to write down the most important bits for faster reference later.

The manager answered another question.

"As far as that night… Yeah, there were truckers in and out, like I told the police, but… Well, we didn't find the bodies 'til the next morning, so…"

The man blinked hard. Looked like a scolded poodle.

"I have the log here. From that night."

He handed the book over. Old-school paper. Mustafa had already seen the photos in the file, but it was still interesting to see the book in person.

"You can see that all the, uh, patrons paid cash that night, so…"

Mustafa's eyes skimmed down the page, noting multiple fake names. John Holmes. Mike Hunt. A.S. Muncher. Peter Pantz.

Nothing there.

She handed the log back over and thanked the manager for his time. Then she started back through the small lobby, passed the closet-sized room with vending machines as she moved toward the exit.

Her mind whirred. So far re-stirring the facts hadn't dislodged anything new.

So now what? Did she just fly into the task force meeting

empty-handed?

She pushed through the glass door. Stepped out into the sun. The Florida air wrapped itself around her like a wet blanket — barely 8 A.M. and already muggy.

The grisly photos of the victims flashed in her head. One face down under the bed. The other draped over the edge of the mattress, legs dangling down so the soles of her feet skimmed the fluff of the shag carpet.

Red gashes in the skin of both corpses. Stark against the otherwise clean expanses of flesh. The cuts looked like lonesome highways on a road map.

All at once, Mustafa stopped in her tracks. She blinked. Twice.

Then she turned back. Stomped up the curb, over the sidewalk, and re-entered the lobby.

She'd seen something. Or thought she had.

She moved back toward that tiny room where the vending machines faced off, let her eyes flit over the space.

Pepsi and Coke machines huddled in one corner. A pair of candy machines filled the opposite one, with one machine in the middle full of plastic triangles of pre-made sandwiches — egg salad, ham salad. All the gross salads were covered.

A cork bulletin board hung on the back wall, almost inaccessible with the machines crushing so close. Flaps of paper hung down over the console there, obscuring it further.

She stepped closer. Peeled back the fliers to reveal what lay beneath.

And now her heart beat faster.

She hadn't seen anything in the file about checking the records from the ATM here in the lobby. Everyone paid cash, eh? Well, this might be just what she was looking for. No camera on the machine from what she could see, but…

Already her phone was out, the outgoing call ringing in her ear. Time to see if the killer left a trace of himself here after all.

☾

At the same time, Detective Bledsoe checked out surveillance footage at Munchie's Truck Stop in Fayetteville. Rather than taking a few hours to sleep like her partner, she'd decided to drive down to this scene herself. She'd watched the sun continue to rise over the black line of the interstate, her sedan coiling down the exit toward the truck stop.

Her eyes felt gritty. Her mouth tasted bad. Sour. She regretted not stopping at home to brush her teeth before she'd hit the road.

The building's owner had given her access to the security setup in the back, with an assistant there to help her navigate the videos. Now she sat in front of a bank of monitors, watching surprisingly high-quality videos of cars and trucks entering and exiting the lot. High-def shit.

"Had some thievery and thought it was worth it to bulk up the security outfit to protect the business," the owner had explained before he left her to it.

She directed the assistant manager to run the footage forward. Pause it. Run it forward. Pause it again. She logged the plates entering the lot one by one.

Painstaking? Yes. Likely to help the investigation? Hell yes. Crazy what a boon technology could be for law enforcement.

The assistant manager needed a bathroom break about forty minutes in, so Bledsoe cracked open the Frappucino she'd bought on her way through the truck stop convenience store. Mocha-flavored.

She took a swig and tried to wash that sour taste on her

tongue away. No help. The creaminess felt good, but the drink was too sweet. Jesus, her teeth felt fuzzy.

She decided to call in some of the plates while she waited. Names and faces arriving on her phone to go with those plate numbers by way of text.

They'd whittle their list of plates down based on what turned up in the other connected cities. Then, with the guidance of the profile, they would start calling dispatchers and establishing timelines for their possible suspects.

Yeah, the process would take time, but it would unearth something. She could feel it.

CHAPTER 18

The sun was blazing overhead when Darger stepped outside the police station for some fresh air. After being in the nearly windowless building all morning, the sudden brightness was somewhat disorienting.

She blinked rapidly, waiting for her eyes to adjust. When they did, she spotted Detective Glenn a few yards from the door, leaning against the wall of the station and puffing on an e-cigarette.

"Started vaping to quit smoking real cigarettes. Thought it'd be a temporary thing. But now here I am, four years later, just as hooked on this damn thing as I was the smokes. How dumb is that?"

Darger studied the thick white plume that vacated Glenn's mouth and nostrils as he exhaled.

"I know it's not technically healthy," she said, "but it's got to be at least some improvement over cigarettes. Right?"

Glenn shrugged.

"My doctor says it's just as bad, but what does he know?"

Darger laughed.

Images still flickered behind her eyes, lingering residue of the work she'd been doing. Over an hour of logging plates from the fresh batch of traffic cam footage they'd received from near the Boston crime scene. The stream of semis pulling into a parking lot seemed endless, and maybe it was. She was still seeing the trucks now even though she'd walked away from the screen.

The tedium of toll road records would probably be next.

Spreadsheets. Fun.

The low purr of a car engine drew Darger's attention further down the road. A familiar vehicle coasted toward them, pulling to the curb and parking. The engine cut out all at once, and Loshak exited the car with two bags of food and a drink carrier filled with white cups.

"There's coffee and donuts in the backseat," he said. "You want to grab those?"

"Got it," Darger said, climbing halfway in to collect the boxes.

"Also, I finally got a call back from Liz Morris at the HSKI. She's emailing us her list of P.O.I.'s right now."

Darger felt a little giddy. A specially curated list of potential suspects… In a serial murder investigation, a lead like that was solid gold.

Detective Glenn tucked his vape pen into his jacket and moved to hold the door open, and the three of them headed inside.

Instead of proceeding back to the conference room, they took a flight of stairs down to the basement. With the rapid expansion of the task force over the course of the morning, they'd quickly realized they were going to need more room. A few detectives had already filtered in from the nearest jurisdictions, and even now several more investigators from up and down the eastern seaboard were en route to join their ranks.

The basement of the station was mainly used for storage — the eastern wall was populated with rows and rows of industrial metal shelves that held boxes of old case files and evidence going back several decades. But roughly half of the sprawling basement was unused, and they commandeered one corner of the empty space for their task force headquarters, hauling in folding tables, chairs, and computers from elsewhere in the building.

Darger dropped the donuts and coffee at the far end of the room, near their newly constructed murder wall, where a photo of each victim had been pinned up along with the date, location, and other pertinent details of the crime. It wasn't much, but the photos made it more than a name on a list. At least now the victims were starting to seem like the real human beings they once were. To Darger, that seemed important.

While Loshak handed out the food and drinks, Darger slid in front of one of the laptops and checked her email. Sure enough, there was a message from L. Morris waiting in her inbox.

She opened the email and stared at the screen for several seconds.

"Is this right?" she said, her eyes scanning down the page.

She sensed the rest of the group huddling close behind her now.

"What is it?" Loshak asked.

"There are over twenty names here. That seems like… a lot."

"You were expecting the HSKI to hand you a single suspect's name on a silver platter?" Loshak asked.

Darger frowned.

"No. But I didn't think there'd be dozens of creeps who would make the list."

Loshak sipped at his drink.

"Once we start cross-referencing these guys with the various surveillance videos and whatever other evidence we've gathered, we'll be able to narrow it down pretty quick. That's my guess. Anyway, you should come eat."

"In a minute," Darger said, her eyes still glued to the screen.

Along with the names of the persons of interest, Morris had sent a brief bio for most of the men on the list.

"Detective Glenn called it," she said, finally wheeling away from the computer. "Most of these guys are either current or former truck drivers."

"Shoot, I was only going off what you folks said in the first place. Blue-collar, not local, travels a lot." Glenn gestured at a map they'd put up on the wall, each victim marked with a red push pin. "Who else but a trucker?"

Loshak rattled the ice in his cup.

"Let's hope you're right on that count. It's just the kind of lucky break we could use."

"Lucky?" Glenn repeated. "How's that?"

"Truckers have to keep records, and they pass through the state weigh stations. If the killer's a trucker, we can track him. If he's not…"

Loshak didn't finish the sentence, and for several long seconds, they lapsed into a thoughtful silence.

Paper crinkled as Glenn unwrapped his sandwich further. He leaned in to take a bite and then paused.

"I never thought about how driving a truck would be the perfect job for a serial killer. Guy can drop bodies all over his route, and it'd be almost impossible for someone to tie them together as being the same perp without something like ViCAP keeping track."

Loshak held up a finger shimmering with bacon grease from his sandwich.

"And bear in mind, not every murder gets entered into ViCAP. So this could be just the tip of the iceberg. There also might be living victims. Women who either escaped or who he didn't kill, for whatever reason."

Glenn wiped at the corner of his mouth with a paper

napkin.

"What was the guy's name you talked about before? The one who killed with his girlfriend?"

"John Robert Williams."

"That's the one," Glenn said, nodding. "Have there been others? Serial killers who drove a truck for a living?"

"Oh, sure. There's Adam Leroy Lane. He killed at least two women and attacked two more before he was caught. He was fond of sneaking into the homes of his victims and stabbing them, usually while they slept." Loshak glanced at Darger. "Who else?"

"Bruce Mendenhall," she offered. "He confessed to murdering at least six women, mostly prostitutes. He later recanted and claimed he was framed for the murders despite his gun being linked to the crimes and mountains of forensic evidence in his truck."

"Then there's Keith Jesperson, aka the Happy Face Killer."

"What kind of serial killer nickname is that?" Glenn asked.

"Jesperson got pissed off when the murder of his first known victim was pinned on someone else. He wanted credit. So he wrote a series of anonymous letters to the police and various media outlets claiming that he was the culprit, and he signed each letter with a smiley face."

Glenn clicked his tongue.

"These guys truly take some kind of sick pride in what they do, huh?"

"Oh yeah."

Darger snapped her fingers.

"Robert Ben Rhoades. I can't believe I almost forgot him. He used the cab of his truck like a mobile torture chamber. He'd chain his victims up and torture them for days and weeks at a time. A textbook sexual sadist."

Loshak grunted.

"Yeah, Rhoades is a gen-u-wine piece of filth," he said and then sighed. "Let's see… there's also Samuel Legg III. Delmus Colvin. Volker Eckert in Germany. Those are just the ones we can name off the top of our heads, but I know of at least 25 truckers who have been convicted in serial homicide cases."

Glenn let out a low whistle.

"Jesus. Lotta sick puppies in the world. Guess it only makes sense that some of 'em have to drive a truck, no?"

CHAPTER 19

For the next hour, there was a frenzy of activity in their basement headquarters. Bledsoe returned with surveillance footage from the Fayetteville scene and a list of license plates to add to those that had already been logged from the other scenes. Any of the men from the HSKI list that could be placed in the vicinity of Big Jon's Travel Center in the past 24 hours and had also been within a hundred miles of an additional murder scene made it to the final suspect list.

By midday, they had pared the list down to five names.

Charles Trotter.

Ed McMurphy.

Ricky Lee Adkins.

Junior Riggins, Jr.

Billy Ray Jones.

A BOLO alert was issued for each man and his truck. While they waited for an update from the cops on the street, Darger and a handful of analysts from the FBI field office in Charlotte started the process of digging into the background of each suspect, compiling as much information as they could on their criminal backgrounds and their personal lives. If and when they got the men into an interview room, she knew these details would be invaluable.

☾

Less than half an hour after the BOLOs had been issued, Bledsoe hustled into the room with her phone pressed to her ear.

"He said OK?" she was saying, and then there was a pause. "Alright. Bring him in."

She hung up and took a deep breath.

"That was one of our squad cars. Guess who they spotted at the IHOP a few exits north of here?"

"Who?"

"Charles Trotter."

Darger's eyes went to the top of their list of suspects.

Next to Trotter's name, they'd jotted down a few pertinent notes. Thirty-eight years old. Originally from Wheaton, Illinois, a suburb outside of Chicago. Current residence was listed as Snead's Ferry, North Carolina, a dot on the map a few hours south of Roanoke Rapids.

"He's the one we have using the ATM near the Miami crime scene?" Darger said.

"Yeah, and the one with two priors for indecent exposure." Bledsoe tucked her phone into her pocket. "He's agreed to come in for questioning."

Detective Glenn came over to join them.

"You two wanna take first crack at him?"

"You don't mind?" Loshak asked.

Glenn shrugged.

"I figure if we got two profiling experts here, we might as well use them."

Bledsoe checked her watch.

"Well, it won't take them long to get here, and I don't know about y'all, but I'm gonna need another cup of coffee for this."

CHAPTER 20

Darger and Loshak huddled around a TV screen with Bledsoe, Glenn, and a few of the other detectives from the task force, watching as Trotter was led into the interview room by the officers who had picked him up at the IHOP. Upon entering the room, he was already talking a mile a minute.

"I'm tellin' ya. The guy's a bum. He was a bum in college, and he's gonna be a bum in the pros. First round pick or no. You saw that bowl game, right? That drop in the end zone against Oklahoma State?"

"Yeah," one of the cops said. "I saw it."

"Hands like flapjacks. See what I'm sayin'? Kid's a bum. Bookmark it."

Darger could still hear the traces of a Chicago accent in his speech.

"Big talker, this one," Loshak said, watching the trucker gab away on the screen.

A schmoozer, Darger thought. Well, maybe we can use that.

"It'll be just a minute," one of the cops said to the trucker, gesturing that Trotter should sit. "You want something to drink?"

Trotter was short and stocky, probably only 5'9" tops, but that broad frame was packed with at least 250 pounds of thick muscle under a sheet of what looked like baby fat despite his age of 38 years. The chair creaked as he settled into it.

"You got Mountain Dew?"

"'Fraid not. The machine's all Coke products. Coke, Diet Coke, Sprite, Monster. Oh, and water."

"Shit, let me get a Monster then."

The cop nodded.

"Be right back."

The group in the observation room kept their eyes on the screen, curious how Trotter would behave now that he was alone in the room.

He pulled a pack of cigarettes from his shirt pocket and set it on the table, batting it over the surface from one hand to the other like a cat playing with a toy mouse.

Even as big as the rest of him was, his forearms and wrists were incongruously large.

"Guy's built like Popeye," Loshak said.

Glenn grunted in agreement.

"Looks more than capable of committing the crimes physically."

Darger studied the man, trying to get a feel for his demeanor. He hunched over the table so his elbows rested on the edge while he toyed with the cigarettes. One might declare the slumped posture a sign of him feeling scared or defeated. The fidgeting a manifestation of his inner anxiety. But Darger didn't get the impression that he was all that nervous. There was something in the shoulders. A lack of tightness. Similarly, his face was a mask of complete indifference. Blank.

The door of the interview room opened again, and the cop set the can of Monster on the table.

"There you go."

"Much obliged," Trotter said, brushing at the stringy brown hair that hung down into his eyes. "I don't suppose I can smoke in here?"

He held up the pack of cigarettes and gave them a gentle squeeze, causing the cellophane to crinkle.

"Nope," the cop said. "Sorry."

A moment later, there was a knock at the observation room door, and the cop poked his head in.

"Thanks for that, Drake," Bledsoe said. "He say anything on the drive in?"

"Oh yeah. Guy's a real chatterbox. He asked why we wanted to talk to him, asked if it was about the bodies they found."

"Interesting. What'd you say?"

"Told him we were talkin' to everyone who was there last night."

"Good answer."

"There's something else," Officer Drake said. "Last night, when we were canvassing for witnesses at the travel center, one of the other truckers mentioned Trotter by name."

Bledsoe cocked her head to one side.

"As in, he liked him for the murder?"

"More like Trotter was a guy who had connections. He's big into the party scene among the truckers, I guess. Guy said that Trotter himself didn't sell drugs, but that he always seemed to know where to get 'em. One of those guys who knows everyone. And he thought that if anyone knew who the dead girl mighta been with before she died, it'd be Trotter." Drake shrugged. "Anyway, just thought I should mention that."

"Thanks again. We'll let you know when we're done with him."

She turned back to face Darger and Loshak.

"You ready?"

Loshak's eyes slid over to meet Darger's.

"I think so. If he's the talkative type, and it seems like he is, we can use that to our advantage."

"Play the 'we're all friends here' game," Darger said.

"Exactly. Lay the charm on real thick, and I bet he'll eat it up."

Darger bobbed her head once.

"Let's do it."

CHAPTER 21

When they entered the interview room, the first thing Darger noticed was the smell of Trotter's cologne, which he'd apparently bathed in. The musky odor seemed dated to Darger on top of being overpowering. It brought back memories.

She'd had a friend in middle school whose dad was a drunk, and he'd used copious amounts of Stetson cologne in a failed attempt to cover the smell of his booze breath. Darger wondered if Trotter was a boozer pulling the same maneuver. Or maybe he just had bad body odor. Or no sense of smell.

Trotter's eyes went comically wide when Loshak introduced them.

"Well, I'll be damned," he said, leaning over the table to shake each of their hands in turn. "They didn't say I'd be talking to the Feds."

"Is that a problem?" Loshak asked.

"A problem? Shit no! I mean, this'll make a hell of a story, won't it? How many people can say they've been interviewed by the FBI?" He leaned in, his voice lowering to something almost conspiratorial. "Hey, I've seen *Silence of the Lambs* probably a thousand times. How accurate would you say their portrayal is?"

Darger glanced from Loshak to Trotter and shrugged.

"Some of it's pretty accurate. Other parts… not as much."

Trotter grinned and slapped his palm on the table.

"That's exactly what I figured! It's Hollywood, right? Artistic license and whatnot."

"Well, Charles—" Darger began, but Trotter cut her off

with a defensive gesture.

"Hey now! We're all friends here, aren't we? Call me Chuck."

"OK," Darger said. "The reason we asked you down here, *Chuck*, is because we're looking for witnesses. We're talking to anyone who was at Big Jon's Travel Center last night. And your name just keeps coming up."

Darger intentionally worded this to sound ambiguous. She wanted to see if he'd break into a flop sweat at the notion of his name being connected to a murder investigation. But Trotter didn't seem bothered. He raised his eyebrows nonchalantly and cracked open the can of Monster.

"Oh yeah?"

"Word around the lot is that you're the guy."

"The guy?"

He brought the can to his lips and took a drink.

"The guy who always knows what's happening. The one who's got all the connections."

Trotter's eyes glittered a second before the smile took his lips.

"Well… I guess I've always been something of a social butterfly," he said, setting the can down. "I have a way with people, you could say. My grandfather called it 'the gift of gab.'"

"So you were there last night? When everything went down?"

"Oh, sure. I was one of the first people on the scene after ol' Hendy started up with the hollerin'. Saw the body and everything."

"Really? I don't think I saw you in the crowd."

Trotter scoffed.

"You mean with the rubberneckers? No, I wasn't among them. You ask me, those kind of people… well… it's just unseemly, is what it is. Like the people who slow down when they see a big wreck on the highway? A bunch of ghouls, the lot of them."

"Makes you sick, doesn't it?" Loshak said.

Trotter shook his head.

"I tell ya, some people just weren't raised right, and it shows."

It was clear that talking to the FBI made Trotter feel important, and Darger decided to lean into it.

"Well, you seem like a pretty observant guy," Darger said. "Can you tell us anything or anyone you might have seen last night? Anything that stuck out?"

Trotter pursed his lips and made a show of thinking hard, eyes dancing back and forth.

"Nothing unusual, really. But you know… I saw her. The dead girl."

"Right. You mentioned that."

"No… I'm talking about before she was dead."

Darger leaned in, genuinely interested.

"You saw Tara Bemis before she died?"

"Sure. She was comin' out of the convenience store. Asked me for a light."

"Do you remember what time?"

"Oh… maybe eight o'clock?"

This aligned with what they knew already about Tara going inside to buy cigarettes a few minutes after eight.

"What did you two talk about?"

Trotter gulped at his energy drink and mopped the back of his hand over his lips.

"We didn't talk about anything. I gave her a light, and that was that. I mean, it wasn't like a family reunion. We didn't know each other or nothing."

"You never talked to her before then?"

"Not to my recollection, but I do come through here an awful lot. And it's like you said… I'm the kind of guy who knows everybody." He shrugged. "So, I suppose there's a chance we'd crossed paths before."

"Did you ever hire her?"

"Hire her? Like for sex?" He let out a bark of laugh. "Look, no judgment on the guys who gotta do that. For some of them, I imagine it's the only way they can get any, you know? But I don't have to pay for sex. Never have. Never will."

"Well, not everyone has your charm," Darger said with a wink.

He laughed again.

"In all seriousness though, if I was going to pay for it, it wouldn't be with no lot lizard. I mean no disrespect, but these girls out here… they're a mess. Can't imagine there's a single one not hooked on drugs. Probably riddled with disease. I can't believe anyone would take that chance, if I'm honest. Maybe that sounds cold, but I just call it like I see it."

He bent over the table, so his face was a few inches closer.

"You wanna hear something real sick? I was on a run a few years back. Stopped somewhere in Georgia, I think it was. One of the lizards had her daughter with her. Kid couldn't have been older than twelve, and mom was selling her on the lot. Can you fuckin' imagine? The depravity. Made me kinda glad I don't have any kids myself, if that's the kind of sick world we're living in."

"No kids?" Loshak asked, though they already knew this from their research into Trotter's background.

"No, sir."

"How about a wife?"

"Nah." He waved the question away like a bad smell. "Tried

it twice. Didn't take."

"Now that surprises me," Darger said.

"Well, what can I say? I'm a hard man to please." He leaned back in his chair and gazed up at the ceiling. "I won't bother sugarcoating it. I know what I want, and I won't settle for less. Now my first wife... the long and short of it is that we were both young. Thought we knew everything, and against the advice of our parents, we got married. Looking back, I can see now how we were both inexperienced with the ways of the world. We tried to make it work, but I think that relationship was just doomed from the beginning. Neither one of us were our true adult selves yet, and at the end of it, we were two puzzle pieces that just didn't fit together."

He drummed out a little rhythm on the table with his fingertips.

"My second wife, boy she was quite the looker when I met her. Pretty little thing. But she was a fair bit younger than me, and I think that may have been the downfall there. She had a... well, I guess I'd call it a lack of motivation. Didn't seem to have any direction in life. If I wasn't there to give her some kind of guidance, she'd just lay around in her PJs all day, watching TV, eatin' Cocoa Puffs. Letting her brain rot. I just couldn't relate to that, being a man of action, myself."

"A man of action?"

"Yeah, you know... if I want something, I develop a plan, and I execute. If I find I'm interested in something, I pursue it as if it were my sole purpose in life. Taught myself to speed-read. I'm fluent in Spanish and French. Even took some cooking classes. I make a mean duck à l'Orange, let me tell you."

"Doesn't part of that come with the job? I mean, you have all this mandatory downtime when you can't drive, so..."

"Sure, but that's the thing. All these guys have that downtime, but do you see them picking up the complete works of Shakespeare? No. You gotta have the drive. A work ethic." He pointed a finger at her. "And most people don't. Anyway, I don't even remember how we got on this whole thing…"

"Your second wife?"

"Oh. Bella. Right. I mean, when it comes right down to it, she got lazy. Gained a bunch of weight, and I know that's not very PC of me to point out, nor am I suggesting that I left her because of it, but it was a symptom of a bigger disease."

"And that was?"

He shook his head.

"Indifference? Apathy? Incuriousness, if that's even a word… Call it what you want, but I just couldn't imagine spending the next however many years with someone who lacked passion like that."

"Let's go back to Tara Bemis. Did you see her talk to anyone else last night?"

"No. Not that I saw. But bear in mind, I laid eyes on her for all of ten seconds. The only reason I even remember is because when I saw her dead, I thought of that quote from Macbeth. 'Life's but a walking shadow, a poor player that struts and frets his hour upon the stage and then is heard no more. It is a tale told by an idiot, full of sound and fury, signifying nothing.' I mean, only an hour before, she'd been up alive and smoking a cigarette with no idea it was all about to end. How wild is that?"

Darger wasn't sure 'wild' was the word she'd use, but she kept her mouth shut. Better to keep him talking.

"Do you have any idea who Tara might have been with last night?"

"Not a clue."

"Any guys you know seem like the type who would do

something like this?"

Trotter seemed to find this a mix of amusing and preposterous.

"Do I know anyone who'd kill a hooker? I sure hope not. Then again, most of these guys get their rocks off jerkin' it to the nonstop porno loop in the lounge. So who's to say what other perverted and depraved shit they're into?" He slurped at the energy drink. "Call me old-fashioned, but I never understood the impulse to whack off five feet from another guy."

Darger saw an opening here and took it.

"But if I recall, you do have an arrest for indecent exposure."

Just like that, the genial smile vanished and was replaced with a stony stare. His new expression reminded Darger of a snapping turtle.

"That was a misunderstanding," he said, his tone as flat as his eyes.

"What kind of misunderstanding?"

"Well, first off, it wasn't anything like I was talking about… those guys chokin' their chickens in the same room together like animals. I didn't drop my pants in front of another *guy*."

Darger cocked an eyebrow.

"The fact that you exposed yourself to a woman makes it better?"

"Look, I was drunk, OK? And it was more of a goof than anything predatory. I did it for laughs. It wasn't like I forced myself on her or something."

"And when it happened again in New Jersey?"

Trotter's eyes bored into Darger's, the anger burning white hot.

This is it, she thought. He's going to get up and leave. I

pushed him too far.

But then he blinked twice, and his mouth stretched back into a smile. He put his arms out on the table, palms up as though in question. Darger caught a flash of a small tattoo on his inner forearm, an anchor rendered in black ink.

He even has a Popeye tattoo, for Christ's sake.

"Hey, what can I say?" the trucker asked. "New Jersey brings out the worst in people, right?"

His eyes scanned the room.

"I don't mean to rush you guys, but how much longer do you think this is gonna take? I gotta be back on the road, and I wanted to swing back over to Big Jon's for the ribs. Have you had them yet? Best in the state. Shit, best in the country, far as I'm concerned."

"Oh, we're almost done," Darger said. "What time did you get to the truck stop last night?"

"Late in the afternoon. Think it was about four."

"And what time did you leave?"

"Once I heard the cops were coming, I knew it was going to turn into a damned circus, so I moved to the rest stop a few miles up the road. I just didn't think I'd get to sleep with all the flashing lights and hullabaloo going on."

"I can imagine. You drivers need your beauty rest, am I right?"

"Damn right! In some ways, it's the most important part of the job, a good night's sleep. I know there's guys that monkey with their logs to drive more hours and take speed to stay awake, but that's just irresponsible, you ask me."

Darger put out her hand.

"Well, thank you for being a good sport. We appreciate it."

"No problem at all. I'd even say it was a pleasure."

His massive hand dwarfed hers as they shook, and Darger

took it as a last opportunity to look him in the eye. She saw a wiliness there. A perpetual amusement. But there was an edge to it. The passion he talked about? Or something else?

When the uniforms returned to escort Trotter from the interview room, she watched him go, wondering all the while if he was the one.

CHAPTER 22

Darger's mind churned as she whisked through the deep air-conditioned chill of the hall. She and Loshak rejoined the detectives in the observation room.

"What'd you think?" Bledsoe asked.

"Hard to say…" Darger glanced at the screen that now showed an empty interview room. "I doubt we saw much of the real Chuck Trotter in there."

"What do you mean?" Glenn asked. "He seemed pretty forthright to me."

"Maybe. But he's a performer. The kind of guy who's always 'on.' He makes a big show of being affable and friendly because he wants everyone to like him. Makes it hard to tell what's true and what's false."

Loshak nodded.

"Kinda reminded me of John Wayne Gacy. The Mr. Popular, life-of-the-party kind of guy. Wants to be everybody's best friend, but in a very surface-level kind of way." Loshak raked his fingers through his hair. "He was pretty slick, but the mask slipped a few times. He didn't like it that you brought up the indecent exposure charge."

"No, he didn't. He let the anger take hold for a second there." She shrugged. "But then it was like he did the math and realized that was less likely to get him a positive result, so he slid right back into the easygoing persona. The guy who doesn't take anything seriously."

"He also edged around answering several of our questions directly," Loshak pointed out. "When you asked if he ever hired

Tara Bemis, he didn't outright deny it."

Bledsoe bobbed her head up and down.

"You're right. He said he 'doesn't have to pay for sex.'"

Glenn snorted.

"Not like the killer is paying them anyway." The detective scratched his chin. "So you think the fact that he's putting on this act means he's our guy?"

"Not necessarily. It could be that he's just desperate for validation. Or it could be that he's figured out that the more likable he is, the more he can get away with."

Darger stared at the empty room on the screen.

"All I can say for sure is that I wouldn't rule him out. He's someone worth keeping an eye on for sure."

CHAPTER 23

Glenn was in front as they exited the observation room, and he turned back to address them.

"You ever put a donut in a toaster?"

"No."

"Can't say I have," Loshak said.

Glenn rubbed his hands together

"Hoo boy, you are in for a treat then."

Halfway down the stairs to the basement they ran into Chief Hall, and Glenn's toasted donut witchcraft was put on the back burner.

"We've got another one lined up for you," he said. "Room 2."

"Already?" Bledsoe asked.

"One of the Halifax County Deputies managed to get in touch with Billy Ray Jones on the CB, and he came right in."

This somehow sounded like a *Dukes of Hazzard* plot detail to Darger, but she didn't say anything.

The chief nodded and handed Loshak a manila folder. Darger could read *Jones, Billy Ray* on the tab in ink that looked almost runny around the edges.

"How'd it go with Trotter?" the chief asked.

"He's a sly one," Detective Glenn said. "We're going to put one of the plainclothes units on his truck, keep an eye on him until we know more."

Darger studied the file over Loshak's shoulder while the others talked. Jones had a modest criminal history. Most of the charges seemed to be drug- or alcohol-related, but there was a breaking and entering charge and, more interestingly, one for stalking.

They returned to the observation room, and Bledsoe brought up the feed from Interview Room 2.

Darger gazed at the screen. Billy Ray Jones was built like a string bean. Tall and thin with narrow shoulders. He reminded Darger of a stretched-out piece of taffy with a tuft of bright red hair on top that stuck up funny.

"Dude looks like a stretched-out Troll doll," Loshak said almost under his breath. "Remember those?"

Darger scoffed.

"Like I could ever forget."

On the screen, Jones picked at the corner of the table where a piece of the laminate top had chipped away. Then he stopped and drummed the fingertips of both hands on the glossy surface. Just as abruptly, he halted his beat to adjust the blue-tinted sunglasses he wore.

"Twitchy son of a bitch," Glenn muttered.

Darger nodded, watching Jones blink and sniff and fidget. At one point, he pulled himself upright in the chair, only to slouch back down some five seconds later. The movement reminded Darger of a puppet being yanked to attention and then dropped all at once.

"I've seen guys get a case of the nerves in there, but this is ridiculous. I keep expecting cartoon sweat drops to start rolling down his face," Bledsoe said. "You think he's on something?"

Glenn scratched at his chin.

"Could be speed. You heard Trotter. Lot of truckers use it to stay awake."

"Or he could be anxious because he just killed three people, and now he's being questioned by the police," Bledsoe said.

"Whatever's giving him the jitters, I think we can probably

use it to our advantage," Loshak said. "He's going to expect us to come in there asking about what happened last night, but I think we should skirt around it for a while. Really drag it out. Keep him guessing."

"That's good," Darger said. "Prolong the wait. He's expecting a release, some relief, once we finally grill him. But if we don't ask…"

"The hamster wheel in his brain just keeps spinning. Faster and faster," Loshak said.

Darger stared at the screen a second longer and felt a tickle of intuition come upon her.

"I think you should go in alone."

Loshak raised one eyebrow.

"Yeah?"

"It's just a hunch, but I think one-on-one will be more awkward for him."

"Like a first date."

Darger chuckled.

"Exactly. And if you get the sense that it's not working out, I can always join you then."

"Alright," Loshak said, nodding. "Let's get to torturing his ass."

CHAPTER 24

From the observation room next door, Darger watched her partner enter the interview room and sit down across from Jones.

Loshak inhaled deeply. When he spoke, his voice sounded deep, almost sleepy.

"Billy Ray Jones."

The agent sniffed a breath like he might say something else. Then he stared serenely across the table at Jones, letting the silence stretch out. Even Darger felt a twinge of awkward discomfort several rooms away.

Jones shifted in his seat and wiped at his nose.

"Uh… was that, like… a question?"

Loshak's eyebrows shifted infinitesimally. He didn't blink.

"No, not a question," Loshak said. "Just stating your name for the record. That's all."

"Oh. Right. OK."

Behind the tinted lenses of his glasses, Jones's eyes twitched back and forth like a ventriloquist dummy's. He clenched one hand over and over, fingers flexing in an odd circular motion as though he were balling up a used Kleenex.

Loshak laced his own fingers together on top of the table. Again, he let the pause stretch into something unnerving before he spoke.

"How old are you, Billy? Can I call you that? Billy?"

"Um… sure." Billy lifted a finger to scratch his cheek, and Darger noticed that his fingernails were gnawed down to stubs. "I'm twenty-seven."

Loshak made a show of writing this down. Hand swooping over the yellow legal pad.

"Twenty-seven years young. Excellent. And what do you do for a living?"

"I'm a trucker."

"Ahh, life on the open road." Loshak smiled faintly. "How long you been doing that?"

"A few years."

"You probably meet some interesting folk on the job. See some interesting places."

"I guess." He licked his lips. "Uh… how long is this going to take?"

Loshak pursed his lips and studied the ceiling. He clicked his pen a couple times and snugged it into his breast pocket.

"Hard to say. Sometimes these interviews are quick. In and out. Sometimes they drag on a bit. Kinda depends on your answers. Why, you got somewhere to be?"

"I'm not feeling too great, to be honest. Flu or something, maybe."

"I see. You need a bucket to puke in?"

"What? No. I just… can you just ask me what you're gonna ask me?"

Loshak opened the manila folder and flipped through a few of the pages. Perusing as if looking for something specific.

"Where was it… doo-doo-doo… ahh… here we go." Loshak inhaled again and nodded. "OK then."

He closed the folder and pulled the pen from his pocket.

Clicked it open.

Jones was practically squirming in his chair now. Darger hoped if he did barf, it wasn't on Loshak.

"I see here you've got a few arrests on your record. Possession. Petty larceny. Possession again…"

Instead of asking Jones a question, Loshak just gazed at him. Slow-blinked once.

The guy swallowed, his Adam's apple bouncing up and down like a ping pong ball trapped in his throat.

"I was a kid, you know. Hanging around with the wrong people."

"I see. And what about now?"

Jones reached up and scratched his head.

"I… I'm not sure I understand the question."

"What kind of people do you hang out with now?"

Jones swallowed again, this time with an audible *gulp* sound.

"The… right ones? I think."

"Good. I'm glad to hear that." Loshak fixed his eyes on him. "Tell me about your work."

The change in subject seemed to rattle Jones. He chewed at his lip.

"What about it?"

"What kind of route you drive, what company you work for… that kind of thing."

"Oh. Well, I work for Bantam Transport out of Valdosta. I just drove up to Philly, and now I'm on my way back."

"Is that a regular route for you? Georgia to Philadelphia?"

The guy's bony shoulders twitched. Shaky.

"Yeah. I guess. Pretty regular. Sometimes I go up to Connecticut." Jones blinked and shook his head as if to clear his thoughts. "I thought this was about those murders last night."

Loshak glanced up from his notepad.

"Pardon?"

"It's just… I don't get what my route has to do with anything."

"Maybe nothing," Loshak said. "What can you tell us about last night? You see anything?"

"Me? No. I mean, I heard about it, but only secondhand. Sounded pretty fucked... err... messed up, from what the other guys were saying."

"And what time did you get to the travel center here in town? Big Jon's."

"I guess it would have been about seven? In the... uh... at night."

This matched up with the time stamp they had of Jones's truck on the security footage. But what Darger really wanted to know was where he had been *before* he arrived at the truck stop.

"And did you drive straight from Philadelphia to Big Jon's Travel Center? No other stops?"

"Yeah. Wait—" Jones rubbed at his nose. "Actually, no. I, uh, stopped at the Pilot outside of Richmond for an oil change."

"And what time did you leave there, would you say?"

"Well, if I got to Big Jon's at seven, I guess it would have been like 5:30?"

Darger felt something in her stomach clench. That was after Dawn Sawiki and Jane Doe had checked into the Cozy Motor Lodge.

Shit.

If Jones had truly been in Richmond until 5:30 P.M., he couldn't be their guy.

Loshak's gaze flicked over to the camera, which had the effect of feeling like he was looking into her eyes. He slow-blinked again.

"He wants us to check Jones's alibi," Darger said, automatically intuiting the nonverbal cue.

"On it," Bledsoe said, phone already out in her hand. "I'll call the service center right now."

The detective stepped into the hallway to make the call, and Darger sent Loshak a text.

Checking his alibi now.

In the next room, she watched Loshak surreptitiously read the text with only a momentary pause in the interview.

"Why not wait until you got to the travel center here for the oil change?" Loshak asked. "They have a truck service center there, don't they?"

"My company has a deal with Pilot," Jones explained. "We get a discount. So I only ever use their service centers."

"Was there a reason you didn't just stay in Richmond for the night?"

"I had another hour or so of driving time left. Besides, I always gotta stop at Big Jon's for a bomb rack of ribs. Good as hell."

Loshak squinted. Darger realized that he looked genuinely interested to hear this.

"You know, you're the second guy to mention the ribs. Better make it a point to try those while I'm in town." He scribbled something on his notepad again. "So you had dinner at the restaurant last night. Went for the ribs. What else did you do?"

"Uh… mostly I slept."

"How do you kill time when you're off duty?"

Jones seemed to have relaxed a bit when Loshak's questions shifted to those specifically related to the travel center, which was perplexing. But now he was suddenly fidgeting again.

"I mean, all the usual stuff. Sleep. Eat. Watch a little TV."

"But surely you must get out for a little recreation now and then. Probably gets kinda lonely otherwise."

Jones shrugged and began picking at his fingernails.

"You ever hire any female companionship?" Loshak asked.

Jones shook his head.

"No shame in it," Loshak said. "A man has needs after all. It's a normal biological function, they say."

Jones kept his eyes down on the table and still now. No more ventriloquist dummy shifting.

"I don't… I don't do that," he muttered.

Bledsoe came back in then, drawing Darger's attention from the screen. The hard line of the woman's mouth didn't get her hopes up.

"Just talked with the manager of the service center outside of Richmond. He can confirm that Jones came in at approximately quarter to five for an oil change and didn't leave until a little after 5:30."

Glenn frowned, and some wordless sound hissed out of him.

"So he's not our guy," he said, jabbing a finger at the monitor. "Wonder what the hell he's so damn nervous about then."

"Way I figure, it doesn't matter much. We're wasting time here. We might as well cut him loose," Bledsoe said.

"Yeah, I'll let Loshak know," Darger said, finding a piece of paper and scribbling down what they'd learned in a rushed scrawl.

She left the observation room and knocked on the interview room door. She could hear the voices go quiet beyond the steel barrier. Loshak answered a second later, and she handed him the paper.

His eyes zigzagged across the page.

"Huh," he muttered.

"Yeah," Darger agreed.

Over Loshak's shoulder, Darger saw Jones remove the tinted glasses and rub at his eyes with a shaky hand. He was breathing funny.

"OK then," Loshak said, turning back to face Jones. "We're gonna let you go now, Billy, but we do appreciate you coming down here."

Jones sat rigid and unmoving in the chair, as if he hadn't heard a word Loshak had said.

"Billy?"

The guy's hand fell away from his face. Arm gone limp all at once.

His eyes rolled back in his head then. Flickering whites exposed. Empty.

His body shook. Violent tremors rattling him in his seat.

The metal chair legs shrieked in pulses over the tile floor. Scooted him back. Shrill squawks like a chorus of injured seagulls.

"Oh shit," Darger said.

She lurched for him. Skirted around the table. She could feel Loshak alongside her.

Jones pitched forward. Slammed his head into the table like his forehead was the face of a hammer and shattered the blue sunglasses lying there.

Then he keeled sideways and crumpled to the floor.

CHAPTER 25

Two paramedics — a man and a woman — huddled over Billy Ray Jones, working with speed. The trucker's seizing had stopped for now, and they were attempting to get Jones to speak.

"Sir, can you tell me what happened?" the female paramedic asked as she slid a blood pressure cuff around his bicep.

Jones groaned, head lolling to one side. His stick figure frame looked all the smaller lying on the floor half under the table.

The male paramedic lifted one of Jones's eyelids and shined a pen light there. The trucker's pupil looked like a swollen black moon. It was so huge Darger couldn't even tell what color eyes he had.

"Pupils are dilated."

"Systolic BP is 190," the woman said. "He's also majorly hyperthermic."

"Heart rate is 130 beats per minute." The male paramedic glanced up. "You said he drives a truck for a living?"

"That's right. What's wrong with him?"

"My guess? Some kind of overdose. Probably cocaine or meth. We better roll."

They hoisted him onto the gurney and unfolded the legs of the thing.

Jones mumbled something then. The female paramedic put a hand on his chest and leaned in, speaking loudly and clearly.

"Sir, can you tell me if you've taken any drugs recently?"

"Something's wrong." Jones moaned and clutched his stomach, as if trying to claw his own gut open. "Gotta get it out of me."

The paramedics exchanged a look as they bustled him into the hallway. It was the man who spoke.

"You thinking what I'm thinking?"

The female paramedic nodded and said, "Body packing."

"Yep. We need to get him to the ER for a CT scan, stat."

Darger, Loshak, and the detectives followed the gurney to the end of the hall, and then the EMTs hustled out the glass doors fronting the building. The ambulance waited there, red lights spinning up top, the back hanging open like a white mouth.

"Body packing?" Glenn repeated.

"He's a mule," Loshak said. "And whatever he's transporting the drugs in — probably a balloon — must have torn. Boom. Belly full of drugs." He shook his head. "It explains why he was so jittery. But also, he seemed confused. I really think he believed he was sick. Makes me think he's not a user. Just a smuggler."

Glenn let out a breath.

"The shit people will do for money."

The gurney clattered and squeaked as the paramedics rolled Billy Ray Jones into the vehicle.

"I bet he has a contact somewhere on his route," Loshak went on. "The contact hands off the drugs. Our man Billy swallows them and drives on his merry way. Pretty foolproof drug mule operation… unless one of the packets bursts, and then it's like an instant overdose. That's how ODB died."

Darger stared at him.

"ODB?"

"Ol' Dirty Bastard. The rapper," Loshak said, sounding

incredulous. "Jesus, Darger, do you know nothing of the Wu-Tang Clan?"

Darger did, but she was always baffled when Loshak was aware of such things.

"You know, even though we seem to have alibied him out, it's a lucky thing we pulled him in," Bledsoe said. "If he'd been alone in his truck when one of those balloons burst? Probably would have been lights out for the kid."

"You should remind him of that when he's staring down a drug trafficking charge that carries a minimum 15-year sentence, Bledsoe," Glenn said, patting his partner's shoulder. "I'm sure he'll drop to his knees to thank you."

CHAPTER 26

Darger stood staring at the murder wall in somewhat of a stupor, not able to fully concentrate. With the adrenaline from Billy Ray Jones's sudden medical emergency having worn off, the fact that she hadn't slept was starting to take its toll.

And evidently, she wasn't the only one.

A few minutes later, Detective Glenn sauntered into the room and spotted Bledsoe in the corner, dozing over an open case file. An impish smile spread over the detective's face. He snatched up a small metal wastebasket from beside one of the desks and tiptoed over to his partner.

"Paging Detective Bledsoe," he said, standing directly behind her and clanging his knuckles against the side of the can.

The sound was deafening and not wholly unlike the crash of a gong.

Bledsoe jerked awake, flailing so violently she nearly tipped out of her chair. When she realized what was happening, she whirled around and glared at Glenn.

"Dickhead! What the hell's wrong with you?"

Glenn was doubled over laughing, so it was a moment before he could answer.

"You're just lucky I didn't stick your hand in a glass of warm water," he said when he'd finally composed himself.

Bledsoe shook her head, still not amused.

"But honestly, Bledsoe, you should go home for a while. Get some real sleep. In a bed." Glenn's gaze circled the room. "You too, Agents. I know for a fact that you've been awake for over

24 hours."

Loshak shrugged.

"I suppose we have to take a break at some point. What do you say?"

Darger opened her mouth to speak, but a yawn overtook her.

"Can't argue with that," Loshak said.

☾

It was a short drive to the motel, and still Darger managed to fall asleep on the ride. Loshak nudged her awake, and she blinked groggily at their surroundings.

The motel was a long L-shaped building, not dissimilar from the Cozy Motor Lodge architecturally, though the parking lot here was much cleaner.

After checking in, they wheeled their luggage into their separate rooms.

Darger left her bag by the door and made a beeline for the bed, ripping away the top bedspread before bellyflopping onto the mattress.

The springs creaked loudly beneath her, and the mattress was firmer than she preferred, but it was such a relief to lie down that she barely cared.

Can't fall asleep yet, she told herself. Better take a shower first. Change out of these clothes, too.

And she'd do it. In a minute.

☾

Darger staggered into the motel bathroom, mouth so dry that her tongue stuck to the roof of her mouth like it was made of velcro. She filled a glass, marveling at the fact that this dumpy little place had actual glasses instead of the shrink-wrapped disposable plastic cups most places seemed to favor these days.

She downed the water and filled the glass again.

There came a rustling noise from somewhere behind her. Barely audible over the sound of the rushing tap, and yet she heard it all the same.

She lifted her eyes. Began to turn around.

And then the shower curtain whipped aside, and an ink black silhouette loomed over her.

She opened her mouth to scream. Felt something brush over her nose. Before she could utter a single syllable, the ligature drew taut around her neck.

Constricting.

Squeezing.

She thought of Dr. Moody's autopsy report.

Asphyxiating.

She flailed. Clawed at her throat. Fingernails plucking at the cord.

And then she shook herself awake.

☾

Darger awoke with her face mashed into the pillow. She rolled onto her side and felt her neck. No ligature. Just a strand of her hair that must have gotten wrapped around while she slept.

As the nightmare-induced panic began to subside, she became aware of an obnoxious trilling sound. Seconds ticked by before she was conscious enough to figure out what it was. Her phone was ringing.

She reached for it, still disoriented and trying to piece together where she was and what was happening.

In a motel room. Fully dressed. Shoes on. Light outside, but not morning.

When she saw the name on her screen — Detective Glenn — it all came back to her.

North Carolina. Three women stabbed and strangled.

Guess that explains the dream, then.

Her eyes went to the clock in the corner of the screen, and she did some quick mental math. She'd gotten a few hours of sleep, at least.

She answered the call and heard the unmistakable glint of eagerness in Glenn's voice

"Guess whose truck was just spotted by highway patrol at a Motel 6 in Rocky Mount?"

Darger smeared a trickle of drool from the corner of her mouth.

"Who?"

"Ed McMurphy."

"That's great," she said. "He's coming in for an interview, then?"

Glenn let out something like a snort.

"Not if he can help it. Says he's on the tail end of his mandatory rest period and has to be back on the road in a few hours, and that if we drag him back here, we're going to make him run late and cost him a job. Claims that we're infringing on his right to make a living. Sounds like bullshit to me, but he's pretty belligerent according to the trooper I talked to. But check this out… the troopers noticed he's got a light out on his rig. So I'm thinking we wait, have them make a stop once he's on the road, and bring him in then."

Darger yawned.

"Have you talked to Loshak yet?"

"No."

"OK, hold on."

Darger rolled off the bed and padded to the door. Her feet scuffed over the sidewalk as she made her way to the next room over. She paused in front of the door. Knocked.

It was a full minute before Loshak answered the door, bleary-eyed and hair smushed in different directions.

"Got Glenn on the phone," she explained. "They found another one of our guys, but he's being… difficult."

She let Glenn lay out the scenario for him on speakerphone.

Loshak inhaled deeply and stretched his eyes wide, as if trying to will himself to wake up more.

"I don't know about this game with the broken taillight," he said, cupping his chin in his hand. "He sounds pretty hostile as it is. I worry if we start playing that way, he'll refuse to talk to us at all."

Darger nodded along with this. She'd thought as much herself.

"Well, we can't just let him walk," Glenn said.

"No. No, but we can concede a little." Loshak blinked and looked up at the sky. "You said he's got another few hours left on his mandatory rest period?"

"That's right."

"Which means legally he can't drive before then," Loshak said, mostly to himself. "And how far away is he?"

"About 45 minutes. Maybe less if you pushed it."

Loshak nodded, making some internal decision.

"Darger and I will drive down there, then. See if we can't convince him to give us a few minutes of his time. How does that sound?"

"Hell, if you want to go the extra mile, have at it," Glenn said. "But it sounded to me like he wasn't gonna talk of his own volition, and that seems awfully shady to me, especially since everyone else has been willing to cooperate so far."

Loshak shrugged.

"Could be just like he says. He's worried he'll lose his job if he doesn't make this delivery on time. Or it could be that he's hiding something else and wants to avoid scrutiny. Or he could be guilty as hell and worries he'll slip up if he agrees to an interview. We'll know more once we go down there and talk to him face-to-face."

"Best of luck with it," Glenn said. "From what the troopers had to say, I think you'll need it."

CHAPTER 27

When they arrived at the Motel 6 in Rocky Mount, the first thing Darger noticed was a North Carolina Highway Patrol Charger parked a few inches from the rear bumper of a semi-truck. Two troopers climbed out to greet them.

"Is that McMurphy's truck you're parked behind?" Loshak asked.

"Yes sir," the officer said. "Detective Glenn called to let us know that you'd be driving down. We just wanted to make sure he couldn't try to take off before then."

"Is he inside or—"

Before Loshak could finish the sentence, Darger heard a door slam and the crunch of boots on gravel. A man as wide as a side of beef appeared then, stalking out of one of the rooms and over to them. His faded Harley Davidson t-shirt just barely clung to the beefy torso. The sleeves had been scissored away long ago.

At first, Darger could only really see his bulk, his splayed arms, the big shoulders arched up aggressively. As he got closer, more details filled in.

Black hair. Deeply tan skin. An angry look folded his dark brow into a pile of fine wrinkles, and a salt and pepper horseshoe mustache framed his mouth, the gray hairs gleaming bright against the dark bronze tone of his skin. The 'stache made Darger think of Hulk Hogan.

"You the assholes fuckin' with my route?" he growled.

Loshak put out a hand.

"Mr. McMurphy, my name is Agent Loshak, and—"

McMurphy glared down at Loshak's hand and spit on the ground. His barrel chest heaved in a breath and let it out.

"I don't give a shit who ya are. Parkin' me in like that is harassment, and I'm gonna report the whole lot of you."

"Mr. McMurphy, we only want to ask you a few routine questions. We understand you're concerned about losing time on your delivery. That's fair. So we took it upon ourselves to drive over here to meet you. If you'll humor us, we can talk here and have you on your way. If there is any disruption to your delivery, I will personally call your supervisor to let them know you were aiding a federal investigation."

The muscles in McMurphy's neck bunched as he clenched his teeth.

"Half an hour?"

"Or less," Loshak repeated.

"Fine. Whatever. Let's get this over with."

They followed him into the motel room. The shades were drawn, and it took Darger's eyes a moment to adjust to the gloomy lighting. Following a strange man into a dark room had her itching to put her hand on her gun, but she resisted the urge.

She blinked a few times, and the details of the space seemed to fade into view. A double bed bracketed on each side by a dated-looking nightstand. A dresser with a small coffee machine on top. A flimsy-looking particle board table littered with beer cans.

The sour, yeasty odor of old beer hit her nostrils then. Pale yellow Coors Banquet cans posed in every possible manner across the room — upside down, sideways, half-crushed into the carpet.

Darger vaguely remembered drinking a tall boy of Coors at a concert once. The taste reminded her of cold, liquid Wonder

Bread in a can. She didn't hate it.

There were only two chairs at the table, so Darger borrowed the one shoved under the desk to make room for all three of them. She pulled out her phone and held it in the air.

"Is it alright if I record this?"

"Knock your socks off," McMurphy said, his tone bitter.

She opened her voice recording app and turned it on.

As they settled into their seats, Darger took the opportunity to study Ed McMurphy.

He had hair as black as a crow's wing and a muscular build that was beginning to stray toward chubby. She knew from his file that he was 37 years old, but he looked older, mostly due to the dark facial hair going white toward the chin and the sun-wrinkled skin around his eyes. The crisscrossing creases reminded Darger of the scales of an iguana. Something about all of him looked sun-charred to her.

There was a perpetually dour look on his face, like he'd only just taken a swig from one of the empty cans and gotten a mouthful of warm, stale beer. She tried to determine if there was any malignance to his expression or if he was just a grim kind of person, but she couldn't decide.

He blinked and looked from Darger to Loshak.

"You said half an hour. Far as I'm concerned, the clock started a while ago."

Darger inclined her head toward the beer cans.

"Looks like you had a little party last night."

"Not unless you count me sittin' here gettin' shitfaced by myself a 'party.'"

"You were by yourself?"

"Just said I was."

"Why not just drink in your truck?"

"'Cause that's a good way to get a DUI. Can't trust the pigs to not write you up even if you ain't on the road."

"Do you get hotel rooms often when you're driving?"

"Depends."

"On what?"

"On where I'm at in the route. On what I fuckin' feel like." He sat back and crossed his arms. "Did you really come all the way over here to give me the third degree on drinkin' a twelve pack of beer on my own fuckin' time?"

Darger studied the closed body language and wondered if there was a way to get him to open up. She doubted it. He wasn't going to make this easy.

"Do you always drink alone?"

He shrugged and pulled the cigarette from his ear, tucking it into the corner of his mouth.

"Not always."

McMurphy produced a lighter from his pocket.

"Uh," Loshak gestured at a sign on the door of the room. "This is a non-smoking room."

McMurphy stared at Loshak while he lit the cigarette. His eyes were dead. Blank.

"I'm sitting here, doin' y'all a favor." He hit the smoke, held it in his lungs for a beat, and then released a cloud of smog from his nostrils. "If you want me to get up and leave, it's no sweat off my sack."

Darger and Loshak exchanged a glance. Darger knew Loshak didn't actually care about the smoking. He was setting McMurphy up. Giving him an opportunity to believe he was running the show. So she played along. Gave an exaggerated shrug that said, *What are you gonna do?*

Loshak sighed and nodded once, as if this was some major concession he was making. He could pull off a good "scolded boy" facial expression when he wanted to.

The corners of McMurphy's lips turned ever-so-slightly upward. It was the first time Darger had seen him smile, though his eyes remained just as dead as before. It wasn't what she'd call a pleasant expression.

"Now, does one of you want to hand me something to ash in or should I just do it on the floor?"

Loshak's eyes searched the room and landed on one of the little Styrofoam cups near the coffee machine. The wrapper crinkled as Loshak removed it. He set the empty cup down in front of McMurphy and took his seat again.

Darger was beginning to see that Loshak had called this one from the start. If they'd tried to haul McMurphy in on something petty like a broken taillight, he probably would have refused to talk to them at all. He enjoyed feeling in control. Asserting his dominance in these silly little struggles over smoking and ashtrays.

So they'd given him what he wanted, and now they'd see if he took the bait. A domineering personality was more likely to brag if he thought he was running the show. And they'd give him every opportunity to do just that.

"So you don't *always* drink alone," Darger said.

McMurphy took a long drag.

"That's what I fuckin' said."

"You ever pay for company when you're drinking?"

He leaned back and let out a snort, as if the question wasn't worth his time. His eyes reminded her of a crocodile's.

Darger chewed her lip for just a second and caught herself. It was clear to her that the casual banter that had worked on Trotter and even Billy Ray Jones wasn't going to fly here. If they wanted answers, they were going to have to come out and ask directly.

"Did you hear about the three women who were murdered

last night up in Roanoke Rapids?"

McMurphy's face remained as stony as ever. Not even the faintest flicker of emotion.

"Don't know how I couldn't. It was all over the radio. You'da thought the president himself was in town the way everyone was all atwitter about it."

"And what do you think about it?"

"What do I think? Good fuckin' riddance is what I think."

Darger raised an eyebrow.

"That's awfully harsh."

"Yeah well, trust me… the world ain't exactly worse off with three less lot lizards in it. In fact, I'd say it could only be an improvement." With the dwindling cigarette still clamped between his fingers, he waved a lazy circle in the air. "I ain't saying I killed those girls, 'cause I didn't, but I didn't shed no tears when they passed either. Shit. It ain't like we're talking about a bunch of Mother Teresas, are we? These ain't the girls anyone is taking to prom, OK? They steal. They deal. They spread disease from crotch to crotch. A bunch of my buddies have been ripped off by 'em. And some of these truck stops are straight-up cesspools thanks to these whores. Like in New Jersey? Christ almighty. You can't swing a dead cat at a New Jersey truck stop without hitting a thieving whore."

He stubbed out the cigarette, the butt crushing into Styrofoam with a faint hissing noise. Then he lit another.

"And what about you?" Darger asked.

McMurphy's lip curled.

"What about me?"

"Well, we looked into your background," she said, flipping open the file she'd brought along. "You're no Mother Teresa yourself, it appears. Says here you plead guilty in 2015 for punching a woman in the face after she refused to perform oral sex."

The somewhat smug expression on McMurphy's face shriveled into something grim again. Darger held her breath, knowing that this might be the end of the interview.

The big trucker tipped back his head. A big sigh swelled up his chest and slowly deflated it.

The quiet in the room seemed to gain weight. Tension. Stretching out. Awkward.

McMurphy stared up at the top of the window frame for almost a minute before he began to talk. His voice came out quieter than before.

"I got this… darkness inside. I'm not sure where it comes from. Maybe it's being on the road. Alone in the truck for weeks on end. Driving shit from place to place. Always hurtling forward. The loneliness eats at you in ways you can't imagine."

He sucked on his cigarette. Let the smoke roll out slowly.

"And I get to thinking about women. About sex. And it becomes like this pulse in my head. It won't turn off. Just a stream of filth in my skull. No release. No satisfaction. I mean, I have release. It's not hard to find some drunk bimbo in any random bar. But somehow it doesn't make the impulses go away. It never does."

Darger felt a chill run up her spine as he spoke but fought to keep her face and body language neutral.

"These impulses. They just thump out of my subconscious. Stuck in my head like lightning bugs in a jar. Trapped with no way out. And it never ends. No relief, you know? I never get a fucking break."

He tilted his head. Seemed to come back to the present.

"When I done what I done…" He pointed two fingers and his cigarette at the file open in front of Darger. "The darkness got the best of me. But I been doing better, I think. Trying to."

Everyone held quiet for a few more seconds.

"Bottom line: I ain't killed any whores, and I don't plan to. You got any other questions?"

Darger swallowed, still feeling unsettled.

"And the assault and battery charge in 2019? When you beat a man unconscious with a wrench?"

This time McMurphy kept his eyes on hers. He smiled. Shrugged.

"Dude got what was coming to him. That's all I can say about that. Besides, those charges were dropped."

"Right," Loshak said. "Because the victim disappeared."

McMurphy scratched at the stubble on his chin.

"I wouldn't know anything about that. All I know is I hope I never see him again." He took a final drag from his cigarette and smashed it into the makeshift ashtray. "Anyway, by my count, your time's up. I guess we're done here."

CHAPTER 28

Back at the station, Darger played the recording of the interview for the rest of the task force. When McMurphy began waxing poetic about his so-called "dark impulses," several of the detectives perked up, their eyes suddenly alight with the possibility that McMurphy could be their man.

"Lord have mercy," Detective Glenn said when the recording ended. "That's one ice cold motherfucker."

"I got goosebumps just listening to the replay," Bledsoe said, stirring a cup of coffee with a wooden stick. "Can't imagine what it was like to actually be in the room with him."

"I can't lie. I was glad I had my sidearm within reach," Darger said.

Glenn shoved his hands in his pockets.

"You think it's him? I mean, it's gotta be, right?"

Darger couldn't stop her face from scrunching into something like a grimace.

"I wouldn't say that."

"Come on. All that shit about the darkness getting the best of him? He practically confessed right there."

"Look, he's a suspect for a reason, and he's a creep no doubt. Nasty. Hostile. Violent. All of the above. He fits the profile. He may have even killed before, given this miraculously missing witness. But did he do these murders?" Darger waved her hand at the murder wall. "I don't know. We've got more names on the list, right? We just don't know yet."

Apparently dissatisfied with her answer, Glenn turned to Loshak. He dabbed his palm into the bristles of his flattop as he spoke.

"What do you say, Agent Loshak?"

Loshak's eyebrows twitched before he answered.

"Is he our killer? I can't say that for certain. Not without real evidence. But do I think it *could* be him?" He hesitated, letting his head bob from side to side. "I do. Right now, I do."

Detective Mustafa, their liaison from Miami PD, crossed her arms.

"I still like Trotter. Anyone that smarmy is up to something."

Bledsoe glanced at her watch.

"What time was McMurphy supposed to get back on the road?"

Loshak's eyes went to the clock.

"Within the next hour or so."

Bledsoe tapped her lip. Stood a little straighter.

"I think I'm going to volunteer for the tail on him."

"You sure about that?" Glenn asked. "You barely squeezed a single cat nap into the last 24 hours."

Bledsoe shrugged.

"That's the job, ain't it?"

"We brought in those extra bodies from the FBI specifically for tailing our suspects."

"I know that," Bledsoe said, already reaching for her bag. "And no offense to your people, Agents, but I got a feeling about this guy, and I'd rather someone who's personally invested in the case be on McMurphy."

Glenn looked at his partner like she was crazy but only shook his head.

"Whatever you say. But you better clear it with the chief. No way am I covering for your ass."

CHAPTER 29

Darger slid into the booth opposite Loshak, the seat seeming to exhale as the padding squished beneath her. While they waited around for another of their suspects to be pulled in for an interview, they decided to grab an early dinner. On a case like this, there was no telling when they'd have another chance to actually sit down for a real meal.

Her partner had insisted they go back to the truck stop to eat, naturally, his plea basically boiling down to one word: ribs.

Their waitress flitted over to their table with menus, then away and back again with the iced teas they'd ordered. Darger figured you had to be quick in a place like this. Some of the truckers were on a prolonged rest period, but others would be keen to get their meal and get back on the road as fast as possible.

She glanced across the table and found Loshak with a pair of reading glasses perched on the very tip of his nose, his expression quite serious as she studied the laminated menu.

"Why are you even looking at that when you already know you're getting the ribs?"

His gaze stayed on the menu, his focus unbroken.

"Sides, Darger. The BBQ platter comes with two sides, which means I have to make an impossible choice. Obviously I have to get the collards, but how do I choose between the creamed corn, the potato salad, and the mac and cheese?"

"A dilemma for the ages," Darger said.

The menu remained clutched in Loshak's hands even after their waitress returned to take their order, apparently still undecided on the debate. Darger ordered first.

"I'll have the fried chicken plate with mashed potatoes."

"Alrighty," the waitress said, scribbling on a pad. "And for you?"

Loshak winced, and his eyes lingered on the menu even as he passed it to the waitress, his mind clearly not made up.

"The baby back rib platter with collards aaaand—"

"Sorry, hon. Ribs are sold out. We got brisket and chicken leg quarters still."

Loshak's shoulders drooped, and he looked so dejected Darger had to stifle a chuckle.

"Well, shoot." He blinked twice. "Gimme the biscuits and gravy then."

"Okie doke. And it looks like you're ready for a refill," she said, pointing at Loshak's empty iced tea glass.

The moment the fresh tea arrived, Loshak snatched it up and drank. He slurped at the straw, his cheeks quirking in pulses.

"Thirsty?" Darger asked in a deadpan.

He detached from the straw like a sucker fish releasing from the side of an aquarium wall, and the space between his eyebrows crinkled.

"As a matter of fact, I am. I think it's that dehumidifier they got running in that basement 24/7. Dries me the hell out." He took another slug of tea. "Anything else you wanna bust my balls over?"

Darger had already tuned him out, though. Her eyes had strayed to the other end of the restaurant where a familiar face clad in a brown janitor's jumpsuit caught her eye.

Dwayne Kunkle pushed through the swinging door that led from the kitchen to the main floor. He wheeled a yellow bucket with a mop handle protruding out of it. His face held blank —

the emotionless, glazed-over look of a man doing manual labor — but for just a second, Darger could see the pale mask his features had morphed into the night they'd talked to him. The thin sheen of sweat beading over his forehead, something waxy in his pallor. He'd been awfully shaken up by the memory of finding the body, and his fear had been oddly contagious.

He turned to her then, and instead of that waxen look, his dead eyes brightened all at once, the bottom half of his face splitting into a broad grin. He waved, and Darger returned the greeting with a nod.

Kunkle left the mop bucket and hustled over to their table.

"Why hello there, Agents."

"Mr. Kunkle," Darger said.

"I'm glad I spotted you folks. Now that the shock's worn off, I realized that in my addled state the other night, I failed to say thank you."

"Thank you?"

"Well, sure. I know a thing or two about being the guy behind the scenes, doing a thankless job that people take for granted. Obviously not on the scale of what you do, but..." He pointed at his eyes and then at Darger. "I just want you to know that I see you. I appreciate you."

"Thank you. That's very kind."

His smile widened.

"Don't even mention it. I can tell you folks are taking this whole case real seriously, and I'm not sure most would do the same for a couple of lot lizards. Anyway, I better get back to it. Enjoy your meal."

As Kunkle made his way back to his abandoned mop and bucket, Loshak finished another iced tea, the straw making that hollow stuttering sound as it sucked the last few drops. There was a joke about "bladder enlargement surgery" on the tip of

Darger's tongue, but then she saw that the waitress was heading their way with a big tray of food balanced on one forearm.

Kunkle touched her arm as she passed, and the woman paused. He leaned in and said something to her, gesturing at where Darger and Loshak sat. She nodded and proceeded to the table.

She placed a plate of biscuits and gravy in front of Loshak, who rubbed his hands together in excitement as he gazed upon the beige-on-beige platter. Then the waitress plopped a second plate before Darger. Steam coiled up off the fried chicken and touched the soft skin beneath her chin. It smelled great.

"Dwayne wanted me to tell you that your food's on him," the waitress said.

"Oh," Darger said, glancing over to where she'd last seen the man, but he was nowhere in sight. "Well that was very generous of him."

"He's a charmer, alright," the waitress said, and then her eyes bugged a little as she did a double take at Loshak's empty glass. "Dang, you ready for another iced tea already?"

He grinned, something in the smile reminding Darger of a precocious kid — a freshly crowned spelling bee champ, maybe.

"Oh yeah. Keep 'em coming."

They had just taken a bite each when Loshak's phone chirped on the table. Darger could read the name on the caller ID — Detective Glenn. They exchanged a quick look, and then he scooped up the iPhone and answered through a mouthful of sausage gravy.

"Yeah?"

Darger could just hear Glenn's voice warbling against Loshak's ear, though she couldn't make out any words — a tiny version of Charlie Brown's teacher. When his eyebrows shot up, her fork froze just shy of her plate.

"OK," he said. "We're on our way."

Darger gaped at him.

"I guess we can forget our peaceful dinner," he said, grimacing at his plate. "They've got the next suspect waiting at a weigh station about an hour north of here. Junior Riggins. We're supposed to head there for the interrogation."

Darger shrugged and took a big bite of chicken.

"Not the first time we've had to eat and run," she said.

CHAPTER 30

Vine-shrouded trees blurred past on the sides of the road. The freeway sliced a black line through the rural green, a strange artery pumping cars through a section of Carolina wilderness.

Traffic thickened as they crossed the state line into Virginia, heading toward the weigh station, and Darger felt a distinct sense of agitation from the other drivers on the road. Cars darted in and out of the lanes. Jerky. Aggressive. It was as if this section of highway had afflicted them all with a restless, territorial energy.

The fried chicken and mashed potatoes she'd pounded down still sat heavy in her gut. Her belly felt that stretched-out ache like it was an overfilled balloon.

Loshak squirmed in the driver's seat. Bouncing from one butt cheek to the other, hands twitching on the wheel.

Darger gave him a look.

"You look like a coked-up Uber driver," she said.

"Too many iced teas," he said. "Yeah. I know. You told me so. Go ahead and laugh it up."

Darger's phone blipped before she could muster a chuckle. Another text from Glenn. She hissed when she read it.

"Holy shit."

"What?" Loshak said. His squirming seemed to intensify, hands popping like kernels of popcorn against the wheel.

"They just searched his truck. Junior Riggins."

Loshak's brow crinkled.

"He consented to a search?"

"I guess so. Anyway, they found several bloody rags at the

bottom of a small trash bin in the cabin area."

Loshak's hands stopped twitching on the wheel. He tilted his head to the side.

"Bloody rags. Jesus. That, uh, seems significant."

"Um. Yeah. That's an understatement."

"Sorry. It's hard to think. I think my bladder is about to rupture."

Darger turned her gaze out the passenger window, looking for the next mile marker. They had to be close to the weigh station where Riggins was being held.

Her eyes flitted along the side of the road. A green sign there said:

Petersburg

6 MILES

Yes. That was right. They had to be close now. Very close.

And then she saw it.

The exit ramp veered off to the right, and the small brick and glass enclosure of the weigh station took shape at the end of the curving lane. It almost looked like a gazebo, at least from a distance. Another green sign pointed a white arrow at the building, the text above reading in all caps, WEIGH STATION.

They hurtled toward it.

CHAPTER 31

Large glass panels took up the bulk of the walls on two sides of the weigh station office that served as a makeshift interview room — one facing the scales where a semi sat even now, and the other facing the freeway in the distance. The thrum of the traffic permeated the background of the scene. A constantly shifting hum.

Junior Riggins, Jr., sat on the other side of a cluttered desk from Darger and Loshak. The trucker's frame completely filled the IKEA office chair, showing the mesh backrest no mercy. The broad, Sequoia-esque torso came with the appropriate oak and maple trunks for arms and legs, something stocky and lumberjack about the whole set. His round face beamed above all that thickness. Deeply tan. A playful twinkle in the pale eyes.

His dark hair was cropped short, just longer than a five-o'-clock shadow, and it formed a severe line that boxed in the top of his forehead. Darger always thought a short forehead seemed Neanderthal-ish, but on Riggins it somehow made sense.

Though his build might have reminded Darger, however vaguely, of Ed McMurphy, Riggins's facial expression somehow waved the notion away just as quickly. A faint smile seemed permanently affixed to the red rims of his lips, and laugh wrinkles grew like bicycle tire spokes from the orbits of his eyes.

Darger tried to stop herself from drawing any conclusions before the interrogation began, but she couldn't hold back one immediate reaction. He looked, for lack of a better word, *jolly*.

Jolly, huh? So why is his truck loaded with bloody rags?

Loshak cleared his throat. A semi-truck horn blared out on the highway, sounding small in the interview room.

"Your full name, for the record."

"Junior Riggins, Jr."

Loshak squinted.

"So your father's name was…"

"Junior Riggins, Sr."

"Uh-huh," Loshak said. "And just out of curiosity, what was his father's name?"

"Marshall Riggins."

"I see. And do you have any idea why we wanted to talk to you today?" Loshak asked.

Riggins sighed.

"I have an idea. It's about Tara and them other two girls, ain't it?"

Darger immediately noticed the fact that he called the girl by her name, suggesting some level of familiarity.

"You knew Tara?"

"Sure did. Been with her several times."

Darger sat back, wondering at his use of the phrase "been with." Did that mean what she thought it did?

"Meaning you… paid for her services?"

Riggins nodded solemnly.

"That I did."

"I have to admit, I'm a bit surprised you're willing to admit that so freely."

He shrugged.

"Why hide it? I ain't ashamed. They're people just like everyone else."

Yes, they were people, Darger thought. But unlike "everyone else," these three women had been brutally murdered. She kept her mouth shut and refocused on what

Riggins was saying.

"These girls… they're lonely. Wounded. That's why I try to treat 'em gentle. You know, show a bit of kindness. Genuine human warmth. I'd never hurt 'em. Cruelty is of no interest to me. You can ask any of 'em. The girls will tell you. Next time you're back over at Big Jon's, ask Monica. She knows me."

"Did you know Dawn Sawiki, as well?" Loshak asked.

Riggins leaned in a little, his face transforming into a mask of confusion, and Darger tried to catalog the microexpressions. Faint puckering of the skin between his brows. A squinting of the eyes. Lips pooching ever so slightly.

Was it real or fake? Darger wasn't sure.

"Who?"

Loshak brought out an enlarged copy of Sawiki's driver's license.

"She's one of the other victims," Loshak explained, passing the sheet across the table.

With a sniff, Riggins brought the piece of paper right up to his face and studied it for several seconds.

"Nope. Can't say that I seen her before."

"How about this one," Loshak said, handing over a morgue photo of Jane Doe.

She'd been cleaned up as much as possible for the picture, the blood and makeup smears wiped away, but she was still quite obviously dead.

Riggins dropped the paper as if it had burned him and recoiled theatrically.

"Jesum Crow! You oughta warn a guy when you're gonna hand him a pitcher of a dead lady."

He rubbed at his forearms and let out a nervous chuckle.

"Woo! Got the goose pimples on my arms now." He squirmed in the chair. "But for what it's worth, I don't recognize her either."

Loshak gathered the two photographs and returned them to a manila folder.

"Mr. Riggins, you submitted to a voluntary search of your truck, is that correct?"

Riggins lifted his chin.

"Yes, sir. I got nothin' to hide."

"When the officers searched your vehicle, they found a small trash bin in the cabin area. At the bottom were several bloody rags."

"Oh, right. You know, I meant to throw that out, but I plain forgot."

Darger was stunned at his nonchalance.

"Where'd the blood come from, Mr. Riggins?" she asked.

His heavy brow lifted in puzzlement.

"I don't know."

"How can you not know?"

Riggins shrugged.

"Mr. Riggins, I have to be honest here," Loshak began. "I find your reaction to all of this a bit strange. If someone told me they found mysterious bloody rags in my vehicle, I think I'd be a little… let's say, *concerned* to know where the blood came from."

Riggins pointed a finger at him.

"I see where you're coming from, my man. And for most people, I totally get that this would be an awkward situation. But with my roadkill projects, it's not all that out of the ordinary."

"Your… roadkill projects?" Darger repeated.

There was a twinkle of pride in Riggins's eye.

"I'm teaching myself how to tan hides. You know, as a bushcraft skill. Only I don't get a lot of opportunities to go out and hunt, what with my work schedule, so I've been supplementing with roadkill. Only stuff in decent condition, obviously. Nothin' too rank."

Darger stared at him.

"You pick up dead animals from the side of the road and… skin them?"

"Sure do," he said, nodding. "And not to toot my own horn, but I'm gettin' pretty frickin' good at it."

She continued staring.

Riggins cocked an eyebrow.

"Not a crime, is it?"

"I suppose not," Darger was forced to admit, though she thought it was awfully strange as far as hobbies went.

"Here's the problem, Mr. Riggins," Loshak said. "The preliminary testing shows that this blood didn't come from any roadkill. It's human."

Again Darger was struck by the man's complete lack of a reaction to this revelation.

"I guess that makes sense," he said, his tone conversational.

"Does it?" Loshak asked.

"Well, sure. Last hide I did was at least a month back. I'm guessing the blood on those rags is fresher than that."

Darger and Loshak exchanged a look. This interview was not going how either one of them had thought it would.

"Help us out here, Mr. Riggins," Loshak said. "First you tell us you don't remember where the bloody rags came from. Then you say they're from picking up roadkill. And now you're admitting they're not?"

Riggins licked his lips. Blinked. Seemed like he was trying to work something out in his head. Then he tipped his head back and smiled.

"Oh, I see where the confusion is! See, I was just saying that

I wouldn't find the bloody rags all that alarming, what with my tanning experience. Blood and guts… that stuff don't bother me."

There was a rush of wind as Loshak sighed.

"OK, so let me ask again… where did the blood come from?"

"Well, I suppose it probably came from this cut on my hand."

Riggins held up his right hand, showing off a deep gash across his palm.

Darger immediately thought of the many lacerations on the three victims. Had Riggins cut himself in a struggle with one of them?

"What happened?"

"Don't remember."

Loshak's face went hard.

"I'm going to have to politely request that you cut the crap. We're going in circles here, and I'm tired of it. Now that's quite a wound you've got on your hand there. Do you really expect us to believe you don't remember how you got it?"

The big man puffed out his cheeks and sighed.

"You're right. And I'm sorry. It's just… well, I'm scared."

Darger felt a sudden tingling in her hands and feet. Jesus… was Riggins about to confess? Her eyes darted to her phone, making sure it was still recording. All good. Then she ran back through the preliminary interview procedure, making sure they'd properly informed him of his rights. Yes. They were gold.

Loshak nodded and affected a more sympathetic expression.

"I can understand being scared," he said, his voice going soft. "But there's no reason to fear us. We're all friends here.

We only want to hear what happened."

"It's just…" Riggins squirmed in his chair now, the first time he'd seemed ill at ease thus far. "Jeez, I don't even know how to say it without, you know, implicating myself."

A feeling of anticipation swelled in Darger's chest. She felt lightheaded.

"Implicate yourself in what?" she said, her voice coming out miraculously even.

"Fuck it," Riggins said. "Easier to rip off the Band-Aid all at once, right?"

He inhaled deeply and held his arms out like a preacher giving some kind of holy pronouncement.

"I got the cut on my hand while I was tripping."

For a few seconds, the only sound was the faint ticking from the clock on the wall.

"You were on drugs?" Loshak asked.

"Yes, sir. My buddy Thor gave me some hella potent shrooms as a belated birthday gift, and I was on a 34-hour reset anyway, so I figured, why not?" Riggins breathed out. "Whew. You know, it's funny, but I actually feel better now that I got that off my chest."

Darger tried to fit this newest puzzle piece with the rest. First the bloody rags. The "roadkill projects." An unexplained cut on the hand. And now psychedelic drugs.

"Anyhow, that's why I'm fuzzy on the details when it comes to my hand," Riggins said, holding up the bandaged extremity again. "See, the way I remember it happening is that I crossed paths with a narwhal, and it stabbed me with his, like, horn thing."

Riggins blinked up at the ceiling, his expression gone thoughtful.

"I don't think he meant it as an act of hostility, though.

Like, I got the sense that he had the capacity to be a nice narwhal… but it was also in his nature to, like, defend himself or his territory or whatever?"

The man tapped out a jaunty rhythm on the table with his good hand.

"After that, things kind of mellowed out, thankfully. I spent a solid three or four hours as a caterpillar, just like, pupating."

"Pupating?"

"In my cocoon. Or maybe it would technically be a chrysalis? It was a blissful experience, though I have to admit, I'm kinda bummed I didn't make it through the full metamorphosis. How amazing would it have been to experience the transformation into a butterfly or a moth?"

"OK, let's go back for a second," Darger said, putting the hippie mumbo jumbo he was spewing out of her mind. "When did you take the drugs?"

"Yesterday… afternoonish?"

"You don't remember a specific time?"

Riggins scratched his head.

"Well, let's see. I stopped at a Micky D's as I drove through Fredericksburg. Had a quarter pounder… That was probably three o'clock."

Darger remembered the McDonald's cup found at the motel room crime scene and had to restrain herself from showing a reaction.

"And I knew that since I wasn't taking them on an empty stomach, it'd take a while for the mushrooms to kick in, so I actually ate them a little before I got to Big Jon's. Had to be around four, maybe four-thirty."

"When did they wear off?"

"I started coming out of it when I heard all the ruckus with the police and whatnot. The noise with the sirens and everything kinda killed the mood."

"Are you saying that between approximately 4 PM, all the way until the time the police arrived at Big Jon's, you have no real memories?"

"Well, like I said… there was the pupating. And then the altercation with the sea beast."

"Do you remember interacting with anyone else in the lot that night? The other drivers? The girls?"

Riggins answered her question with one of his own.

"Have you ever tripped?"

"Can't say I have."

"Well, it's like being in a dream. Hard to separate fantasy from reality. So I don't remember seeing anyone else, but they may have come to me in another form, you know? Like, for all I know, that narwhal was Elvis. Or the Pope."

His eyes went wide, and he stopped.

"Hold up. Is this, like, a Las Vegas-type situation?"

"A what?"

Darger couldn't help but draw a line between Elvis and Vegas and couldn't figure out how sequined jumpsuits and gold aviator sunglasses might figure into the discussion.

"You know… 'what happens in Vegas stays in Vegas'? Confidential, or whatever." He winced. "I guess what I'm asking is, like… you don't have to report this to my boss, do you?"

Darger found it interesting that Riggins was more concerned about his employer finding out about his psilocybin-fueled adventure than the fact that he was currently being questioned in connection with a triple murder.

"No."

"Cool, cool, cool." Riggins chewed his lip. "And then, of course, there's the other elephant in the room… I'm not, like, under arrest, am I?"

Darger thought he was finally realizing what kind of trouble he was in. And then he opened his mouth again.

"For the shrooms?"

Darger sighed. As much as part of her wanted to arrest him, being sketchy as hell wasn't technically illegal.

"No. You're not under arrest."

Riggins smiled and nodded.

"Righteous."

"There's just one more thing," Darger said. "There are some things in your history we wanted to talk about. Your criminal history, that is."

Riggins's smile died off. His tongue flicked over his lips.

"Oh?"

His voice was different now. Flatter. Something about the new tone made the back of Darger's neck go cold.

"Yeah," she continued, watching him closely as she spoke. "Multiple counts of breaking and entering. And larceny. Not the kinds of charges that would usually be of much interest to us, but you stole something rather particular, didn't you?"

Riggins's eyes turned to vacant pits. He blinked once, his gaze shifting over the table. Then he made eye contact with Darger again and held still.

"You broke into your neighbor's house and stole her underwear, isn't that right?" Darger narrowed her eyes. "And it wasn't just your neighbor, it turns out. Because when the police searched your apartment, they found a pretty sizable stash of women's panties."

The seconds stretched out. That cold feeling on Darger's neck went icy. It felt like no one in the room was breathing.

And then Riggins started laughing.

His mouth stayed tight. Grinning. That awful laugh

gibbering through his teeth.

Darger swallowed. She tried not to let the jittery feelings scritching inside show on her face.

And still the creepy clown cackle hissed out, stark in the hushed space. His eyes stayed stony and dark.

That chill crept over Darger's shoulders and reached up to touch her cheeks. She swallowed again.

"Hell, I don't know what to tell you," Riggins said when the laugh finally cut off. "You can judge anyone on their worst day and make 'em look awful bad, can't ya? What you're talking about happened years ago. I did my thirty days. Paid the price for my crimes. I think that's about all I have to say about that."

"Was it the job, you think, that drove you to it?" Loshak asked. "The road. The loneliness."

Offering up a possible excuse to pivot the conversation and keep him talking, Darger knew. Smart.

The trucker's eyebrows scrunched up.

"You mean did I do it because-a truckin'? Hell no."

A half-smile curled his lip now.

"Shoot, you probably heard a lot of that. Everyone blaming the rigors of the job for all their faults. Pretty typical. Everyone is a victim these days."

He shook his head, and his expression softened a touch. His eyes went back to normal so quickly, in fact, that it somehow didn't comfort Darger all that much. The trucker kept talking.

"Some people? They weren't cut out for a job like this. The loneliness crawls under a certain kind of person's skin, pounds in their chest, somehow turns to something restless, something desperate. I mean it eats at 'em and eats at 'em 'til they lose their shit entirely. I've seen it about a thousand times."

He tapped the side of his head with two fingers.

"See, I think we all need a job that fulfills something inside of us. Something that feeds our soul, one way or another. Without that kind of purpose, we're fuckin' lost."

Now he pointed the fingers at Darger.

"So many people think they want the easy life. Lap of luxury. But that's a death sentence, man. Easy is stasis, and stasis is death."

"And driving a truck," Darger asked. "That feeds your soul?"

"Is that so crazy? Out on the road, that's when I feel free. And the job is a challenge, for sure. It tests you. Pushes you right to the edge of all your limits. Physical. Mental. And yeah, maybe even spiritual. Now, I won't lie… sometimes it does feel like pointless shuffling from place to place. An endless journey without meaning. But that just puts me face to face with what we're really up against in life."

He scraped the heel of a hand at his stubble and thought for a second.

"This world can be ugly, and it can be mean. It's mostly cruel and tragic and, maybe worst of all, boring. It can seem like a series of events utterly without reason. An abyss. But you gotta stare that darkness in the face and find the reason inside yourself. Find a way to keep going. Get your dukes up. Scrap and claw. Whatever you gotta do. But find a way."

He blinked again. Stared out at nothing as he went on.

"Barreling along in my truck gets my blood up, man. Gives me this wild feeling like a fire in my belly. The road brings that, what do you call it, existential conflict into stark focus, and it makes me want to fight, makes me want to keep going and going. I ain't just livin', man. I'm attacking life while I can. Just killin' it. For as long as I can."

CHAPTER 32

Traffic pulsed around them as they hurtled south, back to Roanoke Rapids. The restless energy from the other drivers was palpable even through the glass and steel. Everyone in a rush, in a hurry.

"So…" Darger said.

"Yeah," Loshak agreed. "That was… bizarre."

"Do you buy it? His whole story about not remembering anything because he was on drugs?"

"I don't know. The sheer ballsiness makes me tempted to believe him. Most people wouldn't admit to doing illegal drugs in front of two federal agents."

"Right."

Loshak tucked the car into the right lane long enough to let a tailgating SUV pass them. The blinker ticked out the impatience that seemed to hang in the air here.

"On the other hand, he wouldn't be the first killer to make up a kooky story."

"Like the guy who murdered Harvey Milk and said it was because he ate too many Twinkies?" Darger asked.

"Exactly. We've had the Twinkie defense. Now we have the Magic Mushroom defense."

"The drug use does fit the profile. Antisocial, risk-taking behavior."

Loshak nodded.

"And don't forget that the guy said he plays with dead animals for kicks."

"Then there was the stash of underwear some years ago,

and the pile of bloody rags more recently." Darger sighed. "I wish we could have held him until we had the results back on the blood samples."

"Yeah, well, the samples should be at the lab by now, and they've got the green light for overtime hours on it. So hopefully we'll have at least a blood type soon. And in the meantime, we'll have round-the-clock surveillance on Riggins."

They reached the lot outside of the Roanoke Rapids Police Department, and Loshak parked at an angle from the entrance. As soon as they were out of the car, Glenn pushed open the glass door to greet them.

They followed him into the basement. After everyone grabbed a fresh coffee, Darger recapped the Riggins interview for Glenn, and the detective made about five weird faces per second as he took in the odd details.

"A narwhal? He actually said that?" he asked when the story was done.

Darger nodded.

"You said in your profile that our guy is fairly together mentally. So would that rule someone like Riggins out?"

Loshak squinted.

"That's an interesting question. He seemed normal enough in the interview. Sane. Lucid. But if he's telling the truth about the drugs…" Loshak crushed his eyebrows together. "The thing is, psilocybin can cause profound dissociative effects. A disconnect from reality. So I'd expect a killer under the influence of magic mushrooms to display disorganized traits. And that doesn't jibe with the level of planning and sophistication we've seen at our scenes."

"You said, '*if* he's telling the truth about the drugs,'" Glenn said. "Meaning he could be lying. Misdirection, you know?"

Darger shook her head and let out a frustrated breath.

"We discussed that possibility," she said.

Glenn snapped his fingers.

"What if we asked him to take a drug test? Prove that he was actually on drugs?"

Hands on his hips, Loshak's face was grim.

"Problem is, psilocybin is metabolized too quickly for most of the standard blood, urine, and saliva tests. It does linger in the hair for around 90 days, but that wouldn't help us determine whether or not he was high specifically when the murders occurred."

"Well, shit. So much for that idea." Glenn stroked his chin. "OK, so if you throw out the nonsense about mushrooms and narwhals, what was your impression of him? Did he feel like a killer?"

Darger pictured Riggins in the weigh station again, that oddly pleasant expression on his face. It occurred to her, for the first time, that she hadn't found him as off-putting as the others.

"He was a hard one to get a read on. All over the place, kind of. But he was somehow... *warmer* than the others, crazy as it might sound."

"The brightest among us are sometimes bright for a reason: They have the most darkness to hide," Loshak said. "Anyway, that's four names down on the list from VICAP. Just one left to talk to, right?"

As if on cue, the chief poked his head into the break room. He smiled like he knew more than they did, for once.

"Aha. I was just looking for you. County boys just hauled in the next name on your list. He's down there sittin' and stewin', ready and waiting to be grilled by the FBI's finest."

CHAPTER 33

Ricky Lee Adkins made for a pitiable sight on the other side of the table. He looked kind of like a kid both in his gawky build and the frightened expression on his face, big blue eyes opened wide, shoulders stooped as though he were trying to make his stick figure frame even smaller.

A carpet of blond hair cropped tightly to his rounded scalp like freshly mowed sod. The orbits of the eyes were sunken, the hollows of the sockets somehow visible in the plum-shaded flesh.

Darger studied him in the two seconds it took to cross the room, her mind ticking off features one by one. She felt something cold enter her chest cavity as she did.

The trucker's scrawny cross-country runner body sported bony bulges at the elbows, bridge of the nose, and brow — something harsh, distinctly masculine, in the planes of his face and build. These were the primary indicators that he was, in fact, an adult male and not an adolescent.

"Good evening," Loshak said as they trundled into the room. His voice was warm, probing.

Adkins said nothing. He sat nearly motionless in his seat, not moving at all apart from blinking, which he did every second or two. His head angled down toward the floor so intently that it was almost like he was reading something there on the gray tiles, some message etched into the grout lines.

Loshak sat down, and Darger followed suit. She made an effort to scoot her chair back as she did, hoping the screeching noise of metal on ceramic tile might break the spell of stillness cast over the space.

If Adkins heard the shrill sound, it didn't show on his face. The blank expression held steady, his features as static as stagnant water. Lifeless. His complexion almost looked gray.

Darger glanced at Loshak, who shrugged. The agent cleared his throat before he spoke.

"So, uh, Ricky— Is it alright if I call you Ricky?"

Adkins nodded once.

"Can you give us yes and no responses instead of gestures? Better for the official transcript, you know."

Adkins narrowed his eyes. Then he spoke, his voice coming out tiny and breathy. Whispery. Oddly gentle.

"Yes."

His cheeks rippled, head angling up into better view when he spoke.

The skin of his face was pulled so taut it was like it had been vacuum sealed there, stretched like a strange membrane over the bone structure. It was impossible for Darger not to think about the skull beneath that thin layer of skin, the chiseled edges of the jaw and rounded knobs of the cheekbones displayed as prominently as blades.

"Great," Loshak said. "So you know why we were wanting to talk to you today?"

Adkins blinked hard.

"Yes."

Loshak didn't say anything to that. He waited, eyeing the trucker.

Darger understood the play — he wanted to see how Adkins might fill the gap in the conversation. The silent treatment now and again could work wonders in an interrogation setting.

Those being questioned sought a release to their tension,

talked to fill the quiet, and fresh shards of truth often came spilling out in the process. It had worked with Jones.

But the scrawny trucker said nothing. His eyes twitched back and forth once and then went back to their blank stare.

"It's about the murders," Loshak said, and when Adkins still held soundless, he added, "You heard about those, right?"

"Yes."

Adkins seemed to stretch out each of the ess sounds just a little, as though he might be concentrating to avoid lisping or some other kind of speech impediment.

All monosyllables so far. Darger wanted to shake that up.

She leaned forward. Rested her forearms on the lip of the table. Purposely took up more space.

"What do you think about the murders, Ricky?" she said, raising her voice to again try to jar some response out of him.

His eyes flicked back and forth over the grout lines again. Twice this time.

"I don't."

Darger clenched her jaw.

Two syllables. That's technically an improvement, I guess.

Now she leaned back in her chair, metal bits creaking under her shifting weight. She folded her arms over her chest.

Welp. Guess I'm the bad cop.

"You don't think about them, huh? Three girls got butchered, one in the very parking lot where you slept last night… and you have no opinion at all?"

Blink.

"Nope."

Blink. Blink.

"Well, that sounds a little funny to me, Ricky. You know we've already been able to tie you to several of the truck stops involved. Boston. Miami. The one here in Roanoke Rapids, of course. It all lines up with your driving schedule. Any opinion on that?"

The tip of his tongue wet his lips. A pale, pointy thing. White as a snail. Then that tiny voice lilted out of him in a slow singsong.

"Coincidence."

Four syllables, but only one word. Not sure if that counts for anything.

Darger splayed her hand on the folder lying on the table.

"You've had your share of run-ins with the law. More than your share, some would say."

His eyes flicked over the ground again, sweeping back and forth like a pair of pendulums, but Darger noted something new in them. They kept moving this time. She pressed him.

"How about that 'solicitation of a minor' charge? Any light you can shed on that?"

No response.

"'Cause maybe it's just me, but when I hear about a damn near 30-year-old man stalking a high school sophomore, I start getting all kinds of ideas about that kind of person. My imagination runs wild. Maybe I can picture him dumping that body out in the parking lot last night. Maybe I can picture him doing the same all up and down the East Coast. Maybe."

Adkins swiveled his gaze up from the floor. Something demonic flashed over his face as he locked eyes with Darger.

She stared right back at him. Unflinching. But something cold wriggled up her back.

His tiny voice came out clearer. Disgust blossomed in his tone now. Maybe something else, too. Aggression?

"You know something, lady? You talk too fucking much. Running that bitchy mouth. Telling me you know it all. But if you knew anything, you wouldn't be interviewing anyone and everyone, would you?"

Before she could catch herself, Darger blinked, and a thin smile curled just the corners of the trucker's lips. Some victory in that for him.

"I've known a million of you. Behold, the uptight office women who have lost all touch with the real world. All very important, or so they keep telling me. Not that I've seen your kind do much of substance beyond a bunch of yakking. No real work. Lots of big meetings, I'll bet. Pumpkin spice lattes all around, for good measure."

His gaze stayed locked on Darger's. Dark and unblinking. She said nothing. Let him continue.

"Your kind? You're all the same. It's like you strap on a pantsuit, and your shit don't stink no more."

"And what about the girls working the lot?" Darger asked. "Are they all the same?"

His smile broadened a touch, and then he made a dismissive sound with his throat.

"If I'm not being detained, I think I'll get back to my job in the real world. You want to talk more, you can get in touch with my lawyer."

CHAPTER 34

Darger's legs felt stiff as she shuffled out into the hall, the thin layer of industrial Berber carpet seeming uneven beneath her feet. The air conditioner felt stronger out here, too. It reached right through Darger's jacket and shirt to press its chill into her torso. The lack of sleep was starting to get to her.

"So that was kind of a bust," Loshak said, keeping his voice low.

Darger watched Adkins trail down the hall, already well out in front of them and moving pretty good. His slight frame disappeared around a corner, heading toward the parking lot.

"I don't know, I think he told us quite a bit. More than he intended, at least."

"That's true. I mean, he didn't shy away from some fairly misogynistic talk. All that stuff about *uptight office women*." Loshak cupped his chin in his hand. "You got under his skin for sure, and it didn't take much. Whether it means anything for our case or not is hard to say."

Darger blinked at the empty mouth of the hallway where Adkins had been, still gaping like he might reappear there.

He didn't.

"He seemed a little more sophisticated than the others," she said. "Once we got him out of monosyllabic mode, I mean. He was pretty good with words. Surprisingly so. Used a more complex syntax than McMurphy and some of the others. He even alluded to current pop culture during his rant with the pumpkin spice reference."

"Right. So he'd maybe have a little more intellectual brain

power working for him. Which fits the profile."

Darger nodded.

A montage of interrogation clips replayed in her head, flitting from face to face.

She remembered Chuck Trotter smiling, a slow warmth emanating from his demeanor and words alike. He seemed so non-threatening, in fact, that it ironically made him seem sinister — almost a John Wayne Gacy vibe, Loshak had said. And, to put a finer point on it, he had a verified history of violence that validated that suspicion of his disposition — the gap between the sunny surface and the criminal behavior had already been established.

Then there was Billy Ray Jones. The human cocaine piñata. Despite the fact that they'd ruled him out via alibi, she couldn't stop herself from picturing him in the interview room with Loshak. Beady-eyed and sweating one minute, convulsing on the floor the next.

Next she flashed to the grim expression etched into Ed McMurphy's face, smoke twirling around his meaty head. He'd been openly hostile from word one, and he had a history of assaults to his name as well. He'd also had a moment of desperate vulnerability, hadn't he? When he'd talked about the stream of dirt flowing through his head, compulsive thoughts he couldn't turn off. That'd fit with the unsub. Darger felt certain the perpetrator would turn out to have problems in their personal life triggering the eruptions of aggression, one by one.

Then it was Junior Riggins, Jr., in the weigh station with his kooky story and dopey smile. He seemed less overtly threatening than the others, but his history with the stash of women's underwear sure seemed to fit the panty gags found in the victim's mouths, and he hadn't exactly explained away the bloody rags in his truck, had he?

Finally, she landed on Ricky Lee Adkins. His scrawny build. His hairless arms. His soft voice that was almost birdlike. They'd learned little in their interview with him. He'd ranted and then lawyered up.

Detective Glenn rushed into the hall then, wheeling around the same corner where Adkins had vanished. His head snapped around, and when he spotted Loshak and Darger milling near the snack machines, he bolted for them.

"Must be news," Loshak said. "But is it good news or bad?"

Before Darger could answer, Glenn was upon them.

"Got something on Chuck Trotter."

"A new lead?"

"The opposite. A dead end. Turns out Trotter was in Duval County lock-up down in Jacksonville when the Savannah murder went down. Got nabbed on an old bench warrant for writing bad checks."

Darger's mind tried to mold this new piece of information to the rest of what they knew. Neither she nor Loshak spoke for several seconds. She heard Loshak's voice in her head again, a replay of what he'd last said.

But is it good news or bad?

Darger pondered that. Was it good news? Yes and no. They'd ruled out another suspect. That was something.

She pictured Trotter's mugshot pinned to a bulletin board, black sharpie lines x-ing out his name on the list. Another one down. Three to go.

So why didn't she feel good about it?

Though it was technically progress, deep down she felt no closer to cracking the case. They could stop looking into Trotter, but they still had nothing solid, nothing concrete, on any of their suspects, did they?

That feeling of the floor in the hallway being uneven under her legs occurred to her again. It was like the ground beneath this case just wouldn't hold still.

CHAPTER 35

Darger slurped pink goo through a straw, and the creamy fluid coated her tongue. She swallowed before she spoke.

"Long day."

"Oh yeah," Loshak said.

Night had fallen on the drive back toward the motel, and they'd stopped off at a local creamery for milkshakes. Strawberry for Darger. Vanilla for Loshak. The place had come highly recommended by one of the detectives on the task force — Duckworth, Darger thought his name was. And ol' Duckworth had been right. Hand-dipped. Real milk and ice cream. Delicious.

Loshak's phone blipped, and he looked down at it for a second before his eyes snapped back to the road.

"Text from Glenn," he said. "You want to check it?"

Darger swiped and read. She felt her eyebrows climb higher as her eyes absorbed the words on the screen.

"Says the lab sent back more tests on the bloody rags from Riggins's truck," Darger said.

"And?"

"Blood on the rags is A positive. Riggins is AB positive."

"So it's not his."

"No. And there's more. Jane Doe was A positive."

Loshak's tongue clicked as his mouth dropped open.

"Well, that's something."

"Yeah."

"Any word on when we'll have a full DNA profile?"

"He didn't say."

"Ask him to find out if he can."

Darger nodded and fired off a text back. The response from Glenn came back quickly.

Will do.

"Shoot. That's something to look forward to in the morning," Loshak said. "I think I'm too tired to even make sense of it right now."

"Same," Darger said.

Loshak wheeled the car into the lot, and the headlights swept over the motel facade gone mostly dark. They parked and parted ways then.

Darger felt her heartbeat, slow and steady, as she used her keycard to let herself into her room. She flicked on the lights and kicked off her shoes as she crossed the space. Her feet felt like animals freed from pens, toes flexing and squishing into the cool carpet.

Then she sat on the edge of the bed. A deep breath rolled in and out of her.

And suddenly the quiet in the room seemed overwhelming. Eerie. Nothing stirring here but the faint breath of the air conditioning, its icy touch wafting over the floor.

She lay back on the bed and closed her eyes, but she didn't want to sleep. Some electric surge toward the front of her skull throbbed, warning her to stay vigilant, to keep watch.

She had to keep telling herself that it was all in motion now. They had taken real steps toward solving the case today. The DNA tests on the rags and their victims were underway at a lab in Charlotte. The remaining suspects were being surveilled even as she sprawled here. Given the nature of the crimes and the fact they spanned nearly 1,500 miles up and down the east coast, they'd made more progress in a single day than she could have possibly hoped for.

The case wouldn't somehow crash if she weren't awake to drive it. She didn't — couldn't — control all of the moving pieces of the task force. Not even close. She could sleep now, and the work, the progress, would continue through the night.

Still, her mind protested for a while yet, thoughts of doom and pangs of anxiety swirling around each other like it was trying to braid them into a rope.

Images flashed in her head, memories from the case files and interrogations alike. All those faces. Some of them lifeless. Some of them nervous. Some of them jolly.

One of the men they'd interviewed in the last two days was the killer. She was all but certain of it. She just didn't know which one.

She riffled through their faces again and again. And her brain slowed down along with her heartbeat until no other words accompanied the pictures in her head. Just the names.

Trotter.

Jones.

McMurphy.

Riggins.

Adkins.

Repeat.

She lay still, her breath evening out. That litany of faces and names flickered on the backs of her eyelids, over and over.

Nine minutes later, sleep lurched up from the depths of her subconscious and pulled her under.

CHAPTER 36

Detective Bledsoe hunched over the glossy tabletop of her booth at Big Jon's. A plate of food sat before her, but the steak and eggs had only been nibbled at, more smeared around the plate than eaten. She took another drink of black coffee and let her gritty eyes shift to the dark figure across the room.

Ed McMurphy perched at a booth in the back corner, alone and oddly upright. The big guy looked surprisingly alert considering all the driving he'd done today — eyes opened a little too wide, something agitated in every movement he made.

Bledsoe took another sip of coffee as she considered this, felt the scalding liquid screech down her throat. He was probably hopped up on something. Did they still sell trucker speed at the convenience stores? Bledsoe could remember back when Mini Thins and Yellow Jackets were everywhere, semi-legal speed with ephedra as the active ingredient, perpetually on gaudy display just next to every cash register. But she thought at least some of that stuff had been taken off the market over the years. Speed increased productivity, usually an acceptable risk in America, but once a few too many working-class hearts had popped, society clamped down.

McMurphy's eyes swiveled like black marbles in his skull. Searched the room. His gaze locked onto Bledsoe's and held there.

Shit.

She swallowed and looked down at her plate, jabbed her fork into a clump of scrambled egg. The food had all gone dull, that glisten of freshness fading to a filmy matte look like the skin on the top of pudding. How long had the plate been sitting here? At least twenty minutes, she thought. Long enough for the trucker to eat a whole plate of brisket and put in another order.

She glanced up. McMurphy wasn't looking anymore. Instead, he was flagging down a waitress. Getting a refill on his Coke.

So he probably hadn't made her, at least not yet. Probably had no clue that she'd been on his tail all day. The deception rippled a faintly giddy feeling through her gut, but it couldn't quite pull the muscles in her face into a smile. She was too tired for that shit.

She'd caught up with Ed McMurphy at a gas station in Kenly and tracked him all the way down to a distribution center in Statesboro, Georgia. She'd watched him unload his rig at the docking bay. Then she'd tailed him back up to Big Jon's where he was getting a meal and likely spending another night in his truck out in the lot.

Where McMurphy seemed unaffected by all the driving — with the help of chemical aids or otherwise — the endless hours on the road had caught up with Bledsoe in time. Exhaustion wound coils of soreness into her shoulders, stiffness into her neck. Her lower back felt like someone had taken a golf club to the spot where her spine connected to her pelvic bone. Too much time sitting in that damn car seat, body folded in half long enough to crease her back like a sheet of paper.

But help would be here momentarily. She'd be relieved of her duty. She checked her watch. A shift change in twenty-three minutes, officially, would bring one of the field agents from the task force to keep eyes on McMurphy for the next eight hours.

Even with respite so near, Bledsoe could only vaguely

imagine lying down in her bed, feeling that kink in her spine decompress as she sprawled. Sleep seemed more like a distant dream than something she'd actually be doing within the hour.

In a way, she was apprehensive about being taken off McMurphy. She liked keeping an eye on the big creepy fucker, felt more secure being the one responsible, like maybe someone else would let him slip away. She knew the fear wasn't reasonable. Probably.

The waitress circled back to McMurphy's table with another platter — a giant burger and a pile of fries. Jesus, he was eating a lot of food. He shook his empty cup of ice at the waitress and then handed it over for another refill, scowling and muttering all the while.

Bledsoe tongued the inside of her cheek as she watched the poor waitress deal with the buffoon.

Obnoxious piece of shit.

She watched him eat for another few minutes. Tired eyes reading every hostile twitch of his muscles, scanning for meaning in any of it.

The comically large burger made the bottom half of the trucker's face disappear every time he took a bite, and he drenched each fry in ketchup before he ate it, fingers coming away red up to the second knuckle. He ate fast. Chewed with his mouth open. No hidden meaning in any of it that she could see. He was just a pig.

Two things happened simultaneously then that shook Bledsoe awake.

Agent Ruiz entered the restaurant and started over toward her, flashing a big white smile. He would replace her now, and she could go home. The agent was young with one of those fussy haircuts that swooped back on top and was shorn to the scalp on the sides, and his suit fit impeccably, drawing slim at the waist. All told, he looked more like he was about to go on stage to host a reality TV show than tail a serial murder suspect for hours on end. He mouthed "hi," eyebrows jumping, as he wove around a few tables to get to her booth.

The moment the door closed behind Ruiz, it banged open again, something forceful in the way it burst inward, almost violent. Broad shoulders jutted through the doorway then, and Bledsoe inhaled sharply when she saw the face hung up above them. She knew it well.

Junior Riggins, Jr. — the suspect whose truck was full of bloody rags — strutted through the place, looking like Ric Flair or maybe a rooster. Same thing, more or less, Bledsoe figured.

Ruiz sat down across the booth, and Bledsoe gave a subtle nod at the two agents on the Riggins surveillance detail who came in a few paces behind him. Then they all swiveled their heads to watch Riggins march through the place.

His torso swayed back and forth as he swaggered right past big Ed McMurphy. Bledsoe noticed that Riggins kept his head looking the other way.

Staring off toward the kitchen or maybe the blackboard with today's specials?

Or is he specifically avoiding eye contact with McMurphy?

Then she took a closer look at the big trucker sitting in the booth. Really looked.

McMurphy dropped his burger onto his plate with a wet slap and locked onto Riggins. Brow furrowed. Eyes wider still. Those black shark pupils dilating, growing bigger somehow. Head swiveling to track Riggins's path.

He stared. Glared. Didn't blink.

If Riggins noticed McMurphy gawking, he didn't show it. He sauntered over and sat in a booth just a couple spots behind Big Ed.

And McMurphy didn't like it.

He sucked in a big breath and let it out. Sounded like steam hissing out of a vent even all the way across the restaurant floor. Seething.

"Damn. Pretty good chance one of those two is our guy, huh?" Ruiz said, keeping his voice hushed.

Bledsoe's whisper sounded like pages of a magazine rubbing together when it rasped out of her.

"Yeah, maybe so."

She cleared her throat. Took another drink of coffee. Shoot. Maybe she should cut off the caffeine now that home and sleep seemed within a stone's throw.

"What the hell was the stink eye all about with McMurphy there?" Ruiz whispered. "Bad blood? Could they know each other somehow?"

"Hard to say. I mean, McMurphy always seems pissed off about something or other, but his reaction to Riggins was, uh, notable. For sure."

Bledsoe stared holes in the two truckers, one then the other. Their expressions looked exaggerated to Muppet proportions. The glowing Riggins with the smile in his eyes who'd swaggered through the place so carefree he was practically prancing. And then the glowering Oscar the Grouch hunched down in the booth, brow crushed, still fuming over his giant burger.

"They must have some kind of history," she whispered, thinking out loud.

The notion that they'd worked the murders together in some way crossed her mind. Hell, McMurphy was such a damn creep and the blood in Riggins's truck looked awfully suspicious.

Well, shit. That's an idea.

But if they'd conspired in any way, then why did McMurphy seem to hate the other so much? It didn't track. Her tired mind juggled the pieces another couple seconds and then dropped them all.

"I guess it'd be inevitable that some of these guys would end up knowing one another, right?" Ruiz said. "Like at these truck stops, I bet there are crowds and cliques. The drivers. The spotters. The lumpers."

"One dude walks in and everyone yells 'Norm.' Like *Cheers.*"

Ruiz smiled. Studied Bledsoe a second. No courtesy laugh. He looked annoyingly well-rested. Eyes sharp. No bags under them.

After a second, he went on.

"Well, I'm just saying that where there are cliques, there are rivals, you know? Maybe these guys don't get along for completely innocuous reasons. A fight over a parking spot or something dumb. It could be meaningless. Probably is."

They fell silent after that. Watched the two truckers.

"Anyhow," Ruiz said. "I'm on McMurphy now, though I bet there'll be more sleep than excitement in his life for the next eight hours. What I'm saying is, you can take off whenever."

Bledsoe nodded and ate some of her toast. It'd gone cool now. Dry in her throat. The butter greasy on her tongue. But eating it gave her an excuse to stay. Keep an eye on McMurphy for just a while longer.

She wondered how long Ruiz would wait before he prodded her to leave again. And she wondered if she could stomach eating the congealed eggs if it came to that. It'd buy her another chunk of time. The cold steak might be OK, at least.

A couple minutes passed. Her eyes flitted over the two of them endlessly.

Riggins ordered, smiled like he was probably flirting. Then the waitress gathered his menu and left.

He stood when she'd gone, still smiling. Stretched his back and dusted himself off. Then he headed for the men's room. Crossed the floor of the restaurant with that cocky bounce in his step.

As soon as Riggins pushed open the door and stepped into the restroom, McMurphy was out of his seat. Big body lurching. Bolting.

He leaned forward. Head low. Practically sprinting across the restaurant. Weaving around a table.

Giving chase.

Bledsoe choked on a piece of toast. Coughed. Something crusty lodged deep in her throat. Tears welling in her eyes.

Oh shit.

She scrambled for the aisle. Arms scrabbling at the tabletop. Butt sliding over the vinyl seat.

Her sore legs pushed her upright. Back twinging.

And then she was off. Running toward whatever was about to happen.

As McMurphy neared the bathroom door, Bledsoe saw something dark and glossy appear in the big trucker's hand.

She coughed again. Gaped.

McMurphy flicked his wrist, and the straight razor unfolded in his hand.

CHAPTER 37

Bledsoe zipped over the tile restaurant floor. Felt her knuckles brush her holster. Fingers reaching to draw her weapon.

Her eyes stayed trained on that bathroom door ahead. Unblinking and bright. No longer any trace of tiredness there.

The rectangle of glossy veneer stared back — the door a warped mirror stained brown. Next to the *Men's* on the engraved sign, a little cowboy-hatted stick figure gleamed in white lines, grinning like a doofus.

Commotion rippled over the floor. Disturbed the booths like a wave spreading outward from the detonation point of McMurphy and Bledsoe running. Words finally spilled out of the throng.

"Look out! He has a knife!"

Bledsoe didn't recognize the voice. Couldn't tell where it came from. Swiveled her head.

But then she felt Ruiz at her side, and the two of them darted out in front of the others. The officers who'd been surveilling Riggins pumping along just a couple paces behind.

All their steps went choppy as they drew up to the restroom. Feet clapping against the floor.

Every eye in the room watched them now, the chatter cutting out to a hollow kind of quiet. Palpable.

Ruiz lowered his gun and kicked the bathroom door. It thudded like a punted football. Echoed. Burst inward.

And then they all rushed into the harshly lit space.

The bathroom shimmered. Gleaming brown tiles on the floors and walls. Ceramic lacquered to a high sheen. Refracting shards of light like gems.

Bledsoe thrust herself out in front again. Swept her Glock across the room.

Porcelain sinks jutted out of the wall to the right. Mirrors and chrome soap dispensers hung up above. Everything shiny.

Riggins was there to the left. Standing at the urinal with his head cranked back toward the police flooding the doorway. Wrinkles piled up on his forehead like a stack of pancakes, a shocked expression screwed into the features below.

"Holy shit," he said, his voice squeaky.

The cops stopped dead. Frozen. Nobody even breathing.

Bledsoe blinked. Hard. Tried to think. Mind spinning.

Wrong.

Something is wrong here.

"Is there a, uh, problem, officers?" Riggins said, still audibly pissing into the urinal.

Bledsoe looked at Ruiz who shook his head. The other officers exchanged glances.

Then a high-pitched wail shrilled out from behind the stall door. A keening tone. Sharp. Sounded like a shrieking tea kettle.

No.

Sounded like a puppy or a little kid.

Bledsoe whimpered, one little hiccup of sound creeping out of her throat. Some involuntary empathy response to the pain she'd heard in that voice.

Jesus Christ. Does McMurphy have someone in there?

"Oh, shit," Riggins said. "Oh, fuck."

He zipped up and bolted out of there. Shouldering right through the police with the drawn guns like whatever was behind that stall door was twice as scary.

Ruiz gritted his teeth. Veins bulged in his neck like worms

wriggling under his skin.

"McMurphy! Open the door, and come out with your hands on your head."

There was no response from the stall. The only sound at all was a steady *drip, drip, drip* noise. One of the faucets leaking.

Ruiz stepped forward and kicked open the stall door. The latch snapped. The door rebounded off the wall and bounced back. The agent kicked it again, lighter this time.

Bledsoe lurched forward. Jammed her gun and arms into the opening.

And there he was.

Big Ed McMurphy sat on the toilet. His pants bulged around his ankles. Face dark. Jaw clenched.

A pool of red spread over his lap in pulses, hissing when it touched the fabric of his jeans. A steady pattering rhythm as it trickled onto the tile floor.

Not water dripping.

Blood.

He still held the straight razor in one hand. That arm raised and shaking, hand level with his head, elbow locked in an L-shape. It almost looked like he was going to fling the razor like a dart.

Bledsoe blinked hard. Felt a little flutter of breath on her teeth.

It took her a second to realize what the tube of meat in the trucker's opposite hand was.

His own severed penis.

CHAPTER 38

Blood smeared the brown tile floor in the stall. Puddled in the grout lines. Little flecks spattered the wall beyond the pool. Still bright red, still fresh.

Pulling back, police tape crisscrossed yellow lines over the empty threshold where the stall door used to be. The broken latch and hinge left it leaning down into the space, so the police working the scene had removed the door and set it aside.

Darger breathed. Smelled the lavender and Pepto smell of the urinal cakes wafting everywhere in here.

McMurphy was long gone by the time she'd arrived on the scene. She could only stare into the little cordoned-off toilet cubicle and imagine the moment, imagine the shock of the officers who'd burst into the space and found Ed McMurphy sitting there in a bloody mess, his detached manhood still clutched in his fist.

"Genital self-mutilation," Loshak said, appearing just shy of her shoulder. "It's not as uncommon as you'd think, unfortunately. I've seen it quoted that there are dozens of cases per year of self-castration or self-emasculation in the United States, believe it or not. The statistics say that 87% of the, uh, victims are experiencing a psychotic episode when they do it. Drugs or alcohol are involved around 20% of the time."

Darger blinked. Broke her gaze from the stall where it had happened. She looked down at the shiny tile floor instead, a grid of glimmering brown veined with white grout.

"Do we think McMurphy was psychotic?"

Loshak tilted his head.

"Bledsoe did say that he seemed agitated. Tense. Eyes open too wide. And then… well, this. I'm sure he's getting a psych eval at the hospital, but I'm leaning toward yes."

Darger flashed back to the image of McMurphy in the dim motel room, ranting about the dark impulses flitting through his head, that he couldn't control his sexual desires, couldn't find relief. Couldn't turn the tension off. Some part of his brain must have thought this would turn it off for good.

She could still remember what it felt like to sit in the small space with him, the glossy plank of the table the only thing between them. Hostility seemed to radiate from the big man. Dark energy rolling off like a prickle in the air. There'd been something claustrophobic about being penned in with him by those dingy motel walls.

And he'd felt it, too, hadn't he? He'd said as much.

These impulses. They just thump out of my subconscious. Stuck in my head like lightning bugs in a jar. Trapped with no way out.

The sole of someone's shoes squeaked on the tile floor, and the high-pitched sound brought Darger back to the moment. She blinked a couple times and spoke.

"Do the doctors think they'll be able to…" She paused, searching for the correct word. "… reattach?"

Loshak bobbed his head once.

"He's in surgery now, so I guess we'll see."

"They did it for John Bobbitt, right?"

"They typically are able to, I think, but… Jesus."

Loshak leaned over a little, bending at the waist, and Darger couldn't help but notice the way one of his arms crossed over his own genitals as though trying to guard them. He sort of looked like a pretzeled little kid who had to pee.

"You OK?"

Loshak looked down at himself.

"Oh. Yeah. Sorry. Just… I saw some photos in one of the medical studies about genital self-mutilation once. Some things you can't unsee."

He straightened up and shook his head before he went on.

"The case study was a guy who lopped off the works. I'm talking frank and beans both. A 56-year-old retired fire chief, as a matter of fact, father of three adult children. What was left was just a sewed up… spot, I guess. Black stitches. One tiny hole of the urethra. I don't know."

He shook himself.

"It's almost physically painful just to think about it."

CHAPTER 39

While Loshak headed back to the motel to rest, Darger ventured out into the truck stop parking lot. She walked among the few normal-sized cars still snugged near the building, her eyes pausing briefly on the bumper of a Jeep plastered with stickers. Her gaze landed on one featuring a dark winged figure with huge red eyes and lettering that read, "Mothman for President." Darger chuckled to herself and made a mental note to try to find out where to buy the sticker. It'd make a great gift for Loshak.

Harsh bulbs buzzed overhead, spheres of light beating back the night's gloom, and Darger felt wisps of a cool breeze tickle at the back of her neck. She shivered for just a second. Some chill climbed her spine, shook her shoulders, and then fled as quickly as it'd come.

Even with all the trucks huddled around, occupied with sleeping truckers, the place felt strangely still this late. Eerie.

Deeper into the lot, the lights mostly gave way, and the night yawned above her. A cloudy abyss pricked by a few stars. No moon that she could see.

She adjusted her grip on her payload as she neared the sedan facing the rows of semis. She'd known she wouldn't be able to sleep after the bathroom stall bloodbath, so she'd popped into the convenience store and loaded up on junk food — an armload of drinks hugged to her chest, and a flimsy plastic grocery bag of sugar, salt, and saturated fat dangling from the opposite hand.

She hoped with all the snacks to hand out, she'd be

welcome among those working tonight. This was not unlike Loshak's ritual of offering donuts to curry favor with whatever local precinct or task force they were consulting with at the moment, she supposed. Perhaps she'd learned from the best.

I come bearing gifts.

The dome light of the Nissan winked on, and the door cracked open a fraction of a second later. Darger could hear the whispery voice through the opening, a woman's, but the face stayed backlit, shrouded in shadow.

"Agent Darger? That you?"

Suddenly Darger's throat felt dry. She didn't know what to say. Her mind groped for something, reached back to her most recent thought.

"Yeah. I… come bearing gifts."

She winced. It was one thing to think it, but now she'd gone and said it out loud.

Dork.

A man's voice spoke up this time, deeper in the car and slightly muffled.

"Is that Red Bull? For God's sake, hop on in."

Darger felt some strange twinge of relief at the sheer enthusiasm in his voice, internally kicking herself for never quite graduating from that 7th grade level of social awkwardness in times like these.

She climbed into the backseat of the Altima and handed the Red Bull up toward Detective Glenn, whose silver crew cut and loud voice she recognized even in the dark.

"What the hell are you doing here?" she said.

Glenn grinned like a hyena.

"Hey, I sacked out for a good three hours or so in the evening, but I couldn't resist coming out here to watch the lot. Hell, I didn't know there'd be free Red Bull, or I would've skipped sleep altogether."

There was a 50-ish Black woman in the driver's seat, and Darger flipped through her mental Rolodex to bring up her name and background. Detective Barb Mustafa. Miami PD. She'd turned up the key clue at the ATM inside the Forty Winks Motel, or so it had seemed at the time.

Christ, this case is moving fast.

Glenn took the silver can in with a swoop of his arm, cracked it, and took a long drink, all in one fluid motion. The can's mouth glugged gently against his. Then he tipped it back and grinned.

"Oh yeah," he said. "That's the stuff. Thank you kindly, Darger."

"You're welcome. I also have a Coke and an Arizona Iced Tea. Green, I think."

Mustafa reached her hand between the seats.

"I could drink a tea. Thanks."

Darger passed up a pale green 24-ounce can that seemed like it was about a foot tall. Then she offered up her bag of goodies, and the two made their picks. Mustafa opted for Cool Ranch Doritos and Glenn selected a bag of sunflower seeds, both skipping over the sweets entirely in search of something salty. Darger could respect that.

The dome light blinked off, and all the colors inside the Nissan drained to gray. That seemed to relax Darger the rest of the way. She leaned back in her seat and finally let her gaze sweep out over the lot before them.

"So who are we watching tonight?"

Glenn took another sip before he answered.

"Officially, Detective Kassab, out of Boston, and Agent Novak from the Charlotte field office are on Adkins. And us? We're on Riggins."

"Trotter's here, too," Mustafa added. "I know we ruled him out for the Savannah murder, but I'm still keeping an eye on that slimy fucker."

Darger's mind whirred through quick flashes of each suspect — the bright-eyed, gregarious Chuck Trotter, who now looked like a dead end. The scrawny Ricky Lee Adkins with the creepy whisper voice and unabashed hatred of women. And then Junior Riggins, Jr., the free spirit with the bloody rags in his truck.

Her mind replayed one of Glenn's sentences.

We're on Riggins.

It took her a second to process the full ramifications of that.

"Riggins. So you two were in the restroom… when *it* happened."

"I arrived a few minutes after, but Mustafa here saw the whole thing," Glenn said.

The woman let out a noisy breath.

"It was… I don't even know how to describe it. We ran in there thinking that McMurphy was a threat to Riggins, but it sure turned into something else entirely. Fast enough to give ya whiplash, too."

Glenn shook his head.

"This is sick, but I swear to you, on the drive in, I was thinking about grabbing a bratwurst from the restaurant. But… I couldn't imagine actually biting into a, uh, sausage. Not after what happened."

They fell silent for a beat.

"According to Loshak, there's usually a psychotic component. A break from reality," Darger said. "Even so, it's hard to believe that it could be a recurring phenomenon. Something so violent toward oneself."

Both heads in the front seat nodded at that. Glenn

munched a few sunflower seeds as he answered.

"I mean, I get that this is a thing that happens. A recurring phenomenon, like you said. But I can't relate. Chopping off the… the johnson? No thanks."

"I think it's about trying to manage tension," Darger said. "Kierkegaard talked about how the tension between life and death becomes clearest when we stand at the edge of a ledge and look down. Part of us is so overwhelmed by that thin line between life and death, by that open loop of our lives carrying on indefinitely, that we get a faint urge to hurl ourselves over the cliff, to fall into the abyss, into death — not because we truly want to die, but just to resolve that tension. To close that open loop."

She brushed her hair out of her eyes before she went on.

"When we questioned McMurphy, he talked about not being able to turn off his impulses, the dirt and the darkness running through his head. I suspect that's what he was trying to do tonight, even if the way he went about it was insane."

"Here's my question… Do we think this makes it more or less likely that McMurphy is our killer?" Mustafa asked.

"I'm honestly not sure," Darger said. "I guess if McMurphy is the guy, at least he'll be out of commission for a while. Maybe long enough for us to build a case before he can strike again."

Darger opened the bottle of Coke and took a swig. She looked out over the lot of trucks as she did, paying special attention to the rigs Glenn had pointed out. Nothing moved out that way.

"So, Mustafa, you were the one who tied Trotter to the ATM in Miami?" Darger asked. "That was good work."

The detective let out a sigh before she replied.

"It felt like it… 'til we ruled him out."

Darger screwed the cap back on her drink.

"Gotta turn over every rock and see where the evidence leads. That's what my partner always says."

"Where is Loshak?" Glenn asked. "I was hoping to get a chance to pick his brain at some point. I read about some of his old cases when I first joined the force. I think they were why I wanted to become a homicide detective, truly."

"He went back to bed. But I'm sure he'll be delighted to answer your questions and feel ancient doing so. He describes to me, in graphic detail, every time someone asks him to autograph one of his old books."

Glenn chuckled.

"So the great Victor Loshak heads off to bed while his partner brings food to the working stiffs up all night on stakeout duty. Funny. The old man can't hack it, but Violet Darger? She can hang."

Glenn dug in the snack bag and took out a pair of Hostess chocolate cupcakes, working at the cellophane so that the crinkling filled the cabin of the Altima. Just as he started to slide the first tiny cake out of the sheath, his hands stopped all at once.

"Well, lookie here," he said, eyes staring off into the lot. "We've got some action."

"Where?" Mustafa said, head swiveling.

Glenn pointed to the left, handling one of the greasy cakes with his other hand, the tips of his fingers sinking into the chocolate sponge.

"Looks like a couple of the girls trying to sneak back into the lot."

Mustafa's head snapped that way. Darger's too.

Something blurred at the far edge of the windshield. Darkness rippling on darkness. Then the shapes moved in front of one of the white semi-trailers and tightened into focus.

Two girls hustled toward the stacks of slumbering vehicles, one walking funny on high heels in a way that made her look like a strutting bird. Otherwise, they didn't look to be wearing much.

Mustafa fired up the Altima, wrenched the gear shift. The headlights speared the darkness.

And they lurched forward all at once, gravity tugging Darger deeper into her seat. Glenn braced himself with a palm on the dashboard, the other hand trying to shove the cupcake toward his mouth in an awkward way that reminded Darger of watching an astronaut eat in zero gravity.

The scene before the Nissan felt like an action movie shot, Darger thought. The glow of the headlights encircled the running girls, and the windshield pressed tighter on the two figures like a zooming camera lens, closer and closer until they filled the screen.

Lights. Camera. Action.

"I knew it," Glenn said, slamming that hand on the dash and then shaking his head. "Goddamn it. That's Monica. The one with the heels? I know her. Pull up alongside."

Mustafa cranked the wheel to the left, and the Altima glided up along the girls, who now almost seemed to be running in place, still some 20 or 30 feet shy of the truck lot. Then the detective slammed on the brakes, and the car stopped short.

Glenn put his window down and barked through the empty space where the glass had been, his voice straining and solid in that aggressive tone only an experienced police officer can muster.

"Hey! Both of you! Stop right now."

One of the women stopped right away. Bent at the waist. Sucking wind.

The girl in the heels, apparently Monica, kept right on

running, the shoes still twitching her legs in that clumsy peacock swagger.

Something like a growl emitted from deep in Detective Glenn's throat. This time his yell broke up his voice into a rasp.

"Monica! Get your ass over here!"

Monica stopped all at once then. Spine stiffening and arms rising a little, as though she'd been shot in the back and was about to flop over dead.

Both girls turned and slowly made their way to Glenn's open window like a couple of depressed cartoons — their heads low, backs hunched, shoulders sloped down.

The first girl — as yet unnamed — looked young. Innocent. Frightened. The faintest hint of baby fat still showed in her cheeks, on her arms. Maybe 20. Maybe not even that.

Monica's fake eyelashes fluttered like black butterfly wings as she faced the light. Dark crinkles of hair draped around her heart-shaped face. Little twitches seemed to assail her hands and wrists every few seconds, occasionally creeping into her face to wink one eye or shudder one side of her mouth. She was older than the first girl — no doubt — but Darger couldn't read the age with any confidence. Anything from 25 to 45 seemed plausible.

Monica licked her lips as the two of them drew within a few feet of the Nissan. Her expression seemed to change slightly when she recognized the detective, the dark eyes shedding that softness of guilt for something harder.

Something defiant there? Embarrassed? Darger wasn't certain.

"Look. Not tonight, ladies," Glenn said. His tone fell right back into that jocular cadence. Cocky, Hank Schrader energy. "It's too dangerous. I mean, three of your own just got killed last night. You know better than to be out here, don't you?

Monica, I know for a fact that you've been told. Come on."

Monica's lashes fluttered again, that unreadable emotion flaring in her eyes. She shrugged.

Glenn turned to the younger girl.

"What's your name?"

The girl's arms upper arms drew tight against her ribcage, her body language reading more toddler than anything to Darger.

"Kirsten."

"You been working out here long?"

"A few weeks."

Glenn nodded, which quickly transitioned into a head shake.

"Well, maybe you don't know it yet, but this lot ain't safe at the best of times. And right now? We're talking Code Red. Max danger. Air raid sirens should be warbling all across this truck stop. A distorted voice coming over the intercom like, 'Warning. Active serial killer may be lurking on the premises. Please keep arms and legs out of his vehicle at all times. I repeat, don't climb into a goddamn truck with him.' You feel me?"

Kirsten just stared at him for half a second. Then she nodded.

When Monica spoke up, her voice came out harsh. Pointed.

"That's all well and good, but we need to eat. *I* need to eat. Like today. Like now. Not like I can fall back on my *rainy day account* or some shit. Like, we're not out here on a field trip. We need money."

Glenn bobbed his head again. Then he sighed.

He shoved the rest of the chocolate cupcake into his mouth, chewing just twice before he swallowed. Then he leaned forward and dug his wallet out of his back pocket. Pulled out a couple of ten dollar bills. He handed one to Kirsten, who took it, her body language still sheepish. Then he thrust the second toward Monica.

When she went to take it, he held onto it for a second. The green flap of paper was suddenly shoved into the midst of a tug of war. The bill jerked back and forth. Their fingers fidgeting, jockeying to overtake Hamilton's placid face.

Their eyes locked. Some kind of hate in Monica's glare finally came all the way clear — loathing and fury and naked aggression. Darger no longer had any doubt.

"For food, Monica," Glenn rumbled. "Not for crack or crystal or any of that shit. For food."

He let up then, and she ripped the dollar bill away from him. A smile curled her lips, though that pain and resentment still shined in her eyes.

Then the girls stomped off toward the glowing glass front of the truck stop. Monica's heels clomped and echoed over the asphalt like the heavy feet of a Clydesdale.

Darger felt herself breathe. Realized that she hadn't been while they'd fought over the money.

She blinked a couple times. Tried to make sense of what had just happened here.

She'd seen, so many times, detectives and street cops treat prostitutes like they were something subhuman, like they existed only as pains in the lives of law enforcement. Here, she had witnessed just the opposite. Detective Glenn had given the women money out of his own pocket — an act of compassion, a show of kindness.

And yet that look on Monica's face somehow threw it all into question. Why did she hate him so much?

Mustafa wheeled the Nissan back to the parking spot and killed the engine, and the tension of the whole exchange seemed to die along with the headlights. Shut down. Flicked off. The quiet rose to fill the void.

Mustafa sipped her tea. Glenn chewed sunflower seeds in his front teeth like a gerbil. All eyes trained once more on that lot of lifeless semis where nothing stirred at all.

"Well… that was probably the end of our big excitement for the night," Mustafa said. "If we're lucky."

CHAPTER 40

Cold wind riffles the dark coils of hair that frame the girl's face, sends the crinkled strands skimming over the smooth sheet of her forehead like disturbed bits of rotini — a pasta salad squirming atop her head.

Monica feels the little tickle of hair on her skin, just a touch stronger than a breath, though she can barely see the movement in the dark here where no lights reach.

The truck stop still glows in the distance. The sprawling compound looks small enough to be shoved into a shoebox from this far out. Its light doesn't reach her, can't touch her. It doesn't even come close.

Instead, she walks into the gloom. Tromps over the rocky grass beyond the truck stop parking lot, bare feet picking out each step with care — her high heels tucked under her arm for now.

The ground slopes downward underfoot until the dark objects to her left block out the truck stop entirely. Looks like the horizon is slowly swallowing the building.

It's cooler here at the bottom of the hill. She's trekking through that deepest part of the night that drapes fresh humidity over everything, emits a dank chill that sends goose bumps running up the backs of her arms, even at the height of summer.

She stops a second and lights a cigarette, the fire's light harsh in her face and then gone. A pink afterglow hovers where the flame had danced the moment before.

And she takes that first drag. Savors the menthol flavor

spiraling over her tongue, through her throat, into her chest.

Tastes better 'cause it was free.

She sniffs a little laugh to herself. Thinks about Glenn's big square face, handing over ten bucks like he was bestowing some grand gift. Mother Teresa feeding the poor or some shit.

Thanks for the smokes, shitdick.

Then she presses onward. Still picking her way along the fence. Craggy ground stabbing and prodding at her toes and the balls of her feet. All the rocks are somehow sharp here. Embedded in the soil and poking up like teeth jutting out of gums. Shards of broken concrete mixed in like jagged fangs, for good measure.

She shuffles into the darkest stretch yet. Her fingers reach out to brush at the chain links of the fence, rusty and rough. Just making sure it's still there.

It should be close now. What she's looking for. It should be close.

She flicks on her lighter. Adjusts the little black notch on the front toward the plus sign.

The flame grows. A tall ribbon of incandescent orange like a spike of light, rippling gently with her every movement.

Her lighter becomes a torch. Reveals the way. She angles it toward the ground.

She sees the litter first. Sun-bleached trash smashed everywhere. Weathered. Most of it drifted up against the fence like snow.

Crushed Big Gulp cups lie flat to the ground. Empty pop bottles and cans dot the path. Chip bags are caught in the fence, tangled and suspended in the mesh of links. An industrial spiderweb.

She lets her gaze shift beyond the garbage.

It should be there. But it's not.

She lets her lighter go out. The hiss cutting off with a click.

She hobbles forward a few more steps, feeling vulnerable now that the lighter has blown out her night vision. She blinks hard. Tries to see anything but that pink blotch in the shape of the lighter's flame.

After twenty or thirty feet, she flicks the lighter to life again. Flame gouts out of the mouth of the thing.

And it's there.

What she's been looking for — it's there. And she doesn't feel defenseless anymore.

She ducks through the slit in the chain-link fence. Steps one bare foot down on the asphalt of the truck stop lot. Party row. She's already there.

She sniffs another laugh to herself. Looks out at the little sliver of the glowing neon light emitting from the truck stop restaurant in the distance. She knows the police are there — Glenn and the others — so she needs to proceed with caution, keep out of sight.

She takes a deep breath. And begins her duck and run from truck to truck.

☾

Breathe in.

The killer perches behind the wheel of his truck. Set up high at the back of the lot like he's riding atop the sea of semi-trailers before him.

He gazes over the lot at the cops on the other side. Eyes flitting, twitching, smoldering.

Two vehicles. Four LEO bodies that turned to five when that FBI bitch sidled up.

For now, he's just another face in the crowd. Nobody.

Nothing.

But they're close. Closer than they've ever been.

Breathe out.

For years he has stayed invisible. Done his thing. Done whatever the fuck he wanted.

Roamed free. Made the highway his slave. Made all those skinny little things bend and break and bleed.

Whenever he wanted. However he wanted.

By comparison, the new scrutiny feels like a prison. Barred walls closing, closing. Penning him into a box. A cell.

He twists his hands on the steering wheel. Peers out of one darkness and into another.

He can just make out the silhouettes of the heads of the cops in the cars across the lot.

Breathe in.

And he wants to act out. To vent the darkness. To press his hands into some girl's flesh, loop a line around her neck, work his blade until there's no life left in her.

But he can't. Not with the po-po breathing down his goddamn neck.

His molars grit and grind. The sound of bone scraping bone scritching in his mouth.

A shadow jumps in his rearview mirror. Startles him.

Breathe out.

And then there's a knock on the door. Three sharp clicks of knuckle hitting metal.

He waits. Listens. Makes no move.

The door opens then, a slow-motion swing, the tiniest squeak in the hinges.

Breathe in.

The electrical tape he's mummy-wrapped over the dome light blocks the bulb's glare almost entirely. He doesn't think the cops in the distance will see shit, even if they're looking right at him.

The feminine shape in the doorway moves. Climbing in. Her face angles into a wedge of moonlight.

And he smiles because he recognizes her.

Breathe out.

It's Monica.

CHAPTER 41

Darger still sat in the backseat of the Altima as light slowly leaked into the darkness before the windshield. The trailers filling the lot grew brighter, sharper, as the twilight shifted gray hues into the blackened sky. It somehow looked like time-lapse footage to Darger.

After they — mostly Glenn — had confronted the girls trying to sneak into the lot, the rest of the night had gone without incident. Even the conversation in the Nissan had dried up to almost nothing, save for the occasional comment about the array of junk food.

Oh. Yeah. The junk food.

Darger looked down at the plastic trash now scattered around her. The fresh light oozing over the horizon laid the scene bare, exposed the evidence of what she'd done last night while she should have been sleeping.

A spent bag of crunchy Cheetos lay crumpled at her feet. One red rope still remained in the pack of Twizzlers Pull 'n Peel at her side.

And then there'd been the Snickers. King size. Two of them. And the bottles of Coke.

A little pang of guilt twinged in her gut as she mentally tallied the calories, a throb of remorse that pulsed up into her neck. She slid her tongue over teeth coated with fresh plaque.

Then she slid the last Twizzler out of the sleeve and went to work on it.

Something darted in the lot then. A flicker between the trucks. Toward the back of the lot, from the looks of it.

Darger stopped chewing. Froze. Stared.

Just when she was about to ask if the others had seen it, there was another.

A second person zipped along, one of the truckers in just a white t-shirt and boxers, flitting like a blinker in the gaps between the trailers. He sprinted from one end of the lot to the other. Disappeared into the back corner where the angle blocked the view from the Nissan.

"What the fuck?" Glenn said in a falsetto just about under his breath.

He and Mustafa looked at each other. Then they both looked back at Darger in unison.

Darger swallowed the last of the ropey red licorice before she spoke, her voice coming out small.

"Better go check it out."

Darger and the others climbed out of the Altima into the crisp morning air. They crossed the empty stretch of parking lot, picking up into a jog as they moved. Feet quiet. Guns drawn.

That gray predawn light made the way clear enough, but it still left the color drained from the landscape, everything rendered in grayscale like newspaper print. A grid of gray trucks and white trailers, separated by ribbons of black asphalt.

Darger pressed down one of the aisles. Proceeded toward the spot where she'd seen the trucker in his undies vanish.

She hit the last row. Passed the final trucks and drew up on the fence line. Then she took a hard left.

Right away she saw it — a group congregating in the back corner of the lot, gathered around something, though she couldn't tell what.

The whole mob looked like the man she'd seen flitting along the back row — truckers clad in what served as their pajamas. Boxer briefs and a t-shirt for most of them. Sweatpants and no shirt for a couple. Bare feet stepped gingerly on the blacktop as they shifted in the small throng.

Some had their phones out. Talking. The rest were quiet.

Darger caught one stray phrase from someone muttering into a phone — "another body" — and then she was running. Breaking through the crowd. Elbowing. Turning sideways to angle through the gaps.

She reached the empty space beyond the cluster of truckers. Stumbled a second.

And it was there.

The body lay at an angle along the line where the asphalt cut off to dirt.

Naked. Legs folded behind her. Bound.

Crinkled hair. Ashen face. Eyelashes knitted together as though in deep sleep.

Red lines carved over all the rest of her.

Darger knelt next to the body. Let the image come clear in her eyes. She recognized the girl.

It was Monica. The one Junior Riggins had mentioned by name. The one Glenn had given some money to just a few hours ago.

For food.

Darger wrenched her head back around. Stared into the faces in the crowd looming over her, over the girl. She knew the killer was among them.

But the shadows shrouded all of the features, leaving only black smears staring back at her.

CHAPTER 42

Darger sat in her booth at the truck stop restaurant, her eyes still drifting out into the lot where the techs in their Tyvek suits swooped to and from the crime scene. She couldn't see much of the particulars with the trailers in the way, though she knew the process well enough to not need visual confirmation. The CSIs photographed and filmed and scraped and fingerprinted and bagged, documenting the grisly spectacle like always.

Again and again flashes came to her of Monica as she'd been last night. The choppy peacock gait of her walking in her heels. Those fluttering black butterflies of her lashes.

And these shards of memory remained in motion, animated snippets that wouldn't hold still, even if the girl herself now did.

Cold and still and alone. Forever.

An icy prickle swept up Darger's back as the words sounded in her head, the sense of loss suddenly heavy in her chest. Why was grief always a leaden thing? A weight that wouldn't let up.

She swallowed. Took a deep breath and forced her mind to clear. Then she looked at the room around her, noting concrete details to reorient her consciousness to the present moment.

Glossy Formica tabletop. Brown flecked with black in a faux marble pattern.

Little chrome-plated holder for the salt and pepper shakers, a looping piece of steel almost as thin as wire.

Laminated ad for pie sticking out of the top. Whipped cream and vivid strawberries.

Berries as red as—

The pictures flashed again. Scarlet gashes drawn into skin.

She winced. Blinked hard.

But even with the lurid interruption, the technique had worked. She felt more present, more tuned in to the bustling restaurant around her.

Quiet frustration huddled over the small section of the restaurant housing mostly law enforcement on the task force. Mustafa and Glenn sat at the next booth up from Darger with some of the other police who'd been on surveillance last night, all of them now relieved of their duties with fresh teams following the truckers. All their heads bobbed and swiveled and angled toward their plates, but nobody talked much.

Darger had originally sat by herself, happy for the few moments alone to try to process everything, even if it was far too much to work through any time soon. But she hadn't stayed alone for long.

Now Loshak sat across the table from her, his eyes still looking puffy from having just woken up. He took a big drink of coffee before he spoke.

"I've been doing this job for decades. I've seen brazen before. But this? Killing a girl and laying her out with police actively watching the lot? This is on another level. And to pull it off…"

He shook his head. Pursed his lips like he'd tasted something bitter.

"Nothing on the security cams. I guess he'd know their range well enough by now. No witness accounts, either. A whole lot of truckers within an arm's length, and nobody saw anything. Granted, they were all sleeping, but still… This is the kind of risk-taking behavior I would typically associate with a disorganized type, someone out of control, flailing. But it's so damn neat. It's like we're chasing a damn ghost."

For some reason, this phrasing brought to mind her nightmare from earlier. The shadowy figure lurking in the motel bathroom. The sensation of the ligature closing around her windpipe.

Her mind produced a perfect snapshot of Monica then. Of the livid line etched into the pale flesh of the girl's neck. Darger resisted an urge to reach up and touch the skin of her own neck.

Instead, she pushed the empty plate toward the middle of the table, gave herself enough room to rest her arms on the edge. She'd eaten a western omelet for breakfast, spritzing the tube of eggs and cheese liberally with a particular hot sauce at the waitress's suggestion. Pretty good. She typically loved a decent plate of breakfast, but somehow it hadn't seemed fully satisfying this morning.

"I just keep thinking: Is it even one of our guys? Someone from the list?" she asked. "Or is it another face in the crowd?"

Loshak studied Darger's expression, something soulful in his eyes. He took another sip of coffee, his Adam's apple bobbing as he swallowed. Then he spoke.

"Let's not throw the baby out with the bathwater just yet. The odds still favor the profile and the names from ViCAP. Jones and McMurphy were both in the hospital last night, so we can officially rule both of them out. If anything, we're narrowing it down."

Darger sighed.

"Maybe. I guess I look out at the bunny suits flitting around a fresh body, and it sure doesn't feel like progress. At all. Makes me start to question everything."

"I know what you mean, but… we've got to trust the process. Trust the evidence, like always."

Darger hesitated a second. Then she nodded.

Out in the lot, the white clad squad of crime scene techs filed in between the trucks, streams of them following each other everywhere like lemmings.

CHAPTER 43

Darger and Loshak had just climbed back into the car when his phone squawked. He squinted at the screen.

"It's the chief. I'll put him on speaker."

Loshak thumbed his phone screen a couple times and then loaded the phone into the holder jutting out of the dash.

Chief Hall's deep voice throbbed through the phone's speaker, bassy and thick.

"We have an interesting development, and I thought you oughta be among the first to know."

"What is it?" Darger asked, wondering if perhaps they'd been able to match the bloody rag DNA to one of their victims.

"An anonymous tip came into the county hotline. We got a fella out in the sticks between Roanoke Rapids and Snead's Ferry — and, believe me, it's pretty much all sticks between the two… Anyhow, he says that a few weeks back, he saw a struggle between a neighbor of his and a woman at a trailer out in the boonies. At the time, he thought he was seeing a guy helping a drunk girl into his double-wide real late at night. But after seeing the front-page article in the *News and Observer* about the truck stop killings, it occurred to him that this neighbor just happens to drive a truck for a living. Now he's concerned that maybe what he witnessed was something darker altogether."

Darger leaned forward in her seat as the meandering speech went on. She stared at the phone screen like it might make the chief reach his point faster.

"Fairly mundane, as far as tips go," he went on. "The kind that come in by the dozens. But then we ran down the address he gave, and wouldn't you know it? The property traces back to one of our suspects."

Darger's hands balled into fists. Was the chief intentionally dragging this out?

Who is it? she screamed internally. Adkins or Riggins?

"Property tax records show that 1339 Half Moon Road is owned by one Charles Trotter. Not much more than a dirt track through the swamp more so than a real road, mind you."

"Did the neighbor have anything else to say about Trotter?" Darger asked.

"From what I can tell, the guy doesn't know much about him. He's certainly in no position to know that he's on our radar. He just knows he's a trucker and that police are looking into truckers now. In fact, he said Trotter has been 'personable enough' the few times they've spoken, I think is the phrase he used. So we're talking about someone taking a real shot in the dark with the call."

"Lucky for us," Loshak said.

"Indeed," Chief Hall agreed. "Now, I've been in touch with the Onslow County Sheriff, and he's about to send some deputies out that way. The nature of the tip being what it is — murky at best — we aren't trying for a warrant quite yet. But I figure with Trotter on the list, we got good enough reason to have someone take a look, see what they see, and go from there. Maybe it's something. Maybe it's nothing."

"How far is it to the property?" Darger asked.

"Oh, I'd say a three-hour drive from here. Sheriff Pratt gave me some directions for finding the turn-off for the unmarked driveway, in case you're thinking of heading out there yourselves. I can send it over."

Loshak and Darger shared a glance.

"We'd appreciate that, Chief. And thanks for keeping us

informed."

"No problemo. Hey, alright, I've got a few more calls to make, so I'll holler at ya later."

Once the call ended, the interior of the car held quiet for a full second. Loshak stared blankly into the middle distance.

"So we're heading out there, right?" Darger said. "Like now?"

"Oh yeah," Loshak said. "Just thinking. I mean, I'd sort of written Trotter off, you know? He was alibied for the Savannah deal. But then… there are just so many variables to something like this. Hey, what did I tell you about trusting the process?"

He pointed a finger gun at his phone still jutting from the dash.

"Punch the address in, and let's hit it."

Darger started working at the phone. Fingers swiping and punching.

Loshak started the car, yanked the gear shift, and they lurched into motion.

CHAPTER 44

Miles of North Carolina wilderness filled the land between Roanoke Rapids and Snead's Ferry. Bright green vines of kudzu clogged every inch between the trees — the kind of thick, choking growth that only occurred in humid climates, Darger thought. A quick flash of an Alaskan rain forest gleamed in her head, fevered memories of slogging through it in the rain, in the dark, danger lurking all around, but she pushed the images away as quickly as she could.

Her fingers looped into the little hand hold jutting out of the door, textured plastic brushing wrinkles like laugh lines against her skin. The tactile experience again helped her stay in the moment. She stared at the emerald blur out the window, walked herself through how they'd gotten here.

A few lush fields of tobacco, soybeans, and some sort of vine — maybe sweet potato? — had occupied the roadsides during the early part of the journey, but the woods swelled with each passing mile, overtaking more and more of the terrain. A teeming, constricting, creeping thing. Not just dominating the landscape, crushing it.

Eventually they'd fled the asphalt, moving out of the hills, and followed a couple of dirt roads into the swamp. Here the foliage shifted again. Willows poked out of the sludge, slumped things with weeping, hairy-looking fronds. Lily pads floated atop the sparse sections of water, and cattails likewise thrust out of the sludge.

A placid AI voice on the phone ordered Loshak to take a left turn on Half Moon Road, and he did. The dust that kicked up behind the car in a cloud arced right along with their turn.

"I think this is it," Loshak said, taking the second driveway on the right, per the instructions they'd received.

They crested a hill, and Darger caught her first glimpse of the trailer up ahead.

The structure sat on a shelf of raised land, just a few feet higher than the swamp all around it. Pea gravel ran along the border between Trotter's lot and the bog, a touch that almost gave off the feel of a beach of pebbles around a private island.

The double-wide itself was a handsome thing. Clean white with a gabled roof and a porch on one corner. Clearly a newer model trailer in damn near mint condition. Not quite the dilapidated look she'd subconsciously anticipated.

Still, it was a creepy spot. Isolated. Some tension in the air here. Something gloomy about the big willow looming behind the house.

Drawing closer, more details emerged. Windowpanes inked black squares and rectangles into the white siding. A couple of rusting cars sat in the driveway, somewhat offsetting the clean, sturdy look of the trailer and lot, making it look more like what they'd seen plenty of on the way in.

Must be some kind of county law. You've got to have a couple of non-functional vehicles in prominent display on your property or there's a hefty fine.

Loshak veered onto the gravel driveway, and hunks of limestone pinged against the undercarriage. It wasn't until they were halfway up the drive that the deputy's cruiser came clear.

The two deputies sat on the hood of their vehicle, one with his arms crossed over his chest. The other had his thumbs looped in his belt.

The latter stepped forward with a big grin on his narrow face. He was the one who spoke first as Darger and Loshak climbed out of the car, introducing himself as Jenkins.

"Heard y'all were coming out, so we figured we'd wait on you. All take a look together. Hell, I figure if you've got FBI help at your disposal, you might as well use the dickens out of it."

He pumped Loshak's hand with gusto. Then he gave Darger's arm the same treatment.

"Well..." Loshak said. "As federal agents, our help doesn't always get such an enthusiastic welcome, so I'll take it."

"It was Jenkins's call to wait," the other deputy said, raising his tone into something strident. His grin looked just a little wolfish. "I'm Bedard, by the way. Personally, I thought we should go on and take a look and then get gone, FBI help or no. I mean, we're taking a cursory glance at some trucker's trailer. No warrant or nothing, so... I don't see how the FBI brain trust is going to be a big boon in the effort, but whatever."

He stood back. Arms still crossed over his chest.

Darger fought to keep a smirk from curling her lip.

No frantic handshake, then? Fine. Be that way.

"Don't mind my partner's arrogant demeanor," Jenkins said. "He was raised a Duke fan, so he don't know any better."

They walked toward the trailer, four sets of feet crunching at the bed of rocks underfoot. Jenkins stepped out in front.

Darger let her eyes flit over the squat structure, top to bottom, sifting for any useful detail. Nothing stuck out right away. The place looked just as clean up close.

They tried knocking on the front door first, though they knew for a fact that Trotter was already hundreds of miles from here, rocketing north on I-95. Jenkins pounded on the screen door, made it rattle against the jamb. No response, of course. The deputy turned back, and they started working their way around the double-wide.

The two deputies circled the beaten-down cars, leaning close, cupping their hands to each rear windshield to peer inside.

Darger and Loshak trotted from window to window around the side of the trailer to do the same there. Loshak scooped up a five-gallon bucket along the way, and Darger understood what he meant to do with it seconds later.

She stepped up onto the orange bucket to see into the next window, a short clerestory frame set near the roof. Nervousness flared in her gut for a second as she lifted herself onto the makeshift step, some part of her certain that her boot would punch right through the plastic bucket bottom, but it held.

She took a shaky breath. Then she shined her light into the darkened space, only able to see a thin ribbon under the black curtain material in the way.

"Blackout curtains," Loshak said. "Makes sense. This thing is probably like a toaster oven when the sun beats down on it."

Darger swept her light over a swath of linoleum, just able to make out the bottom edge of the fridge and a small oven. A few knickknacks sat on the counter — a lighter, a blister pack of nicotine gum, an orange tub of Gatorade in powder form. Nothing of use for their purposes.

"This is the kitchen," she reported. "Not much to see."

She hopped down from her perch, and they moved on.

As they rounded the back of the trailer, a faint pond scum stench wafted near every now and then, blowing in off the swamp whenever the breeze picked up. An algae-like odor — green with a hint of funk. Darger could tell by the way Loshak's nose wrinkled that he could smell it, too.

She looked out over the back of the property. The willow glistened just along the swamp's edge, a slouching giant.

"Guess he owns six acres out here," Loshak said. He, too,

was looking over the lot.

Darger looked around. Spied bog in all directions.

"How many of those acres are stanky swamp, I wonder?" she asked.

Loshak sniffed out a laugh.

"I heard Deputy Jenkins call them *h-wetlands*. Hitting that h-sound really hard at the beginning, you know. H-wetlands."

He plopped the bucket down in front of another window, and Darger did the honors. The plastic cylinder shook once but held firm beneath her.

She peered into the tiny gap beneath another curtain. Let her light lance into the space. She could see a bit more this time, though it took a second for the details to resolve.

The back of a TV rose up from a plank of lacquered wood. An HDMI cable and a pair of thinner lines, perhaps speaker wires, snaked out of the thing and weaved out of view.

She tried to look past the flat-screen to see anything else on the tabletop, anything that might give them probable cause or something to justify a warrant. More trinkets filled the TV table. A matchbook. An Xbox controller. One of those stress-relieving foam squish balls in the shape of a tiny human brain.

Darger let out a breath. Again, nothing of use.

She climbed down. Feet pounding into the dust along the cinder block supports.

"Nothing here."

"Well, we've got another window or two to check, at least," Loshak said. "I think the deputies went around the other side, so maybe they'll spot something."

Doubt welled in Darger again as they walked toward the next window. She felt a heaviness in her upper back like it wanted to mimic the willow's posture.

"What do you think about the timeline discrepancy?" she

asked. "At the time of the Savannah murder, Trotter was hundreds of miles away in a Florida jail cell."

Loshak blinked before he answered.

"What do I think? I think Trotter didn't commit the murder in Savannah, obviously. His alibi is airtight on that front. We even have surveillance footage — video evidence — of him in his cell that day. But that doesn't necessarily rule him out as a suspect for the other crimes."

Darger stared at the ground. They crunched over pea gravel as Loshak went on, kudzu shoots creeping over the edges of the rocks.

"We're talking about a serial murder case spanning some 1,500 miles over a period of months and possibly years. There are just so many variables to consider that I think all we can do is look at all the evidence and see what it tells us. For example, the Savannah killing could be coincidentally similar to the rest, unrelated. Or Savannah could be the work of a copycat. We've seen that before. We just don't — can't — know until we look at everything."

Darger raised a finger.

"See, I don't buy the coincidental angle. At all. Piquerism, especially on this level, isn't common. The odds of such a similar set of murders right along the same interstate being unconnected? No way."

"Well, it's not impossible, but you're probably right. I'm not sold on any particular angle at this point. Still gathering facts, you could say."

That was when the yelling started.

"Holy smokes!" an enthusiastic voice let out, obviously Jenkins. "Jeez!"

"Uh. We've got something over here," the second voice, Bedard, added, something serious in his rising lilt.

Well, well, well… look who's suddenly interested in calling in the FBI's help.

Darger led the charge toward the source of the voices, she and Loshak zooming along the back of the house. They found the deputies peering into a low bedroom window along the side of the trailer, bigger than the rest. Unlike the others they'd encountered, the curtains here were drawn aside, the full pane of glazing exposed.

Darger stepped closer. Pressed her nose to just shy of the glass. Her eyes adjusted to the soft gloom of the trailer's interior.

A card table took shape on the other side of the window, and one gleaming object rested on the center of its flimsy surface, set at an angle.

A hunting knife.

CHAPTER 45

Darger felt her chest expand, a big breath inflating her. Her eyes danced over the glinting steel of the blade, fresh hope welling inside along with the wind.

Then she let her breath out, and that hope seeped out right along with it. She let her gaze drift to the back wall of the room, taking in the details beyond the card table, piecing together a context for all of the information here.

"Let me take a wild guess," she said. "Pretty much everyone in the county is a hunter."

Both deputies nodded.

"It's certainly the majority, ma'am," Jenkins said. "Turkey and deer, mostly. A cultural thing passed down through generations. I started when I was six or seven."

"Same here," Bedard said.

Darger pointed at the glass. Wagged her finger back and forth along the odd stick-like forms jutting out of the back wall, mostly up high.

"And it wouldn't be all that weird to have a hunting knife in a room full of racks of mounted antlers?"

Even the enthusiastic deputy seemed to lose his fire all at once, his posture sagging before Darger's eyes.

"I mean…" Jenkins said. "Probably not."

"Shit," Bedard said, shuffling back from the window. "I really thought we had something here."

"I wouldn't say the knife is meaningless," Loshak said. "But its existence is certainly not evidence of anything."

"Surely not enough to get a warrant," Jenkins said. "Dang it all."

Darger took a few paces away from the group and found herself back out front. Alone with her thoughts, which she didn't mind. Though she couldn't decide what she thought.

If Trotter could be ruled out for Savannah — and he could — it'd be a lot neater to rule him out of the rest. Cleaner. Let them trace all of it back to one hand, one perpetrator, and it'd be easier on every part of the process. Even with a mountain of forensic evidence, this kind of case could be tricky to prove in court. If the story were murked up considerably by Trotter having a solid alibi for *some* of the murders, it'd be that much more difficult.

Darger found herself stepping up on the front stoop again as her thoughts swirled. For a second, she didn't know why, and then it hit her.

Her senses sharpened all at once. Peach fuzz standing tall on the back of her neck. All of her focus streamlined onto the front door, eyes trying to bore holes into the thin flap of the storm door.

Something here. She could feel it like a throb in the air.

She opened the screen door. Stood on tiptoes and got her face right up to the square pane of glass in the door beyond it. She found another window unblocked by blackout curtains — the gauzy drapes here shrouded little of the view.

She took a long time looking over a shadowy living space. Cheap couches with wagon wheel artwork squared off. It was neat — no mess — which she hadn't expected, but it was consistent with all else about the home and property — well-maintained.

So Trotter was capable, detail-oriented, sophisticated. She'd thought as much when she'd interviewed him. If anything, that fit the crimes and cover-ups better than a messy place would.

Something meticulous about it all.

She got out her flashlight and tried shining it in. Aimed it at the shadowy corners where the gloom morphed all the details into dark blobs.

Her pulse pounded in the side of her neck as she swiveled the light around, some part of her suddenly sure she'd find something. Right here. And right now.

But she scanned and scanned again, and there was nothing there. Just more random baubles and gadgets. An open pack of Starburst on an end table. Another Xbox controller next to a throw pillow on the couch. A Mitsubishi mini-split for heating and cooling jutted out of the wall. It looked just like the one in Darger's hotel room.

Nothing.

She stepped back. Blinked. That momentary confidence dashed all at once.

Shit.

She felt hollow. Lost again.

She let her fingers ease off the side of the screen door. She was just about to let it swing closed when she saw it, and then she snatched the aluminum frame, pried the door wide again.

A smear curved just under the door handle. It'd gone brown with age, but when her flashlight beam swept across it, she somehow saw a flash of the original hue.

Blood red.

CHAPTER 46

Darger's breath went feathery. It felt like bubbles of carbonation were climbing up the walls of her skull and gently popping along the folds of her cerebrum — two flutes of champagne dumped into the brain pan.

Every time she blinked, she saw it again. That blood smear curved like a quarter moon under the brass-colored door handle — that was their express ticket to the next phase of the investigation, and they'd almost missed it.

She wobbled out onto the gravel driveway on legs gone shaky with adrenaline. She sidled alongside Loshak's car and braced herself with a palm pressed flat to the driver's side window.

She could hear the crackle of the radio somewhere off to her left. Jenkins was already calling it in, his Carolina twang coming out a mile a minute to a dispatcher who kept asking him to slow down. After perhaps ninety seconds, the talk cut out.

Jenkins rushed over the gravel then, choppy steps, each footfall crunching like a spoonful of Grape Nuts. Finally, he wheeled around the edge of the car and caught sight of Darger still bracing herself with one hand on the car.

"Just talked to the home base," he said.

His eyes looked open too wide, like a spooked horse. He smiled for a fraction of a second, and then he directed his rapid-fire cadence at her like a fire hose on full blast.

"The folks from the state crime lab are already on their way out, and Sheriff Pratt himself is talking to the judge now about a search warrant. Shouldn't take long now. Yep, it's all happening. The real deal. Mighta just cracked this one wide open."

Darger stared at the ground as Jenkins rambled on, listing off a few more clichés. The bed of sharp rocks gazed back at her. Nonplussed.

"Good frickin' eye back there, by the way." He turned to crow at his partner. "Hey, Bedard. What'd I tell you about taking full advantage of the FBI's help? Huh? I mean, my God, don't you ever get sick of it? Being wrong all the damn time? Getting your nose rubbed in it again and again. Goodness."

Bedard bellowed back, offering Jenkins a way to keep his mouth quiet with a part of his anatomy.

Darger got a quick vision of the near future. Once they had the warrant, they'd tear Chuck Trotter's handsome double-wide apart, hunting for anything that tied him to the crimes. Maybe they'd find something, and maybe not. Either way, this would vault them ahead in their investigation, giving them a primary suspect or ruling the guy out once and for all.

But all of that could wait. For now, Darger wanted to hold onto this flash of bliss, that bubbly feeling in her dome.

Somehow, she knew it wouldn't last.

CHAPTER 47

Thirty minutes later, Darger sat on the front end of the car, fingers and thumbs all atwitter at the screen of her phone. A light breeze fluffed her hair, but even the distant stench of swamp wasn't enough to break her concentration. Not when she had her hackles up like this.

That excited, drunken feeling of finding the blood smear had all but vanished within fifteen minutes. Then she'd gone right back to work.

Some fresh stab of doubt had crept into her gut as they waited for the warrant and the techs. It could just be the typical butterflies — waiting had a way of feeding anxiety more often than not — but she didn't think so this time.

Jenkins looked up from his own phone to call out an update.

"OK, it's official. The warrant has been approved. The rest of the cavalry is about ten minutes out yet. Aside from the folks from the crime lab, we've got a three-man strike team who'll bust in first and secure the scene."

"That was fast," Loshak said.

Jenkins bobbed his head once.

"Way it was told to me, we got lucky with the judge. We were expecting to be limited to only items relating to the girl mentioned in the tip call, but he opened up the search parameters to include anything relating to the I-95 case. Basically, we'll have free run of the place. If there's anything here to tie Chuck Trotter to the crimes, anything at all, we'll nail him. Sure as you're alive."

Darger nodded, eyes still locked on the screen.

Her doubt had put her on the scent of something. She'd decided to vet the tip call the best she could. It'd been anonymous, as most tip line calls were, but that didn't mean that poking around was without use.

Following up with the dispatchers, she'd found that they did have a phone number for the call. Unfortunately, the tip had come in on a burner cell phone. Untraceable. Was that suspicious? Maybe. It certainly fired up some wariness in Darger's mind. But it ultimately wasn't evidence of anything untoward on its own.

Now, she'd requested the recording itself be forwarded to her phone, which should arrive any second.

"Still looking into the tip call, huh?" Loshak said. He was eating Doritos, two fingers dipping into the single-serving bag and scissoring out one orange triangle at a time. "Find any juicy leads in that gift horse's mouth?"

"Not yet."

Her phone blipped. The text with the audio file had arrived. She thumbed the icon and watched the circle fill as the file downloaded. When it was done, she brought the phone to her ear.

The North Carolina accent stammered and sounded sincere. Reminded her of Jenkins's tone, though this voice was deeper, maybe older. She listened twice and brought her phone back down to her lap.

The man's story was just as Chief Hall had relayed — a man had seen Trotter engaged in what appeared to be a drunken struggle with a "female companion."

"Not the first time I seen somethin' like that, and I was raised to mind my own, you understand," he'd said.

Only now, having read about the murders in the paper, he

wondered if there might have been something sinister afoot.

"If something unfortunate befell that young lady... well, I'd feel responsible, I guess," the caller had drawled.

It all sounded reasonable enough. Except for one detail.

Trotter's trailer was barely visible from the road, and the foliage was so dense, Darger couldn't see any other houses from the property. She had to figure that was reciprocal — the neighbors couldn't see Trotter's place from their properties either.

He did say he was a neighbor. Maybe he was taking a walk in the woods.

In the middle of the night?

Darger jammed her phone back into her pocket, frustrated. Was something really off here, or was she just being paranoid? Letting the doubt win out over reason?

"Anything good?" Loshak asked. Then he tipped the tiny bag to shake the Doritos crumbs into his mouth.

Darger shrugged one shoulder.

"Not really."

"Anything bad, then?"

Before she could answer, a crew of vehicles stormed up the dirt road behind them, kicking up noise and dust. Everything happened quickly from there.

A police van and a few unmarked SUVs zigged and zagged into the driveway, parking at angles, rear wheels spinning up handfuls of gravel and flinging them. They killed their engines one by one, the cacophony of growls cutting out to nothing.

Then the strike team filed out of the van, all geared up in Kevlar body armor, black cargo pants, and helmets domed with clear visors. Their boot treads fell heavy on the crushed rock.

The back door of the vehicle slid open, and out came the compact door ram — the Blackhawk Thunderbolt CQB looked sort of like an engorged night stick with a big looped handle on top. One of the tactical officers wielded the thing, fingers laced around the handle, the bulky strike bar hanging off to the side of one hip. His body language reminded Darger of a video game character brandishing a Gatling gun.

The dust cloud still hung over the road as the strike team jogged up toward the double-wide. With all the gear on, they sort of looked like part of a football team clad in black, jogging onto the field.

Two of the officers stood to the side, one holding the screen door open, while the third man took the battering ram to the locked door. He gave it one good swing, slamming the plate into the plank of wood.

The deadbolt snapped and burst. The top hinge buckled. The door exploded out of the frame with a splintering sound and fell backward into the room, a floppy thing dangling by the two bottom hinges.

Everything held still for a second. Motionless.

And then the three tactical officers streamed over the threshold and into the shadowy place.

CHAPTER 48

The strike team locked down the 700-odd square feet of the double-wide quickly. Thirty seconds after breaching the door, their voices chimed over the radio in harmonic unison, like a barbershop quartet down only the bass singer.

"All clear."

Darger felt the muscles in her neck and chest release. A long, slow exhale rolled out of her. She squinted then, made herself take in the big picture.

The whole scene seemed to take a breath at the announcement. One kind of tension — the immediate safety of the trailer's interior — had subsided, but now the search of Trotter's place would begin. This part, though perhaps lacking in danger, ultimately carried bigger stakes from the task force's perspective. Their chance to nab a brutal serial killer — or rule Trotter out as a suspect — would play out here and now.

Darger set her jaw. Let her eyes flick over the dozen or so members of law enforcement still huddled in the driveway.

Go time.

All of the personnel waiting outside seemed to come unglued from their positions then. The swarm of techs, a couple of detectives, the deputies, and Darger and Loshak — everyone stirred, rising from the cars and SUVs they leaned against, all of them suited up already. Some spontaneous exodus pulled them out of the driveway and funneled them toward the door of the trailer.

Darger fell into the single file line, a CSI in front of her and Loshak just behind. They poured into the doorway like that, the open mouth of the trailer slurping them up.

Darger's heart glugged as she passed through the threshold. She couldn't help but gape at the wounded wood where the deadbolt had been ripped out of the strike plate. Something violent showed in the cratered bit of lumber.

That single file procession broke up as soon as they were inside, and all the pieces scattered.

The techs fanned out into the space to get to work, breaking up into smaller groups that went room to room, a couple already filming everything to document the process for the official record.

The detectives and deputies went their own way, somehow always looking like they were moving against the grain as they walked among the more orderly CSIs.

Darger found a clear spot along the kitchen counter and tucked herself into a kind of cove there, trying to stay out of the way of all the foot traffic. Loshak joined her, huddling close. It made her think back to her days of going to college parties, feeling awkward and out-of-place and trying to become one with the wall.

"So, what do you think?" Loshak said behind her, keeping his voice low. "Horror show or nothing burger?"

He grinned like a goofball. His face looked small encircled in the white vinyl of his suit, the fabric cutting off most of his forehead and part of his chin, somehow making him look like a weird beakless bird.

"What do you mean?"

"I mean, do we find something here or not? Are there grisly details lying in wait in one of these rooms? Is Trotter our guy? Or do we come up empty? Find nothing."

Darger watched through a doorway at the far end of the double-wide as one of the techs bagged the big hunting knife from the card table. They'd want to test that for blood as quickly as possible.

"I don't know," she said. "Aren't you the one who's all about letting the evidence dictate the narrative?"

Loshak's eyebrows crinkled against the vinyl.

"Well, yeah. Obviously. But I'm asking for your gut feeling. You usually have an instinct for these things. Seems like it's usually right, too."

Darger glanced around the place again as she thought about it, and signs that an actual human being lived here started jumping out at her one by one.

A kitten calendar adorned the wall just next to the fridge, the little tabby cat in this month's photo delighted to be tangled in pink yarn.

Mounted on the fridge door with a Pizza Hut magnet was a photograph of Trotter himself, beaming from the driver's seat of his truck.

A creepy painting of a hobo clown on black velvet hung in the living room. Big eyes and bigger mouth. Only slightly terrifying to Darger's aesthetic eye.

Under the TV, a few well-thumbed paperback novels filled a shelf — horror and suspense titles by Dean Koontz, Robert Bloch, Karin Slaughter, and Jack Ketchum sticking out at a glance.

Then she noticed the figurines near the books. More hobo clowns grinned like banshees, their odd postures and big shoes rendered in ceramic with brightly colored paint details.

A book of New York Times crossword puzzles sat on a coffee table, a pencil stuck in the middle like a bookmark.

She saw them everywhere she looked — reminders that this guy had interests, engaged in culture, even if he also maybe did awful things. Something about the quirks gave her goosebumps.

Loshak's questions replayed in her head.

Is Trotter our guy?

I'm asking for your gut feeling.

Horror show or nothing burger?

She searched her feelings. Tried to put all the jigsaw puzzle pieces together, figure some way to make everything fit.

"I don't know," she said, responding finally. "I really don't know."

A holler in the utility room snapped her head around that way. She sensed Loshak jump, startled into something of a short hop.

One of the techs was screaming his head off in the small room just off the kitchen, clearly excited about something, but she could only make out every fourth word or so.

She exchanged a glance with Loshak, and they headed that way. A throng of other bunny suits fell in behind them.

Darger peered around the corner first, eyes going wide at what lay in front of her.

The tech sat before an overturned hamper, dirty clothes cascading to the linoleum at his feet. Towels. Socks. Boxer briefs. A few t-shirts, most of them black or dark blue.

But it was the lone pair of jeans atop that pile that stood out from the rest. Splotches tinged the denim in uneven dark shapes, the nearly black smudges stark against the blue like continents on a globe.

Chuck Trotter's jeans were covered in blood.

CHAPTER 49

Darger stepped aside to let the others into the small laundry room, and the mass of white suits backed up behind her burst into the opening. A slew of bodies crammed through the doorway all at once, Tyvek suits crinkling and sliding against each other with swishing shower curtain sounds.

The lemming squad of techs flailed around the jeans, all aflutter at the sight of the blood. It looked like a bizarre ritual, something prehistoric. Strange, white-suited creatures circling a bloody altar, looks of awe contorting every face. Mass reverence.

Darger watched the faux ceremony through the doorway. Focused on her breathing. Steadied herself the best she could.

She found her heartbeat surprisingly even. Perhaps a little elevated but hardly approaching a gallop.

That was good. She wanted to keep her head here. She couldn't jump out ahead of the evidence — the concrete, definitive evidence.

Something still felt off about all of this. Something…

Loshak turned to look at her then from his place just inside the laundry room doorway. The smile plumping his cheeks faded as he read her expression. He quirked his head to the side.

"You're still not sold?"

"I don't know. Maybe."

Loshak trailed out of the laundry room, and the two of them returned to their out-of-the-way spot along the kitchen counter.

"What are you thinking?" he said, keeping his voice low.

"Just feels like there's still something I'm missing, I guess."

He held still for a second. Then a slow nod rocked his head up and down.

"I can see that. I mean, I think it looks pretty good at this point. We've got a blood smear on the door. A pair of blood-stained pants. But there's still a lot to sort out."

He seemed to watch her out of the side of his eye once he was done speaking, slow-blinking like an iguana.

Darger shoved off the lip of the countertop and wandered through the double-wide, moving away from the roiling excitement in the laundry room. She wanted to get a closer look at the living room, though she wasn't sure why.

A few Blu-ray cases sat next to the row of novels — an eclectic mix of movies on display here. Numerous Tom Cruise titles dominated the left side of the stack, ranging in popularity from *Top Gun* to *Cocktail.* The right side intertwined quirk with horror, *The Royal Tenenbaums*, *Evil Dead II, The Peanut Butter Falcon,* and John Carpenter's *Halloween,* among others.

Darger couldn't decide why she was focusing on these details. Why did Chuck Trotter's relationship with pop culture keep pulling her closer like a moth circling a bulb? She didn't think it could mean anything, for or against him.

Serial killers were fans of books, music, and movies just like anyone else. The history had been documented well enough.

John Wayne Gacy loved REO Speedwagon and Elton John.

Leonard Lake was obsessed with the John Fowles novel *The Collector.*

David Berkowitz, AKA the Son of Sam? Huge Hall & Oates fan.

BTK, Dennis Rader, sent a packet to police including the cover of the John Sandford novel *Rules of Prey.*

The Night Stalker, Richard Ramirez, was obsessed with AC/DC, and a piece of their merch eventually got him caught. He'd lost his AC/DC baseball cap in the chaos at one of the crime scenes, and it became evidence in his ultimate conviction.

Ted Bundy preferred talk radio to music.

Like we needed more proof that he was a psycho, Darger thought.

The list went on and on, and few knew it as well as Violet Darger. So… what?

She turned in a full circle, let her eyes drift over the trailer from one end to the other, trying to figure that out. Nothing came to her. No epiphany. No psychic impulse or gut feeling.

What was she looking for, really?

An identity.

Not his face or his name. She knew those already. The identity inside. Psychology, personality, philosophy, ideology. Whatever you wanted to call that mixed-up set of values and traits that drove a person's behavior.

She was scouring the home like maybe she could piece together a picture of who he really was from what lay on his bookshelf, sprawled on his coffee table, hung on his wall. But she knew it was nonsense.

His self would stay hidden within the walls of his skull, encased in bone, no matter what they found here today. Even if they pinned the murders on him, unearthed the evidence to prove it beyond a reasonable doubt, some of the specifics in Chuck Trotter's head would forever stay concealed there, perhaps hidden even from Trotter himself. It was, she thought, the reality for all of us.

She took a deep breath. Felt her ribcage swell as her lungs filled. Held the air inside.

Maybe it was time to tamp the paranoia down a bit. The evidence against Trotter was mounting.

So let it mount. Don't try to fight it.

If getting tunnel vision and making leaps without evidence was bad, wasn't preemptively doubting solid, physical evidence equally bad, in its own way?

Let it be. Go with the flow. Trust that the truth will come clear in the end, if you follow the information with an open mind, heart, and eyes.

She let the big breath out in a slow, even whoosh. Some kind of airiness crept over her as she did, a buoyant feeling in her head.

Camera flashes strobed in the laundry room doorway, where many of the techs still gathered. As Darger watched from a distance, some of the CSIs filtered out of the small room and went back to searching the rest of the double-wide.

The search would stretch on and on from here. More than likely, they'd be here for hours, but Darger felt open to whatever they would find now. The tension had fled her like the knots in her brain had come loose, the conflicted feelings replaced by a lightness, an ease.

She wandered toward the room with the card table and mounted antlers and stepped inside. There was one tech here, and Darger was careful to stay out of her way. The CSI was photographing everything, working her way around the space, opening every drawer in the desk, sliding back the slatted closet door, documenting it all.

Darger marveled at the antlers jutting out of the wood paneling, not fully understanding the urge to cut off the animal's horns and mount them bare. Taxidermy always made her think of *Psycho* even in the best of cases, but a stuffed deer head made a little more sense to her than the severed antlers here. Something ghastly about the slice of skull that connected the two sides, like a bone cup. Her shoulder blades shimmied as she stared at one.

She completed a lap around the perimeter of the room, took in another small shelf of thriller paperbacks, a few framed family photos that didn't look to be of this century, a desktop scattered with bills marked PAID in an all-caps scrawl, red ink. Then she found herself back at the doorway. Just when she was thinking that the master bedroom was the only room she hadn't gotten a look at yet, someone yelled from there.

"Got something!" a female tech's voice blared.

Darger ran that way, Loshak falling in beside her along the way. This time they were the last to arrive, stopping just outside the doorway and craning to get a glimpse past the crowded doorframe.

Someone had drawn the curtains, and boxes of golden light slanted over the blue carpet here. More wood paneling shot up the walls. A floral bedspread covered the queen-sized mattress, green stems and pink petals intertwining in an endless repeat. There was something so granny-ish about the pattern that it was hard for Darger to believe that Chuck Trotter, with his Popeye arms, actually slept here.

But what drew her eye lay just before the bed.

The techs all huddled around a metal toolbox with the lid hanging open, that astonishment once again smoothing all of their features as they gaped at the contents. Everyone in the bedroom held rigid, bodies taut.

Another ritual. Quiet this time. Motionless.

Darger stepped close and peered down into the shadows inside the box.

CHAPTER 50

The standard serial killer trophy stash formed a haphazard pile inside the small metal box at Darger's feet. She eyed what she could as the techs recorded the open box with both photo and video evidence. The CSIs wouldn't really dig in until they had what they needed in the can in terms of documenting the discovery of the toolbox.

Polaroids of women in distress lined the top of the pile. Wide eyes. Parted lips. Frightened expressions etched into the folds around the brows and the orbits of the eyes. Perhaps twenty such photos, by Darger's estimate, though there could be more tucked out of view.

A couple of photo IDs jutted out of the side of the stack. One from Vermont. Another from Georgia. It looked like there were more of these as well, but Darger couldn't be sure yet.

A class ring, too, bulged out of the pictures. A gaudy gold thing as chunky as something a mafia don might wear on his pinkie. Black bold lettering listed the graduating year — 2016.

Wads of lacy fabric tufted the bottom of the box. Lots of black and red. Some turquoise and one patch of purple clashed against the rest. Even with what little she could see, Darger knew what it was. Women's underwear.

Trophies. A box full of trophies.

It was like every item on the serial killer memento checklist could be marked off, all in one little box under Chuck Trotter's bed, barely out of plain sight.

She swallowed. Mouth gone dry. She shifted her weight from foot to foot, her boots squishing into the carpet.

"You're thinking it's too neat," Loshak said, as though plucking the words from Darger's head. "Too… convenient."

He stared at her, his face still framed in the circular cutout of the bunny suit. Something inquisitive blazed in his eyes, made him look less like a bird now and more like a cat.

"But it's kind of undeniable on some level, right?" she said. "I mean, this is beyond damning."

Darger thought about her choice of words. What kind of evidence was beyond damning? Definitive. Were they there yet? Maybe not, but it was getting awfully close.

She snapped her head around then, scanning the room anew. She started up high. Took in a rattan ceiling fan. A thrift store-salvaged dresser with a couple of black bottles of Axe Body Spray on top, flesh-toned gouges veining the dark wood. A nightstand with a John D. MacDonald paperback and an empty water glass. Another hobo clown painting ate up a chunk of the wall behind them, his white face stark against the black velvet canvas. This one wore a smile that could only be read as menacing.

"Another creepy clown painting. Cool," Loshak said in a deadpan.

After that, Darger's eyes swept lower. Blocky wood trimmed the mesh point where the floor and wall met. She traced the pale line along the floor until it butted into a large white vent with tilted slats like ribs. It looked like a cold air return for a furnace. Pretty nondescript.

Except…

Darger lurched into motion. Stumbled over the floor and knelt next to the vent. She peered through the gaps between the tines, seeing only shadows on the other side. Then she looked closer at the vent.

Screwdriver marks scuffed the places near the screws,

which had been painted white to match the vent but also looked to have been marked up some. The scrapes were minute. She wouldn't have noticed if she weren't looking specifically. Leaning in closer, she could see that one of the screws was loose, a sliver of silvery thread showing where it stuck out of the screw hole.

"What is it?" Loshak asked, behind her all at once.

She glanced back at him, saw his expression change as he focused in on the vent.

"This place is heated and cooled with these wall-mounted mini-splits, right?" she said, raising her arm and pointing at the HVAC unit on the wall. "No ductwork involved."

"So why the vent in the wall?" Loshak said.

"Exactly."

They called over one of the techs who snapped a few photos and then got down on his knees to unscrew the vent cover from the wall. The metal slid out of place with ease. One nitrile-gloved finger accidentally plucked a musical note out of one of the metal slats, sounded like some strange instrument between a banjo and a steel drum.

The rectangular cavity in the wall gaped, shadowed by the paneling around it. Darger could see, though, that there was no ductwork there, confirming that the vent cover was a decoy. This was a stash spot.

She swallowed again. Felt a little prickle crawl over her scalp like static electricity.

The CSI clicked on an LED penlight and brushed its beam into the hole. Naked lumber stared back. Studs and plywood. Pink floofs of fiberglass insulation had been shoved off to the sides to carve out the hiding spot.

After photographing the opening, the tech pulled out a stack of stickers of a clown face, and Darger gritted her teeth.

Jesus, enough with the clowns already.

The tech handed over five copies of the same sticker featuring a wrinkly clown face. Little teeth poked out of his big gums in an open-mouthed smile. Raccoon blackness encircled the eyes. Darger thought the image seemed familiar, but she couldn't place it.

"Have you seen this before?"

"What, the sticker?" Loshak said. He shook his head. "I don't think so. Why?"

"I don't know. I just thought—"

The CSI cleared his throat, which drew Darger's attention back to him. He swept his flashlight into the hidey hole, and they all gave it one last good look.

Nothing. Nothing there.

"Huh," Loshak said. "Well, that was an anticlimax."

"Yeah," Darger said.

That throb on her scalp died away all at once. Even after the tech had shrugged, clicked off his light, and moved on, Darger held still, staring into the empty hiding spot.

Behind her, the techs had started digging through the contents of the toolbox, laying out the Polaroids, licenses, and personal effects of countless victims. She turned to watch as they photographed the array in wide-angle shots — all the trophies spread over the blue shag carpet in the creepy killer's lair. This was the money shot, the one that would be blown up and mounted on a poster board as People's Exhibit #32 in Trotter's trial. It was almost like getting a few hundred kilos of drugs laid out on the table for a photo op after a major drug bust, Darger thought.

The techs fired off photo after photo, making sure they had multiple angles, a multitude of media-ready shots. Only then would they get in close to document each and every item individually, a tedious slog that would take time.

Darger walked closer. Examined the photos. She recognized a few of the faces from the files — these were their murder victims all right. But there were more. Additional women, and she knew what that meant. More bodies waiting out there to be found.

She let her gaze fall on the toolbox sitting there next to the bed. Empty now. A hollow shell with its mouth hanging open, as though shocked to be discovered and plundered so.

Then she looked back at the stash spot where the phony vent cover had been, her eyebrows lifting. She turned her head back and forth a couple times.

Box.

Hiding spot.

Box.

Hiding spot.

"So… I'm thinking our hiding spot behind the vent is about the right size to house the treasure chest toolbox," she said.

Loshak was nodding along even before she'd finished.

"We can have the techs measure to be sure, but yeah. Just eyeballing it, it looks about right."

"So here's my question," Darger went on. "What are the odds that we would have missed it?"

Loshak squinted.

"You mean, had the toolbox been back in that little hidey hole?" He pooched out his bottom lip. "I mean, it's certainly possible. The vent cover was a clever enough ploy, and it looked natural. Had you not spotted it, I think it could have been overlooked."

"So then why was the toolbox practically out in the open?"

Loshak's squint intensified. But a voice behind them interrupted before he could answer.

"Not to stick my nose where it don't belong," Jenkins said, "but the interior of Trotter's truck is visible in several of the shots of the girls."

He pointed at three of the Polaroids laid out next to the portrait of Trotter from his fridge. There was no doubt about it. That was definitely Trotter's truck in the photographs.

"And look at this one here."

Jenkins held up one of the Polaroids, and Darger took it from him.

The girl in the photo looked familiar. It took Darger a second to place Debra Smith. In the personal photos she'd seen, even in the victim's driver's license photo, the woman had always been smiling. White teeth on full display. The corner of her eyelids crinkled. Cheeks puffed up into two balls of rising dough.

Here in the Polaroid, Smith's expression was all too grave. A slackness pulled her cheeks down, and her lips dipped at the edges. Her eyes were big and clear and opened wide in terror.

Darger blinked a few times, staring at the photo, her gaze drawn back to those frightened eyes every time she tried to look away. Finally, she pried her eyes away from the victim and saw what Jenkins had meant her to see.

The man's hand jutted into the foreground of the photo where he had a hold of the girl's wrist in what looked like a death grip. Yanking. It was clear by the angle that the hand belonged to the photographer. Immediately Darger felt what he must have felt.

That hand lurching out like a striking snake. Grabbing her arm. Squeezing the tiny bones in her wrist. Wrenching her around for the photo.

Smile for the camera, honey.

The pop of the flash. The bright light bursting between

them. The image captured here, her terror captured here, forever, and spat out the mouth of the camera as his souvenir.

Darger blinked hard and broke the spell. She locked in on that important detail once more, that little black swirl in the center of the photo, and then she handed the photo back.

There was no doubt now. No doubt at all.

Darger thought back to that strange moment in the interrogation room with Chuck Trotter. The smiling doofus sat across the table from her with something childish in his eyes, not quite innocent and not quite sinister. During an awkward silence, he'd turned his hands up on the chipped laminate tabletop, a gesture as though to ask, "Anything else?" And in those two seconds, she'd seen it there — the little black anchor inked into the creamy flesh of his inner arm.

The man's forearm in the photo had the same tattoo.

CHAPTER 51

Chuck Trotter's voice sounded unnaturally deep pumping through the speakers in Deputy Bedard's cruiser. The two deputies sat in the front with Darger and Loshak crammed into the backseat, all of them focusing on that singular source of stimulus — Trotter's words pouring through the stereo.

With the volume up so loud, every detail in the trucker's speech came clear, every little rasp and lilt and juicy lip noise cooing right in their ears. It felt like he was sitting in the car with them, which made Darger uneasy. She couldn't decide if it was that or the blasting air conditioning that had puckered goosebumps onto the flesh of her arms.

"Any word on what's causing traffic to back up on I-95, northbound?" Trotter said. "I'm just past exit 166. Over."

Another voice answered him almost immediately.

"That you, Trotsky? It's Sebas," a husky voice said, something different and folksier in the southern accent at play here. Maybe Alabama, Darger thought. "We've got a full-blown clusterfuck of an accident up here. Little Ford hatchback just about exploded. Front end all burst outward, bits of it strewn everywhere like confetti, and then the son of a bitch caught on fire. Still smokin' and everything. Black as squid ink. Ran into a pickup truck that got pretty fucked up its ownself. Possibly one or the other was going the wrong way on the freeway is what I figure. It's that bad. Gonna be a scrape job for the driver of the hatchback, too. Poor bastard."

Trotter's response seemed too cheerful given the nature of the conversation. He purred into the CB mic like a pleased kitten.

"Really, I say the folks who gotta clean it up are the poor bastards. Peeling melted roadkill off the asphalt in *this* heat? Uh-uh. No thank you, sir. Good to hear from you, though, Sebas. Sounds like we're heading the same way. I'll be stopping off at the Champion just outside of Chesterfield tonight. Care to meet up for a few beers and/or laughs? Or a lot of beers and a lot of laughs?"

Sebas chuckled a smoker's wheeze into the mic.

"Hell, when you put it like that, how can a guy say no?"

The background static of the radio cut out, and Bedard tapped his finger on his phone.

"That's the end of the recording," the deputy said. "Agent Zhang, who is following Trotter now, forwarded the file to me. She says it was recorded about twenty minutes ago."

"How'd they manage to record it?" Loshak asked.

"If you can believe it, she held her damn phone right up to the speaker on the CB," Jenkins added from the passenger seat, his eyes so bright they almost struck Darger as manic. "Crazy how damn good an iPhone microphone is, huh? Technology is frickin' bonkers."

Loshak sat forward in his seat, just about sticking his face up to the cage cordoning the back of the cruiser from the front.

"So we know where Trotter is headed, and we can intercept him. How far is he from his destination?"

Bedard's phone blipped, and he read a text while Jenkins answered Loshak.

"Couple hundred miles," Jenkins said. "And given the traffic situation, they think we'll have at least three hours to work with. Possibly more. Sheriff's on the horn as we speak with the Jersey field office. They're coordinating with the task force to set up a roadblock to nab Trotter. The exit leading to the truck stop he mentioned will make the perfect bottleneck."

"What about this Sebas he's talking to?" Darger said. "Any word on who that might be?"

"They're tracking him down through the dispatchers at the various trucking companies we've been in touch with. I don't figure he'll be difficult to pin down if his given name truly is Sebastian, first or last. Not too many of those running around, you know?"

Bedard held up his phone then and waggled it back and forth.

"In the meantime, we just got orders to get y'all to the airport in Raleigh," he said. "You've just won an all-expenses-paid trip to a truck stop in beautiful suburban New Jersey, and if you act now, we'll throw in that set of steak knives."

Jenkins shook his head.

"You see what I'm dealing with?" he said. "Duke fan."

CHAPTER 52

The flight from Raleigh to Philly took one hour and four minutes from gate to gate. Darger hadn't flown on a full-sized chartered jet all that many times, and she found the experience strange, somehow over-stimulating, even with the plane virtually loaded with the familiar faces of members of the task force.

She drank a ginger ale once they hit max altitude, and Loshak whipped out two packets of those bright orange crackers sandwiched around stale peanut butter, one sleeve for each of them. The combo settled her stomach and her nerves, as it usually did.

It seemed like every time they flew, Loshak was foisting the orange crackers on her. She considered that for a moment, and her eyes narrowed.

"Wait. We didn't know we'd be flying when we set out this morning. Do you always have these crackers on your person, in like a secret pocket, or what? Do you travel with a case of them?"

Loshak gave her a faint smile as he chewed, orange crumbs dotting his lips.

"A gentleman never reveals his secrets."

He shoved another neon orange square into his mouth while maintaining eye contact, his mannerisms somehow delicate and prissy in a way that seemed amusing.

When the plane touched down, they didn't dally, darting down the jet bridge and into the sunny confines of Philadelphia International. They survived the throngs of congestion mobbing the various terminals and fled the building in a walk that approached a jog. Detective Bledsoe directed traffic from there, calling out orders and pointing two fingers here and there in a way that reminded Darger of an executive chef ruling over a bustling restaurant kitchen.

Most of the task force headed for a fleet of black SUVs waiting in a row in a lot just across the street from the building. A Mercer County Sheriff's cruiser sat just beyond the glass doors leading out to the parking lot, one Deputy Alvin Spells out of the car and ready to whisk Darger and Loshak some 46 miles northeast to the Champion Travel Stop in Chesterfield Township, New Jersey.

Spells was burly and dark-skinned with bright eyes and a neat salt and pepper beard of hard angles. After he flagged them down, he introduced himself quickly, shook both their hands, and then gestured toward the back of the cruiser. Darger sensed great excitement in his body language, especially as he lunged back into the driver's seat, a type of enthusiasm which she appreciated.

"We're the ones getting escorted?" Loshak said, almost under his breath. "Jeez. Are we getting the VIP treatment?"

Darger scoffed.

"You think riding in the back of a cruiser instead of an SUV is the VIP treatment? You know drunks piss in the backs of these things. Like all the time. A police cruiser is basically just the mobile toilet that carts you to the drunk tank, as far as the drunk and disorderly are concerned. The rental place probably just ran out of SUVs or something, and the Bureau didn't want us showing up to the scene in a minivan or hatchback or whatever, so they arranged alternate transport. Anything not in the FBI standard black would be unbecoming of a federal agent, after all."

They climbed in then, and Darger thought she detected a faint acidic smell. Sharp. Not a urine stench necessarily, but… what else could it be? She looked at Loshak, and his shoulders sagged, whole upper body shriveling like a deflating balloon.

"Fine. You win. We're riding in the pee cart. Happy?"

"What's that you say?"

The interrupting old man voice came from the passenger seat, where another deputy's head wheeled around, fleshy and round like a jack-o'-lantern set atop the shoulders of a White man in his late 50s. The twin white caterpillars of his eyebrows leapt up his forehead, leathered skin perpetually crinkling around his eyes, like his whole face was a flexing baseball mitt.

"Uh. Nothing," Loshak said, leaning back in his seat as the cruiser swept into traffic.

"Uh-hah," the deputy said, his pronunciation of the word funny and loud. "Well, I'm Deputy Wilcox. I've heard all about you Feeb profilers, believe me, so I'm pleased to meet ya."

"Likewise," and, "Same," Darger and Loshak said over each other.

"Me and Spellsy, we'll get you up to that truck stop in no time. My partner, he's a real good driver. Fast, you know? Well, no. I take that back. Maybe not that good. But definitely fast."

Spells chuckled at that, and then they swerved up a looping entrance ramp onto the freeway, all four of their heads and shoulders leaning just a little to the right as the car swooped. The blinker tick-tocked a few nervous heartbeats. Then they merged into traffic and the ride smoothed out some.

"We've got over two hours yet until the suspect will be incoming," Spells said, those bright eyes meeting Darger's in the rearview. "We'll get you two there in plenty of time. Hell, I'm excited to see the festivities myself. I've been at this gig thirteen years, and I've seen a lot, more than a lot, but I've never seen anything quite like what we're talking about here. A roadblock to stop a truck-driving serial killer. That's some kind of spectacle, you know?"

"Should have popped some kettle corn," Wilcox said. "In case things get lively. Hopefully for him more than us, of course. Heh. Heh."

As promised, Deputy Spells drove like a maniac, weaving in and out of lanes and somehow seeming to gain speed the whole time. His moves, though aggressive, felt confident to Darger. Something assured in them. She still gripped the handhold next to the door handle the whole time, but not that hard.

The cruiser chewed up the highway — a rocket, silver as a beer can, hurtling toward Chesterfield Township where the truck stop lay in wait. The mile markers throbbed along the side of the freeway like a blinking light. With Spells shaving minutes off what should have been almost an hour-long drive, they'd be there in no time.

"You think we got assigned to the pee cart on purpose?" Loshak whispered, leaning close to Darger. "Like an intentional diss?"

"What? Twenty minutes ago, you thought we were getting the big shot treatment."

"Well, I've been convinced otherwise, haven't I? Anyway, a rift between interdepartmental agencies like that, say a beef between CIRG and the BAU? That'd be something, wouldn't it? Seems plausible enough to me."

Darger just stared at him for several seconds.

"Agent Loshak, please try to deal in reality."

CHAPTER 53

Half a dozen police cruisers flanked the sides of the exit ramp. Their drivers milled nearby, waiting for the go-ahead to roll the roadblock into place.

It was just getting dark. The sun sank in the distance, and a creeping shadow spread over the land from the opposite horizon. It looked to like a gloomy puddle washing over the fields and roads.

She adjusted the binoculars as she swept them across the scene, fine-tuning the focus. She tried to read signs in the body language of the officers hanging around the cars, hoping to ease her own mounting anticipation.

Instead, she perceived only max tension in the air around the cops. Twitchy mouths and shoulders. Fidgety fingers. Everyone nervous. Everyone waiting.

She and Loshak sat in the truck stop lot, watching the roadblock from a distance of perhaps 150 yards. Both had a pair of 'nocs up to their eyeballs. He munched from a bag of Combos — pepperoni pizza-flavored — fingers fishing into the crinkly bag and shoving pretzels home without ever looking away from the site of the impending spectacle, almost like he was watching a movie instead of a real-life police operation.

Darger swung the binoculars away from the police, tracing up the exit ramp behind them to survey the setup again. She was impressed with how well the ramp would work at blocking off Trotter's view. Between the hill and the overpass, he wouldn't see the police until he was three quarters into the curling ramp lane, and by then, there'd be no way back. They were fortunate that such a good bottleneck had fallen into their laps, assuming all went to plan.

The steady crunch of Loshak's snacking cut out then, the sudden lack of sound somehow ominous like the chirping of crickets going silent in a dark alley. Then the agent gasped a little.

"It's happening," he whispered, and Darger could somehow hear the flecks of half-chewed pretzel caught in his throat. "He must be getting on the exit now."

She jerked, swiveled her binoculars back just in time to see the cops at the roadblock burst into motion.

Bodies lurched. Doors slammed. Taillights flared bright, tinting the asphalt red.

The cars rolled into place to cut off the roadway. Four cruisers set on diagonals formed a tight formation toward the center of the lane, with the other two cruisers each cutting off the shoulder on either side, the outside cars at hard ninety-degree angles relative to the flow of traffic. Altogether it looked pretty formidable.

While the cars were being parked, a couple of officers about fifty feet in front of the roadblock tossed spike strips over the asphalt. Enough to span the entire lane.

The flashers came to life then. Red and blue lights glowing and twirling over everything.

The police in the cruisers climbed out then and took position behind the opened driver's side doors of each of the vehicles. Guns drawn. Ready to point out at the empty lane ahead of them.

The inside of the car suddenly seemed deathly quiet. Made it feel like they were watching a silent movie. Darger licked her lips.

She heard it before she saw it. The drone of the diesel

engine changed pitch as the semi shifted gears in the distance, growing louder as it drew near.

And then the big rig coiled around the ramp. The blocky front end appeared there, headlights cutting into the dusky light of the late evening.

The truck seemed to hesitate as it got closer. Looked like a nervous animal slowing, sniffing.

The cops braced themselves against their opened doors, hunched one by one, and extended their guns before them, arms resting on the wedge of the roof and the door.

The whole scene seemed to take a strange breath, the semi's headlights bobbing in the distance, the night flexing around them as it prepared to unfold.

The engine roared louder then. Trotter picked up speed. Barreled forward.

"Jesus, he's going for it," Loshak murmured.

Darger adjusted the binoculars. Watched the truck grow blurry and then sharpen into focus. She saw the dark line at the bottom of her field of vision where the spike strip lay.

He rushed for it. Bore down on it. Faster, faster. Either unafraid or unaware of the prickly obstacle in his path.

The front tires exploded when they hit the spike strip, a pair of audible blasts heard even at a distance. The truck kept going, tires popping one after another until the black tatters spinning around the rims caught and rolled the spike strip over and out of the way.

The semi careened. Danced over the asphalt. Flitted left and then right on shredded tires as though the wind were batting it around.

But it kept going. Hurtling forward. Not really slowing.

The truck jackknifed. The tractor lodged to the left. Pinched against the trailer on an angle.

Still the forward momentum kept on. Plunged it straight down the single lane like a bowling ball. Tattered tires flinging scraps of rubber everywhere.

Darger stared into the binoculars unblinking. Felt a little breath shiver against her bottom lip.

The semi's length became hard to fathom — a missile launched at the roadblock. The weight of the trailer behind it making it a giant battering ram.

Twelve tons of metal headed for the line of cop cars. The big bang became inevitable. A matter of seconds.

Three.

A couple gunshots rang out, sounding pinpoint small against the angry growl of the diesel engine.

Then the police all fluttered out from behind their cars. Exploding away like spooked pigeons bursting off a power line.

The officers dove for the edges of the asphalt. Hurled themselves into the drainage ditch, tumbling down the slope and rolling into the muck at the bottom one after another.

Two.

The truck's course seemed to steady into a hard line. A final stiffening. Bracing for impact. It looked like a strong safety lining up to launch himself helmet-first into some shrimpy wide receiver's chin, delivering the concussion protocol blow.

One.

Darger winced. Clinched her upper arms against the sides of her ribcage. Kept her eyes open.

The truck slammed into the two center cruisers with an incredible crash, violence ringing over the night. The cab bucked once as it connected, something virile in its body language. And then everything seemed to shatter around it.

The police cars burst out of the way. Thrown back in a surge like plastic toys caught in a wave lapping up on the beach.

The front end of the truck exploded into shards. Metal shredding. Twisting outward from the exposed engine block.

Somehow it was the most aggressive thing Darger had ever seen.

Sparks burst from the bare rims now, the front tires long gone. Naked metal ground grooves into the asphalt, all of it bedazzled in glittering orange flecks.

The motor moaned once — a deep sigh, something mournful in it. The pitch shifted into something lower, clunkier. A death rattle. And then the drone of the diesel engine guttered out.

Quiet. Empty.

Still the semi scraped forward. Stubborn. Its full length skidded through the roadblock, and then it coasted to a stop in the intersection beyond.

The whole thing almost seemed to settle further down once it stopped. A wounded animal hunching, curling itself into something smaller.

Black smoke fluttered from the broken place where the hood used to be. Liquid tendrils rising and curling.

The scene otherwise held still. Eerily silent. Motionless.

Holy shit.

Darger swung the binoculars to the truck's windshield. Scanned the dark glass. Looked for any sign of movement in the shadows there.

Nothing.

Nothing.

And then the driver's side door lurched to life. The blue sheet of metal hiccupped once and angled into the night.

Chuck Trotter flung himself into the open. Plopped down to the road in a Spiderman pose. He hopped up and sprinted for the truck stop, legs jittering, a bolting rabbit.

He leapt the ditch between the road and the compound. Shinnied up the chain-link fence like a spider monkey. Legs looping over the top and folding beneath his bulk as he hit down on the opposite side.

He picked himself up again and loped toward the sprawling dark before him. One leg hitched now, his gait uneven.

Three paces later, his silhouette melted into the endless rows of semis cluttering the lot.

CHAPTER 54

Darger lurched out of the car, feet clopping over the asphalt. She listed hard to her left and then got her balance, picked her knees up higher as she darted in a straight line, building speed.

She sprinted for the shadowy gaps between the rows of trucks ahead. Gun drawn. Eyes sharp. She could feel Loshak alongside her more than she saw him, some little flicker of darkness throbbing out of the corner of her eye.

She tore over the parking lot. Saw the asphalt blur past underfoot, the textured flecks of rock and macadam scrolling, scrolling, almost black now as the light fled the sky.

That wall of semi-trailers loomed ahead, seeming to grow as she drew closer. The mostly white boxes glowed a purple hue in the dusky light, a little gauzy around the edges.

And she could see the other police swarming the lot, too. Perhaps a dozen in dark uniforms. Guns out. Arms and legs pumping. Voices barking a mess of commands and bursts of radio chatter she couldn't understand.

They hit the back lot in a wave, and everyone fanned out. Splaying into the rows. Disappearing into the dark places between the trucks.

Darger held her breath as she entered the labyrinth of trailers. The gloom enveloped her, darkness shrouding all of her in that purple murk.

She slowed to a jog. Footsteps softer now. Quiet. Her heart hammered in her chest, each beat thrumming up into her neck, into her head, thumping like a timpani in her temples.

The frenzied chatter seemed to have cut out at once. All

held quiet now with just the buzz of the lamps somewhere overhead adding a sizzle of white noise to the procession.

A single diesel engine grumbled somewhere off to the right, faintly audible as she moved among the seemingly endless line of trucks. Sounded stark, almost lonely.

She slowed further, creeping now. Head swiveling in search of the faintest twitch or flutter in the shadows. Her eyes adjusted as she advanced, details drawing sharp even in the half-light.

Loshak was gone, she realized. Probably stalking the next row over.

She inched up to the back of the first trailer, that thrum of blood in her head intensifying, the drumbeat galloping faster and faster. Electricity lurched and spit and itched behind her eyeballs.

She wheeled around the corner. Thrust her Glock into the empty space. Swept the muzzle all the way around.

Nothing.

Vacant.

She kept going. Scampered on to the next row. The tip of her tongue pressed hard against the roof of her mouth like it was trying to hold it in place.

Her thoughts spun out nonsense fragments. Pounded out words that didn't accumulate. Her mind somehow working hard and getting nowhere like a gerbil spinning on its wheel inside her head. Sprinting in place.

Something stirred in the shadows next to her. The darkness rippled like the surface of a lake.

Darger froze. Gaped. That itch behind her eyes grew frantic, thrashing.

The truck door to her left jiggled. Gave off a click just louder than parting lips. The metal panel swung open slowly.

Darger squared her shoulders and lifted her Glock with a shaky arm.

CHAPTER 55

The trucker climbed down from the truck in slow motion. He looked like a sloth descending from his tree, one hand gripping the steel loop of the grab handle, his back to Darger as he stepped onto the first foot rail and then the second. The whole process was soundless save for the tiniest aluminum ping as each foot touched down.

Darger crept forward. Lined the Glock up with his back, center mass. She felt a bead of sweat weep from the corner of her brow and sluice down to her jaw.

Her eyes pinched to slits. He was right there at the end of her gun, gliding to within arm's length and totally unaware of her presence.

There was only one problem.

It wasn't Chuck Trotter.

A man with skinny limbs and a little potbelly descended before her — a bystander in the wrong place at the wrong time. Strands of greasy hair trailed out of the mesh of his ball cap and snaked over the back of his neck.

Darger's molars clenched, jaw muscles trembling around them. Then she hissed at him.

"Get back in the truck."

He wheeled his head hard to the side.

"Huh?"

"FBI. Get back in the truck. Now."

He disobeyed the order. Lowered himself to the asphalt and turned the rest of the way around. His voice went whiny.

"But I'm all out of scratch-offs."

"Back inside. Now," she said through gritted teeth.

He glanced down then, his eyes bugging out when they landed on her Glock, which was now angled at the ground. He blinked twice, shoulders jerking back as Darger moved the gun.

"Aw, hell," he muttered.

He started back up the pair of steps on the side of the truck, suddenly moving much faster than any sloth. The door clicked shut behind him, and his shadow stared out the driver's side window, the dome bulb lighting his head from behind.

Darger took two breaths, and then she hustled on. Pivoted around another corner, pointing the Glock into the gloom once more.

Movement there. Liquid shapes shifting in the darkness.

She lifted her gun a few degrees to line up the shot. Steadied her arms and her breathing. Something cold prickled over her scalp.

But it was another cop. One of the uniforms from the roadblock, bulked up with body armor. She'd watched him through the binoculars, recognized him by the bristly top of his buzz cut as much as anything.

He gave her a look, eyes snapping from hers to the Glock and back again. He jerked his head in a single nod when she lowered her weapon.

Then he moved on. Broad frame disappearing beyond the next semi.

Darger inched forward in her own aisle. That lone grumbling engine in the distance cut out, clinked a few times, and then held quiet. Thoughts pounded through her head now along with pulse.

Part of her wondered if anyone here would let Trotter into their truck. Try to hide him. That'd complicate the search.

They'd be aiding and abetting a serial killer. Obstruction of justice on multiple counts of felony murder. Way too high a price for any reasonable person to pay, but…

He'd been planning to meet someone here, and he seemed to have friends everywhere. Darger pictured his grinning face across the table from her in the interrogation room, like a gregarious child's.

Whoever he was talking to on the CB. That'd be a good starting point, if they had to search truck by truck. The earlier CB conversation gave them probable cause.

They had the ally's name, she thought, or at least a strong suspicion of a name. *Sebas* was what Trotter had called him on the radio. Sebastian… something. Darger's mind whirred, trying to remember the last name Detective Bledsoe had mentioned on the flight.

But the sharp crack of a gunshot off to her left disrupted the thought.

CHAPTER 56

Darger didn't hesitate. She ran toward the sound of the gun shots. Zigzagged deeper into the lot.

The sound came from somewhere in the back corner of the vast rectangular parking area. And more shots rang out even now, metallic thunder cracking open the night, the slightly different pitches and rhythms telling her plenty even if she couldn't see anything yet.

A gunfight.

A gunfight in a truck stop parking lot in New Jersey.

Jesus Christ.

She tried to block the next words, but the voice in her head wouldn't be denied.

Chuck Trotter's last stand, then.

Does he think he can shoot his way out?

Or is death by cop what he wants deep down?

A shiver crawled over the skin of her back, made her stomach wriggle.

Her feet still pattered at the asphalt, gritting and pounding, long strides propelling her forward. She zipped past row after row of trailers, the hulking boxes whooshing by in pulses on both sides.

And the sun was gone all at once. Sucked down into the horizon now. The last glimmer swallowed by the hungry night.

The shadows swelled to cover everything even as she ran. Creeping over the pale walls of the trailers. Suffocating everything in their murk.

The filmy glow of the streetlights didn't touch the back of

the lot. They left it to the gloom.

Darger ran for the darkness, took that headlong plunge into the abyss as she had so many times. She wasn't alone this time, but it sure felt that way for the moment.

She sprinted up the back row. Swallowed hard as she crossed that barrier into deepest shadow.

She saw a pair of cops there. Two Kevlar-vested shapes ducking behind the back of one of the trailers.

One of the officers leaned out with his gun. Fired two shots, orange light flitting at the end of his arm.

The gunshots barked, splitting the night. The bullets *thuff*ed funny in the distance, where they hit something Darger couldn't see.

The sounds echoed off the blacktop, off the metal walls of the semi-trailers around them. Vibrating sharpness that fluttered everywhere. Echoes wavering like the peals of a struck gong.

Then the cop ducked back into cover. Huddled behind the rearmost wheel well of the trailer.

When she got up alongside them, she saw what they saw.

Trotter had taken cover in the back corner of the lot. Maybe fifty feet beyond them. He was squatting behind a concrete divider along the fence, his big bulk just visible there when he moved.

He jerked upright while Darger was watching, rising from the shadows, his eyes two gleaming black spots in the gray smear of his face. Wet spots that disappeared for a second when he blinked.

But it was him, that was for sure.

Then she saw the gun in his hand. A 9mm leaping up. Jerking twice. Flame snorting out of the muzzle.

She heard the whoosh of the bullets coming for her. The air

disturbed by the projectiles, whistling and sucking.

And she ducked into cover.

CHAPTER 57

Darger stayed down. Upper back pressed against the trailer's back tire. The thick axle probably offered the best cover here, angling a slice of steel between her and the trucker's gun.

More shots rang out. Peppered the asphalt. Skipping through mud puddles with hissing, sloshing sounds.

A ricochet whizzed up off the blacktop and shuddered past. The air shivered around it. Too close.

He's aiming low. Skipping 'em in like stones across the top of a pond.

It was smart of him. Their position was weak, with nothing but the rubber of the tires offering cover just along the ground.

Darger peered down at the pair of wheels she leaned up against. The steel rims offered decent protection, a piece of concave armor almost like a helmet for her ribcage, but the dark donuts beyond that provided only thin layers of rubber, hardly any defense. At least there were two tires there, the dual rear wheels doubling up on the flimsy coverage.

As if on cue, Trotter fired off three more blasts, and one of the bullets punched the inner tire. It hissed as it deflated. Lisping sibilance. Sagging.

Someone was yelling then in the next row over. Darger peeked under the trailer, chin cranked back over her right shoulder.

Another trio of police had set up behind one of the other trucks. One of them had a bullhorn pressed to his mouth, telling Trotter to surrender, the officer's voice distorted as it propelled through the cone-shaped speaker.

"Throw the gun into the open and get down on your belly with your hands over your head."

The gunfire ceased all at once, those words seeming to hang in the air. Both sides waiting now, wanting to see what would happen next.

Darger leaned back toward the edge of the tire facing the concrete divider where Trotter hid. She took a breath and peered out that way again.

The big trucker was nowhere to be seen, ducked back behind his cement wall. Even his shadow was no longer apparent there.

The cop manning the bullhorn waited a few breaths before he went on.

"This can't go on for long, Trotter. Not with you alive. You're pinned down and low on ammo, son. Give it up."

All held still for a beat.

Quiet.

Tense.

Trotter bobbed up again. Gun jerking his hand.

More gunshots. Both ways.

Darger fired off a few rounds, the Glock bucking against the web of her palm. There was something satisfying about the feel of the recoil, the clear sense that violence was being dealt from the barrel of her gun.

But Trotter was quick, bobbing and weaving in and out of cover. All of Darger's shots went over the cement barrier while he was down, piercing the empty space where he'd been a second earlier.

Muzzle flares strobed the scene. Orange flickers bursting and sparkling everywhere. Incandescent.

Bullets thwacked into the concrete in front of the trucker. New holes pocking the pale gray surface. Perforations that kicked up little clouds of powder that roiled like smoke in the orange blasts of light.

Trotter disappeared again. Going down funny all at once. Something arched in his back that reminded Darger of a sewer rat skulking back into a storm drain.

Something… limp?

The scene held still again. All eyes narrowed on that sheet of concrete now pitted like an acne-scarred face.

Then the yelling started.

"Is he hit? Who has eyes on him?"

"Dude got popped."

"I think I got him! Yes sir, I think I did."

Nothing stirred behind the cement barrier. No sound, no movement.

Darger's breath was shallow. Thin and whistling between her teeth. Her face felt flushed and warm and strangely heavy like it was an IV bag full of hot fluid.

She could only stare at that shadowy corner where Trotter must be, eyes scanning all the details endlessly.

That thick slab of concrete. The post behind it where the two sheets of chain-link fence met.

He was already penned in a cell in a way, she realized. Would he end up in another one after this? Or was it already too late?

A couple of the flak-jacketed officers from the roadblock crew crept out into the open, that bristly buzz cut moving out in front. They pointed their guns at the little shelf of concrete now scarred with tiny craters.

They drew up on the barrier in slow motion. Silent. Staying low. Bent at the knees, at the waist. Combat boots stepping with care.

The silence was electric after all the gunshots. Hollow and

strange. Somehow empty and brimming with tension at the same time.

Buzz Cut stopped in his tracks. Brought a fist up. The other officer froze behind him.

They stood there. Stock still. Chests inflating and deflating slightly out of time with each other's.

Then Trotter bobbed up again and blasted.

CHAPTER 58

It all happened at once.

Trotter's gunshot cracked. Echoed funny off the concrete in front of him.

Orange light washed over half the trucker's face in a flash. Cast thick shadows under his brow and along one side of his nose and jaw. His lips parted a quarter of an inch, and he had the tip of his tongue clenched between his teeth in concentration.

The buzz cut cop took the bullet square in the chest. He stood up straighter, shoulders pinching against the sides of his neck. Then he staggered back a couple of steps and twisted to the side.

But his vest took the brunt of it. Darger could see it. The coppery glint of the shell mushroomed on his Kevlar like a smashed penny on a railroad track.

He brought his free hand to the place where the bullet had pounded him in the ribs. And he made choked little sucking sounds like he couldn't breathe, his lips wiggling around his teeth, flecks of spit flying everywhere.

The other cop darted forward as that played out. He stomped toward Trotter, legs coming out of their crouch to push him up to his full height.

The gun thrust at the end of his bent arm. The hunk of metal jutted from his hand.

His bicep bulged. Forearm flexing.

He squeezed the trigger.

And the gun barked. Shrill. It snorted metal and flame.

He squeezed again. Again.

The trucker ducked, upper body folding up like an accordion. But he wasn't quick enough this time.

The first round pierced Trotter's neck. A clean red hole punched there in the front.

A jagged venting of meat erupted where the exit wound tore out the back. The trauma was ragged, a missing puzzle piece torn from the side of his neck. A sheet of blood pulsed in the place where his throat had just been.

Trotter let out a big breath. Gurgled where the bullet had opened him up.

The next two bullets speared the trucker's forehead. Poked twin holes in the flesh, each ringed with a froth of blood on impact.

The rounds exited the back of his head, shattered the crockery of his skull on their way out. Shards of bone coming free like tectonic plates, the rounded dome coming undone.

Trotter grunted once. Eyes flickering, flickering. Staring at nothing.

And then he fell behind the concrete wall, limp body flopping like a felled tree. He landed face down.

CHAPTER 59

Red and blue lights twirled over the asphalt, glowing stains flitting over the ground and the sides of the trailers. Darger walked among the motes, her own footsteps somehow loud in her ears, even in the bustle of the scene.

Officer Buzz Cut — the one who'd taken a bullet in the vest — sat just inside the back doors of an ambulance. A couple of EMTs poked and prodded at his chest, and it wasn't until Darger got close that she could see what they were looking at.

The kidney-shaped bruise just beneath his left nipple looked like a purpled blotch on a Doppler weather map. It wrapped partially around his side from there, as if the jet stream might blow the storm over onto his back.

To Darger, it appeared more like the work of taking a Nolan Ryan fastball in the chest than anything a tiny slug of metal could possibly do. She could still picture the coppery flattened thing adhered to his vest, so much smaller than the dark mark it'd left behind in his skin.

Buzz Cut winced and sucked wind as a nitrile-gloved finger pressed into the center of the purple blot. Then he caught Darger's eye and laughed a little bit.

"Broke two ribs," he said, giving the barest of shrugs. Then he smiled bigger.

Darger tilted her head. She read the nameplate on the balled-up shirt lying next to one of his hands.

"So… is that smile embarrassed or proud, Harris?"

He hissed out another laugh, harder this time, and then he flinched again and cupped a hand just shy of the abrasion on his chest.

"Both, I think. Jesus, don't make me chuckle like that. It fucking kills."

Darger nodded and moved on, pressing deeper into the throng. Police still swarmed the lot, some out among the trucks, others here in the partitioned parking area closer to the building.

The lemming squad of techs was back, streaming everywhere in single-file lines, just like they had earlier in the day at Trotter's lair. Black-suited agents stalked the grounds, talking into walkie-talkies and somehow looking vaguely supervisory even if they never seemed to be doing anything of consequence — a couple even wore their sunglasses despite it being full dark out.

Total commitment to the federal agent stereotype.

A variety of blue and brown uniforms also waddled about, representing two sheriff's departments and the local PD. All of them had a little pep in their step, shoulders back and chests out, or so Darger thought, and that made sense in her opinion. They'd gotten their man, hadn't they? And they hadn't lost anyone in the process of taking him down, either. A win-win. High fives all around.

Once again, the lookie-loos gathered just beyond the sawhorse barrier that formed an orange line in the middle distance. Onlookers smoked cigarettes and gawked at the procession of police. They looked more or less identical to the crowd that had gathered outside the truck stop in North Carolina not so long ago. The homogeneity of it struck Darger. Would the two crowds have been so uniform twenty years ago? Thirty? She thought maybe not. What did that say about the direction of the world? Darger couldn't see how it could be a good thing.

She caught up with Loshak on the other side of the lot, near a white van with a Burlington County Coroner seal printed on the side. A pair of coroner's assistants loaded a gurney into the back, white vinyl shrouding the body.

"This is him?" Darger said as she got close.

Loshak glanced at her and pumped his head once.

The wheels of the gurney retracted as it slid home into the cargo area, Trotter's body bag shaking along with the motions. The yawning space at the back of the van suddenly seemed to take on a tomblike feel to Darger — somehow made more than the back of a van in this moment.

The doors slammed shut then, and that moment of reverence seemed to cut off all at once. The two men climbed into the front seat, and a second later the engine rumbled to life, taillights flaring. The van looped out onto the road and rolled away.

Something nagged at Darger still as she watched the vehicle shrink into the dark horizon. She chewed her bottom lip. Her next thought came out loud, surprising her.

"Wish we could have talked to him again."

Loshak held silent for a second before he responded.

"Trotter?"

She nodded.

"Just to try to figure out the loose ends, you know? We could have straightened all of the details out, but now…"

She pictured him again in that interrogation room, some fresh flash coming to her of how mild-mannered he'd seemed. Better at hiding the darkness than the other suspects — she'd thought so even at the time. So much better that he'd get to take some secrets to the grave, as it turned out.

"Oh hey," Loshak said, eying his watch. "The plane is leaving in twenty, per Detective Bledsoe. I figure when we get back down to Carolina, we can get something to eat."

Darger squinted at him, thought she spotted something mischievous in the faint grin not quite overtaking his lips.

"You got big meal plans or something?"

He just smiled harder.

CHAPTER 60

Darger's stomach still felt squirmy from the short plane ride as Loshak pulled their car into the lot at Big Jon's. She looked around a second, eyes scanning the normal cars parked near the building then shifting to look over the rows of trailers lining the back lot.

Pink light glinted on everything, shimmering from the neon bulbs above, twisted into the sign's lettering like balloon animals. The reflected glow made all those dark windshields look like strange mirrors flushed with a coral hue.

The familiarity of this setting struck Darger. The brick facade of the building, the crowded lots, the gleaming balloon letters of the sign shimmering above it all. She'd spent hour after hour here this week, spent a good chunk of it here in the parking lot staring out at the expanse, and every detail seemed to have become commonplace. Routine. Almost comforting in some way that only known places can be.

With Chuck Trotter dead on a morgue slab in Trenton, New Jersey, and the bulk of the homicide cases closed, she hadn't known if she'd ever see this truck stop again. And now here they were just over an hour later, a pair of moths drawn right back to those rosy neon bulbs as soon as it got dark.

Loshak parked the car, and Darger shook her head in the passenger seat.

"I can't believe that this is where you want to eat. After all the hours we've spent here. I mean, truck stop food. That's what you want?"

"Ribs," he said, biting the word off a little aggressively.

"What?"

He swung his shoulders around and gave her a look like she was an idiot.

"Like I was going to miss out after everyone recommended the ribs."

"One such recommendation came from Trotter himself, in case you've forgotten."

"Yeah, well, there's no accounting for taste. Just because he was a serial killer doesn't mean he can't be a connoisseur of great food." He yanked the key from the ignition. "And surely you've seen the signs. All those blue ribbons and the little trophies in the case next to the greeter's podium? This place supposedly has the best ribs in the entire tri-county area, Darger. They absolutely slayed at the most recent Ribfest in Asheville — a clean sweep in the three main categories of sauce, flavor, and overall rib experience. I couldn't let this opportunity pass."

He shook his head. He had a faraway look in his eyes. Almost mournful. Darger bit her lip to keep from laughing.

"I had to come back. Had to see what all the fuss is about. Hell, you know we'll never be back here, right? How often do we get down to North Carolina, at all? This is a once-in-a-lifetime thing. And if I blew it? If I missed out on Big Jon's famous Carolina-style ribs? I'd be kicking myself for the rest of my life."

Darger turned a palm up between them.

"Are we still talking about ribs? Because this seems a little too deep. Too… Freudian," she teased. "Did you have a bad experience with pork as a child?"

"You ever have Carolina-style sauce?" Loshak asked, ignoring her. "'Cause it's a whole 'nother beast, I'll tell you that."

"Here we go."

"See, it's vinegar-based. Tangy as hell. Maybe even a little sour. Not all sweet like the sauce you find in the Midwest, nor smoky like what you'll often come upon in Texas or the Southwest. Nope. In the sauce world, Carolina barbecue stands alone. For my money, it's at the tippy top of the list. No lie. It's something special."

"In the sauce world," Darger repeated. "Yes. Of course."

They climbed out of the car and hoofed it toward the bright glass of the doorway. An air-conditioning unit buzzed on the roof and trickled condensation out of a tube just bigger than a straw, the runoff drizzling into a bed of gravel off to the left of the door.

Inside, that air conditioning spread a chill over the floor of the place that made it feel empty despite a healthy enough crowd occupying most of the tables, both truckers and non. The greeter led Darger and Loshak across the restaurant, and they were seated in a booth way in the back corner.

Loshak ordered a full rack of ribs, as expected. After some hemming and hawing, Darger opted for ginger and soy-glazed salmon, at which point Loshak grabbed his chest as though he were having a heart attack.

"Salmon!" He spat the word out as soon as the waitress was out of earshot, glaring at Darger. "Are you doing this just to troll me?"

Darger laughed and almost spit Dr. Pepper everywhere.

"No!" she said, pausing to catch her breath. "Calm down, weirdo. Jesus, I don't like ribs."

Loshak's mouth hung open long enough to mouth-breathe three breaths.

"You don't… like… ribs?"

"I find the gristle-to-meat ratio off-putting. Nor do I enjoy the sensation of gnawing on a bone. Plus they're messy. I hate having sticky hands."

Loshak grumbled something at that and glugged down some iced tea, his eyebrows twitching.

Detective Glenn caught Darger's eye from across the room, and he lifted his glass of Coke at her as though in a toast. She raised her own glass back at him.

The food arrived within a few minutes. They ate.

Loshak got sloppy right away, the vinegar sauce smeared all around his mouth and even up onto his nose. Darger vacillated between laughing internally and being almost disgusted as she watched him suck soft meat off the curved bones, something frantic in his eating that brought to mind a gluttonous medieval king.

But Darger's thoughts quickly drifted back to the case. She remembered Trotter's final moments, eyelids fluttering around eyes gone blank, his body flopping to the asphalt face down.

"You think he did it on purpose?" she found herself asking out loud. "Trotter's death, I mean. You think it all played out how he thought it would?"

Loshak took another sip of tea.

"You mean, do I think he set up the suicide-by-cop scenario on purpose? Maybe. I mean, anyone could see he was in a hopeless position. To not surrender at that point is a form of suicide, even if he hadn't been planning it before that.

"A lot of these guys — the ones putting themselves in a position to get shot by a cop — there's something a little more histrionic at play, I think. The guys are making a public scene in some way. Yelling. Or outright attacking people or the police. Trotter ran until he was cornered."

He took another drink of his tea before he went on, ice tinkling against the sides of the glass.

"There was a famous suicide-by-cop case in Los Angeles in the early 90s. A guy threw a pedestrian down, yelling about God. Then he walked down the street and tossed an unarmed security guard over the rail of a bridge. When the guard grabbed the rail and dangled, the perp unhooked his fingers. It was about a 30-foot drop onto a sidewalk below, and the security guard broke both ankles."

Darger cringed, picturing the guy's feet hitting the concrete and flexing too far. Loshak kept going.

"When the police arrived and gave chase, the offender continued yelling about God, and then he turned toward the police with a jacket wrapped around his hand.

"The responding officer, thinking the perp was armed, shot him. But the guy kept walking toward him, getting shot three more times as he grabbed the policeman, and they both fell to the ground. He died shortly after, wounds to the neck and chest. He was, of course, unarmed. I remember people comparing it to that Michael Douglas movie *Falling Down* at the time, like this guy couldn't take it anymore, I guess, and just went on a rampage. To me, that case has more of a public element than what we saw with Trotter, that histrionic characteristic I was talking about, but I guess it's hard to say."

Darger fell quiet for a few seconds, idly stirring her straw in her drink.

"You know what's funny?" she said, staring at a square of light reflected on the glossy tabletop. "When I think about the version of Chuck Trotter we met in that interrogation room, I just have a hard time connecting him to these crimes. I know he did it, like I understand that *that's* factually the case, and I can even see some of the bits and pieces psychologically that explain the behavior, the way he matches up to the profile. But, on a gut level, when I think about the guy, think about what it felt like to be in his presence, he just seems harmless to me somehow. Like someone's chatty neighbor, always out in his driveway washing the car or something mundane like that."

Loshak shrugged.

"I know what you mean. He didn't feel like a monster in the room. That's not terribly uncommon, but the regularity doesn't make it any easier to process. I said before he reminded me a bit of John Wayne Gacy. When you watch footage of Gacy in interviews, you know this guy did all these awful things, but he just seems like… a dork, I guess. Benign. A talker. Like you said, just like someone's neighbor. And I did get that feeling talking to Trotter."

"They hide themselves well," Darger said. "You could look at it that way. The disarming traits we're talking about? It's the perfect camouflage."

Then she caught sight of something across the room, something that fixed her eyes in place right away.

A familiar broad frame filled most of a bench seat in a booth in the opposite corner.

Junior Riggins.

He sat by himself, eating chicken and waffles, eyes shifting everywhere.

The facts of the case replayed in her mind — the bloody rags in Riggins's truck, the odd interview where he claimed to treat the prostitutes like royalty or some such nonsense. So far they hadn't matched the DNA from the rags to any of the known victims. But that didn't necessarily rule anything out, did it?

"Hey, don't turn around, but we've got company in the back corner."

Loshak froze with a crooked rib a few inches from his mouth, lips glistening the maroon shade of the sauce. His eyes widened.

"Who?"

"Riggins."

"Riggins. He of the bloody rags and magic mushrooms?"

He wrenched his whole body around and stared at Riggins across the room. The movement was fast enough to catch the trucker's eye, and he stared back at them. Darger couldn't read the expression on his face. It was mostly blank, which seemed at odds with what she remembered about him. He'd been all smiles back when they'd interviewed him.

She kicked Loshak under the table, and he practically jumped out of his seat.

"I told you not to turn around," she hissed under her breath.

"What? Oh. Right. Yeah."

He shrugged and went back to work on his ribs. Darger fought down a chill.

"It never really felt resolved with him, did it?"

Loshak sucked a wad of meat off the end of a bone.

"You mean Riggins? Yeah, I guess not. I mean, we never found a match for the blood on those rags. That leaves a pretty big question mark."

"You think he could have been involved in the cases where Trotter couldn't have done it?" Darger asked, thinking out loud. "Like the Savannah murder."

Loshak stopped chewing. Squinted.

"You mean Riggins as a copycat? Or maybe an accomplice of sorts? I mean, it's plausible enough, but we're an awful long way from proving anything like that."

Darger could just see the dark shape out of the corner of her eye, a hulking thing getting closer. She'd averted her gaze from Riggins once he'd spotted them, but now she had to look, had to check.

He was up. Walking. Heading right for them. That jackal grin split the bottom half of his face into a wedge of glistening teeth.

"Christ," Darger whispered. "He's coming this way. Like right now."

Loshak dabbed a napkin at his mouth, perhaps removing a quarter of the sauce.

"How do I look? Am I clean?"

He jutted his chin and pursed his lips at Darger to draw her attention fully to his saucy mouth. She winced at the sight.

"Uh… not even close."

"Shit."

He drew a fresh napkin from the dispenser and scrubbed his face furiously, smearing orange goop everywhere, slowly swiping some of it away.

Riggins strutted up to their booth, bent at the waist, and leaned over and put one hand on the table.

"Well, well, well… The FBI always gets their man, huh?" he said through smiling teeth.

"That's the Mounties," Darger said, and Loshak nodded.

The jackal grin wavered slightly.

"What?"

"That's the unofficial slogan for the Canadian Royal Mounted Police. 'They always get their man.'"

"Oh. Well, them, too, then."

The grin came back, bending toward a rictus. The silence between them stretched into something uncomfortable, and then Riggins went on.

"Anyways… I just wanted to offer my congratulations. Y'all did it, just like I knew ya would. Another perp behind bars. Just like on TV and shit."

Loshak ran a finger over the blade of his nose before he responded.

"Uh-huh. Well, thanks."

Riggins nodded and walked back toward his booth on the opposite side of the restaurant. Darger kept her eyes trained on his back as he strutted away.

CHAPTER 61

Loshak tore open the little packet, and then he smeared the wet nap over his lips and chin. Faux lemon scent permeated the booth, and Darger slid to the open edge of her seat to get away from it, but she couldn't look away from Loshak's scrubbing job.

He worked in circular motions, the small white square slowly taking on the hue of barbecue sauce. This was the third moist towelette he'd taken to his skin, and somehow sauce still shellacked the bottom of his face, some greasy layer of it seemingly stuck there, glistening.

"It's like I painted eight coats of the stuff on me," he muttered to himself. "I might need turpentine or something to strip this."

He eyed the bill sitting in a tray next to his elbow. He stopped scrubbing and dabbed the cleaner of his two hands at the inside pocket of his jacket, and then he patted at his pants. His eyes went comically wide.

"So I, uh, think I left my wallet in the car."

"I can cover it, if you want."

He shook his head.

"Look, I'm the one who demanded we come here, so it's my treat. But, um… you want to run out to the car and get the wallet while I keep working through the de-saucing protocol? At this rate, it shouldn't be more than 45 minutes or an hour until I'm clean, so..."

Darger laughed and scooted the keys over the tabletop, skimming them off the edge of the table and catching them in her cupped hand. She glanced toward where Detective Glenn had been sitting, but he was gone now.

She caught sight of Riggins for just a second as she turned to cross the restaurant floor, but the trucker had his head down now, his attention focused entirely on the last of his meal. Somehow that made him seem less threatening — just a guy spearing a triangle of waffle and scraping it through a puddle of syrup. Nobody eating waffles looked scary, Darger thought.

She pushed through the glass door and stepped away from the building. The chatter died behind her as the door swept closed.

The temperature had dropped several degrees while they ate. A cool breeze whispered over Darger's neck and arms, and when the wind picked up, that chill cut right through her shirt.

She started into the rows of cars. Looked off to the left where all the semis were parked, those rows of trailers where just this morning they'd found a body, though it already felt like days ago. A faint shiver crawled over her skin, made her shoulders twitch, and she knew it wasn't from the cold this time.

And then she stopped dead a few feet shy of Loshak's loaner, her feet planting themselves beneath her involuntarily. An image flashed in her head. The stack of wrinkly hobo clown face stickers from Trotter's double-wide, those big gums and square teeth flaring on the screen in her skull.

The sticker had seemed familiar right away. Could she have seen it in the lot? Maybe plastered on one of the trucks. And would that even mean anything? She didn't know, but her gut told her to take a look anyway. More information never hurt.

She slowly turned, scanned the dark sea of vehicles surrounding her, that pink gleam still glinting down on them from the sign. Her eyes skimmed over the regular vehicles near the building, but soon they ventured out toward the back lot again.

She recognized the truck in the distance. Second row, all the way to the left. The flame decals on Riggins's cab practically glowed where the neon light touched them. The usually orange fire had been tinted the pale shade of grapefruit juice in some places, closer to bubble gum in others.

Darger walked that way, pace increasing with each step. She wove through the SUVs and pickups mostly cramming the closer lot, with just a few sedans and compacts mixed into the mob. All the while her eyes stayed on that semi cab ahead.

Her mind stayed blank at first. That image of the truck growing closer became the only thing she was conscious of, like she was being pulled through a tractor beam toward it. As she got about halfway there, though, the doubts suddenly welled in her.

Riggins owned his own truck. She remembered that from the file. That fit the notion of him putting a bumper sticker on it more than most drivers.

But where would he even put a sticker? Somewhere on the cab, obviously, as the trailers would come and go, but would inside make more sense than outside? Maybe so. And she *had* seen photos of the inside of his cab, from when the cops had searched and found the bloody rags. She tried to recall the photos, tried to force her mind to remember, to envision the sticker in this new context, but the image wouldn't come.

No matter. If she was quick about it, she could climb up and try to peer through the windows.

The sticker itself would be proof of nothing, of course. Even if a creepy clown sticker very tangentially pointed to a link between Riggins and Trotter, it wouldn't have any bearing on Riggins's connection to crimes or lack thereof, not by itself.

So… what did it all mean? She didn't know. Yet.

It could be nothing, it could be something. She'd take a look, and then she'd know.

Darger turned sideways to sidle between two SUVs, the jutting rearview mirrors giving her obstacles to work around. She kept her head trained on Riggins's truck in the distance.

The tiniest scuff nearby — a rubber sole on gritty asphalt — set her teeth on edge. She just had time to turn her head, to see the dark shape blur into motion.

Something lurched out of the shadows and grabbed her. One arm wreathed around her shoulders. Another took her low, around the belly.

She tried to reach for her gun. Couldn't. Arms pinned to her sides. Hugged tightly against him.

She swiveled her head. Saw the face of her attacker pressed close, eyes all wide and psychotic, lip drawn down to expose the bottom row of teeth, sneering like a bulldog.

It wasn't the face she'd expected.

But it's not him.

It's not him.

It's—

His hand jerked. Something dark there, clutched in his fingers. His arm catapulted up over his head, thrusting the object into the light.

The nickel plating glinted pink in the neon glow. The matte rubber grip looked dull next to that vivid gleam.

He had a gun. Just as she realized this, the thing leapt.

The butt of the gun arced downward. Conked the top of her skull and rattled her brain around.

She blinked. Looked at the dark smear of his face now going double. She had time for one thought before everything went black.

Not you.

CHAPTER 62

Darger rose from the darkness in stages.

The buzz in her head came back first. White noise throbbing there, a swelling and waning whoosh that reminded her of waves sloshing against the side of a boat.

Then the scent of pine assailed her nostrils, sharp and cloying. Not real pine, she realized after a second. The artificial kind.

She could picture the perfect angles of the little green shape, like a Christmas tree cookie cutter, before she could think of the words.

Air freshener.

The pine smell is an air freshener.

I'm in a car.

The notion jolted her memory, rolled the footage in her head, and she could see it all again, the whole scene lit in the coral glow of the neon bulbs outside of Big Jon's.

That pumpkin face pressed close. The butt of the pistol swinging toward her head. And then the impact shattering it all into pink shards that dissolved into black.

She opened her eyes. Found herself staring up into the sky. Moon and stars and the burning bulbs hung up over the parking lot.

Then the windshield took shape — a dark frame in the foreground. The edge of the dash was there, too, its jutting edge rendered in shadow.

She was slumped to the side in the passenger seat, practically lying down, her head hovering just a couple inches over a pair of cup holders. The reality slowly dawned on her — the car wasn't moving, wasn't running. They were just sitting in the parking lot.

How did that make sense?

She snaked her fingers down to her holster.

Empty. Of course.

Then she tried to sit up, and something cinched her throat closed as she did. One short cough barked out of her, and then her wind cut off.

She jerked a second, tried to fight it, fingers scrabbling at the cord pinching her neck, but the line only drew more and more taut with every movement. She lay back again, found a sliver of windpipe open enough to breathe through.

And he was there. A silhouette slumped down in the shadows veiling the driver's seat.

Dwayne Kunkle. The janitor from Big Jon's.

It didn't make sense.

Did it?

She ran back over the past few days, remembered interviewing him as an eyewitness that first night. Recalled how he'd paid for their lunch the next day. He'd stayed close.

No brown jumpsuit tonight. Kunkle wore a Hawaiian shirt unbuttoned to his mid chest. Cargo shorts adorned his legs.

Must be here on his night off.

Keeping an eye on us still.

He had a ligature around her neck, some kind of slipknot, his forearm slowly unflexing, letting the line go slack now that she was keeping still.

His eyes blazed, black pits shining in his face, somehow visible even in the darkness.

He spoke, bit off his words, voice raspy and hushed and spurting in the gaps between his clenched teeth.

"Keep real fuckin' quiet now, bitch. You understand me? If I'm getting caught, you ain't gonna be breathin'. Trust me on that."

He waved the hand tucked close to his belly, and Darger saw the faintest glint of the nickel-plated gun in the darkness.

Shadows flitted outside the Jeep. Slouching torsos elongated in silhouette. Long limbs swinging.

People in the lot.

That's what he's hiding from.

They both held still and silent. Watched the shapes fluttering beyond the windshield.

And then she saw them. Three figures walking just a few yards away from Kunkle's Jeep. Not just people. Police.

The trio of uniformed cops fanned out into the lot from there, going their separate ways. They walked funny, slow, squeezing between the tightly packed cars.

Were they looking for her already? Or did they just finish eating, and now they were headed home?

She swallowed into a sore throat. Felt her eyes flicking back and forth over the man walking just past the passenger door, his back to her as he turned sideways to get skinny enough to pass the jutting rearview mirror.

Help is so close. So close. Just on the other side of the glass.

Kunkle gave a sharp tug on the rope, and it tightened around her throat again.

Water welled in her eyes. A hot, swollen feeling filled her head.

The cops trundled away. The little shapes of them in the overhead mirror grew smaller and then melted into the dark contours of the cars filling the lot, all of the darkness congealing into one entity somehow.

When they were out of sight, the rope let up again, and

Darger breathed. Felt the air dry and harsh in her throat.

Gone.

She was alone now. With him.

An animal smell occurred to her nostrils then. Something musky, sweaty, gamey like questionable meat, funky like a wet St. Bernard — *his* smell, she knew. Foul.

A few breaths after the cops had fled from view, he sat up. Leaned over the steering wheel and started the vehicle. The engine purred, and the headlights blinked to life before them, splashing over the brickwork of the truck stop's facade.

He waggled the gun again.

"Remember what I said," he said, his voice gravelly. "Real fuckin' quiet, bitch. Like absolute silence. You got that?"

Darger hesitated a second, let her eyes shift over the angry folds of his eyes and nose, the Elvis sneer of his top lip. Then she nodded.

He shifted the Jeep into gear, the ligature pulling a little bit as he did. Then he adjusted his grip on the rope, drew it just to the edge of choking her.

"Good girl." He smiled in the dark. "You know, they say you FBI types are cold. Tough. Like she-devils or some such. But look at ya, a well-behaved little thing, cowering there. Man, I'm tellin' ya. I'm pretty sure you cunts are all the same, no matter how they try to dress you up."

A laugh sniffed out of his nostrils.

The vehicle drifted forward, cranked to the left. To Darger it felt like they were floating through the lot, somehow made weightless in this moment. So slow, so normal, they'd be innocuous to any onlooker.

They swung past the front of the building, and Darger caught just a glimpse of Loshak in the side mirror, pushing through the glass doors seconds after they'd rolled past. He had his head down, hands working against each other, still swiping a wet nap over his fingers.

The Jeep rocked down the ramp leading out of the lot, and they eased onto the road and started building speed. Loshak disappeared behind them, lost in the dark. Even the glow of the truck stop slowly grew tiny in the rearview until the gloom swallowed it entirely.

CHAPTER 63

With the truck stop out of sight behind them and the road empty and dark ahead, he jammed on the accelerator. The Jeep perked up, engine humming at a higher pitch. All the trees on the side of the road smeared into a dark blur.

Darger waited. Breathed while she could. Deep breaths. She'd let the scene settle before she made her move. Lull him, if she could.

They tore along like that for a while, a bullet in the dark, weaving their way out onto rural roads that seemed less and less familiar to her. Tree branches reached over the asphalt here, a bunch of gnarled arms extending from the edges of the tobacco fields, and willows slouched everywhere in the distance, droopy heads of hair along the horizon.

Beside her, Kunkle shifted in his seat. He tucked the gun under his thigh and settled back into position.

He lit a cigarette, orange flame flickering under his chin for a second. Then the fire was gone, and the red cherry of his Camel stood alone in the darkness.

He cracked his window, and the night air sucked at the narrow opening like someone slurping the dregs out of a paper cup with a straw.

Darger let her eyes roam over the interior of the Jeep, the trickle of the wind whipping her hair around in her face. The dash lights glowed purple toward the top of the dashboard. The various gauges were lit well — the orange needle pressed toward 95 on the speedometer and trembled like it was about to pop — but the lights didn't reach very far down.

She stared into the dark folds of shadow beneath the knobs of the stereo until she was finally able to make something out there. A shaky breath entered her lips, cool wind rushing in from the night outside.

This would work. She hoped.

Now she watched him out of the corner of her eye. Waiting. Waiting.

He busied himself with his cigarette. Hooked the tube into the corner of his lip. Took a drag. Flicked the ashes in the crack along the top of the window while he exhaled smoke.

OK. Go time.

Three.

Two.

One.

Darger wrenched herself upright. Careened her shoulder toward the passenger door, crashing that way.

He huffed a wet sound and jerked on the rope. Ripped the cord back his way all at once.

She stopped short like a dog sprinting to the end of its leash, and then she came crashing back down. Gagging. Hard.

She tried it again. Hurled herself into the dash this time, hands scrabbling like mad, high and low, churning like hamster paws working at the wheel.

He yanked again. Harder this time.

Even her gag cut out to silence now. She could see the veins pulsing in her eyes, red blotches twitching and disappearing over and over. Worm patterns fluttering and fading.

Heat flushed her face. She could feel it turning her flesh red even if she couldn't see it. Fevered liquid filling her skull, tremoring in her cheeks.

He wrenched the rope down. Harder still. Bounced her head off the center console and ground her face into the cup holders.

The rope gnawed at her neck, took her high on the throat. Every little filament of cord grated into her skin, constricted her neck so tightly it felt like her eyes might pop out.

Her vision started to darken. Her view of the cup holders went swimmy along the edges.

And only the hammering of her pulse in her head seemed real now. It throbbed in time with those veins flaring scarlet lines over everything, grew louder until all other sounds were blotted out.

He jerked her upright all at once. Slapped her in the face with the hand still gripping the rope.

Her head snapped around hard, dead-ended at the point where her neck could rotate no further. The bright pain in her cheek and jaw flared a fraction of a second later.

He grabbed her chin and muscled her head back around. Slapped her again. Backhanded this time.

Bright motes exploded in her field of vision. Sparks bursting upward from a campfire.

She just saw his gritting teeth, those bulldog teeth, and then there was a flash of bright red, pain thrumming through her skull, and she shut her mouth. Powerless. At his mercy.

She realized that he was talking to her, that maybe he had been for some time.

"Calm the fuck down! Alright? Jesus! Don't you see that there's nowhere to run?"

She blinked. Stared at the dark shapes shifting around like blots in a kaleidoscope.

He slapped her again, and she felt something pop where her lip mashed into her teeth.

"I asked you a fucking question, bitch. You ready to calm down now or what?"

She hesitated, just like last time. Then she bobbed her head once. Felt so submissive as she did.

"Good." He shook his head. "Christ on a pony. Not one of you ever listens. I swear to God."

He let up on the rope, and cold wind scraped into her neck. Sounded like someone scratching a match over a strike board. It stung the whole way into her throat, too. Didn't feel good at all, physically, beyond the muted sense of relief in her lungs.

Still, she breathed. Forced deep heaves in and out fast. The murky shades of the Jeep's interior crept back into her field of vision, that darkness relenting, at least a little.

She turned her head toward the window. Watched the endless swamp roll by, the edges of it catching the light from the headlights, lily pads and snatches of overgrown mud puddle glowing for a second as they rushed past.

From the corner of her eye, she kept her focus on the small, silvery dot. Could only barely make it out in the dark, but she knew it was there. Knew that any second now, it would happen. It would happen. It had to happen.

He talked. Something idle in his voice.

"I'm the one who called in the tip on Trotter. You smart enough to figure that out yet, or no? He would have taken the fall for it all, had things broken right. Hell, they almost did."

He sucked on his cigarette.

"Not that he wasn't guilty as sin, mind you. We worked together, I guess you could say. Me and Chuck, I mean. We go way back. Figured out at some point that we shared a common passion. I saw some magazines he had. Mentioned that I could see he was a man of refined taste. It took off from there. Hell, I'm the one who turned him onto the wonders of binding with rope. Heh. See, sometimes he drove the truck, and sometimes I drove it. It was the perfect deal to alibi both of us, ya know? But he had to blow it for both of us. Had to hit close to home. I told the motherfucker so many times — don't shit where ya eat. But I don't know. Guess he had, uh, impulse control problems. Heh. Heh."

He ashed the cigarette out the window. Hit it again.

"I thought I was in the clear, but then what do I see but you poking around in the goddamn parking lot. Walking right toward my Jeep like you had a bug up your ass. I knew you were going to be a fuckin' problem. So here we are."

They both held quiet. He let a breath out of his nostrils all slow, like he was releasing steam.

He was just going to speak again when it happened.

Something clicked. Metallic. Loud enough to shut him up.

That little silvery spot within the shadows of the dash lurched finally. It leapt about a quarter of an inch toward her. Darger grabbed it. Wielded it.

She only saw the bright red coils for a second as she turned and jammed the Jeep's cigarette lighter into the side of his neck.

CHAPTER 64

The lighter sizzled against his throat, emitted a smell like charred pork. Sickly sweet.

Darger could feel the thing sink into the meat of his neck, the top layer of flesh melting away, disintegrating to ash within a fraction of a second and crushed out of the way, the lighter plunging deeper, deeper.

He screamed through clenched teeth. Vocal cords shredded. A howl of great pain.

Some falsetto fizziness screeched atop the throatier warble. Little flecks of spit spritzed between his teeth in pulses.

His hands sought hers, spidery fingers crawling over the back of her wrist. He tried to pull at the clawed-up fist wrapped around the lighter, still jamming it into his throat.

But Darger ripped her hand away before he could get a hold of her. Jerked free of his loose grip.

The lighter gleamed a second between them. Arcing. The brightness of its orange coils had faded to a sunset shimmer. A little dull compared to the harsh glow it'd held before, but still plenty hot.

She tossed it into his lap.

It bounced once and rolled down the declining slope of the bucket seat. Disappeared up the leg of his cargo shorts.

He gaped at his legs. Blinked once. His lips popped as they parted, and then he whimpered. A hiccup chimed deep in his throat.

He swatted a hand at the dark place where the orange glow had vanished. Mashed it around in a blind scramble. It looked more like he was trying to swat a bug than anything.

A faint sizzle hissed from within the khaki folds of his shorts. Then a new smell arrived — the acrid stench of burning hair.

He screamed that fizzy gurgle through his teeth again. Throttled himself up and down in his seat, bouncing like a baby in a high chair.

She caught just a glimpse of one of his kicking legs as they passed under a box of moonlight, a white and blue flip-flop dangling from his foot.

Darger grabbed the rope extending from her neck with both hands, gave it a firm tug, putting her weight into it. The rope held for a beat, then it wrenched out of his hand all at once. The sudden slackness in the line crashed her shoulder into the car door, pain jolting up into her neck.

But she was free.

The Jeep had slowed during the skirmish. Now it careened back and forth over the asphalt, lurching hard to the right and juddering over the gravel along the shoulder.

That orange needle on the speedometer now hovered somewhere just shy of 40. It would have to do.

Darger gripped the door handle. Took a breath.

She bashed her aching shoulder into the window as she tugged the door latch toward her. The door resisted, fought her, but finally it swung out into nothingness, that chill wind suckling in the vacancy.

The dark knobs of the gravel flitted past along the ground. A rolling sheet of dirt beneath.

She blinked. Took another breath. Stared at the lumpy blur of the earth.

He screamed harder behind her. Breathing heavy. He jammed freshly burned fingertips into his mouth, whimpering around them.

Another breath. Shaky this time.

Darger heaved herself out of the moving vehicle and into the night.

CHAPTER 65

The scrolling ground caught Darger on the side, her hip and shoulder touching down simultaneously, and suddenly the ground wasn't scrolling — she was. She skidded over the gravel and twisted into a barrel roll.

Gravity dragged her down the grassy slope into the ditch, slanting, pulling, rolling her down into the dark. The stars and the dewy grass tumbled by one after the other. Dizzying.

Then she splatted at the bottom. Her momentum cutting out all at once with her face down.

Wet sludge enveloped her. It felt like cold mud hugging her slowly, slurping and sucking until it submerged her whole. Trunk, neck, shoulders, and head engulfed in gloop.

And then she was pushing herself up. Standing. Splashing and stomping and stumbling up the slope on the opposite side. Clods of mud peeled away from her and slapped at the ground.

She ran for the swamp.

The land tilted down underfoot. The dark expanse of flat wetlands lay before her, silvery moonlight touching the top of the water, reeds poking up every few feet in clustered silhouettes like cowlicks. She trudged into it, feet plunging into the muck with sloshing bathtub sounds.

The bugs droned everywhere here. An endless collective chirp that buzzed over the flat land.

The Jeep's brakes squealed somewhere behind her. A hard stop. He must have gotten the lighter by now.

But she didn't look back. Not yet.

She sprinted deeper into the swamp, into cover. Picked her

knees up high to try to maintain speed.

Her fingers wormed under the rim of the rope around her neck. Pulled. Loosened the binding a quarter of an inch at a time. When the loop was big enough to fit over her jaw, she ripped it free and tossed it off into the weeds.

Then she massaged at the grooved place where the rope had gnawed at her throat. Little braided indentations brushed back at her fingertips. It was like she could feel the texture of the rope embedded in her skin in a perfect imprint. She could already picture the angry mark it'd leave, a purple coil of bruising like an inky snake tattoo.

She kept running, kept pushing herself. If he gave chase in his flip-flops, and she figured he would, every second of her lead would count. She would make sure of it.

The Jeep growled louder behind her, the drone of the idling engine giving way to rage and movement once more. The tires squawked and then caught on the pavement. And then the headlights swept her way, splashing out over the swamp.

Shit.

She glanced back as the row of extra lights on top of the vehicle flicked on. The six rounded halogen bulbs emitted a warm yellow glow. Impossibly bright. It reflected from all the patches of wetness between her and the vehicle, shards of jeweled refractions shimmering where the water moved.

The Jeep eased forward in slow motion. Seemed to hesitate. Something nervous in its movements.

Then it lurched and flung itself over the edge of the shoulder in a jolt. It bobbled out of sight for a second, jumped the ditch, and mounted the other side, headlights and then tires climbing back into view.

The SUV came roaring into the swamp, headed right for her.

CHAPTER 66

Darger kicked her way through the sludge, water flicking everywhere. Her ankles slopped through a few inches of wet and another few inches of gelatinous muck below that.

The thick stuff grabbed at her feet, at her ankles, formed suction cups around the soles of her boots and tried to rip them off her feet.

She veered hard to the left, still moving deeper into the wetlands. She couldn't outrun a goddamn Jeep. She knew that. So she'd have to try to outfox him somehow, someway.

The swamp smell rose up and wafted around her — the green stench of algae, of seaweed, mixed with something more potent like raw sewage. The odor seemed to hover in the air, a bodily scent like a cloud churning along with her motions.

She glanced over her shoulder at the headlights blazing through the night, at the even brighter floodlights above them. The beams swept over the water and found her.

Then the engine roared again. The Jeep seemed to lift a little as it accelerated, tearing through the bog.

She tried to follow the shallows, veering whenever the water got deeper. Anything to keep her speed.

She meandered more than serpentined. Parted the reeds with her arms to forge new paths.

But it wasn't a lot of use. The water kept getting deeper as she got out away from the road.

Ankle-deep. Then calf-deep. Then knee-deep.

When the water got up to her thighs, she knew she was in trouble.

She kicked her legs, tried to pick her knees up, but she was going too slow.

The Jeep loomed closer. Gaining on her.

The ground dropped out from under her then. The water was suddenly waist-deep in all forward directions.

She couldn't run. She could barely move.

The lights swelled around her, brighter and harsher, and the Jeep's growl grew louder, closer. The fine details of the engine's rumble suddenly made discernible — the guttural *ka-chunk* pattering like hummingbird wings, the gnaw and gnash of the gears.

Too close. She dared not look back.

Still, she pushed forward. Kept her legs churning. Leaned her whole body to try to gain gravity's aid, at least a little. It was all she could do.

Her fingertips skimmed over the surface of the water as she ran. Arms splayed for balance, rotating at her sides.

Her hip grazed something hard under the surface, her momentum pounding her against it, and then her whole body inflected to the left in a stumble. Wobbly steps threatened to dump her face down in the muck.

She reached a hand out toward the hardness — a tree stump under the water, a huge willow probably, the sheared-off remnant about three feet wide.

The lights jumped over the glimmering surface around her. Drew her gaze back to her pursuer.

The Jeep bore down on her, bobbing as it rocketed over the swampland. Little clusters of cattails exploded out of its way, smashed flat into the mud.

She got her balance back and turned. Some bitter taste rising to her gorge. It was too late to get away now, but what else could she do?

Her legs plunged through the water. They'd gone half-numb now, felt like strange stilts vaulting her along in slow motion.

She listened for the inevitable sound of defeat: the Jeep pulling up alongside her and slowing. He'd jump out, press that gun into her back, and force her back into the vehicle.

But the vehicle didn't slow. It kept going. Engine screaming louder, its thundering heart fluttering, accelerating.

He's trying to hit me.

All those lights speared her in the back. Too big now, too close.

The Jeep charged the last few feet. An angry thing coming in hard.

Darger dove.

CHAPTER 67

Her body flailed in open air. Laid out flat. Arms and legs akimbo. She dropped toward the water.

Falling.

The Jeep rushed past before she hit down, the front end just missing her. The left fender grazed the tread of her boot and kicked that foot up in the air in a ragdoll flourish.

Then the lights skimmed past her and away, and she saw just a glimmer of their glow rushing over the water and cattails beyond — their yellow hue somehow seemed greasy like a blotted stain on a fast food bag.

She struck the sheening surface of the water. Hands then arms then head submerged.

The dark fluid of the bog lurched around her, swallowed her whole. It made a little squelching sound as it did, sucking just like when her boots had been caught in the mud.

Black muck surrounded her. Cocooned her. It blotted out her vision, her hearing reduced to gloopy sounds — that odd hollow of water cupping her ears. It gave off a din of white noise like the ocean in a shell.

And then she felt the wake of the passing Jeep jolt through the water, through her. The surging ripple spread outward from the tires, a wave that wouldn't break.

The cold struck her then, delayed by shock for those first few seconds. The wait somehow made the chill punch harder.

Numbness bloomed in the meat of her, all four limbs going frigid and anesthetized right away, the core of her cooling a beat later. Her hands felt like bricks of ice at the ends of her arms.

She hurled herself forward and tried to swim. Sliced her arms through the wetness. Churned her feet with legs going rubbery.

It worked. It was just deep enough here that she could push off and get some forward momentum.

She pressed deeper into the swamp. Stayed underwater to try to conceal her position for as long as she could.

Then the reeds poked up. Clusters of weeds tangled around her wrists and ankles, raspy stuff and green stuff working together to slow her, sticky blades of grass attaching themselves to her face and weaving into her hair.

No way forward.

Fuck.

She thrust herself upright, the water bursting around her as she stood. She wheeled around, head and torso rotating. Sheets of liquid plummeted from her chest, from her back, slapped at the surface of the swamp with a series of smacking sounds.

And she looked out at a world still half obscured by the muck clumped to her brow and cheek-bones. The dark swamp stared back at her, gloomy and indifferent.

But then the red glint flared over everything — the Jeep's taillights not far from her. Her stomach dropped — she'd barely distanced herself from it.

The vehicle whipped around, sending up a spray of black water in a semi-circle. The bright lights swung back to light her up, made the muscular SUV look like an insect with too many eyes.

She swallowed. Felt naked and cold with those yellow lights on her. Exposed.

The Jeep screamed again, coming straight at her.

CHAPTER 68

Darger turned back the way she'd come, running back toward the shallows. His voice played in her head, raspy and fevered, something he'd said when she was still in the Jeep.

Don't you see that there's nowhere to run?

The engine boomed out over the hollow of the swampland. A baying hound closing in for the kill.

She broke away from a nest of reeds and swam while she could. Pushed her feet off the sludgy bottom and propelled herself forward, her body a blade knifing through the water.

His headlights glinted off the top of the water. Reflected shards of brightness shot everywhere in watery flutters. The swamp looked disturbed. Haphazard ripples running through it, wrinkling it into choppy shanks.

Darger swam, her head gliding along just above the surface, and she kept looking at the water, eyes scanning the darkness, scanning the darkness. Trying to see something — anything — there in the wetness.

She could hear the tires thumping over rough land somewhere behind, its noises growing ever louder.

She burst through another stand of cattails, plants slithering around her wet figure. And then she dove forward again, swimming through the next clear patch of water.

The Jeep slurped through the bog off behind her, the lights bouncing over everything around her, the glare reflecting off the top of the water like glass. Then the vehicle dipped lower, and the headlights were gone all at once, plunging Darger into darkness for the moment.

She elbowed through another section of reeds and lily pads in the gloom, and she stood again when she reached the next open section of water. This was it. She thought this was it.

She rotated her torso back and forth as she waded forward. Her arms out wide. And she ran her hands through the black water before her.

It should be here.

Right here.

Shouldn't it?

Her fingers splayed. Clawed at the swamp's surface with each step forward. Cold liquid swirled around her hands, a water fountain feeling touching all the webbed places between the digits.

But the fingertips found nothing. Just water. Empty wetness everywhere. It all looked the same.

Darger swallowed hard. Felt a sandpaper lump shift in her throat.

It's not here.

She thrashed now. Arms swinging back and forth harder. Seeking. Whimpers venting through her nostrils.

It's not here.

I'm lost.

Got turned around.

The bright lights of the Jeep rose up over the marshy land. A cluster of spotlights reaching their brightness over the mess of black water and reeds, beams finding her, trying to lance her straight through.

The SUV juddered over the bumps in the muck, uneven thuds and splashes ringing out as it hit ruts and potholes.

THUMP-THUMP-SPLASH.

THUMP-THUMP-THUMP-SPLASH.

THUMP-SPLASH.

Darger's eyelids jiggled, wetness spreading over her field of vision, just like the wet smeared over the rest of her. The tears refracted in the bright light now surrounding her, a thousand little flares bursting out of the wetness.

And then her sweeping wrist hit something. Something hard.

She backtracked. Found it again.

There.

She stepped closer and ran both her hands over the ragged surface. The little wood fibers along the top had gone slightly mushy out here in the wet. But the thing was solid underneath that. Hard as concrete.

She blinked again, and the tears leaked out of the corners of her eyes, trailed over her cheekbones. She talked herself through her discovery, a calm internal voice piercing her panic, shaky breaths flowing in and out of her.

The stump is there. It's there. An old willow stump.

It was about three feet in diameter, she thought. Set almost waist high in the wetness, with the top just two or three inches beneath the surface. It held the girth of a side of beef and was rooted into the ground firmly enough to hold up a few thousand pounds of tree, even in the ever-sloughing mud of the swamp.

This will work.

It has to work.

She stood up taller. Backpedaled on tiptoes. Kept her shoulders squared up with the stump.

The Jeep weaved in the distance, still rocking up and down as it busted through plants and troughs in the sludge. Then the SUV aligned itself with her and steadied, picking up speed again.

The engine screamed out over the flatness of the bog, the

vehicle a raging hulk she could no longer really see beyond the glare of the lights.

She kept backpedaling. Her whole body knotted up, every muscle drawn taut, braced for impact. Her chest shook and hiccupped with each shallow breath, tension thrumming inside her like a thousand plucked filaments.

The Jeep rushed for her. Drew a straight line right to her.

The eyes of the headlights grew bigger, brighter. Filled her field of vision. Something jubilant in the oversized bulbs, in the body language of the vehicle charging those last few feet like a silverback gorilla.

Aggressive.

Triumphant.

Oblivious.

Darger squinted. Held her breath. Her stomach wadded itself up into a ball of tight flesh like a clenched fist. Her jaw muscles flexed and unflexed over and over.

It finally happened in slow motion.

The Jeep slammed into the trunk and stopped all at once.

The impact emitted a resonant crack that rang out over the flatland like a thunderclap. It echoed off the surface of the water and hung in the air, shivering — a bang loud enough that Darger felt its vibration rumble through the earth and rattle her sternum.

The front end of the vehicle crumpled around the hunk of wood, instantly made concave.

The hood buckled and wrinkled like a snarled lip.

The grill caved in.

All the metal bent into impossible angles, the Jeep hugging the freshly exposed tree trunk.

The rear end hopped up and slammed back down, and then the thing went still. Spent. All that force expended and absorbed by the stump.

The surging liquid around the Jeep kept going, rushing for Darger. A wave rolling for her, over her, rising up onto her chest, her throat, her chin. Cold wetness climbing her.

The engine whined its dying note over the scene, whimpered out some higher tone. Pained.

She blinked once. Heart slamming.

She stared at the uncoiled scene of violence before her. Struggled to process what had just happened.

That wave relented. The water fell back from Darger, rushed into the vacancy around the vehicle, around the stump.

The engine gurgled and died and hissed steam in the hollow quiet following the crack.

The sudden emptiness was immense. Made Darger's skin crawl.

But there was something else. Something moving still. Something it took her eyes a second to catch up to.

A dark bulk had crashed through the windshield. Ejected from the driver's seat and thrown into the bog.

CHAPTER 69

Everything held still. Dead. Silent.

Even the bugs kept quiet for now, their endless chirping cutting off hard at the moment of impact, the air heavy with something that made them shrink back.

Darger waded forward. Moved for the spot where Kunkle's body had hit the water, legs swishing through the swamp in slow motion.

Two of the Jeep's floodlights still glowed over the top of the water, the black ripples moving there the only sign left of the violent spectacle that had just occurred.

There was something eerie about that, Darger thought. How something so violent, so momentous, could be over so quickly. That the worst of our real-life nightmares flare and die in three seconds, somehow changing everything forever in the time it takes to draw two breaths.

And it occurred to her — not for the first time — that death always worked that way. One second you were alive. The next second you weren't. No one could escape that final second. You could put it off, perhaps. Hide from it for a while longer. But it always found you in the end.

Her fingertips skimmed over the top of the water again, arms pumping in time with her forced march.

When she got close to where he went in, she slowed and started patting around under the surface, just like she had when looking for the stump.

A burnt smell touched her nostrils, and she realized that coils of smoke now fluttered out of the broken front end of the

Jeep. The wisps looked like inky spiderweb strands where they floated through the floodlight beams.

A single bug trilled somewhere in the distance, a sign that all would return to normal sooner than later, a sign that this climactic moment was already over, already past. Darger shivered then, a fresh chill shuddering through her.

The water exploded in front of her. Kunkle's top half burst out. Arms flailing.

He beat at the glassy surface of the marsh. Tendrils of liquid splashing everywhere.

A guttural screech split his lips, torn from his throat. A squawk. A wail.

The high-pitched rasp coming out of him made the hair on Darger's arms stand up. He sounded like a wounded cat.

Then he slumped forward. Still again. Silent again.

Darger crept that way. Barely able to see him as he lay just beyond the reach of the pair of still-functioning floodlights.

She treaded close. Found his still figure there.

And her eyes adjusted to the dark as she stared down at him.

The shadows mostly held him. His open eyes looked black. Face all folded up in pain.

His eyes flicked to hers.

Jesus, he's still alive.

But she saw no recognition there. Just an animal blankness. Some kind of shock.

The tip of his tongue pulsed between his teeth.

Darger let her gaze fall lower on his being. She saw that angry circle where the lighter had cooked a coin-sized slice of his neck.

And she saw the shape jutting from his back, the dark stain on his shirt around it.

A stake of wood just thicker than a cigar plunged into his gut and exited through the small of his back. A smaller stump, just bigger than a sapling. Dark clouds bloomed outward from the place where the wood embedded itself in his flesh.

When he was thrown from the Jeep, he'd been impaled.

CHAPTER 70

Darger patted Kunkle down, searching for his gun or hers. He lay still even as her hands slid over him. She thought he must be unconscious now, probably going in and out.

Her search came up empty.

The guns must still be in the Jeep.

She trudged back to the wreck, water rippling in her wake. She tried the driver's side door first, found it jammed shut, the metal folded funny along the hinges.

She sloshed over to the rear door. This one swung free when she gave it a tug. She braced her hands on either side and hauled herself up and out of the muck.

The cold hit her instantly, the night air nestling itself into all that wetness. She started to shiver.

She eased herself into the back seat, leaving a trail of muddy smears.

Darger spotted Kunkle's phone wedged in the corner where the dash met the windshield. She snatched it up. Found the screen shattered into an elaborate spider web pattern.

She pressed each of the side buttons. Swiped at the screen. Nothing.

The phone was dead.

Of course.

She tucked the phone into one of the cup holders and began searching again. She had no idea what Kunkle had done with her phone and sidearm. Hopefully he hadn't tossed them.

She sifted through the assortment of random junk littering the back seat. A small flashlight, a spray bottle of Armor All, a single grease-stained work glove, two half-empty bottles of water, crumpled grocery store mailers, a pair of neon green plastic sunglasses, the wrapper from a granola bar. But no gun and no phone.

She crouched down and reached under the back of the driver's seat. Came up with a coil of the same rope Kunkle had wrapped around her neck. She flung it away. The only item under the passenger side was a small portable air compressor.

A bolt of pain shot through Darger's foot and up her leg. A cramp in her toes.

She squirmed there on the upholstery for a few seconds, gritting her teeth and waiting for it to pass.

Must be the cold.

When the cramping subsided, she took a breath. Thought for a moment.

The last she remembered, Kunkle had his own gun tucked under his thigh. If it had still been there when he crashed, where would it have gone? Ejected along with him or...?

She leaned into the front of the Jeep, eyes scanning the dark interior. Her hand flailed against the ceiling until she found the dome light and turned it on.

She squinted and blinked against the sudden illumination. Caught a glimmer of that nickel plating almost immediately.

She slithered forward on her belly, stretching across the driver's seat and ducking under the steering wheel. Her fingers reached. Fumbled around the gas pedal and the brake. And then she had it.

She scooched herself backward and took a moment to study her prize.

A 9mm Smith & Wesson. She made sure the safety was on and tucked it in her waistband.

With a final glance around the inside of the Jeep, she

grabbed the flashlight and lowered herself back into the scummy water.

CHAPTER 71

Darger waded back to where Kunkle remained, slumped in the water. She gripped the front of his hair and lifted his head. His eyelids fluttered, opened halfway.

She aimed the small beam of the flashlight directly at his face. The yellowish light gave his face an eerie cast. Cheeks sunken. Eyes glazed.

"Where's my phone?"

His mouth twitched once and then went still. She thought he wasn't going to answer, wondered if he were even fully conscious, but then he spoke.

"Fuck you."

She gripped his hair a little tighter and traded the flashlight for the gun she'd tucked into her waistband. She swept the barrel toward his temple, watched his eyes jerk to try to watch the weapon thrusting closer, closer.

"Tell me what did you do with my phone."

Breath huffed from Kunkle's nostrils in angry little puffs.

"I ain't goin' to prison."

Darger lowered the gun. She was wet and freezing. The only thing she wanted was to dry off and get warm, but she didn't want Kunkle to know that. She forced her body to be still. Resisted the reflex to shiver.

"Well Dwayne, you're not really in a position to negotiate, are you? The way I see it, you have two choices: Tell me where my phone is so I can call for help, or sit there, impaled on that branch, and bleed out. Slowly."

He glared at her, mouth puckering. For a split second, she

thought he might spit on her.

She suddenly wished she'd brought the rope from the Jeep. She wondered how long this game would go on if she tied a ligature around *his* neck and gave it a few tugs. Let him feel the life literally ebbing away from his body. His consciousness fading with the thundering of his pulse in his ears. See how he liked that.

When his silence continued, she released her grip on his hair and let his head drop. His face slapped into the water and popped up a second later, spitting out swamp juice.

She swiveled around and started to move away, in that involuntary slow motion enforced by the water and the mud.

Kunkle's head snapped up higher.

"Hey! Where are you goin'?"

"Back to the road. I'll flag someone down and get help that way." She glanced back. "I'll try to remember where you're at. But you know… my head does feel a little funny. I might forget."

Kunkle wriggled a little, kicking his legs as if that might free him.

"You fucking bitch! You can't just leave me here!"

Darger slogged another several paces forward.

"Hey!"

His tone had gone high-pitched now. Whiny and desperate.

Darger continued ignoring him and pressed on, water rippling around her.

"Fine! Fuck! There's a storage compartment on the tailgate door. Your shit's in there."

Darger veered toward the back of the Jeep. Thumbed the latch and found her things exactly where he said they'd be.

She added her own gun to her waistband arsenal and then took up the phone before returned to the stump.

She paused a few yards from Kunkle, phone in hand. He stared at her, the blue glow from the phone's screen reflecting off his eyes. Was he sneering or grimacing from the pain? She didn't care either way.

She smiled at him as she dialed 9-1-1 and pressed the phone to her ear.

"Who's well-behaved now?"

CHAPTER 72

Darger stood on the side of the road, watching the medivac helicopter hover over the swamp a few hundred yards away. The air current from the rotors etched strange ripple patterns onto the surface of the water.

A spotlight illuminated the activity below where two flight paramedics loaded Kunkle onto a rescue litter. Half a dozen straps were secured across his body, and then the paramedics gave a signal to the chopper. The neon orange stretcher began to rise into the night.

Loshak came striding down the ditch to stand beside her, a paper cup clutched in his hand.

"Did I hear right?" he asked, extending the steaming beverage toward her. "The fire department used a bow saw to cut Kunkle loose and left the branch in him?"

Darger brushed a mud-caked strand of hair from her cheek and took a sip. It hurt like hell to swallow — her throat felt like she'd tried to swallow a cheese grater. The feeling of the liquid oozing down her esophagus and into her belly was a more pleasant sensation, at least. Warming her from the inside out.

"The paramedics wanted it left intact," she explained, her voice coming out in a hoarse croak. "They said removing it in the field is too risky."

Mylar crinkled as she pulled the emergency blizzard blanket a little tighter around her shoulders.

The stretcher was almost to the open door of the helicopter now.

"OK," Darger said with a nod. "I'm ready to go."

Loshak bit his lip, looking her up and down.

"What?"

He winced.

"It's just… the mud."

Darger opened the front of the blanket and studied herself. From the waist down, she was coated in varying thicknesses of muck.

"Well, so what? It's not like it's your personal vehicle. The Bureau will have it cleaned."

"Yeah, but… the smell." Loshak wrinkled his nose. "It's, uh, not great."

"Gee, I'm sorry," Darger said, her teeth still chattering despite the thermal assistance from the blanket and coffee. "Next time I'll try to have my standoff with a serial killer in a swamp that isn't directly downstream from a pig farm."

"I'm just saying… it's a three-hour drive home in that car."

Darger sighed. She supposed he had a point.

She waggled her elbow at the nearby ambulance.

"Maybe we can grab some extra blankets from the paramedics. Lay them over the seat."

CHAPTER 73

Hot water streamed over the crown of Darger's head, down the nape of her neck and onto her shoulders.

She watched the water slap against the floor and spiral down the drain. It ran clear now, but for the first ten minutes, it'd been a cloudy brownish color.

Over the patter of the running water and the hum of the automatic fan, she heard a muffled female voice echoing down the hall outside.

"Shower Customer Number 78, your shower is ready. Please proceed to Shower Two."

Darger had been Shower Customer Number 77. The idea to use the truck stop rent-a-shower had sprung into her mind the moment she'd spied the pink neon lights of Big Jon's Travel Center.

Hot showers.

It would have only been another fifteen minutes to their motel, at the most. But the idea of staying in her wet, muddy clothes a second longer was more than Darger could stand. And so she'd insisted that Loshak pull over immediately and let her out.

It was worth it, she thought, grabbing the bottle of shampoo she'd bought in the convenience store and lathering her hair for the second time. A fruity scent — mango, maybe? — filled her nostrils.

Her thoughts meandered as she soaped and rinsed. She wondered if Dwayne Kunkle had arrived at the hospital yet. Whether he was perhaps even now in surgery. Would he survive?

Do I even care?

Darger turned off the water and wrung out her hair. She grabbed one of the fluffy white towels from the rack in the corner and started drying off.

There was a knock at the door. Tentative.

"Yeah?" Darger asked.

Loshak's voice.

"It's me. I've got some clean clothes for you."

Darger secured the towel around her and moved for the door, feet smacking against tile. She unlocked the door, opened it a crack, and Loshak passed the clothes through.

"Thanks."

"No problem."

Darger dressed quickly, relishing the feeling of being clean and warm and dry. As she pulled the shirt over her head, she caught a glimpse of her reflection in the mirror. The dark purple mark ran the full circumference of her neck.

Images of Kunkle's many victims flashed in her mind then. The matching ligature marks around their necks. The girls who hadn't survived.

And suddenly Darger was filled with regret.

I should have waited. I should have let him die in that swamp. Impaled on that stump. A slow, painful death. No mercy.

But maybe that wasn't for Darger to decide. Maybe that was the true difference between her and the Kunkles and Trotters of the world.

Unlike him, she didn't believe it was her right to play God.

CHAPTER 74

It was five days before Kunkle was in any condition to speak. Darger met Loshak on the sidewalk outside their rooms that morning for the drive to the hospital.

"You sure you're up for this?"

She nodded as she rattled the handle of her door to make sure it was locked.

"Because Kunkle's still hopped up on the good drugs," Loshak went on. "Doubt he'll give us anything useful today. We're just trying to lay the groundwork for future interviews. So I can handle it alone if you want."

"I can do it."

He raised his hands in front of him in a placating gesture.

"Alright. Had to ask."

They took US-64 west to the hospital in Durham. As they settled into the monotony of the highway, Loshak speculated on the best strategy for their interview.

"Did he strike you as the bragging type? A Bundy or Gacy?"

"I don't know," Darger said. "He did admit it. And he seemed awfully talkative before the shit hit the fan, back when we thought he was just a witness."

Loshak adjusted his grip on the steering wheel.

"I can see him being the kind of guy who will tell us everything at first. One of the guys who almost wants to claim credit for his nasty deeds. It's only later, when it comes time to face their punishment, that they try to deny it."

Darger stared out the window at the green blur of trees whizzing past.

"In some ways, it doesn't matter whether he cops to the murders or not," Loshak said. "Because he's going to have a hell of a time denying the kidnapping and attempted murder of a federal agent."

☾

Dwayne Kunkle's room was easy enough to find — it was the one being guarded by a pair of state troopers. Darger exchanged a nod with the men as she crossed the threshold.

Inside, the former janitor was propped up in the bed, eyes closed. His face was a mosaic of bruises, cuts, and scratches from going through the windshield. Darger smiled a little to herself when she saw the angry red spot on the side of the neck where she'd burned him with the lighter.

"Good morning, Dwayne," she said.

His eyelids fluttered, opened, then went comically wide.

"If you come any closer, I'll scream," he said, patting around for his call button. "You can't touch me. I've got witnesses."

Darger raised an eyebrow and glanced back at Loshak.

"Calm down. We only want to talk."

Kunkle glared at her.

"Yeah, right. After what you done to me…"

Darger let out a half-laugh.

"Me?"

"Kidnapping me," Kunkle said. "Putting your gun on me, like some common criminal."

A shoe squeaked in the hallway, and then a voice came from behind them.

"Unbelievable! I step out of the room for five minutes to get a coffee, and already you're trying to skirt around my client's right to an attorney."

The man speaking had dark hair with white wings at his temples. Something about his pinstripe suit and gold watch screamed "defense attorney."

"And you are?" Darger asked, though she already knew.

"Gregory Fennich of Fennich and Associates."

Darger made brief eye contact with Loshak. Kunkle had lawyered up, then. So much for hoping he'd turn out to be a Bundy-style braggart.

Fennich was still rambling on.

"You know, I've heard of police harassment, but this is beyond the pale."

"No one's harassing anyone," Loshak said.

Fennich scoffed.

"Please." He swiveled his head, turning his attention on Darger. "You know, I've read up on you, Agent Darger. You've got quite the reputation."

"Do I?"

"Oh yeah," Fennich said, his tone full of disdain. "The magazine covers? The commendations for bravery and valor? You might have fooled the press and the higher-ups at the FBI into believing you're some hot shit FBI profiler, but I know your type. I've seen a million of you law enforcement fame whores. Now, I'll be generous and assume that at some point, you had good intentions. Maybe you were even decent at your job. But somewhere along the line, you got addicted to the attention. Became obsessed with getting all the glory. And you quit caring about right or wrong."

Darger blinked.

"I have no idea what you're talking about."

"No? Then explain to me how it is you ended up in that Jeep with my client," Fennich said. "Isn't it true that you were frustrated by the fact that local law enforcement got all the credit for solving the case when they captured and killed Chuck Trotter?"

"Are you cross-examining me now?" Darger asked.

"And isn't it also true, that in an effort to get your name back in the spotlight, you concocted a story in which my client was some kind of accomplice to Trotter?"

"If by 'concocted a story,' you mean, 'followed the facts.'"

"And, in fact, you became so obsessed with the idea that my client had something to do with the murders — despite the fact that they'd already been solved — that you accosted my client in the parking lot of that truck stop. You drew your weapon and forced my client into his vehicle and made him drive out into the country, where I can only imagine you planned to execute your own twisted version of justice."

Darger shook her head, not quite believing what she was hearing. She'd been prepared for a wacky story from Kunkle, but *this*? This was insanity.

She turned her gaze on the bony janitor where he lay in the bed.

"And this?" Darger pointed at the bruise encircling her neck. "How do you explain this?"

Kunkle squinted. Leaned forward.

"Why, Agent Darger. That's quite a bruise you've got there. What happened?"

He feigned sudden surprise.

"Ya know, I've heard tell of this. It's called… auto-erotic asphyxiation, I believe. A dangerous and potentially deadly sexual fetish."

Darger almost laughed.

"There's rope in your Jeep that matches this mark and the marks on all those dead girls, Dwayne."

"I just got the cheap stuff from the Home Depot. Sounds like a terrible coincidence," Kunkle said, folding his hands in his lap.

"So *I* kidnapped *you*? That's your defense?" she asked.

"Please don't speak directly to my client," Fennich said.

But Darger wasn't speaking to anyone anymore.

She really was laughing now. Hard. A big belly laugh rolled out of her in a stream that bounced her shoulders, and then the chuckling veered into a babble of nervous giggling.

Kunkle gaped from his bed, fingers balling up the edge of the blanket. He looked like a frightened child.

The lawyer flinched and took a big step back from Darger, like she was having some kind of fit that might be contagious.

She could only stare back at the two men.

Then her eyes fell on Loshak, who wore a vaguely bemused expression.

Oh my God.

I've got to get control of myself.

She tried to rein herself in, tried to stop the giggles, but she couldn't. The laughter seemed to burst through her, hissing and popping out no matter how hard she tried to clench up.

Fennich stared at her for another few seconds, and then his top lip twitched. When he spoke, his voice came out breathier than before, less solid, less confident.

"I don't think it's funny."

"Well, I do," Darger said, and then she laughed harder.

Tears now brimmed in her eyes. Her cheeks ached.

She managed to compose herself enough to make her way to the door and let herself out of the room. She shook her head as she did.

As she crossed the threshold into the hall, she turned back for just a second.

"Yeah. Good luck with all that."

Epilogue

Darger sprawled on the couch, remote in hand, queuing up the night's movie on the TV. When she caught a whiff of popcorn in the air, she got up and went to poke her head in the kitchen.

Owen was contorting an ice tray in his hands, trying to shake the last cube loose.

"What can I help with?" she asked.

His eyes slid sideways over to her.

"Not one thing," he said. "You're supposed to be on the sofa, recuperating."

"I told you, I'm fine."

"Oh please. Your voice isn't even back to normal yet."

"So?"

"So, I've seen the way you wince every time you swallow something."

"You know, you're right. Carrying a glass of iced tea to the living room would surely impede the healing of my throat."

Owen narrowed his eyes at her sarcasm before handing over the bowl of popcorn.

"My, that Yankee pride bruises easily, don't it?"

Darger snatched up a piece of popcorn and chucked it at him before returning to the living room.

When Owen came in a minute later, she moved her feet to make space for him.

"Time for the real masterpiece," she said, pressing the Play button.

The opening credits began, white text on a black screen polka-dotted with stars. Five letters appeared in fragments until the title was spelled out completely.

ALIEN.

Owen reached over and switched out the lights.

☾

Midway through the finale, Owen's eyes went wide, and he clicked his tongue.

"Ahh, I get it now."

"What?"

"Why you're such a die-hard for this movie." He tweaked one of her toes. "You're Ripley."

Darger eyes went to the screen. Studied Sigourney in her white tank top and tiny panties.

"Uh, I *wish.* She's like, six feet tall."

Owen opened his mouth to say something else but was interrupted by the ringtone on Darger's phone. He leaned over and read the name on the screen.

"Loshak."

"Ah crap," Darger said and held out her hand.

She thumbed the Answer icon and shoved the phone against her ear.

"Another one? Already?"

"No, no," Loshak said. "I'm just calling with a little update."

"Oh. Good," Darger said and felt genuinely relieved. She was not ready to go back on the road again. Not just yet.

"Thought you'd be interested to know that we finally solved the mystery of the bloody rags in Riggins's truck."

That got her attention.

"Do tell."

"Well, they tested the DNA, as promised. No match on any of our victims. No surprise there, now that we know Riggins wasn't involved. But then they ran the bloody profile against Riggins's DNA."

"But I thought the blood on the rags didn't match his blood type," Darger said.

"It didn't. But they compared the profiles anyway. Turned out to be a fifty percent match."

"That would have to be a parent, sibling, or child of Riggins himself."

"Exactly. And based on the exact sciencey details I don't remember, they knew it had to be a sibling. So Bledsoe did a little digging, found out Riggins has a sister."

An uncomfortable feeling crawled into Darger's stomach.

"Uh oh."

"Yeah, that's what she thought, too, at first," Loshak said, sounding amused. "But she was able to track the woman down. Denise Riggins is alive and well in Rutland, Vermont. Says that a few weeks back, Riggins gave her a ride to work in his truck, and she got a bloody nose. Apparently a routine thing for her. Some medication she's on gives her some absolute gushers."

Darger laughed.

"So… not a narwhal."

"Nope."

The TV screen caught Darger's eye.

"Here's a question for you," she said.

"Yeah?"

"Do you think I'm like Ripley in *Alien*?"

Loshak snorted.

"No offense, but we're talking Sigourney Weaver, in her prime."

She smirked over at Owen.

"That's what I said."

"You're being too literal," Owen said, apparently following the conversation despite only hearing her side of it. "I meant, you're like Ripley in *spirit*. You're the final girl. Fighting the homicidal monster with nothing but your own moxie. It's also why the second movie doesn't do it for you. Ripley as a soldier with big guns and the mechanical loader is an entirely different archetype. Not your style at all."

Loshak made a thoughtful *hmm* sound on the other end of the line.

"Now that I think about it, Ripley *is* pretty mouthy to her superiors. Bordering on insubordinate. She's also convinced from the start that she's right and the only one who's got it all figured out," he said.

Darger raised her eyebrows.

"Um, maybe because she does have it all figured out? If anyone had bothered listening to her, the alien never would have gotten on the ship. Everyone else *died* because they ignored her."

"Mhmm. Yeah," he said. "Maybe there are some similarities after all."

"Goodnight, Loshak."

"Enjoy the movie."

Darger hung up and resumed playing the movie. As Ripley aimed the grappling hook, Darger shook her head.

"Now how can you prefer the second movie over this?"

"I thought we agreed to disagree," Owen said.

Darger tilted her chin defiantly.

"I'd never admit defeat so easily. If the facts haven't swayed you, perhaps there's another way to persuade you."

She ran one foot up Owen's thigh, and a slow smile spread over his lips.

"I'm listening."

Darger froze.

"On second thought, I just remembered I'm supposed to be… *recuperating.*"

Owen's teeth flashed with a grin.

"You're going to play *that* game, are you?" He latched onto each of her ankles and gave her a yank until she was half in his lap. "Well, there are plenty of things we can do that require very little effort on your part."

Darger slid one hand around his neck and gazed at him through her eyelashes.

"Do tell."

"It's easier if I show you," Owen said.

He leaned in and pressed his lips to hers.

☾

The night holds still now over that stretch of highway just past the exit leading to Big Jon's Travel Center. At first glance, a lull in the traffic renders the scene in a still life.

No moon. No stars.

A cottony smear of clouds marbles the sky in grays and blacks. Occupies that expanse above. Fills it with vapor that looks solid and tufted from the ground — something that seems to carry weight but doesn't.

No headlights spear the murk. No cars jockey for position in the lanes. Not even so much as a rabbit stirs in the clover along the roadside.

This section of the interstate is almost deserted. Almost empty.

Almost.

Lightning bugs provide the only movement here, the only life. The mindless things flit without purpose, tiny wings carrying them across the sky in silence.

So the hollow night stretches up from the vacant asphalt, a vast opening between the stratosphere and earth, and the empty space seems to hold more meaning here just now, a kind of hushed reverence blanketing this stretch of road.

The fireflies flicker and gleam and blink on and off against the creamy gloom of the heavens. Yellow flares in the darkness. Those pinpricks of light that glow for just a moment and then are gone so quickly.

COME PARTY WITH US

We're loners. Rebels. But much to our surprise, the most kickass part of writing has been connecting with our readers. From time to time, we send out newsletters with giveaways, special offers, and juicy details on new releases.

Sign up for our mailing list at:
http://ltvargus.com/mailing-list

SPREAD THE WORD

Thank you for reading! We'd be very grateful if you could take a few minutes to review it on Amazon.com.

How grateful? Eternally. Even when we are old and dead and have turned into ghosts, we will be thinking fondly of you and your kind words. The most powerful way to bring our books to the attention of other people is through the honest reviews from readers like you.

ABOUT THE AUTHORS

Tim McBain writes because life is short, and he wants to make something awesome before he dies. Additionally, he likes to move it, move it.

You can connect with Tim via email at tim@timmcbain.com.

L.T. Vargus grew up in Hell, Michigan, which is a lot smaller, quieter, and less fiery than one might imagine. When not click-clacking away at the keyboard, she can be found sewing, fantasizing about food, and rotting her brain in front of the TV.

If you want to wax poetic about pizza or cats, you can contact L.T. (the L is for Lex) at ltvargus9@gmail.com or on Twitter @ltvargus.

LTVargus.com

www.ingramcontent.com/pod-product-compliance
Lightning Source LLC
Chambersburg PA
CBHW020605310726
48979CB00008B/1356/J

* 9 7 8 1 9 5 4 2 0 3 1 4 3 *